" 'Don't you hate it when this happens?' " he read. "They left you a card with a phone number? Now, that is handy. If only more criminals could be this obliging. Police work would be so much more straightforward. Have you seen a psychiatrist recently, Mr. X?"

"No."

"No. Well, we'll see. Zara, our Health and Safety Executive, will have to put an Odysseus Hat on you while I'm out of the room. I'm required to inform you it's a routine restriction, after the Hesketh Case, and does not affect your liberty status." The Zone Traffic Securities cop strutted to the door, opened it, and left us in silence as the noise of his feet clipped down the corridor and faded. I stared at Zara with a sinking feeling of bored dread. Surely she wasn't going to do what I was thinking.

"Up," she said. I scraped the chair back across the floor and stood wearily. Zara nodded in approval, then sniffed and approached several shiny seven-foot metal tubes, and I sighed with despair. She bear hugged one, staggered over to me, climbed uncertainly onto the chair, heaved the thing up, and plonked it over my head so that it slid down and hit the floor with a clang. It was wildly dark, and there was barely room to move my arms. I turned my head and, twisting a touch more, found one tiny eyehole. I squinted through it and saw Zara taking up her stoic position by the door again.

"Excuse me," I shouted, my voice echoing around the cylinder. "Is this really, honestly, necessary?"

"Health and Safety." I faintly heard her voice filter through.

"Health and Safety? I could die and you'd never know."

"Well, it is Health and Safety," came the shrugged, flat reply ...

OUTRAGEOUS FORTUNE

WITHDRAWN

Tim Scott

BANTAM BOOKS

OUTRAGEOUS FORTUNE
A Bantam Spectra Book / June 2007

Published by Bantam Dell
A Division of Random House, Inc.
New York, New York

This is a work of fiction. Names, characters, places, and
incidents either are the product of the author's imagination
or are used fictitiously. Any resemblance to actual persons,
living or dead, events, or locales is entirely coincidental.

Book design by Karin Batten

Bantam Books, the rooster colophon, Spectra, and the
portrayal of a boxed "s" are trademarks of Random House, Inc.

Library of Congress Cataloging-in-Publication Data
Scott, Tim, 1962–
Outrageous fortune / Tim Scott.
p.   cm.
"Bantam Spectra book."
ISBN: 978-0-553-38440-6 (trade pbk.)
I. Title.
PS3619.C6855O98 2007

813'.6—dc22   2006102878

Printed in the United States of America
Published simultaneously in Canada

www.bantamdell.com

BVG   10   9   8   7   6   5   4   3   2   1

To Michael Marshall Smith. For his inspiration and encouragement. His thoroughly good nature.

And his Long Island Iced Teas.

Acknowledgments

Thanks to my editor, Anne Groell, for her passionate support, astute comments, and warm sense of humor; to everyone else at Bantam who has helped on this book, and to John and Sian for a place to stay. Thanks of a very different kind go to my dad for my unique education. And to my mum for her courage and strength.

And, finally, to Bearsuit for being a band not like any other. Ever.

Art is the lie, which helps us understand the truth.

—*Pablo Picasso (1881–1973)*

All things are subject to interpretation; whichever
interpretation prevails at a given time is a function of
power and not truth

That which does not kill us, makes us stronger.

—*Friedrich Nietzsche (1844–1900)*

PART ONE

Don't Ever Do This

In the confused moment of death, we all find ourselves truly alone, with only what little sense of who we actually are, and our love for others to guide us.

1

Fuckers," I whispered to myself as I looked at the small pristine business card held lightly between my fingers. On it were the words:

"Don't you hate it when this happens?"

It was printed in a rather fetching raised font, something like Arial Black, or maybe even Charcoal. In the bottom right-hand corner, inexplicably, I noticed a phone number.

"Fuckers," I repeated, feeling like there was just too much new information to take in, and my brain had temporarily crashed. "Fuckers," I added quietly, after a pause.

I looked around, but everything else seemed pretty much the same as it had the night before. The advertising billboards smeared with a huge poster for Chocolate SleepAwake—a good-night-wake-you-up drink, which sent you to sleep gently, then woke you up a bit later at exactly the time it said on the tin. There had been a court case the year before when a woman claimed she'd bought a tin of eight-ten, but it had woken her up at seventeen minutes past each hour, every hour, then sent her to sleep again three minutes later.

And it had done it for ten days solid.

She tried to claim damages, but the courts laughed at her case. Justice was more like an infection these days. Sometimes it was about, sometimes it wasn't.

"Why couldn't she just buy an alarm clock like everyone else?" the judge demanded somewhat flippantly in his summing-up.

I wondered exactly what the hell to do next, which was made doubly difficult because my mind resented facing the awful truth of the present and kept trying to skid off elsewhere.

Fuckers. Fuckeeeeeeeeeeeeers! I thought, gazing at the array of pipes around my feet. A man in a sharp suit and Christmas-present tie walked past, looked awkwardly at me. Meeting my eyes, he nodded a smile.

"Morning," he said.

"Fuckers!" I said pleasantly, making a kind of look-what-happened-to-me gesture with my arms, which was not a gesture I could ever remember making before.

"Exactly," he said, without breaking stride.

Yes, everything else on my street was pretty much as you'd expect. The smell of oil from somewhere, the neon advertising sign that picked your name up from your C-4 Charlie and turned the whole fluid color screen into a personal ad, which had all been very state-of-the-art twenty years earlier but now was sad and neglected. Part of the screen had crashed, and for the past three months it had got stuck on a Jessica E21, and no one had come to fix it. Yes, the bikes still wound ceaselessly past on the freeway, and inside the shabby Laundromat were the time-honored mix of bored students and worn-out mothers. The flags at the gate out of Chillout fluttered in the distance. Everything was as it had been the night before, when I headed off to the all-night bar six blocks away to see Emma.

And create my first disaster.

The evening had started fine. The usual warm, friendly mix of chatter—and then somehow we'd drifted into a humongous argument, I really couldn't even remember about what or why.

She was perfect for me.

She was organized, pretty in a no-surprises sort of way, and not altogether paranoid. So why had I upset her so much that she had walked out and left me to sink a surprisingly large amount of alcohol on my own? I know I felt she was generally motivated by fear and I found that immensely frustrating. I wanted to shake it out of her, say "Come on! Forget about what other people will think just for once!" Maybe, this is why I argued with her; maybe I wanted to make something give because I was kidding myself we were a couple, when I knew deep down we were just a convenient distraction for each other.

I looked around. Everything was the same, exactly as you'd expect. Everything that is, except for the stupendously large hole between two buildings in the exact spot where my house used to be.

"Fuckers," I said again. "Someone stole my fucking house."

It happened. Not so much now, or maybe it didn't get as much news coverage since the novelty had worn off, but house stealing was inextricably part of the state culture. Once someone invented a means of stuffing solid matter down to a hundredth of its size, it became the crime all respectable drug gangs wanted a part of. Houses were generally stolen to order now, for rich people who couldn't be bothered to go through that whole thing of buying furniture and spending hours lamenting over curtain colors and fretting over bathroom fittings. They simply looked through one of the many catalogues that did the rounds on the Dark Side and put a check mark against the one they wanted. Then some guys came along and stole it, and took it to a new location, usually in another state a long way away.

In the old days, gangs had stolen all the houses they conceivably could, but then often found they couldn't shift them. I'd heard of a place out in the desert in Mexico where there was a scattering of New York penthouses and condos from Florida. They languished at odd angles to each other with no roads and no services, and no one living there except a few students who went out to party now and again. I always fancied going there.

This was definitely a moment to light up a cigarette, but I fought the urge. Sure, I could call in Zone Securities. I could wait around for a tired cop in a seen-better-days uniform to come down and nod in a "there's-one-born-every-minute" kind of a way. Yeah, I could answer a bundle of questions. But we'd both know my house was long gone.

When a bad thing happens, it asks you who you are. And if you're not sure, the bad thing gets inside you. It finds a place to hide and you carry it around. I didn't have a particularly good grip on who I was. Too much stuff had stirred up my head. Too many moments of confusion had knocked me off course. I wanted so much to tidy up the loose ends of my life and start again, but they just kept unraveling, as though some hidden part of me was pulling at the threads.

"Don't you hate it when this happens?" I said in a barely audible voice, slipping the business card into my inside pocket. "They steal my house, and they leave this." If I hadn't been so pissed off, I would have loved them for it.

I took one last look at the hole—they'd sealed off the water and gas and vis-media like professionals—and made a decision. What I quite clearly needed more than anything right now was a

Long Island Iced Tea. No. Actually, what I needed were about forty-six Long Island Iced Teas, one after the other.

And I would have headed off to find them straightaway if, at that moment, I had not been accosted by a whirlwind of old newspapers that flew at me like they were out to make some sort of point, or were incensed I hadn't read them properly.

I batted them out of the way, knowing with a sinking feeling that the approaching howl I could hear meant I was going to see something bad when I got them off my head. And there it was: a GaFFA 6 helicopter hovering about twenty feet off the ground. Not state-of-the-art, the GaFFA 6, but tried and tested. You weren't a proper gang if you didn't have a GaFFA 6. There was a thick smell of smoke from the engine, which didn't seem altogether healthy, and a slick, impenetrable roar from the rotors. The paintwork was scratched up and the logo on the nose too beat-up to make out properly, but I could see quite clearly the two eight-millimeter machine guns, and they were definitely fixed on me.

My mind reeled. Maybe the guys who stole my house wanted to tie up the loose ends? But that seemed unlikely, because this was much too over-the-top a way of going about it. Whoever was in there had been in a hurry to get here, but why? I reckoned I had a wild, outside chance of taking out the pilot if I could get hold of my gun before being riddled with holes, but instinct told me to hang back. If they'd wanted me dead, whoever they were, I would be dead by now.

A rope fell out of the open side door and a small figure in black slid down and landed about ten feet away. The helicopter yawed away and was gone.

"You're probably wondering what I'm doing here," said the figure. "My name is Caroline E61. We've just identified you as someone who would particularly benefit from our new range of encyclopedias." This girl then handed me a large volume bound in blue with the inscription ST. MARK'S ENCYCLOPEDIA, VOLUME ONE: AARDVARK TO ARCHITECT.

"What?" I said, staring at it.

"You're exactly the sort of person who would benefit from our new range of encyclopedias," she repeated. "You can't beat books, can you? We identified this moment from your Medi-Data stream as a time when you're particularly emotionally vulnerable, and therefore much more open to a sale."

"What?" I said again.

"Have a browse; there's really no pressure. Everything from Agua Moose to Zxxth."

I stared at the book, then looked up and caught myself noticing that her eyes were a searing light blue. "Someone has just stolen my house," I said, pointedly laboring each word.

"Well, what better way to start afresh than with a new set of fifty-six encyclopedias?" she chirped back, unmoved.

"Look," I said, "I really don't mean to be rude, I honestly don't, but I'm having a bad day, so please, would you mind if I just told you to fuck off?"

She paused, tilted her head slightly to one side and looked at me. Was she smiling? I couldn't read her expression. I'm normally pretty good with these things, but I suddenly felt strangely out of my depth. A door had opened somewhere and I had blundered through, and I had a terrible sensation I had blundered into a world I did not understand.

"Can't 'fuck off,' as you put it, I'm afraid," she said, with an edge to her voice. "I'm a limpet saleswoman. We're a new breed. Go everywhere and do everything. I shall be with you for the entire next twenty-four hours. Haven't missed a sale yet, and I don't intend to start with you." She took out a small handgun and glanced over my shoulder. Now she was scaring me.

"Look," I said, trying desperately to sound purposeful. "Look,

I really don't want any encyclopedias, and I don't exactly think you'll be able to follow me about, so let's leave it there."

I turned and walked away. I expected her to follow but she didn't. This was incredibly confusing. What did she say she was? A limpet encyclopedia saleswoman? Coming out of a helicopter? It really did not add up. I walked self-consciously toward the road to find a taxi and was about ten steps from her when I realized I was still holding the encyclopedia. I turned to find she hadn't moved. I walked back and offered her the volume.

"Yours."

As she took the book she tugged it, pulling me toward her. Suddenly I was way too close to her face. Those searing blue eyes were awesome. "I'm awfully tenacious," she whispered, and I felt the tingle of her breath.

"Good," I said without meaning to. "Right, I mean." Then I paused. "OK." I turned toward the road and flagged down a taxi Rider.

It was definitely time for a surprising number of Long Island Iced Teas.

2

The Crossfield 2000 swooped through Chillout and headed toward Classical and Classical Trance. The 2000s were big enough for three adults with an additional child scoop on the back and an engine like a raging bull getting its own back on the Spaniards for all that bullfighting. I swayed with the bike on one of the cambered corners, snug in the crash suit. It was supposed to be automatic, adjusting to your size, but invariably they got jammed. This one was tight about my waist, but not unbearably so, and at least the air-conditioning was working.

We swayed right into a corner and headed for the bridge over the river that marked the divide between Chillout and Classical. Was that woman following us? I glanced around just as the driver accelerated and nearly went off the back of the bike. I didn't notice anyone among all the other bikes; it was just the usual mad ballet of machines as we crossed the bridge and entered the gate that led to the neatly trimmed lawns of Classical.

The well-kept, carefully painted houses, the sublime sense of order, the pristine bikes, pristine children, and pristine lives of people you suspected had themselves so well sorted, the closest they got to a major crisis was if the dog got muddy paws on the kitchen floor. We passed one of the massive, color fluid signs that lit up saying: "Shhhhh!"

Classical was good on a Sunday morning when you woke up with a woman you loved and the sun was shining and you bought the papers and wanted to share a park walk—when you wanted to share one of those endless, perfect mornings when suddenly life makes sense. I'd had days like that. I know I had. I'd even had them with Sarah, my ex-wife, but when I looked back into my mind for them they were so buried in a past that was fogged up by too much confusion, too many spilled moments, too many wrong turnings, that I didn't know whether they were a truth I could reach again. Maybe I was damaged goods now, and those moments of utter peace and happiness were things that I would never be able to touch again.

The bike roared over a junction, triggering a huge PLEASE BE QUIET! sign that flashed doggedly, and the taxi Rider throttled back, knowing the Classical road noise checks were pretty rigorous. They were a pain in the ass like that.

I was heading for The Most Inconvenient Bar in the World because I needed space and time to think all this over. And The Most Inconvenient Bar in the World—or Inconvenient as Mat and I habitually called it—had both of those in spades. It prided itself on being located fantastically inconveniently. Not only that, it was almost impossible to get to the bar and get served, or, in fact, ever to find any sort of place to sit. A new road was built making it almost vaguely accessible a year before—which had pissed off the management so much, they had moved the whole bar six blocks away, to a much more inconvenient location in the Thin Building.

The Rider kicked into fifth with anticipation as he saw the gate out of Classical and into Compilation. I checked about again and sensed someone was out there in the gaggle of bikes keeping tabs on us, just far enough back not to cause suspicion, but maybe I was just paranoid. I swayed with the bike as we swooned gently over into a huge cambered bend and flew into Compilation. The road blurred past inches below my knee before the Rider flicked us upright, and we rocked neatly between a couple of old Crossfields crawling in the outside lane.

I loved bikes almost as much as I loved Long Island Iced Teas, but not quite.

We were in the shopping district of Compilation and Compilation is a silly zone. Full of multistores and people who don't know where else to be. Full of the sort of people who try and avoid decisions like other people try to avoid going up to the bar when it's their round.

Society had started to be based on music about fifty years before, almost by mistake. No one planned it; it just sort of evolved, then got accepted, the way things do if they feel right to a large body of people. Towns and cities had grown ridiculously large by the end of the twenty-first century, then inevitably they fractured. And when they fractured, they broke into tiny tribes based on music.

Chillout, where I lived—had lived; *fuckers*—was a cool place. Nobody hassled you much, not even Zone Traffic Securities. You didn't get lots of pointless leaflets through the door, and people in the stores were mostly pretty chilled. The architecture was all rather nicely curved and beautiful too. Dance, it has to be said, had some excellent stores. Rap was a bit showy for me, and zones like Skiffle were pretty much dead.

The whole setup made some sense, since music defined people as much as anything, and it was kind of lovely in a heart-warming sort of a way, living in a community where you had something vaguely in common with most of the other people who lived there. Of course, I had friends in other zones. Mat lived in Rave and Teb was over in White Noise. I never understood that, but that's Teb for you.

We swept down an alley, and the bike skidded to a halt.

"Close as I can get," said the driver.

"Yeah, I know." I took his fire-wire and plugged into the tiny socket on my wrist to validate the money. Some smart newswriter had labeled them "Jab-Tabs," and the name had stuck.

"Thanks. Have a power day," said the Rider automatically.

"It's too late for that, really," I said.

"OK well, whatever," he replied. "Sorry I trod on Mr. Grumpy's toes there," he added in a rather unexpected children's character voice, then, with a squeal of tires, was gone.

The alley was a dead end but for a small low door that hung off its hinges. The green paint flaked off in shards and someone had written: "This revolution is for display purposes only!" in white paint above it. I was right on the edge of Compilation, in a kind of no-man's-land before you got to Trance. There was a noise of someone playing a hand drum echoing around the buildings. Sometimes it felt like it was close enough to grasp, sometimes much farther off. Just a homeless person I guessed, passing the time. I swung through the green door that led into the shell of the old building; the roof was missing now and the place was full of rubble.

I picked my way through and out the other side to the river, crossed the footbridge, and glanced down.

The river was empty. It had been removed for cleaning some months before and the company concerned had gone bust. Now nobody could find it. There had been something about it in the newspapers.

I reached the other side of the bridge just as the sun poked out from behind the clouds, and I began to feel my fingers warming up. They were always freezing up on bikes and turning blue because the circulation had been damaged. A hangover from getting frostbite on a mountaineering trip years before.

In the distance was the Thin Building, and in spite of everything I just stopped and gazed, and desperately fought the urge to light up a cigarette. God, I could do with a drag.

The Thin Building had been abandoned by the buildings around it, which had fallen or been pulled down over the years for one reason or another, so now it stood there undaunted and alone. In the daylight, it was beautiful in a quite different way than I was used to.

Nobody bothered with this part of town. Nobody built stuff here—no new Well-Malls, no Public Access arenas, no twenty-four-hour Ziffer Sniffers Alarm stores—just acres of architectural bits and pieces. There were stacks of old fireplaces and classical doorways and chimneypots and a whole host of stuff that maybe at one time was in some sort of order and now just seemed to be dotted at odd angles. I wound my way past a huge staircase spiraling up into the nothingness of the sky and almost tripped over the edge of an ornamental fountain. The area around the Thin Building was supposed to be a reclamation yard, but it was more like a graveyard for stuff. Driftwood from houses long since gone, each an echo from a different past that no one could remember anymore. Now they sat out the ends of their days here, as though paying homage to the Thin Building.

My mind flicked into alert mode as I heard the noise of bikes echoing dully across the waste ground and looked around. But there was no sign of anyone there at all, though the growl of engines was unmistakable. I looked again. I was beginning to think that maybe it was some trick of the wind, then I clocked them, up on the roof of the old Water Bank over the empty river.

How on earth did they ride up there? There were three or maybe four Riders, silhouetted against the rising sun, and there was something about them that made me uneasy. I looked away as the sun became too bright, and when I looked back they were gone. I quickened my step; I was exposed here, and I didn't feel comfortable with it.

The Thin Building came about like this. Before planners became outlawed and all fled to South America to live in exile, they had decreed the new building was only allowed to be twenty feet wide, but four hundred feet long and two hundred forty-six stories high. The reason was a secret—because, they said, no one else was qualified enough to understand. That the architect managed to create the beautiful structure before me was astounding or, maybe, just plain lucky. Seeing the Thin Building made me feel that, despite everything, there was a sense of order buried somewhere within us all—a discernible truth that, if we could only find it, would make things an awful lot clearer. Maybe it was a sense there just might be a God, after all.

Or maybe that was all just a lot of bullshit I kidded myself with.

I pushed open one of the huge brass doors that always filled me with a sense of my own importance and insignificance in equal measures and stepped into the lobby of the Thin Building with its vast curved ceiling and pale marble floor. The elevators were right at the far end in a semicircle, which was a good two-hundred-foot walk, and the whole lobby was cool and deserted. Except, I realized, for an old man sitting on one of the alabaster benches, soundlessly asleep. My footsteps echoed on the marble like pistol shots across an alpine valley, but they didn't disturb him. I stopped when I drew near and saw he had a kind, well-worn face. "Look after yourself, old man," I whispered, and walked on.

"Morning," said the elevator.

"Inconvenient," I said automatically, stepping inside. It was on the top two floors.

"Oh yes!" said the elevator. "No problem. No problem-o." The doors closed with a pleasingly solid swish-cum-clunk.

"Knock, knock," said the elevator hesitantly.

I yawned.

"Knock! Knock!" it said, more confident this time.

"Oh. No jokes please." I closed my eyes.

"Oh, come on," said the elevator. "Knock! Knock!"

"I've had a bad day."

"Come on! It's a good one. Knock! Knock!"

"Please," I said, and kept my eyes firmly closed. Then finally the door opened and I breathed a sigh of relief and stepped out. I paused, turned around, and stepped back into the elevator.

"This is only one sixty-seven."

"It's as far as I go," said the elevator.

"What? Oh all right. All right." I sighed. "Who's there?"

The doors shut.

"Norma Lee."

"Norma Lee who?"

"Norma Lee I'd plummet and kill you, but today I feel good. Get it?"

"I get it."

"It's a bit of an elevator joke. It's going the rounds."

"Wonderful," I said, without conviction. "Are we there yet?"

"Yes," said the elevator. "Here we are."

The doors opened and I stepped out to be greeted by a low hum of voices and warm, distant laughter. I glanced out of the window and saw a Rider picking his way gingerly through the reclamation graveyard. That was unusual. It was an "FBZ"—a Forbidden Bike Zone—and even around here in Compilation the security people would give him a hard time. Then I noticed a second bike and a third, then a fourth, all weaving slowly toward the Thin Building from different sides. I didn't have a good feeling about any of this.

"Kids must have been mucking around with the circuits of number four elevator," I said to one of the balding bouncers, absentmindedly. "It's telling jokes again."

The bouncer shrugged.

I nodded, realizing he was so uninterested in what I had just said he could have won some sort of award. I put the Riders out of my mind, shouldered my way past a gaggle of girls so pretty it was frankly annoying, and headed for the bar in a small room in the far corner. It was, as I expected even at this time of the morning, packed.

Some people claimed that Inconvenient hired actors to come in and pack the bar if there weren't enough customers, just to make sure it was always incredibly inconvenient to get a drink. I'm not sure I believed this and I never bothered to find out, because it just didn't matter. I took a deep breath and bludgeoned my way into the melee, avoiding some haircuts that had been gelled into such a state they had become dangerously sharp. When I was about twenty feet away from the bar the crowd—as always—became too solid and I was wedged in. I scanned the bar in the small gaps between the heads in front of me and felt my heart leap. Eli was serving. This was good. This was more than good.

Eli 32N and I went back a long way. So far, in fact, I couldn't even remember how we'd met—or maybe I didn't want to exactly, because it had been a bad time for all of us. Eli was the woman I wish I'd married, but for some reason we'd gone down the road of being good friends. Timing, I think, had a lot to do with it. And once that happens, once friendship goes beyond a certain point, some women like Eli see your faults, your human- ness, the fact that you're not that unattainable magic they crave, and there's no going back.

I twisted my hips and found myself rather closer than I would have liked to a large man with a beard covered in droplets of sweat. Over my shoulder, I clocked the doors on elevator four opening, and out walked a girl with a rabbit-up-the-ass expres- sion and wearing way too much makeup, who marched up to the bouncer, said a few words, paused, then stomped off indig- nantly. I smiled. I didn't think people actually stomped like that in real life.

My right hand was now free and I stuck my index fingerprint on the screen on my left wrist and woke up my Skin Media phone. Skin Media was still relatively new and felt itchy some days, as though you had a tiny patch of sunburn on your wrist. There were also stories of some people who had the Skin Media picking up aircraft frequencies, or being woken up at night by the taxi chatter from Buenos Aires. I wasn't one to go too big on new technology, but I signed up with everyone else when it was clear Skin Media was working out. I edged my left wrist up near my mouth.

"Phone, get Eli for me, will you?"

"You have four messages," said the phone.

"OK, never mind that now. Just get Eli."

"Sure, sure. Just thought you might like to know about the messages."

"Come on phone!"

"I am an answaphone. What's the point of me taking all these messages if you never listen to them?"

"Phone, just get Eli will you?"

"OK. They're all from Emma, in case you were wondering."

"Phone..."

"I'm doing it! I'm getting Eli now. Emma rang last night when you were drunk; man is she pissed with you! I'm ringing Eli. I'm ringing."

Eli picked up. "Jonny X67, you old retrograde, how's it going? I can't talk too long, I'm working."

"I know," I said. "I just need a favor."

"I'm not dating you, Jonny X. We're friends . . . remember?"

"No, it's not that, Eli. I'm seeing Emma now anyway—we're getting on really well—though I still don't understand what is with you. Why does becoming good friends mean you can't become lovers later? Anyway, doesn't matter at the moment. Listen, I'm about twenty feet from the front of the bar. Can you serve me, please?"

"Jesus, Jonny, I'll get sacked. You know the rules here."

"Please, Eli, I'm having a bad day."

"Thought you said you and Emma were getting on really well," she said playfully.

"Yeah, I kind of lied, and anyway it's more complicated than that; I'll explain later. Please, Eli, I know you can do this."

She heard the desperation in my voice and relented. "OK. OK, Jonny, just this once. Long Island Iced Tea?"

"Yeah. Eli, I owe you."

"Yeah, so what's new?" She hung up. I craned my neck past a man with bulging afro hair and caught a glimpse of her. She was talking to someone else on her Skin Media phone and was scanning the crowd. When she clocked me, she smiled, shook her head, then scowled in a way that made her beautiful.

I smiled too, and suddenly felt immensely insulated from everything around me, enveloped in the warm pleasure of simply knowing I had a really good friend. And I would have happily stayed in that wonderfully warm state of mind if two heavy hands hadn't thumped down on my shoulders and dragged me backwards.

"Trying to get served before your turn?" growled one of the bouncers, who looked as if age and probably too many cheese-burgers had eroded his figure to the extent he was now border-ing on paunchy and unfit. Even so, I didn't doubt he could still hit me tremendously hard. Another bouncer with a thickset shaven head, a neck like a tire, dangling earrings—and also, I couldn't help noticing the word OTTER mysteriously tattooed on his forehead—stared at me in a way that stripped away any courage I might have been harboring. I tried to keep from looking at the earrings.

"Well," I began, "no, I . . . There's a misunderstanding. You see, I phoned Eli. The noise was . . ." They stood me upright against a wall in a quiet corner away from the crowd. "I was only asking her if . . . nice earrings," I said suddenly, unable to contain myself any longer. The bouncer wearing them smiled and there was a pause big enough to drive a train into.

"Well, it's your lucky day, isn't it?" said the other one. "We owe Eli. You're coming with us."

I felt myself relax and smiled with the sudden joy of someone who has just put down more bricks than they really had the strength to carry.

The bouncers led me down a small, cramped set of back stairs that ended in a dark, low-ceilinged room, with a floor of uneven stone. We all crouched to avoid cracking our heads on the beams.

The overweight one motioned me to one end of the room and I glanced about, catching sight of what appeared to be an old DJ setup in the dim recesses, with the words IF YOU DON'T DANCE WITH DAN, YOUR MONEY BACK! blazoned across it. Looking at the general appearance of the thing, I was reasonably confident Dan went bankrupt pretty quickly.

Above us I could hear the shuffle of feet and guessed we were under the bar. The murmur of muffled music started up and I caught the raw-edged smell of cigarette smoke in the back of my throat. I breathed it in. Suddenly I really, really knew I had to have a cigarette. Just one. I felt for the packet I'd bought the previous night but managed not to open.

"Now," said the bouncer knocking the roof above his head, "you know what this is?"

"No," I said, without thinking too much.

"This is what people dream of. This is a trapdoor, which comes up right at the front of the bar at Inconvenient."

The other bouncer—the one with OTTER tattooed on his forehead—started sniggering.

"Right," I said, slightly distracted by this and still struggling to locate the packet of cigarettes.

"Here's the plan," said the overweight one, unfolding a large thick piece of paper. It was a blueprint of the floor plan of Inconvenient. I marveled at just how thin the building really was.

"We kill the lights here," he said, looking up at me to see if I was following, and I let my hands drop from their cigarette search and nodded sagely. Otter suddenly sniggered again. I glanced at him and did a double take; he already had his hand on a rusting, old, and frankly dangerous-looking electrical power switch.

"I open the trapdoor here," continued the overweight one, jabbing the plan. "I go up, clear a small space in the confusion of the darkness, then you follow me up. OK?"

I nodded again and backed it up with a strange shrugging gesture, which was supposed to indicate how impressed I was.

"Eli serves you, I flap the trapdoor shut, and we make our escape here, where the crowd is thinnest. Sweet as a moose. Any questions?" he said, neatly refolding the plan and tapping it on his hand before slipping it carefully back into his jacket pocket.

"No," I said, trying to contain my bemusement. I have to say I was warming to them though. I mean . . .

"OK. Synchronize watches," added the overweight one.

"Why?" I asked, without thinking, and wished I hadn't.

His shoulders sagged in disappointment at the question. "Why? Because"—he sighed—"it's good practice, yeah? Always do things properly. Then it becomes automatic. OK?" He shook his head. "Christ," he said under his breath.

"OK," I said. "OK," I repeated, more upbeat, trying to retrieve the situation.

"On my mark," he cried. "Mark! We go in one minute," and he crouched ready, looking at his watch with utter concentration. Insanely distracted by my new urge for a cigarette, getting a backache from the constant stooping in this small space, we waited pointlessly. I looked about, smiled at Otter when I caught his eye, then found I was making a tocking noise with my tongue.

"Sorry," I said, aware of the overweight bouncer staring at me with bulging eyes.

"Three, two, one, mark," he hissed. And I have to hand it to him; the plan worked beautifully. The lights went out, I heaved myself up through the trapdoor after the bouncer, stood up feeling for the edge of the bar, and there was Eli. Enough light spilled from some machine somewhere so that I could just make her out. She handed me a huge Long Island Iced Tea.

"Jonny X, what are we going to do with you?" She smiled. "Do you know why I do these things for you?"

"Because you love me?"

"Because you remind me of my brother."

"Yeah," I said.

She plugged a fire-wire in and out of my Jab-Tab with such force it almost took my arm off.

"Now get out of here!" She smiled and without warning the bouncer dragged me off through the crowd and sat me unceremoniously in a chair at a corner table that, moments earlier, would surely have been occupied. There are no spare tables in Inconvenient. There just never are. If there is an empty table, it gets removed by the management and put in storage. The lights blinked on again, and I looked about.

"Not bad," said Overweight. "Twenty-six seconds. Next time we do it in twenty." And he pointed at me, raised his eyebrows, and was gone.

"Thanks," I said as he left. "Thanks," I said again, more to myself. I took a deep breath and stared at my Long Island Iced Tea.

For the first time in a bit, things were looking up. I was in Inconvenient, I had a huge Long Island Iced Tea, and somewhere to sit. People would kill for the position I was in. Now I felt comfortable enough to think properly about everything—to run over the events of the last few hours, to try and put some sense of order back into who I was, and to make an attempt to take charge of my life again.

The clock showed nine-forty. At this time of the morning, I should by rights be at work, but I suddenly realized I had almost completely forgotten about work. No matter how much I liked my job, and I really did, the whole idea of it seemed like a strangely distant memory. Like something that no longer even applied to me, as if my whole past life had mysteriously gone out of whack while I was looking the other way. Or worse, had never really existed properly in the first place. What the fuck was happening to me? I'd never felt like this before.

I held that thought and wondered about my house. Maybe I was just getting old and couldn't cope with unexpected things going off like that. In the past I went in search of the unexpected, daring it to happen in a crazy, youthful way. But now things were different and I had gone soft, or maybe had just got older, and that edge I'd felt so keenly when I was younger was blunted now by too much of the crap of life.

I took a sip and felt the liquid course through me. I was thirty-two and I was a dream architect, designing dreams for anyone who would pay—mainly the incredibly well-off, obviously, because it still wasn't a cheap habit by any means. I designed the images, constructed the story, then fed it all into a computer program that converted my designs into a small candy-covered tablet with the client's name neatly embossed on the top. They took the dream an hour before going to bed, and synthetic brain cells in the tablet traveled into the brain via the bloodstream and shed their load of images and dialogue. I'd written a lot of dreams for a lot of people, and I'd only fucked up really badly once.

And now I'd lost my whole dream library. Hundreds of dreams I'd written over the years were filed away in my house, and I deliberately didn't keep a backup at work because security was so lax. Many of my clients would have been distinctly embarrassed to have their dreams splashed over the magazines, so I had a secure place for them at my home. Now it would be excruciatingly tricky to pick up the serial dreams of many of my clients without my library.

"Fuckers," I whispered, and retrieved the business card from my inside pocket. "Don't you hate it when this happens?" I read again. And then looked at the tiny print in the bottom right-hand corner.

"This just can't be a phone number," I said almost inaudibly to myself. "Phone, try this number will you? One, eight hundred, 'a,' 'a,' 'r,' 'r,' 'g,' 'h,' 'h.' "

"OK," said the phone. "It's ringing."

Someone picked up. "Eddy-yo!" called a voice.

"Who's this?" I said.

"Who's that?" came the reply.

"Are you the punk that stole my house?" I said, and felt my pulse increasing.

"Oh man, is that you? Hey!" he called to someone farther off. "It's the Moose we stole this house off!" Then he added, "Neat place. I mean neat. Know what I'm saying? I love the bathroom fitting—"

"Listen, I want my house back and I want it back now, understand?"

"Whoa. Whoa—man! Listen, you know we can't do that—this house was an order from an important client, but listen, we can't find the corkscrew."

"What?" I said.

"We can't find the corkscrew."

"Or the vis-media remote!" called a voice in the background.

"That's right, or the vis-media remote. Where are they man? Come on!"

"You steal my house and want me to tell you where I keep the media remote?"

"Yeah, Moose. Give us a break here. It's my friend's favorite program in ten minutes, and he'll be in a bad mood if he misses it. What's that program you watch called, dude?"

"*Sarah the Space Chicken,*" called the voice in the background.

"*Sarah the Space Chicken.* Know what I'm saying? Come on—give us a break, here."

"Listen," I said, "listen..." I trailed off, hearing the sound of bikes echoing from somewhere. And then the doors of elevators two and three opened, each revealing an identical Rider, dressed in black on a smoking black Crossfield, holding what could only be described as a very large gun.

A second later, the doors opened on elevators one and four and revealed two more identical Riders. The Rider in elevator four was rather smaller—in fact, much smaller—and had clearly just fired several rounds into the elevator control panel. Inconvenient had seen many things, many spurious attempts to get to the bar quickly, and few of them worked. There is no doubt that everyone else in Inconvenient regarded the four Riders as just another group of guys trying to get served in under an hour.

I knew instinctively they were wrong.

I knew instinctively these Riders, for reasons yet unfathomable, were there for me.

3

My plan was quick and I have to admit not entirely foolproof. I dived under the table and, as luck would have it, I did it at the exact moment all four of them roared out of the elevators and began blasting the shit out of everything.

A large proportion of the people waiting at the bar didn't move. When you've waited for that long at Inconvenient, you're loath to lose your place—even in the face of four very large and surprisingly aggressive Riders, pumping shotgun rounds randomly about the place. I could almost guarantee there were people here now who would be leaning over to the person next to them, and saying, "You know, this is nothing, you should have been here yesterday."

But frankly, this was something—and from a safe distance I would have found the level of destruction really quite impressive. But close-up, it was genuinely terrifying. I drew my gun, feeling that if I was going to fire it, now would be the perfect time—but I couldn't see anything through the dust.

"Man, I'm listening, and I'd say you have really upset someone there. You're having a bad day today, aren't you?" said the voice on my Skin Media phone in a sudden lull.

"What?" I cried.

"I said, you're having a bad day. When I have a bad day, I try and sing a song to alleviate the stress. You should try it."

"Listen," I shouted, as a vast lump of the ceiling crashed down on the table above me, "I want some things out of my house, OK?" Something inside my head had stirred without my actually being conscious of it, some distant memory, but I couldn't risk putting it into neat thoughts yet, so I just let my instinct talk and see where it led me. "Now, the vis-media remote is fixed under the table in the lounge, OK? I'll give you that for nothing, but you'll never find the really good lights in the bathroom, or work out how to operate the stairs to the roof garden and loads of other stuff, unless I tell you. So I'll make a deal with you. The books and things I want from the house, for the information you need."

There was a pause. "Hello?" I shouted above another huge, dust-flaring explosion.

"I'm listening," said the voice. "And you know what? I'm kind of warming to you, Moose. I think we've got a deal."

"I'll call you to arrange the handover." My voice trailed off. One large motorbike wheel had stopped, pointing at the table, then a second one, and a third and a fourth. Hemmed in by the four huge tires, I decided it was pretty hopeless to remain under the table.

Clearly they must have a fix on my C-4 Charlie so, slowly, I peeked out. As I feared, four huge shotguns appeared in the swirl of dust, each an inch from my nose. I instinctively dropped my gun and, before I had even properly stood up, found myself yanked onto the back of one of the bikes.

The bouncers had rallied in the period of calm and, as the bikes screamed about the bar like caged tigers searching for a way out, smoke pluming from the tires, they poured fire in our general direction, wreaking final havoc to any parts of Inconvenient still in one piece. I took a peek over the shoulder of the Rider in front of me and saw rather worryingly that we were headed for the bar—where, incredibly, there were still people waiting to be served. With a screech of power, we cut through the debris, and die-hard customers leapt onto the counter and headed for one of the giant windows. I didn't like the look of this, so I did what I always do in very bad situations: I closed my eyes.

I'm sure it's for the best. I'm sure in battle training with the most hardened of special forces troops they have a lecture one day, when their commanding officer says: "And if things get even worse than that, remember, you can always close your eyes." Well, it worked for me. With my eyes closed I heard the roar and felt the smash as the bike bucked through the gigantic glass window, but I didn't actually see it.

When I opened them again, things weren't a great deal better. I found myself plummeting through the freezing sky, surrounded by four large blurs of men in black coats and four spinning Crossfields. I realized I was about to die and felt a confusingly deep regret that I wouldn't have a chance to see the limpet encyclopedia saleswoman again. There was something about her. Her of all people.

And this would have been almost my last-ever thought if one of the Riders hadn't bear hugged me with one huge hand and pulled a ripcord with his other. A spurt of shiny black material swept out of his backpack, and with a massive jolt a chute opened and I found myself floating rather peacefully in the iron grip of a Rider, down past the midfloors of the Thin Building.

Who were these guys? Everything was out of kilter; the normal rules of life just didn't seem to apply anymore and I couldn't work out why. We sank toward the ground in a small, spiraling group. My head was now jammed to one side of the Rider's chest, and I could see only a small area below. As I watched, one of the Crossfields came into my view, falling gracefully end over end until it hit an ornamental fountain and exploded theatrically in a burst of metal shards. But we were drifting sideways fast, and my view of the dead bike was soon lost.

The wind was picking up and pulling us south toward Jazz. And, as I guessed, it wasn't long before I saw the tops of buildings below whipping past at an alarming rate. Either these people were very talented Glider-Riders toying with the elements, ready to pull off an extraordinary maneuver, or they were complete novices totally at the mercy of the screeching wind.

I had a terrible feeling it was the latter.

We skimmed a tall building and I kicked one of the aerials, snapping it clean off, so it snagged on my foot. For a moment I struggled to shake it free until eventually I felt it fall away, then with horror saw we were now dropping down between the buildings and flying along a narrow corridor over the main freeway at terrific speed.

We were definitely in Jazz. Here the buildings were a weird mixture of everything, so that a ground floor would be maybe in a classical style, but the next two floors would be modern and so on. Builders just did a floor each, then let someone else carry on. It was a silly system, and it was things like that which had made Jazz a scapegoat for a lot of the tension between the zones in many cities about twenty years back. I forget which ones it was exactly now—Punk I think, and Brass Band and Underground

Shopping Beat and maybe Wah-Wah. They formed a military pact and attacked Jazz, ostensibly on the basis that they didn't think Jazz was actually music, but it wasn't really about music. It was about intolerance, stupidity, and insecurity—the things wars were always about. The Jazz Wars lasted for three years until there was a settlement, but the people in Jazz had never quite got over being picked on like that and were ultradefensive to talk to.

We swung wildly, dropping in sudden jolts as we hit windless pockets between the buildings. The freeway below was packed with bikes. Either we were going to get killed by the traffic, or we were going to get killed by hitting one of the buildings. The options weren't good.

Another terrifying drop, and we skimmed the road. I swung my legs up to my chest to avoid one of the bikes speeding toward us. There were few options left and I braced myself, now frankly annoyed that I was going to die in a head-on collision with about forty bikes and I had absolutely no clue as to why.

Suddenly, we swung left into a small sheltered alley and the turn sucked the lift from the chute and we stalled, pausing agonizingly for what seemed like an entire minute though in reality it was probably about half a second, before plummeting the last five feet to the ground.

We landed unceremoniously in an open Dumpster. After a moment I pulled myself together, cleared the rotting food off my coat, and clambered unscathed but dazed onto the ground.

I was in an alley somewhere in Jazz, and I wasn't dead. By rights, I should have been grateful, but I wasn't; I was steaming with annoyance. The Rider disentangled himself from the chute and approached me. Above I heard a dull crunch and looked to see one of the other Riders smacking his helmet forcefully into the brick wall just above us and crashing down the last ten feet.

"Ahhh. My ankle, my ankle," he cried, bouncing off the side of the Dumpster. "You said these things were easy but I think I've broken my fucking ankle, Jeff." And he rolled about, somewhat theatrically, on the ground.

"Death. My name is Death," said the other Rider tersely.

"That is the last time I trust you, the last time. I can hardly walk. Oh shit, there's a hole in my pants and I love these pants! These are my lucky pants!"

"Just shut up about your pants and find War and Famine!"

"Who?"

"The other two. Go on; I'll look after the Package." And he turned to me. "Did you have a good flight, sir?"

"No, I fucking didn't," I said as my general feeling of relief and annoyance beat back any sense of fear. "Would it be too much to ask what the fuck is going on here?"

"Jonny X, you are having a bad day today, aren't you? Well it's going to get better soon because we have a special surprise waiting for you. We are going to look after you with the utmost care." And with that, he punched me with a curving uppercut, and I was only vaguely aware of the noise of the punch landing on my chin and the sharp twist of my head as I fell deeply unconscious.

In this state, I dreamed vividly. Normally I don't remember my dreams, and I can trace the moment that it all began to twelve years earlier, when I was training to be a dream architect. As students, we had access to the hardware to make dreams at a fraction of the cost. OK, the quality wasn't as good—some images would get lost or stories jumbled—but basically we had the chance to have as many dreams as we wanted, every night. And I took full advantage. The safety limit was three a week, but there were a lot of things I didn't know how to deal with going on in my life back then—like Eli's brother, Jack, dying—so I used the dreams to escape. Sometimes I was taking ten a night.

Designer dreams are vivid and stay with you well into the day, and for a while it was a great release; a glorious window into another world. But after a while it's like eating too much candy and your brain becomes restless for something else. Something with more depth, something with some kind of substance and meaning.

We'd all read the theories of Sigmund Freud and Carl Jung at college, and we'd immersed ourselves in long, late-night brandy- and coffee-fueled arguments about their beliefs. Were genuine dreams compensatory? Were they a way for our subconscious to give us warning of dangers ahead, if only we could interpret and understand them?

The theories seemed to have weight but what was certain is that designer dreams didn't do that. They were just window dressing, and maybe worse than that; maybe they fucked up your subconscious in a way no one properly understood.

So, with no head space for my own dreams I began to feel drained, unsettled, and unattached. And when I found myself saying things and doing things I didn't recognize as me, I knew I had to change my life quickly.

So I just stopped.

I left designer dreams alone completely. Now I don't even take up the complimentary quota of dreams I'm allowed by Easy-Dreams, the company I work for. Instead I give them all away to friends—mainly to Teb, whose head is so much on another planet already it doesn't seem to make any difference. Sometimes now, I have moments of unfathomable despair when I find it hard to get a grip on who I am. I can't adequately explain it, but I put this feeling down to that time of my life.

So it doesn't take a genius to work out that I don't remember my dreams now because something in me doesn't want to. It's one of those ironies I liked—a well-paid dream architect happy to give other people dreams, but who hasn't remembered one of his own for twelve years. But that was all in the past and the dreams I had now in my state of utter unconsciousness were outrageously vivid and comforting, in a way that was unlike any designer dreams I could remember.

It was an unbelievable release, a huge sigh of relief—a wonderful peacefulness that things would turn out right if only I could just keep going. So many images coursed through me that when I woke I felt settled and chilled out and I lay there, happy just to be.

Up above, a ceiling fan covered in dust thwacked the air gently, even though the room was cool. Then, after another minute, it suddenly occurred to me that I didn't know where the hell this place was. I went to sit up and found I was strapped down to a bed. I turned my head to one side and saw a row of old metal hospital beds, parked up neatly against a wall, and elsewhere random bits of ancient medical equipment standing about hopelessly. I glanced to the other side and there was nothing much, just more beds and a blank wall. I looked back at the ceiling fan and became aware of a dull ache from my jaw.

The pain triggered the memory of all that had happened in the past few hours, and it crashed over me in one gigantic wave of cold reality. Even while I was half-wondering if I really believed it all to be true, I knew deep down that it all was.

What on earth was it they wanted from me? From *me*, for God's sake? I was just a normal guy; I got up, went to work, came home, and on a good night had a beer with my friends. So why me? There had to be some reason. I turned the thought over in my mind. Some craziness of my ex-wife, Sarah? No, even she wasn't that mad. Emma, my girlfriend? We'd had one argument; surely this would have to classify as overkill even by her standards. My house... What did that guy say about my house? Something had stuck in my mind. It had been stolen to order, yeah, but there was nothing unusual about that. It must have made it on to one of the books of an estate agent on the Dark Side somehow. And then the limpet encyclopedia saleswoman; she said she got information that I was emotionally vulnerable from my Medi-Data stream, but that information was supposed to be guarded from the Dark Side by a zillion systems.

I sighed and tried to shake these thoughts off. Right now, I decided, I needed to escape, and fast. I strained against the white canvas straps pinning my arms neatly down to my sides and tried to gauge just how far up shit creek I actually was, and whether or not I had a paddle. Somewhere, I had once read that one of the great rules of escape is to do it early; the longer you're a captive, the fewer the chances you'll have to get away. Up until now, I had only usefully applied this information to bad parties where I found the secret was to get away within the first ten minutes of arriving. If you left it any longer and it was a particularly bad party, you could easily get trapped into listening to someone ranting on about the social implications of washing up or something.

I froze abruptly and listened. I could hear voices somewhere outside the shabby, fingerprinted double doors on my left. Then they stopped and I heard the clack of a woman's footsteps in a long corridor. They echoed on for an age and finally died away into silence. I breathed a sigh of relief, feeling this might be the best chance I'd have to get away. This time, I tried to slide my right arm out from under the strap, but the canvas webbing rucked on my sleeve as I tried to pull it free and it scraped against the skin on my forearm, holding me tight.

Then, without the slightest warning, the double doors at the far end exploded open with a muffled boom and a huge man in black strode in purposefully. I guessed he was one of the Riders. He reached my bed, stopped, glanced me up and down and seemed about to say something, but instead nodded and turned away.

"Wait!" I said, almost involuntarily. "Wait. This is all"—I didn't know what I was trying to say—"crazy." I finished up somewhat ridiculously.

He held up a large hand that I took to mean "Shut the fuck up," then nodded again. What was it with him and the nodding?

"You want some porridge?" he added, after a pause.

"Porridge?" I repeated.

"Yeah, you know. Yum, yum. Porridge."

"OK," I said, knowing that while porridge wasn't my number one priority—or even probably in my top one hundred priorities—at least this seemed like some kind of development.

He grabbed the metal end of the bed and swung it behind him, sending me sliding out into the middle of the room. The bed came to rest against a piece of medical equipment on wheels that had the words ALWAYS RINSE blazoned across it in big black marker pen. I found myself wondering what was supposed to be rinsed—the machine or the patient? The big guy was just to my left now, and as I turned and looked up at him, I felt a chill. There was a blatant scar on his neck, about two inches long, where his C-4 Charlie had almost certainly been removed. For some reason I found this deeply shocking and I tensed up involuntarily.

Here was physical proof of the kind of world I now seemed to be a distinct part of. Yes, sure you heard stories of bodies turning up without a C-4 Charlie, but I had never ever met anyone who had actually done it. Maybe I should have guessed. That's why the Riders rode through the Forbidden Bike Zone around the Thin Building without a care; they were invisible to the authority computers.

I knew there was a business in removing C-4 Charlies on the Dark Side. They even tried to fit new ones, but it didn't work.

Like the Jab-Tabs, the C-4 was all tied up with your DNA, and that made it impossible to replicate. Being caught without a C-4 Charlie was unthinkable. If you were very lucky, you wound up exiled to somewhere in Europe like Belgium, but much more likely you ended up extremely dead. Zone Securities and the City Caretakers reasoned that if you removed your C-4 Charlie, you had something big to hide—and therefore, as far as they were concerned, had as good as admitted your guilt.

The Rider grabbed the frame of the bed and slung me crashing through the double doors. I felt them bounce along the sides of the bed and flip-flap behind us as we passed into a dimly lit corridor with flaking paint walls. Suddenly I didn't like this. I was strapped to a bed, being pushed around an old deserted hospital by someone who was quite possibly a psychopathic killer. I tried to distract myself by taking in the surroundings.

Hospitals had all gone out of fashion twenty years earlier, when equipment and drugs crashed in price, and they had been replaced by street corner clinics and Well-Malls—each unit specializing in a different bit of the body. Some were cheaper and more disreputable than others, but word eventually got about which were the best. There was a lung clinic on my street that I never got particularly good vibes about; it always looked empty. I turned my head to see more clearly what was off to the side. We were passing doors at regular intervals, most of them closed, but we came to one hanging off its hinges. Inside was a small arsenal of weapons. Before I had time to look again we were past it. We burst through another set of shabby double doors and the Rider stopped.

"Famine," he called, then paused, but there was nothing but grimy, water-dripping silence. "Famine!" he called again with a heavy hint of tried patience. "Open the fucking door, can't you?" There was a pause, and another man I took to be one of the other Riders appeared in the corridor.

"What?" he said. "Ohh," he added, seeing me, and held the small door open as I was pushed through.

This room was warmer, and from what I could see had been made more homey in a chaotic sort of a way.

There were a few chairs, stacks of various bits of electrical things, motorcycle magazines, a set of beat-up golf clubs, and on one wall I recognized an old pinball machine with its lights blinking on and off methodically. But the thing that struck me most forcibly were the walls, spray painted with strange, bulging graffiti. Everywhere I looked were three-D words with extravagant white highlights twinkling off them, like a toothpaste ad on drugs. As I began to read them, I realized they were quotes from somewhere. Somehow, this all didn't feel very promising as regards my life expectancy.

"Would someone please, please, explain to me what the fuck is going on?"

4

I married Sarah when I was twenty-five. We had an apple pie wedding, as Mom would have said. The sun shone, everyone looked smart and young, the person who married us wasn't too smug, and the photographer wasn't drunk. Mat made a surprisingly funny and rather touching speech—there's a naive, soppy, romantic side to him that still gets him into all kinds of trouble—and everyone danced under the stars. We were married out in Big Sur, where there are still forests that can mend the soul and a shoreline that catches your breath.

I remember looking around the table while we were eating and realizing what an exceptional bunch of friends I had—genuine people you could call on anytime, whatever the situation. Sarah, my wife, was gorgeous—with a clear mind and a get-up-and-go sort of nature, soft skin and chocolate brown hair—though somewhere in there was an insecurity too. I knew it was there when I married her, but it seemed to grow overnight and during the years that followed no matter how hard I tried to set her on her feet, she kept leaning on me harder and harder. And when she fell, she said it was all my fault.

I watched her character shrink before me and I felt so helpless. The spirit I'd loved her for had turned into fear, so that she no longer thought she could cope with the world; was so scared of the thought of being on her own that she crushed the present, suffocating any joy from life, and turned everything into a battle for survival. I knew this was not right—not for us, not for people who had a house and food and friends. And the more she clung to me, the more we both drowned, sinking under an invisible sea of desperation.

I tried. I really did, but she fought the truth of what was happening, thinking it would kill her, when I knew it was the only thing that would have set us free. And in the end, one day I left; but knowing it was for the best didn't dampen the pity I had for her. I rode down to Big Sur and sat on a rock watching the waves explode below and cried—with relief and with sadness and with guilt.

But mainly with relief.

I miss the old Sarah, but in truth I can hardly remember her. How or why this all happened I don't know. Technically we're still married and I see her sometimes. My door is always open to her, but there's no going back. I didn't have the apple pie life Mom had hoped for, after all.

I rang Mat that afternoon, and he dropped everything and swung by on his bike with two boards on the carrier and a couple of wet suits and we went surfing. That was always Mat's solution to everything. Him and Teb are so different like that. The waves were about four-foot on the push of the tide, with a slight offshore breeze just whipping up the tops. So we paddled out side by side along the rip and sat out the back waiting for the bigger sets that came in now and again, bobbing on our boards.

But now, thinking about it, there was something about this whole memory of Sarah that didn't somehow click. It was as though she had been laughing at me all along, smiling underneath. I couldn't explain that feeling at all. Yeah, there's something about Sarah that seems all wrong.

Anyway, we spent that afternoon catching the surf and sitting out the back, just as Mat and I and Eli's brother, Jack, had done so many times before in another age, all those years ago.

We do a lot of weird things in our lives. We want things, we love people, we strive to achieve stuff, but in the end it boils down to one question. The whole of life can be boiled down to one question: "What the fuck was that all about?" Maybe we don't think we ask it, maybe we think we avoid the question, but we all have our own unique answer, assembled over days and years; it's our lives.

I couldn't tell you what I thought the point of life was. Somewhere back when I was young, I would have given you an answer and believed it too. But I had gone backwards somehow, found a world that looked just like the one I used to move around in; but this world was somehow harsher and more complicated, as though my head had been filled with glue. Now when things got tough, all that I felt was: Keep going. If I could only just keep going. Then I'd end up somewhere else, and maybe that somewhere else would be better.

And as we sat out the back that day, I went through the whole thing in my head. Knowing I was free now and knowing that I mustn't make the same mistakes again; knowing the past was clawing at me, but also knowing that going forward was the only direction that mattered.

We surfed until the sun began to set and fired up the clouds so they glowed with the same soft crimson as a young woman's breathless cheeks, and for the first time in a long while I was able to let myself feel grounded again. I was able just to be me, as though my soul was finally content to settle down into the pit of my mind, and the moment seemed to consume me with its Day-Glo purity and truth. Mat turned to me as we sat out the back in a lull. "Deep down, this feels like it means something, doesn't it, Jonny?"

I nodded.

"Not all of life feels this real," he added, watching the sun sink gently into the glassy ocean, and I knew what he meant. It was as though someone had suddenly turned up the dial marked "life" until the intensity was shouting at us, and all blurred edges created by things like hate, greed, and jealousy were straightened out at a sweep. I wanted to trap the feeling somehow and lock it down inside myself so that in times ahead I could revisit this place at this moment, with such an explosive clarity it would make me understand that, underneath it all, everything was all right. But I also knew, deep down, that was impossible.

Memories fade, no matter how much you try and keep them alive. Things change. Shit happens.

So, I just looked across at Mat and smiled, breathing in the moment so it felt like it was living deeply and wholly inside of me.

5

"Relax, Package," said a Rider.

"What the fuck is going on here? If you don't mind me asking," I said, suddenly consumed with enough irritation to smother my fear and probably kill a badger at twenty paces. Two of the Riders edged in, and their puzzled, standoffish expressions reminded me of the faces of some people in our office who one day found the photocopier was having a breakdown. It was crying it was under too much pressure and couldn't do color anymore, and one of the secretaries had had to take it home for the weekend.

The bearded Rider stared calmly at me, but his thoughts seemed elsewhere, and I took in the full extent of the rivulets of scars etched into his forehead. They had clearly seen their share of bad sewing.

No one said anything, and after a minute I closed my eyes and tried to think of clean, peeling lines of waves at Todos Santos Island, and the time I'd paddled out at dawn with Mat at Thor's Hammer and watched the sun rise over the dunes. But the image just kept collapsing, like a nighttime dream drowned by waves of consciousness in the sunlight of the early morning.

"Porridge," reiterated the bearded Rider, without breaking his lost stare.

"You're not giving him porridge?" sang a wiry voice abruptly. The bearded Rider's eyes jolted back into focus. I could just see the one who had spoken: a thin Rider who seemed nearly half the size of the other three. He had a wiry, chirpy, overloud voice that ran up and down words the way a squirrel scampers about a tree. "Give him CornConfetti instead, Jeff; don't be so mean. Or those Rici-Rici-Pops things. They're not bad with sugar. And there's Chew-Kings somewhere. I knocked off a planeload. Remember?"

The Beard simmered with such force it probably showed up on the Richter scale, then turned purposefully. He slid a large shotgun smoothly off his back and stuck it unemotionally in the small Rider's throat.

"My name," he whispered, "is Death! Can you please get that into that round, waxy-haired thing you use as a head?"

"Knock it off," said one of the other Riders, crumpling some paper. "If you two are going to kill each other, I'm seriously quitting."

"Death." The bearded one spoke in a dry, even voice, with words that seemed heavy enough to make holes in the floor.

"Not anyone can deal with the Alpha grid. Or keep the Zone Security guys at bay. They're tricky. You've got to know how to deal with the wire gates on the GlobeNav. I worked hard at that, you know. You guys haven't a clue," the one crumpling the paper babbled on.

"Thank you, Famine, I'll bear that in mind," the bearded one said, without removing the shotgun from the chirpy one's throat.

"Took me an aeon, and I had Virus Propelled Grenades. Do you know how tricky they are to use?"

"He said shut the fuck up, didn't he?" the chirpy one yelped, breaking out of the corner. The bearded Rider sighed, then slipped his shotgun smoothly back to its holster.

"Death. Got it?" he mouthed under his breath.

"Actually no!" said the chirpy one kicking over a chair, with renewed gangly vigor. "You're not being Death just like that. No way. I've decided I'm Death."

"What?" said the Beard.

"I'm Death now," said the chirpy one. "Me. I am. OK? Harry R45 is now Death. Everyone got that?"

"Oh, well done! Well done. Bravo!" groaned the bearded Rider, slipping half a glance in my direction. "OK, let's see what the Double E wanted. You are . . . Pestilence," he said, shoving a piece of paper at the other guy. "It was decided at the meeting with the Double E. And the Double E will personally stuff your lucky pants down your lucky throat if you don't get that into your lucky, fucking head!"

"Pestilence?" said the chirpy Rider. "Pestilence? La-di-da Pestilence! My friends will blackball me if they think I'm called Pestilence! It sounds like some kind of deodorant."

"Get used to it," said the Beard.

"No, no, no. I'm being Death, end of story. You can be Pestilence. What the fuck does that mean anyway? Why should I be a deodorant?"

"Conversation over," growled the main Rider. And at that moment, my whole world suddenly filled with the wild grin of the fourth Rider as he slanted a handgun to my head.

"What's pestilence, dude? Come on! Let's hear what you have to say on the subject!" Sweat slithered down his forehead. "What's pestilence? Tell us, college boy. You tell us all. Nice and loud."

"Don't kill him! Not now!" called Famine. "You guys. He's not expendable like the Ringer; you remember that. If he shoots now, I'm seriously quitting."

"Easy," said the Beard. "Easy with the piece, War. OK? He's really valuable."

Sweat coalesced in droplets on War's forehead as he leaned over me, and it was a wonder he hadn't been served some sort of court order, because his smell must have been in breach of all kinds of health restrictions.

"What's pestilence? I want to know!" he cried. "No secrets, little boy."

"Pestilence," I croaked, trying to find some strength to my voice. "Pestilence is an epidemic . . . like a swarm of locusts. It's a huge . . . pain in the ass, basically." And then I turned and locked eyes with the one who didn't want to be called Pestilence. He had deep, almost black pupils that jerked and flicked, almost spinning about his head like the reels of fruit on a slot machine. "A massive pain in the ass." I enunciated every single word in his direction. It was a crazy thing to do, but the guy had the kind of chirpy character that ripped away my fear with irritation.

There followed a pause that I'm sure would have won most of the awards at the International Festival for Film Pauses. It would have won "Deepest Pause," "Longest Pause," and "Most-Worrying Pause." And possibly "Pause Most Worthy of Special Mention." It would have swept the board. Those awards lasted ten years before the sponsors pulled out. There was some scandal when "Best Foreign Pause," "Best Reasonably Long Pause," "Best Short Pause," "Best Pause Translated from a Foreign Language," and most of the other awards all went to a Scandinavian film about a puffin who had learned the concept of elegance. Especially when it turned out the director was sleeping with one of the members of the panel.

The bearded Rider leaned over and very slowly drew the gun out of the hand of the manic one. War didn't flinch, staring into my eyes like he was trying to find my soul; just as you might look for a large fish that was hiding under the weeds of a crystal clear river.

"Porridge," said the bearded one, tossing the piece onto one of the old upholstered chairs, where it bounced like a dropped toy.

The door clacked shut and War smiled at me, pointing two fingers at my head and making a "pcchhh!" noise like he was firing a gun, while Famine smiled on witlessly.

If I ever get out of this, I thought, I'm going to eat more garlic or whatever it was you're supposed to do to stay healthy, and I'm definitely going to take up smoking again. I really, really could do with a cigarette, and I tried to imagine the deep pleasure of inhaling one now, but the taste of the first drag lay agonizingly out of reach.

"The great day of wrath is come, who shall be able to stand?" one bit of spray painting said in bulging letters. And farther along, half-obscured by the pinball table, another said: "And power was given to him over the four parts of the earth, to kill with sword, with famine and with death and with the beasts of the earth."

No mention of shotguns or porridge, I thought, staring at the grimy ceiling. "And the power was given to him over the four parts of the earth." I ran it over in my head. What four parts? The words rang a bell in my brain, and I knew I knew where those lines came from, but for some reason I couldn't bring it to mind. And the more I ferreted around my head, the more the memory just sidestepped me, like a bullfighter playing with a bull.

In the end, I had less sense of what the answer could be than when I started. All I was left with was a distant clang of familiarity that was too far off to hear clearly, like a warning buoy for a ship chiming somewhere in the dead fog.

"Come on, Dukey!" cried the Rider who had put the gun to my head. And twisting around again, I saw he had started to play a handheld Game Guzzler. He was still sweating like the teenager at a disco who could never understand why he didn't get the last dance. I watched his huge, ripped-up hands flick at the keys, and I could almost imagine he had swallowed a furnace a little earlier, which now caused this excess of heat and made his eyes flare with sparks.

"The great day of wrath is come, who shall be able to stand?" was painted just behind him. I sighed, wondering how I would ever make sense of all this. And as I lay there, I felt a strange silence sink into the room—a very particular sort of mildewed silence that was immensely depressing.

It reminded me of the faceless, tragic breakfast rooms I had encountered in countless motels when I had been on the road for EasyDreams, and the sensation shivered through me, even here, with a hollow, dry-rotted clarity. Those mornings had always been the same, with the same dull breakfast-cutlery-chinking silence. The same tired uncertain smiles on the faces of the waitresses. The same dampened rattle of Spanish voices at the other tables. The same wither of sunlight that dropped painfully on the dried-up furniture. The same stench of people passing through, the carpets sodden with the presence of strangers who'd gone ahead, or back, in a ceaseless trawl around that lost underworld of shuffling travel, and here it was again. The same rootlessness. The same sense of being on the edge of life, in some backwater that nobody cared about.

The same pockmarked, down-at-the-heel, lost-to-humanity silence.

"Don't do that with your hat!" War screamed at the Game Guzzler, but I hardly heard him. Despite myself, I was thinking about those damned motels and how, at the end of the weeks, I'd come home with relief, finally feeling I was in a place I could breathe properly again, and spend time with Sarah. On the fleeting Sunday afternoons, we'd hold each other and talk about our dreams. Or read books on the deck of our wooden house while our black-and-white cat, who we named Possible Horse, would claw at my lap with his white-whiskered, head-nuzzling paws, and his solid build and powerful purr would make him vibrate like a jackhammer. In my mind's eye I saw myself sitting there drawing in the gentle warmth of the winter sun on my back and hearing a distant clang of a train edging its way through the town, nosing the kids off the track.

I really loved books. They were one of the things I used to get emotional about. At a party, I could remember seeing the eyes of a good-looking woman glaze over as I had gone on about my passion for them with a childlike, religious fervor: the way you could slip them into your pocket; the way they took you into your soul, like a secret, unexpected journey. I wondered why reading from a screen seemed too transient, brittle, and temporary; maybe it was as though a final decision about the order of the words had yet to be reached.

I hadn't learned then, as a teenager, that talking with that kind of earnestness about something can be exhausting to listen to, and that those sorts of girls were far more impressed by my friends who lied to them anyway, claiming they were the brothers of someone famous. Truth is not generally the keenest weapon but I had persevered with it, stubbornly thinking that in the end it ought to come out on top, but it had never really seemed to prove me right.

"Phase one incomplete. The Duke of Wellington cannot be tempted with bananas," enunciated the Game Guzzler crisply. I sighed. I really hated those machines and would gladly have reintroduced penal colonies for those who were caught with them.

"The Duke of Wellington will be sick if you feed him furniture," the thing burbled on, seemingly getting more confident and content. The door clacked open as the bearded Rider swung in, injecting some energy into the docile quiet.

"Porridge," he said grimly, "nice and fucking fresh," like this was something virtually unique. "Get the Package out of there. Come on!"

"Level two!" growled War, not raising his eyes.

"Come on!" said the Beard. "Leave it."

"The Duke of Wellington will be sick if you feed him furniture," the machine reiterated in the same deep tone that I was more used to hearing from someone giving a commentary about the life cycle of an oak tree or something.

"Level two? Jesus, War," said the bearded Rider. "To get to level three all you have to do is not feed the Duke of Wellington the furniture. Weren't you supposed to be a teacher once?"

"I *was* a teacher," said War looking up from the screen to some distant point, as though he might just be able to see his class three-quarters of a mile away. "Who's making all that noise?" he said. "See?"

He plonked the machine down and I felt him loosen the straps holding my arms. The main Rider indicated with a tiny rock of his head that I should sit up, and I swung my legs stiffly off the bed, awakening a throbbing ache of pain in my jaw where his punch had landed. I touched it gingerly, reassuring myself it wasn't as big as it felt.

The Rider handed me a bowl of sweet-smelling porridge with a spoon standing perpendicular in the middle. I lifted a dollop of the steaming stuff slowly into my mouth and found it was warm with a thick texture. The chirpy Rider came in closer and made a strange guttural growl, and smiled at me.

"Porridge, eh?" He nodded. "You like porridge! Porridge for the Catch. You like that stuff, eh?"

"It's lovely," I said, but it came out flat. I thought he was going to turn away then, but he continued to stand there, rather too close to my face, and watch me eat just like a dog hoping for a scrap. I took another spoonful and he followed me intently, grinning, then turned around and grinned at the other Riders. When he looked back, I noticed a flash from his mouth and saw that one of his teeth seemed to have been replaced by a brass round of ammunition.

"So, Jonny X, you want to know why you are here, eh?" He smiled.

"Yes, that would be good."

He seemed to find this funny and repeated it more loudly for the others to hear. "He wants to know why he's here!" The Riders all smiled, happy to play along with him for now. "We shoot the hell out of a bar and give him a flying lesson and he wants to know why he's here!" The others continued to smile in a self-congratulatory kind of a way and I nodded uncertainly, not ready for this change of mood.

"I'm Jonny X; I want to know why I'm here!" yelped the Rider—an impression that bore no resemblance to me at all. He was on a roll now. "Why am I here?" he cried starting a weird walk. "I'm Jonny X, why am I here? I must be here for some reason!"

A gunshot choked all life from the atmosphere.

Bits of ceiling sifted to the floor in the dead, severed silence, and the chirpy one was left marooned in the middle of the room, a forced smile stuck to his face like a bit of tape. The bearded Rider resheathed his smoking shotgun on his back.

"We're professionals. We're not some kind of fucking circus."

"Professionals," echoed War. "Pro-fession-als," he enunciated again, right in the face of the chirpy one. He took a chair and scraped it along the floor toward me and sat down. The atmosphere was roller-coastering wildly, and I had no idea what was going through their minds, or how dangerous this all was; but I sensed that this was probably how they lived from day to day, in a jumble of drama and confusion. They filled in time with it, feeling it was somehow necessary to always push the boundaries.

The small, jumpy one who didn't want to be called Pestilence looked at me from the pinball table where he had ended up and grinned. Once again, I felt like I caught a flash of the brass round of ammunition stuck there in place of one of his teeth, and the image went into my head in one lump, as though I had unexpectedly swallowed it whole.

War put his mouth next to my ear. "We have a little job for you, Jonny X," he whispered, and I realized no one else could hear him. "A nice, simple little job."

I sighed because, frankly, I couldn't see that whatever he was likely to suggest was going to be "simple" or indeed "nice." I didn't think they had got me here to weed a window box or something.

"Know what we are?" cried the jumpy one from across the room.

"Leave it," cut in the Beard.

"We're the chosen ones," he said, grinning. "We are the four Riders. You understand?"

I felt War breathe into my ear without paying any heed to anyone else.

"We need help with a very special target," he whispered, raiding my thoughts so that all I heard was his voice. Automatically, I ate the porridge.

"What are you saying?" called the bearded one. "Don't tell him the target, all right? The Double E gave instructions for us to wait."

"Our target," whispered War, pressing on softly and pausing only to wet his lips, "our target is . . . God." His voice was barely audible even an inch from my ear, then he finally pulled back, smiling.

"God?" I coughed, in the midst of some porridge.

"You told him?" growled the Beard. "I don't believe you just fucking told him! Fucking mental case amateur."

"We have been hired to assassinate God," whispered War, unperturbed. "The creator of the entire fucking universe. And you, little man, are the key!"

The bearded Rider pulled him back by the shoulder. "You're a liability."

"No, no, no. I am a professional." War smiled. "Pro-fess-ion-al."

I felt a wave of cold uncertainty sweep over me. Something was very wrong here. This was definitely not the sort of situation they teach you how to deal with at night school, although I'm quite certain they could get a reasonable grant if they chose to start a course. No doubt a sizeable group of married mothers would dutifully sign up and be rather too conscientious about the whole thing.

"What do you say to assassinating God, Package? Reckon you got the guts?" added the one who didn't want to be called Pestilence.

I nodded imperceptibly, hoping to buy some time, while inside my head I was shouting, You're all bonkers! You're all bonkers! You're all completely bonkers!

"What about your house?" he went on. "You do that? You get that organized?"

"No," I murmured.

"No? What about the girl from the chopper? She know you?"

"No."

"All very weird. No one steals houses anymore, not without us knowing about it."

"Forget it," droned the bearded one. "Now, we have things to plan."

"No way am I going clothes shopping with him again," Famine said.

"All right, cool it." And he turned back to me. "So, now you know all about it, Jonny X. We'll see you in the morning for some action."

And with that, he caught me with a thumping uppercut.

I half heard his fist connect with my jaw before I leapt into a thick, black swirl of unconsciousness.

6

In this dream I was alone, and the sunlight reflected in a blinding sheet off the wide, curving field of smooth snow.

I glanced at my feet and saw I had on my old climbing boots, the ones that had worn out years ago, and over them were the familiar, hard-to-tighten blue crisscross straps of my crampons. I was breathing hard, drawing in huge lungfuls of air that seemed to be light and empty of any substance. My legs ached, feeling heavy and bulky as I pushed methodically through the caking snow. The slope wasn't unusually steep but I stopped after a while to regroup my senses, leaning on the top of my ice ax and adjusting my hood and snow goggles with my left hand as best I could while still wearing my clumsy overmitts.

It was then I saw the figure plodding away up the slope ahead of me. For a second I was disoriented, wondering who it could be, then suddenly I knew. It was Eli's brother, Jack, and we had come out here together. While I was watching he stopped, turned toward me, put his ice ax above his head and pointed excitedly. I stood there and smiled, just savoring the moment, wondering what he had seen. It was so good, being here. It was better than good. I turned and felt a lash of excitement as I glimpsed the vista he'd been pointing at.

We were above most of the other peaks now, and could look across mile after mile of sculpted white mountains, sleek and graceful with their pure hard sides and pitted edges, shading to black where the rocks poked through. It was like looking down into the jaws of time. A sharp, crisp, snapping crack came from somewhere, followed by a low ominous rumble that ran around the inside of my head. I turned back to look up the slope, but Jack was swept from view amid a wash of snow that was thrown up by the boiling noise. I struggled to breathe. I was coughing. The explosion seemed to carry on ricocheting inside my head and I fought against it, now knowing it was a dream, but I couldn't seem to shake it off. I battled with it, but it was like being trapped inside something I couldn't control.

I kept going, fighting it, and suddenly my eyes opened and I was breathing heavily.

7

It was dark and I was awake. Just.

There was dust everywhere, and my eyes were still heavy with sleep and fought to make sense of anything. A small pile of rubble seemed to have collapsed in the corner, coughing up more dust in bulging clouds. I heaved myself up and berated my mind for not being up to speed more quickly. More noise. Something metal falling.

Wherever I was, it was all but destroyed and the explosion had been real. I had sucked it into my dream. A small light danced about in the darkness, picking out fallen beams and snapped pipes until it settled on me. It looked like a tiny, blinding, shooting star. A black-gloved hand appeared with the fingers outstretched, and a woman's voice said: "Come with me if you want to buy a set of encyclopedias."

I was knocked sideways and backwards and several other directions in confusion.

"I really don't want to buy any encyclopedias," I said, groggily. "I don't have the shelving, for one thing."

"We have," she said, "about ten seconds to get out of here before a sizeable proportion of hell breaks loose, and I don't mean the cafeteria bit."

I thought about it for roughly a tenth of an instant, then grabbed her hand. She forcefully yanked me up and I flapped after her like a kite pulled by a seven-year-old on a windless day. Rubble lay strewn in ankle-snapping piles, and my feet scuffed and floundered on the uneven surface as we flew into the impenetrable dust.

God knows how she has any idea where we are going, I thought.

There were shouts from somewhere, and the dull, empty, hollow explosion of a shotgun firing, and more rubble falling. I was accosted by the image of the jumpy Rider leering at me with that damned round of ammunition stuck in among his teeth, and it finally woke me up, as if lightning had lit up my mind and set fire to the remains of my sleepiness. Was this woman rescuing me? And if so why? And then it occurred to me just how mad the Riders would be—like a bunch of bears that have just found out they've had their honey stolen. Along with their wallets.

Another gunshot cracked the air, this time closer, and my lungs ached. My mind was still playing catchup with events, and I realized this had to be the same woman who had come out of the helicopter and tried to sell me those encyclopedias. It had only just clicked. Somehow I was being rescued by an encyclopedia saleswoman.

We ducked under a fallen beam and slid into a long, empty room. For a sliver of a second, part of my brain tracked away from everything and saw how the moonlight coursed in through the tall windows, picking out the swirling dust in long shafts. Then I felt my feet ache as we clattered over the wooden floor down to the far end. The noise echoed flatly and reminded me of being in a school gym. I was beginning to feel an excruciating pain creeping up my arm as she held my wrist with the weight of a felled redwood.

We slammed, thwick-thwacking, through a set of double doors, and she hooked me sharply right as, almost immediately, the doors exploded off their hinges under a barrage of fire. She skidded to a halt and looked me in the eyes. I thought she was about to say something, but instead—with hardly a flicker of movement—she somehow jettisoned me out of an open window, headfirst.

I found myself on the ground outside and before I even had time to think, she was there, hauling me onto the back of a bike.

And then we were gone.

Crash suits hummed into place amid the roar of acceleration and the smell of oil as we choked up a tiny alley. The bike slewed around a bend, hemmed in by tall, gray concrete walls, then she flicked us upright and hit the throttle.

Suddenly, I had faith in this woman and realized she had the sort of confidence that could burn a path through a dark forest. I couldn't be sure how many encyclopedias she had sold, but she could certainly handle a bike.

We leapt onto a freeway and I guessed we might be on the outskirts of Rap or Heavy Metal. It was just a feeling gleaned from the thrown-together buildings I could make out in the distance, because those weren't zones I ever hung out in, and this freeway wasn't especially distinct. The neon aura of the glow

lamps shot past, one after the other, strobing in the blurred, vibrating darkness, and I felt the bike lurch and kick sideways as
we rode a bend that must have been greased with oil.

The shock of the escape had touched a nerve inside of me,
maybe because I hadn't been properly awake, but the idea of dying now seemed real and cold and lonely. I had hoped that, in
the moment of death, my life would all add up to something that
would be realized in a flourish of understanding and peace. But
this had made me see I could be wiped out in a flurry of trivia
and my last thoughts might be confused and meaningless, and
somehow that was more surprising than the idea of being consumed in a sheet of pain.

I tucked my head in closely to Caroline's back just as the bike
seared into a long, sweeping bend, and we galloped inexplicably into thick darkness. A whole swathe of glow lamps
were out, and my lungs tightened as I wondered if this was
some kind of trap set up by the Riders.

I glanced ahead over Caroline's shoulder and saw a plasi-
screen loom forward in the blackness, and on it a dark girl with
bold, high cheekbones poked her finger at us and her easy,
smooth voice filled the speakers in my crash suit: "Grr! Ha! Bang!
Jonny X, time you took out a new sort of life insurance? Yes? Take
out a policy with us today, you son of a bitch!"

The marketing people of that company had clearly been either up all night or having a very strange day when they thought
that one up. The irony about life insurance didn't escape me, but
I was more taken by the fact my C-4 Charlie was broadcasting
my existence loud and clear to anyone who cared to listen, and
I felt a sickness in my stomach.

The Riders had traced me once with my C-4 Charlie, and I
didn't doubt they could do it again. Didn't doubt that, even now,
they probably were bearing down on us with their ludicrously
oversized shotguns. I gripped the bike tighter with my thighs

and stared at the ground, wondering why this woman had bothered to come after me. Did she really understand what she was getting into? Again, the leering image of the Rider with the ammunition round in his teeth plastered itself around my mind.

It had been a bad day, I thought. A very bad day, and I wanted a cigarette more than anything. But I never had managed to find the packet I had bought the night before, and I couldn't see Caroline being keen on the idea of stopping off to get some. She jinked deftly between a couple of other bikes and inside my crash suit I rocked from side to side like a rag doll. I tried to get the thought of the satisfaction a cigarette would give me out of my head, and wondered again why the hell she had come after me. It couldn't just be about trying to sell me those encyclopedias again, could it? I had never even heard of limpet saleswomen, and I guessed there had to be more to it than that. But at least she was on my side and I was grateful. I'd had precious little go my way in the past twenty-four hours and whoever she was, she didn't appear to want to kill me.

The way things were, I had to regard that as a bonus.

She throttled back after half an hour or so and slithered off the main freeway, powering down as we hit a deserted junction. The empty quiet was unnerving and unexpected. Shorn of our speed, I felt stupid and conspicuous, as if we stood out like the only piece of bread at an annual convention of wild ducks.

Plasi-screen signs flashed and I tried to take a bearing on where we were, but it wasn't anywhere I knew offhand. It was probably outside the music zones, and people always said they lived "natural" out here.

"The rain shower you're approaching is brought to you by Merryweather Hover-Umbrellas," said a man on a screen with a smile so shiny he could have used it as an alternative source of renewable energy if they found a way to store it. "Merryweather," the man bustled on. "If you haven't got one of our

Hover-Umbrellas you're a loser!" Some other people appeared on other screens.

"Loser! Loser! You're a loser, Jonny X."

Frankly, this sort of thing wasn't helpful.

A rain shower erupted right on cue, triggered by a local cloud machine that must have been somewhere about. Caroline throttled the bike away from the junction, picking her way through a series of small roads flanked by a mixture of small-time malls and bars that seemed to be mostly dead, and there was a strange, foreign peripheral feel to the place, as though it was outside of the normal run of life. The warm rain teemed down, and I found my crash suit had a big leak. I was soon soaked through, shaking the water out of my eyes to see anything at all. Being outside the music zones, the advertisers tended to feel more courageous about giving their customers a hard time; they probably didn't even have a license to be drizzling rain on everything like that.

Caroline took a left down a small track by the side of a low one-story building just as the rain eased off, and we wound our way up through a series of hairpin bends that ushered in a crisp chill to the night air. It was mostly forest now, and I abruptly caught the sweet smell of the wet pine needles. It was reassuring something so sensual still existed.

My body temperature began to drop alarmingly as we climbed higher, and I hoped wherever we were going wasn't much farther. Still, I wouldn't have put it past this woman to carry on until we were in Michigan. The violent intensity of the Riders' presence was dimming in my mind, or just being overwhelmed by the shouts of cold from my body.

But we did keep on going and it was interminable.

Climbing up through the trees on this tiny track, accelerating occasionally when it flattened out, then climbing again. What was I doing here? A thought sniped at me from left field that this whole thing could be something to do with the International Board for Random Events.

The International Board for Random Events (IBRE) came into being when experts became worried that computer models were on the verge of being too precise at predicting future events. So to safeguard world trade markets, the government had formed the IBRE, which was given carte blanche to create random events that no computer could predict. What these random events were and how they were generated was a fiercely guarded secret. I couldn't see that they were behind this though. It was all too small-scale. Maybe the whole IBRE thing was a fabrication anyway, invented by someone to keep the traders' minds at rest.

The bike wound around another hairpin and I glimpsed a pinprick of scarlet as the red fire of dawn slipped through the trees. It wasn't hard to understand what the Aztecs had been on about worshipping the sun, because seeing the dawn always woke something in my soul. It was the one time of day I could believe almost anything was true, and I could have believed all kinds of things were true now, except my hands were full of the jagged burrs of frostbitten pain, which jabbed me away from dreaming.

8

Later, I slept.

I heard the engine cut out and forced my eyes open from a heavy, thought-drugged, soul-aching half sleep, and found the bike being rocked onto its stand.

The door to drowsiness still lay open in my head and half dreams flitted around like bats, caught in the light of my consciousness for a brief second, with the same bright candor that still pulsated from a memory of a theater show I had seen when I was small.

And then they were gone.

I tried to focus; where were we? Poking out from among the pine trees was a small cabin with a turf roof and a deck that rode out from the side of the hill like the upturned palm of a hand.

"Come on," hectored Caroline, hustling me off the bike. "Get inside. Hurry up."

I crept painfully off the bike, forcing blood into the stiffness of my legs and around the bruises that had frozen rigidly, like leaves in pond ice. I hobbled up the wooden steps, suddenly aware again of the damp, honey-sweet smell of the wet pine needles that lay in rafts on the forest floor, and made my way through the flapping mosquito-mesh door, then the main door itself.

The cabin was stiff with cold. It hadn't been used for a while, but a log fire was laid out ready in the hearth.

"Here," called Caroline, throwing a thick gray blanket at me. "Take off those wet things and use this till I get you some clothes." She struck a match and the smell of burnt sulfur drifted around the room on a thin wisp of smoke. The flames in the fire nibbled, then snapped at the twigs, crunching the paper hungrily as it came to life. I ditched my clothes, leaving them in a heavy, damp pool on the floor, and it felt like shedding the last vestiges of my past as I wrapped myself in the blanket, pinning it securely into place, and stared at her.

"My C-4 Charlie will have them buzzing up here before too long," I said. "And they are surprisingly dangerous people."

"It's OK. I cloned your C-4 Charlie while we were on the bike and sent it to a thousand different places." She handed me some coffee. "They won't know you're here."

"Oh, OK," I said, not exactly understanding what she was on about but feeling that any explanation might not make things much clearer, anyway. "Where are we? What is this place?"

Then it struck me.

This cabin seemed familiar. No, it was more than that, and

yet I couldn't place it. A shard of a memory had dented the surface of my consciousness, and the ripples fanned out through me, but my head was too full of other stuff. Too stirred up by old events that didn't mean anything and pointless people from the past who had swamped who I was, so I couldn't find jack shit in my head. "Have I ever been here before?" I added lamely, saying it simply because I felt it.

"Shouldn't think so. It's a safe house. They don't generally make the holiday rental market," she answered, tilting her head to one side with a searching stare. The same look she'd given me when we first met, and again that feeling as though she was testing me, seeing if I understood what she was saying behind the words, but I was way out of my league here. I was floundering like a new kid on his first day at school.

"Why does an encyclopedia saleswoman need a safe house?" I said, feeling the bizarreness of the sentence in my mouth and listening to the words enter the room as though they were being spoken by someone else.

She shrugged. "People come after me sometimes. It's a high-risk business. You wouldn't believe the hoods I have to deal with."

"Really?" My head spun. "You sell encyclopedias. It can't be that high-risk, can it?"

"You are way out of touch. It's on the front line these days."

"Is it? Well then, why not work in a store in a mall and sell them there instead?"

"Come on," she replied. "Do I look like that sort? Those store kids are just amateurs." I stared at her in confusion.

"Do I know you at all?" I said, almost involuntarily.

"No." She answered quickly. " 'Course not. But I know you. Married to a Sarah X eight years ago, no children, but one cat—"

"Whooa!" I said, holding my hand up. "You're out-of-date. We separated quite a while ago. Officially we're married, but that's it."

She paused. "Oh. Company records a mile or two away from reality, as ever. One day, one of their mistakes is going to be serious for someone in the field. You know about RMPs?" I nodded.

"Yeah, so do they. So. Do. They. That's all they seem to do." RMPs were a new teenage craze. You popped one in and it stimulated a random three-second memory that was lodged in your head with an almost real-life intensity, as though someone had suddenly shined a torch on one piece of highly colorful hieroglyphics in a lost, dark, ancient Egyptian tomb. It was the sort of thing the young jet set did after dinner parties, or kids messed about with when they were meant to be working. You were only supposed to do a couple every twenty-four hours. People who'd swallowed a whole packet had had their heads fried in a weird explosion of memories that came at them so fast and with such intensity, it seemed as though they were trying to exist in several distinct realities all at the same time. Their brains just couldn't deal with it.

"Tell me, have I missed the bit where you explain to me why you blow up an old hospital and take me to a safe house in the middle of nowhere? And are you sure I don't know you from somewhere? Perhaps a long time ago?" I added, after a pause. "A party or something? I've a friend called Mat C21. You know him?"

There was silence for longer than there should have been as we looked at each other, and it was an easier silence than by rights it should have been. Somehow—and inexplicably—I felt calmness slide through me, and a flare of something deeper.

"Here we are," she said, finally handing me a volume. "In here are all the answers you could ever need. Have a good look through. That's just a few of the A's, but you'll find color pictures and diagrams detailing clearly and concisely all aspects of the universe and more."

"I'm not being deliberately difficult, honest to God," I said. "I just really don't want any encyclopedias, and can you please tell me what is going on here? My house got ripped off, some Riders kidnap me, then you come after me and try and sell me a set of old-fashioned books. What is all this?"

"I'm really sorry about your house, that's a bummer. I'm sure it is, but I don't want you to lose sight of the fact that these are a treasured collection you can enjoy at your leisure to discover the mysteries of the universe and even share with your wife. Perhaps your wife loves you a lot more than you realize."

"What do you mean?"

"It doesn't matter, it doesn't matter. Jonny X, the bottom line is I'm a limpet saleswoman and I'm remarkably tenacious. I have to be. My neck is on the line every time I go for a kill."

"A kill?" I repeated.

"A sale. We call them 'kills.' Forgive me. I forgot you're a civilian. Now, I don't usually have the trouble I've had with you, but it's all part of the job and that's cool. I live with that. But your twenty-four hours is nearly up and I am going to get mountains of grief from my boss if we don't complete real soon, so I'd appreciate it if you would have a look through, then I'm sure you'll want to do a deal and we'll all be happy." She handed me the volume, nodded, smiled, then slipped out the front door, clacking it shut behind her.

"What?" I said out loud, quietly shaking my head and sitting down.

It was coffee in the mug. One sugar with just a tiny amount of milk, exactly as I take it. Even when I explain to people how I like my coffee, they get it all wrong, but this was perfect. I couldn't even begin to think how she had come to get it right by chance, unless her research people had their good moments too.

But this woman was still a confusing enigma. Surely she

wasn't a limpet encyclopedia saleswoman. There was no such thing, was there? Though to be honest, I had heard of selling fads that were pretty strange; there had been one for Wise Head Golf Clubs. These were golf clubs that adjusted the angle of the golf club head a moment before you hit the ball so that all your shots always went straight. They called it the "power of the nuclear bomb" for some ludicrous reason, which made no sense to anyone except some advertising marketing men. Anyway, they had programmed loads of golf balls to follow people who visited certain golf courses. The only way to get rid of them was to say "A wise head makes a wise player," but you had to say it about fifty times to get rid of all the balls. I think in the end someone went and burned the factory down and the company didn't get much sympathy from the judge, who was a bit of a player himself.

I'd never played golf in my life; I guess I'd never seen any evidence to suggest that it wasn't a hugely pointless and dull game best left to middle-aged men who thought they had something to prove or needed to get away from their wives. Or both.

Maybe these encyclopedias were being sold with a similar sort of fervor; but as I leafed through this volume, pleasant though it was, it did seem like a gigantic, cumbersome dinosaur from another age. A bit like the way the Two-Tone Zone now insisted everyone wear a hat and a suit in all of their bars, or they got an on-the-spot fine.

I sat down, flicked through, and saw it was pretty much as I had expected: a lot of stuff beginning with "A," coupled with simple, tidy explanations and neat line drawings. Surely there was more to these encyclopedias than that? Surely, for her to go to all this trouble, there had to be more in here than this childish-looking content? I laid the book randomly open at a picture of an Aeolian harp and tried to see deeper. I really did not need a set of encyclopedias, however much this woman tried to sell them. That was it. End of story. Still, it was better to be here than with those Riders by a factor of about six trillion.

The image of them jogged something in my memory, which seemed to be thawing out from the damp cold, and I eased myself up and walked stiffly over to the shelves. I ran my finger along the acres of smart volumes until I came to the P's, pulled the book down and sat flicking through the pages until I found it. "Pestilence."

" 'Pestilence—an epidemic disease causing a high mortality rate,' " I read out loud. Well, I hadn't been far off. Maybe the Riders would be interested in a set. I scanned down the page where it ran on about pestilence. " 'One of the Four Horsemen of the Apocalypse alluded to in the Bible, in the Book of Revelation. The others being Famine, War, and Death.' " I smiled ruefully.

So that was it.

That was the connection between their farcical struggle with their new names and this crazy wish to assassinate God. Something made some kind of sense.

"Piece of the jigsaw," I said softly, then contemplated that I had never actually ever done a jigsaw myself, even as a child, and it would probably be some sort of service to mankind's credibility if they were outlawed. I had a vision of some aliens having got hold of the ten-piece jigsaw of Mary Poppins my sister had been given one Christmas, putting it together, nodding to each other, and posting a note to the rest of the universe to never bother visiting earth.

Ever.

I shook myself back to the present and realized my mind must be tired as hell to be wandering off among such left-field thoughts, and I took another sip of the excellent, rejuvenating coffee. The Riders were naming themselves after the Four Horsemen of the Apocalypse and that presumably explained all the writing on the walls. I looked up "apocalypse" in the A's, found it, and scanned down to the bottom of the page.

"Four Horsemen of the Apocalypse," it read. "The end of the world, described in the Bible by the Book of Revelation, is heralded by the appearance of four horsemen who ride the earth bringing death and destruction on four different-colored horses." I took another sip of coffee.

So what could possibly connect all these things? Four Riders pretending they had come out of the Bible and wanting me to assassinate God. An encyclopedia saleswoman who had saved my life. And a group of thieves who had stolen my house and didn't know where the vis-media remote was. I clutched my coffee mug. Then I set it down, searched through the pockets of my sodden clothes, and retrieved the card those punks had left among the remains of my house. The number was in my Skin Media phone now anyway, but I thought I might as well hang on to this in case my phone had a nervous breakdown or something.

" 'Don't you hate it when this happens?' " I read aloud again.

Maybe I should give them another call and try and organize that meeting. They had seemed open to the idea, and my dream library books could be the key to sorting this whole mess out. I touched my Skin Media phone.

"Geesh, have I got some good messages for you!" sparked the phone immediately and part of me wished I hadn't woken it.

"OK. Cool it," I said, trying to keep the thing from mouthing off.

"Emma rang and left another really long message," it cried excitedly. "Boy, is she ever mad!"

"OK," I said, "I'll give her a call later and explain."

"Explain what? Why you are 'selfish and self-obsessed'?" cried the phone happily. "Or 'devoid of normal human responsibilities'? Or 'lacking in the most basic skills and sensitivities necessary for a relationship'? There was also something about resizing the shape of your kidneys. Can I go into that? It was really graphic."

"She was that mad?"

"Yup. It was terrific."

"Right," I said, feeling tiredness and frustration slice through me; this was one mess I could try and sort out now, before it grew any larger. "Call her now, then. Go on. See if I can sort this out."

The phone hummed happily. It liked nothing better than phoning people, and got stroppy if it was ignored for too long. It was some clever marketing thing that they programmed into its character, which I found had got much worse over time; the idea was it encouraged you to use it more. Only, of course, it wasn't clever. It was just incredibly annoying, like so many things marketing people do. In fact, like pretty much all the things I could think of that marketing people do.

Emma's voice clicked on the line. But it was just a message. She wasn't picking up.

"Hi, this is Emma, I'm having my hair developed all day. If that's Charlotte, leave me a salacious message. And if that's Jonny, this is going to cost you so much cake, you bastard!"

I sighed. There was something not quite right with us. Something not quite right with this relationship, as though we were speaking totally different languages and neither of us had realized it. But right now I didn't want to go delving to see what that feeling meant.

"Emma. It's Jonny. Hi, I just want to apologize. Cake is definitely on me. I've had a crushingly bad time. Someone stole my house, which, as you can imagine, wasn't good; and all kinds of other stuff have made things even worse. I'm sorry if I've been insensitive, you don't deserve that and I'll call you really soon when things are not so crazed. I'd like to give this another

chance. You're a really great person and we could get on fine...
did we really argue about smoking?" I paused, not even sure
whether we had argued about it or not.

My memory of her seemed to be torn into shreds that were
billowing in the breeze.

"Did we really go to that bar together that night? Sorry, I'm
talking nonsense, so... I'll be in touch really soon. Love you," I
said, clicking off with a tap of my finger and feeling that I had
stirred up even more confusion in my head than before I started.

"And there are three messages from Zone Traffic Securities,"
the phone hummed on.

"Right; good," I said, still thinking about Emma. "What?" I
suddenly jerked, as this information seeped into the relevant
part of my brain.

"You were the lone rider on a machine speeding and crossing
three FBZs yesterday and were required to turn yourself in by
midnight last night. I guess you've missed that one a bit.
Important, do you think?"

"Caught speeding yesterday?" My head ached at the news. "In
three FBZs? But... I wasn't... Yesterday afternoon..." I thought
back. "I was... unconscious," I finished, trying to wrench my
thoughts into some sort of order. "It wasn't me. There's been a
huge error."

"OK. They seemed pretty certain though," said the phone. The
room suddenly felt very quiet. It was a nasty silence, which
seemed to gather around me and say "Oooooooooh dear."
Getting on the wrong side of Zone Traffic Securities was a sure
way to ruin your life in a very dull, long, drawn-out, bureau-
cratic kind of way.

"Not Zone Traffic Securities too," I said with resignation.
"They really are a tight-assed bunch of persnickety wankers."

"Thanks for the big welcome," said a voice behind me, and I

felt a cold shiver arrow down my spine. I paused, then turned very slowly to see a thickset man with a moustache like a flock of toothbrushes. He was wearing a Zone Traffic Securities uniform and pointing a gun directly at my head. "Here's a tip," he added. "When you've gone to all the trouble to hole yourself up in a hideout and you've cloned your C-4 Charlie, don't use your Skin Media. It kind of gives the game away."

I made a small, strange, pointless gesture that involved raising my shoulders and turning out my palms and said, "Ahh." The door rattled open and three slightly overweight Zone Traffic Securities blokes and a woman bundled Caroline E roughly into the room.

"Wildcat!" exclaimed one of the men.

"Derek, bring Buzzy 34 in here. We got a couple of Exosets need booking," the woman sang out at her voice com.

"Q-ten to that," came the hissed reply. "Is this an R-forty-one?"

"I don't have a fucking clue," said the woman. "Just land the goddamn chopper."

No doubt I was just another dispatch number to them, another small-time nobody, another zap-file, another face in a line of faces that didn't mean anything other than it was all part of the day-to-day routine. I tried to meet Caroline's eyes as we were herded, stumbling, back outside. I wanted to know what she was thinking, wanted to know if she was still on my side and if she had some plan; but her features seemed worryingly cold, dead, and expressionless.

A couple of other Zone Securities personnel were outside, looking bored, and after a second or two Buzzy 34 popped up above the tree line and skated to a landing in front of the cabin. I felt a hand in the small of my back push me roughly toward the GaFFA 8 chopper, then a lot of things happened at once. The face of one of the Zone Securities blokes on the edge of the clearing crumpled with panic, while a sickening crunch resembling a watermelon being imploded with a baseball bat came from behind me. I spun around to be caught instantly in the giant grip of the thickset Zone Security bloke, but beyond him I saw Caroline E swerve off, trailed by a line of gunfire, leaving four of the Zone Traffic Securities mob scattered on the ground.

"It's a six-seven," cried the pilot, and they acted quickly, heaving me into the floor of the Buzzy and piling in as the rotor blades screamed us off with such a crazy yaw over the trees that one of the guys rolled across the chopper floor and clean out the door. The tree branches below must have broken his fall, because we heard his shouts a few seconds later.

"What kind of a fucking takeoff was that, Jackson? Jackson? Jackson, come back here with that thing! Come on. Don't play games with me!"

"He knows the rules," nodded the chopper pilot like a teacher at a primary school, turning to everyone in the back. "Second time in two months he's done that. It's six-seven for Christ sake! A six-seven! Not just some three-eight." The Buzzy groaned higher into the sky, and it was clear he wasn't turning back.

"I am not walking again!" cried the man's voice, more distantly, from below. "I'm not fucking walking back again! Please? Come on! Please? It's miles to anywhere! Come on! Baaaaaaaassstaaards!"

The rotors clobbered and cracked the air overhead as the pilot threaded us down a series of frenetic, controlled airways, via several airspace holding "lounges." I lay in my blanket on the chopper floor where I had been dumped, while the Zone Securities Unit lolled in their jump seats. They didn't bother to slide the door shut, or take much notice of me. They figured I wasn't going to leap, and they were right. I looked out as we skimmed through the sky and realized we were way out of town, perhaps up toward Nevada, but I couldn't tell for sure. Another time, I might have enjoyed the flight, but now things had closed so far in around me I felt suffocated and strangely resigned. My past life was hemorrhaging and bleeding away and I didn't understand why; I didn't have a fucking clue.

After fifteen minutes we reached the sea, and as I looked out I saw Half Moon Bay and below us, Elmar Beach. A break I had often surfed with Mat and Eli's brother, Jack, and it was a steady three feet today I guessed. And as I looked, someone took off and ripped a shortboard along the face, and it felt like staring down at my past life.

"It's like he thinks I could break a six-seven," the pilot was saying over his shoulder. "Next he'll want me not to use standard voice com procedures, or reverse a J-fifty-four."

"You're a pain in the ass," said someone to the pilot.

"I know," replied the pilot with a huge smile. "It's great, isn't it?"

I let his voice slide into the background and stared back out at the sea. Maybe I could find someone at Zone Traffic Securities who would realize the Riders were for real, however unlikely that seemed. Maybe I could find someone who would understand that I couldn't have been speeding and that none of this was my fault. Maybe, if I could just find someone at Zone Securities who would act independently and fight the system.

Surely there had to be someone there like that.

9

When I first met her, Sarah had a young room-mate called Tanya. I remember her because she went about the house theatrically banging doors and constantly striking poses when anyone was about, like a second-rate catalogue model who had forgotten she was not at work.

I got the feeling that unless she reminded you she was there, she was scared she might actually cease to mean anything.

Later, I wondered whether she had been using this show to drown out the alarm bells ringing in her head, trying to tell her she was living a cold, obvious lie. It was as clear to everyone else as if she'd given them a pamphlet on the subject, but she patently refused to admit it to herself. She thought she was exuding this persona of cosmopolitan confidence and soulful artistic wit; but it was just an awfully thin, cracked sheen, covering a rather sad, lost girl who copied things other people did to invent some sort of personality for herself. She was like a weird amalgam of people she respected, or had seen on the EtherMat, or read about in trashy magazines; and she found it a constant battle to keep all these disparate bits together.

And then I began to understand that we can have an image in our head of how we think the world sees us, and it's easy for that image to be way off, just as it was with Tanya. Pointless pretenses don't fool anyone for very long, however deeply we try and live them. And someday, somewhere, and sometime, we have to face up to ourselves; the selves that other people see.

We really do.

I was beginning to feel I was going to have to face up to a lot of things. I was beginning to see that my old life was losing its ability to support me. I was beginning to feel that I would have to find some kernel, some nugget at the heart of my soul, that was actually me—and somehow I felt if I could find it I wouldn't drown, no matter how much grief came my way.

10

"Right, forgive me, but I want to make sure I've got all this straight," said the Zone Traffic Securities captain, with sharp, severe features, as I sat still wrapped in my blanket in a grimy room somewhere in the bowels of Zone Securities that felt like it had been shunted up to make space for other, more important rooms. The atmosphere seemed to suck the personality from me.

It was as though too many lost souls had been here before and soaked the walls with a particular kind of hopelessness.

"You were unconscious at the time of the bike offenses, but were on the back of a bike ridden by someone who'd had his C-4 Charlie removed, so it looked like you were the one speeding. That's what you're saying?" he said, the collar of his shirt so crisp I suddenly thought it looked like it must be made of icing sugar.

"It really happened like that. Do you think you might have some camera footage taken in Jazz yesterday?" I said, trying to work a relationship with this guy, but I sensed he had an almost impenetrable barrier made of businesslike directness around him that was going to be difficult to puncture. It seemed like Frank Sinatra's voice coming in from somewhere—or one of those Brat-Pack singers anyway—and I recalled from somewhere that the Zone Securities HQ had been relocated to Easy Listening.

There was an irony in there, and lots of jokes were made in the newspapers about how easy it was for the police, spending all their time listening to ridiculous stories made up by their suspects; but I think the reason the new HQ ended up here was because the zone wasn't popular and land was cheap.

"Honestly, why would I make something up as stupid as that?" I said, trying to get him to bite.

"Because you're a desperate, rather lowlife criminal?" the man answered eventually, with a rise in his voice.

"Yeah." I smiled, trying to take this as a joke. "I was being rhetorical, I guess."

"And I was being a sarcastic wanker?" said the man, pushing his gaze into me like a magician slipping knives into an assistant. He accompanied this with a weird sort of nonsmile.

"No, no. 'Course not, didn't mean that," I said, realizing that telling the truth had definitely not been the right decision at all. Now there was no going back; I was like an arctic seal pup who had never been in the sea, but had now strayed onto a slope of ice that was rather steeper than expected. There was only one way I was going, and that was down. "I was just trying to explain and get things straight," I said, scrabbling furiously.

"Exactly. Well, let's leave that for now. So these invisible men kidnapped you, but then miraculously you were rescued by a woman who eluded my colleagues and she was...who again?"

"An encyclopedia saleswoman, sir. I know that sounds crazy—I know it does—but you can look them up."

"Right, well, so was she the one to steal your house, or was that a rabbit from the planet Zinklon?"

"That was some punks." I sighed, reeling inwardly. They had made the connection with my missing house. I didn't think they'd be organized enough to know it was gone.

That was the annoying irony with big establishments—they could be ruthlessly efficient when they chose to, and hopelessly incompetent the rest of the time, when you actually needed them to do something.

"You have your house stolen and you don't report it? Isn't that strange? Normally when houses vanish like that, people are trying to cover up something. Lose their pasts somehow. Are you trying to cover up something in your past, Mr. X?"

"No, I've nothing to hide," I floundered. "I've even got the number of the punks who stole it. Here, please. Call them and sort it out. I'm not being obstructive about this." I handed him the card. The man took it neatly between finger and thumb and examined it like it had been picked out of a sewer.

" 'Don't you hate it when this happens?' " he read. "They left you a card with a phone number? Now that is handy. If only more criminals could be this obliging. Police work would be so much more straightforward. Thank you for leaving your number. When would be a convenient time to arrest you for the armed robbery?"

A burly woman stood by the door, but otherwise the small room was empty except for several bizarre, tall, shiny, metallic cylindrical tubes in the corner. They must have all been about seven feet high. He got up to leave, unable to keep a sneer from his face.

"Have you seen a psychiatrist recently, Mr. X?"

"No."

"No. Well, we'll see. Zara, our Health and Safety Executive, will have to put an Odysseus Hat on you while I'm out of the room. I'm required to inform you it's a routine restriction, after the Hesketh Case, and does not affect your liberty status." The man strutted to the door, opened it, and left us in silence as the noise of his feet clipped down the corridor and faded. I stared at Zara with a sinking feeling of bored dread. Surely she wasn't going to do what I was thinking.

"Up," she said. I scraped the chair back across the floor and stood wearily. Zara nodded in approval, then sniffed and approached the shiny seven-foot metal tubes, and I sighed with despair. She bear hugged one, staggered over to me, climbed uncertainly onto the chair, heaved the thing up, and plonked it over my head so it slid down and hit the floor with a clang. It was wildly dark, and there was barely room to move my arms. I turned my head and, twisting a touch more, found one tiny eyehole. I squinted through it and saw Zara taking up her stoic position by the door again.

"Excuse me," I shouted, my voice echoing around the cylinder. "Is this really, honestly, necessary?"

"Health and Safety." I faintly heard her voice filter through.

"Health and Safety? I could die and you'd never know."

"Well, it's Health and Safety," came the shrugged, flat reply.

"This is ridiculous..." I began, but my voice halted of its own accord, as though it had fallen off a cliff; somehow I knew I had already plumbed the depths of her conversation. I sighed, breathing out deeply, and tried to think positively. This will pass, I told myself. Things will get better. I wouldn't always be standing inside a seven-foot-tall cylindrical tube for pointless reasons of Health and Safety.

Frank Sinatra's voice crooned around me, sounding like he

had been shrunk to only six inches high and was standing in the bottom of a very deep well. "Blue moon, Da di da da da dooo."

A long time ago, when I had been in first grade, our teacher had told us the story of the Englishman Scott of the Antarctic. He wanted to be the first person to the South Pole but came second to Amundsen, the Norwegian, then froze to death on the way back. In England, they hailed him as a hero. Many years later, when I read about it more closely, I found out that the Englishman, Scott, had been really a bit stubborn and frankly a bit stupid, and that the bald facts suggested he was not really a hero at all but more of an arctic joyrider. Sure he was brave to go to the South Pole rather than sit at home eating cakes; but his death was pointless and unnecessary and owed more to stupidity than to heroism. That's when I began to understand that people don't pride the truth above a good story.

Up until then I thought truth was all that mattered. I thought that's what we were all fighting for, and some people were dying for. Sure, truth can be complicated, can be gray instead of black-and-white.

Or mauve.

But the point is, just because it's difficult and can't be boiled down to one sentence, or isn't amusing, doesn't make it any less valid.

"Truth corrupts," I once heard a politician say with an alcohol-fueled smile, and I could see he was serious. "It gets people confused, and we don't want that."

But he was wrong.

Sure it can bore people. Sure it can be dull and difficult, but it is worth striving for. A story that's a lie is convenient and often very funny, but it really is a slippery slope. Accepting a lie about small things primes us to accept bigger lies next time, and it's the thin end of a very large wedge. Somewhere in this country, we lost the skill of encouraging truth and instead embraced lawyers and marketing men to whom truth is something of an out-of-fashion embarrassment.

The man from Zone Securities was just another person who didn't care about the truth. He was stuck in the rails of believing whatever was easiest, just like he had been taught. We pride so many things above truth—right down to who can shout the loudest, which may well be a hangover from our Neanderthal past, but we really need to move on from that.

No wonder our society is so fucked.

I heard the door open, squinted through the eyehole, and saw a man I didn't recognize. He was shorter and wore a smart light suit, had well-groomed hair, and was carrying a folder. "Would you like a cup of coffee?" I heard his muffled voice echo.

"Yes, please," I cried, my spirits lifting.

"I'm sorry. Can you hear me?" he called louder.

"Yes," I cried.

"Would you like a coffee?" he enunciated slowly, and held up a steaming plastic cup.

"Yes, I would," I shouted as slowly and clearly as I could.

He smiled and nodded to Zara, who grudgingly moved toward me and vanished out of my line of vision. I felt a jolt, then light flooded over my feet as she slowly heaved the tube off. I felt my arms free up and ducked my head out of the thing. Zara staggered off the chair and waddled like a penguin over to the corner, where she dumped it with the others.

"Sorry about the Odysseus Hat," this man said.

"Health and Safety," I added.

"Ah! You know. Ridiculous isn't it?" He smiled and handed me a plastic cup of coffee.

"Thank you," I said, and decided to try and make some positive effort with this man. "I'm here for driving in some FBZs, which really wasn't—"

"Yes, yes, I know." He held up a hand good-naturedly. "My colleague was called away on some sort of...business."

He ended vaguely.

"This is your wonderful card, is it?" he said, handing me back the printed card I had found at my house, just as the door flapped open and another burly woman in a Zone Securities boiler suit backed her way into the room, pulling a hand truck with another seven-foot-high cylindrical metal tube on it.

"I think you've the wrong room," the man in the suit announced.

"Oh, sorry; whoops!" the burly woman replied, looking around and nodding at the door. "Thought this was twenty-four. Oh yeah, twenty-four is the other one, with the blood on the floor," she said, and started back out.

"I wasn't there!" came a muffled cry of a woman from the tube, whose words shunted out of her at the speed of a wild lawn mower. "How could I? I've never been to Idaho, why would anyone in their right mind want to go to Idaho? I hate Idaho, almost more than Cincinnati. OK, I hate Cincinnati more than Idaho I admit, but it's a close thing, really close..." Then the door of the room shut, cutting off her voice.

"Sorry," said the man, regaining the sheen of his composure. "Yes. We've checked your story out, and it makes a surprising amount of sense."

"Really?" I said, knocked back by this sudden change of fortune.

"Yes. To let you into a little secret, the Surveillance Vis link has been hacked into," he said conspiratorially, "and it's someone's idea of a joke to play *Chico the Dog* twenty-four hours a day onto all our surveillance screens. Very funny, eh? As a consequence we have no visual data at all at the moment. But the really annoying thing is, there's no episode thirteen."

"What do you mean?"

"Well, Chico goes from being stuck on an island in this swollen river which is rising a foot every few minutes at the end of episode twelve to jumping from a balloon and landing on a trampoline at the start of episode fourteen, and we don't know what went on in between. It's kind of bugging everyone. But it's a silly thing and we have someone working on it, so really, don't worry. The point is we have solid eyewitness reports confirming these Riders as you describe them. How about that?" I nodded and took a sip of coffee, trying to absorb the news and trying not to let my relief run away with me. The coffee was excellent. Really, extraordinarily excellent and just how I like it.

"So, clearly, there's no case against you and you are, as of this moment, a free man."

"Free?" I repeated, still treading carefully.

"That's it. Free," he chirped. "Get yourself out of here. Have a good lunch. Go and kiss a beautiful girl for me."

I hesitated; there was something not quite right here.

"All definitely sorted?" I found myself saying, setting the cup back down on the table. "Free?"

"Yes," he said. "That's it. Good-bye." There was a pause and I started toward the door in what felt like a peculiarly weird, hanging silence.

"No, not really," he cried, clapping his hands and laughing. "You're not free. Good God, no! And you believed me! You believed me just like that! Your face was such a picture. I wish you could have seen it. Oh, you bought that all the way to Alaska! I can't believe it was that easy! I don't know how I kept a straight face!" He laughed in the direction of the large woman, who remained totally expressionless. "That makes me feel so good! No, no, no, no, my colleague checked the column marked CLB. I've no idea what that really stands for exactly. Nobody does. We call it the 'complete load of bullshit' column. It means you're in with the Half-Gones. I really wish you could have seen the look on your face! So, I'm required to inform you we'll contact your next of kin et cetera, et cetera." I looked into his beaming face. "You have to admit, you fell for that like a poo from a seagull didn't you? Never mind," he added with a wink, then turned briskly and left.

Zara was standing over me with the Odysseus Hat and the next thing I knew it dropped down, snuffing out the light with a muffled clang.

11

I felt a great swathe of resentment hammer through me as the darkness inside the Odysseus Hat drained away my senses. Perhaps it should have been a conciliation that at least the Riders weren't shooting at me, but somehow it wasn't. Whichever way I turned, my previous life seemed to be dimming quickly into a foreign past, like watching an idyllic tropical island receding from the deck of a clanking, grimy, steaming ship.

Maybe this happened to other people too. Maybe they'd had their lives swallowed up by events they didn't have a fucking clue about and had entered this same bonkers, twilight world where different rules applied, where they no longer had control over anything they could shake a stick at.

I banged my forehead gently against the wall of the Odysseus Hat, trying to get a grip. There was no point trying to get out of the tube now because I didn't doubt that would cause enough paperwork to precipitate some sort of forestry crisis.

All I could do was wait.

And then, without explanation, something came to me, like a stone falling in the waters of a still pond. One of the Riders had called the other Jeff, and I had known someone called Jeff.

Somewhere.

The name was well used in my mouth, yet I couldn't put a face—or anything else—to it, which was odd. And then I had the weird sensation that this thought had been there all the time, sitting there in my mind as big as a boulder, but I hadn't been able to see it. Jeff. Why was that familiar?

A jolt. Inexplicably something began nibbling at my feet, and I tilted my head down to see a slice of light cutting in at the base of the tube, and felt something being slid in under my shoes. A thin metal plate edged its way between me and the floor, then there was a pause, followed by a stomach-churning whip as the Odysseus Hat tipped back, cracking my head with a sickening jolt on the metal. Then the whole Hat vibrated and I scrabbled and twisted to find the eyehole, and saw flashes of the wall and the doorframe slide past.

We were moving on some sort of hand truck, probably like the one I had seen the Idaho woman being pushed about on. And now that I thought about it, I couldn't remember where it was they said I was going.

I kept my eye on the peephole as best I could as we edged into the corridor. Another Odysseus Hat flashed past with a metal gleam, then I saw open office doors. In one I caught a glimpse of a man with his feet up on the desk and a pencil in his mouth, holding a sheet of paper. Another two Odysseus Hats shimmered past, followed by the thick wedge of blue from the uniforms of the Zone Traffic Securities women pushing them. Another office. Then another office with a blank day planner on the far wall, hanging at a rakish angle, and in the foreground I caught a fleeting glimpse of the man who had first interviewed me. He was smiling broadly and presenting a birthday cake to a young, flushed girl, amid a group of people who were all singing. Clearly, my case hadn't lingered on his conscience for too long.

More doors.

Then left down another corridor and I smacked my forehead on the metal tube as we snapped to a jarring, bone-aching halt. Squinting out, I saw a uniformed woman gesticulating theatrically amid a commotion of raised voices, and an Odysseus Hat rolling across the floor with a pair of legs sticking out, as helpless as a tortoise on its back.

We moved on, leaving the scene in chaos, and I saw the walls of the corridor skate past, interspersed with more Odysseus Hats being wheeled in various directions, and I sighed. What had happened to the world? Had it always had a soft underbelly of confusion and chaos, only I had not known it was there, or perhaps just chosen not to go looking for it?

On the face of it, the universe was such an ordered place, all the planets doing their thing, exactly as Einstein said they would. But then someone discovered quantum mechanics, which seemed to show that very small things, like atoms, just did exactly as they wished and were unruly as a drunk teenager with a shopping cart. Maybe on some level we all strove to echo that inconsolable balance between confusion and order; perhaps we were all programmed to try and put things into some sort of system, but there was another part of us that knew deep down there was no point.

I was yanked upright with a clang as the Hat snapped vertical and rolled on its lip slightly, before settling again. I felt a slither under my feet and the metal plate was gone. I strained at the eyehole and could just make out several other Odysseus Hats in a haphazard line, leading to what looked like a cupboard door. A woman in a Zone Securities uniform was ushering one of the Hats into the cupboard. She closed the door, heaved down a worn, stiff, oversized handle, and there was a distinct and quickly receding cry. When she opened the door again, the Hat was gone. Then she ushered the next one into the cupboard. As I watched the next Hat vanish, I really didn't have a good feeling about this, because wherever they were going, I sensed it wasn't going to be ideal.

The queue of Hats in front of me melted away quickly, until I could distinctly hear the gentle singsong voice of the woman through the metal.

"Forward we go, darling," she said, and I felt the Hat scrape across the floor and had no choice but to go with it. "There, well done—a little bit more, my darling. That wasn't so bad, was it?" she cooed, as the peephole went black and I realized I must be inside the cupboard.

I heard a clunk.

Then the stale air seemed to open up and embrace me in one of the longest pauses I have ever known.

12

The record companies had scrambled for power when the cities fractured under their own weight, and politics crumbled in on itself. There had been a massive leadership vacuum and the music companies were at the height of their influence. It seemed natural they should step in.

Everyone knew who they were and they already had a huge, hierarchical structure in place to deal with the dull stuff. They shaped the cities into music zones, which hurt at first, but once it had all settled down it seemed to work out. Music was our elemental-defining characteristic—or at least, that's what everyone was told at the time.

There still was a government that pouted and argued and

generally went about the place stirring up apathy, but it hadn't had any power for years—mainly, I think, because people had just got bored with it all. It had become so ridiculously petty and savagely inward-looking that if you wanted power, you bought your way into one of the big music companies, such as B. Gets F.B.T., Empty Vessels, or Bacca!Bacca!Woof!Woof!, which had all been top of the pile at one time or another, as the power had ebbed and flowed.

The Zones themselves became run by small elected groups from the people who lived there, but the Music Boards had found a zillion ways to bend and fold decisions as they wanted.

True, they had more influence in some zones than in others; they still were strong in Urban Dance and Blues, but their power was waning in Klick Track, Wah-Wah, Techno, and White Noise, where they didn't have much of a say anymore. But most often, I guess, it was somewhere in between.

Zone Traffic Police was a strange anomaly that no one could quite explain, and if you brought the question of their power up at a dinner party, people shrugged their shoulders in a "that's-how-it's-happened" kind of a way. Somehow Zone Traffic Police had quietly edged its way into a niche of power across all the zones.

And I mean all of them.

They had maneuvered themselves into a position where no one could tell them what to do. Not without giving them a ridiculously large bribe, anyway.

How was it that a bunch of traffic wardens wielded more power than all the politicians put together?

Maybe it was because everyone realized that traffic was a big deal. Everyone wanted the traffic system to work, and the only way was to let someone run it and turn a blind eye as to how they went about things. After all, people thought, it was a dull job and thank God someone wanted to take it on. That's the best way I can explain it; but why the traffic police had grown to take over other areas of the law, I don't exactly know. I really don't. Why the traffic police dealt with homicides and music copy infringement was just one of those bizarre things, and might have had something to do with budgets and streamlining, but more likely someone deep inside the system was wielding power for the hell of it.

Either way the Zone Traffic Police enjoyed their elevated position. The people there flexed their arms, they strutted about and treated people like they were in first grade.

Every dog has its day, and this dog was having such a good day it was barking with so much excitement, you thought it might explode.

13

The floor abruptly vanished and my head smashed the top of the Odysseus Hat as I sank with it like a stone.

The empty, never-ending fall crunched my stomach into a tiny hard thing until I was eased into a long, sweeping, downward slide.

Then a slingshot of a left-hand curve.

I was flattened achingly against the inside wall of the Hat in the thick vibration-roar of a body-rattling, furious blackness.

Bizarrely random snapshot images of memory flashed through my brain as though shaken free from inside my head by the frenetic pummeling: on a longboard at Steamers Lane; an emotional male opera singer I had seen somewhere; waiting at the altar. But not an altar I recognized.

Then the left-hand bend snapped right, jettisoning me across the Odysseus Hat, and I whacked my nose with a hard, brutal thump. What is it about getting hit on the nose? Why does it hurt out of all proportion? My face streamed with pain, but a pinprick of light in the metal hat hauled my attention back. I tried to keep myself steady enough to look through as we tore along, but my head was thwacking the sides of the tube like a jackhammer. I caught a frenetic glimpse of some kind of canteen, way down below. But the scene snapped away abruptly as I creamed into another searing right-hand bend that was swamped in reams of inky darkness.

What was the point of all this? Whatever happened to elevators and stairs? I could feel the raw bruises aching on every inch of my body, and the sensation took me back to being wiped out by a wave the size of Oregon on Todos Santos Island. I had sat on the beach for a good hour after that just getting my head back together.

More random images crashed through my brain: Habakkuk handing me something; an acacia tree in an atrium.

Suddenly, a thumping drop brought the Hat down again on my head, then I was into another long, sweeping, downward curve before the vibrations eased off and the speed was reined in. A rattle, like we were skating over rollers, and we slid to a halt. I heard a well-oiled humming noise and felt the Hat tip until I dropped like a dead sack onto my feet, with the Odysseus Hat still over my head.

I became suddenly aware of my own breath and realized I was snorting like a cantering horse. I just stood and tried to let the memory of the vibrations drain from my body, but my legs felt mugged of energy.

"Sally H78?" a voice said impatiently, and I realized it might have been speaking before and I'd not been tuned in to it.

"What?" I shouted.

"Are you Sally H78?" came the muffled male voice again.

"No!" I cried.

"Well, where is she?"

"I don't know." I answered with irritation, still trying to get my head into gear again, but I couldn't see where the eyehole had spun around to.

"Oh, Rill. Rill!" called the voice. "We've another Wombat in the system. I bet she's stuck in one of the overheads!" Then aimed at me: "Did you see her at all?"

"No," I shouted. "I can't see a fucking thing."

"Oh, this is all I need. I'm supposed to be off at six, you know. Typical. You sure you didn't see her in one of the overheads?"

"No," I said slowly. "I am stuck inside a seven-foot-high metal tube, in case you had missed that bit."

He snorted, as if this wasn't much of an excuse. "I know where she is. She's in the overhead on level two. She's jumped the points. Anyway, what do you want?"

"Want?" I asked.

"Yes. What do you want?"

"A . . . a cigarette if you've got one. That would be great."

"Yeah, like I can do that." He snorted again. "I take it you're Jonny X? Or am I going to be here all night?"

"Yes. That's me."

"Thank Christ. Says here you're in with the Half-Gones. Have you been decommed?"

"What?"

"Decommissioned."

"I've really no idea. I'm here for speeding and entering a—"

"Right, OK, says you haven't here. I'll get you to Section Decom; I've got to find this damned Sally woman now."

"Please, why don't we just use the stairs?" I cried. "I can walk, you know. Wouldn't it make everything much simpler and less fucking painful?"

"Yeah, but not as cost-effective, apparently," he answered, after a pause.

Again I felt the slither of metal under my feet and again the head-cracking jolt as the tube was tilted back. Then, the now-familiar, steady rumble of the wheels vibrating up through the metal sides like the sound of some oversized cat purring. We were moving, only this time I couldn't see anything and somehow I cared less and just lay there. I'd had the stuffing knocked out of me and my mind had been shaken off its mountings, so I just let the occasional shouts from outside filter in without paying too much attention.

"Oy, Natter! You seen Bishop anyplace? We've a Wombat in the system, and I need him to check the overheads in section two! His voice com is dead as a dodo!"

Something shouted back I didn't hear, then: "In a dress? Well, he shouldn't be in a fucking dress at work should he? We've said he can wear the women's shoes, but that's it!"

And later: "Tessa 34? I'm supposed to be off at six. You want to deal with a Wombat Retrieval? There's a bonus in it." But mostly I just let my thoughts wander—and they didn't wander very far or with any great intensity.

"Here we are, mate—Decom. Someone'll pick you up later," I heard him snort, then it felt like he thumped the side of the tube a couple of times good-naturedly before snapping it upright and sliding out the heel of the hand truck from beneath my feet.

The echo of the thump roused my senses. Where were we? Decom? What was that all about? A massive thunk on the roof of the Odysseus Hat sent a sharp shock through my veins and I tensed as white light streamed in over my feet and the Hat began to slide up and away. As I squinted into the growing brightness, the tube was yanked off and I could see nothing because the intense whiteness of the light bleached away all my vision. My ears buzzed at the disappearance of the constant metal echo, and I stood generally dazed and uncertain, feeling like a cat that has been plonked down in the snow for the first time and can't make sense of the world. Machines groaned and spat in an erratic symphony of noise, but through it, I heard a bright, perky woman's voice over a PA:

"It is illegal to cross the yellow line. Please do not cross the yellow line or you may be harpooned."

I blinked, taking in the new scene in tiny slivers as my pupils fought to shrink down to narrow slits. An old lady in a heavy tweed skirt was standing about twenty feet to my right on a raised platform, with a cluster of grimy, jutting-armed, heavily bolted, overused machines about her, while a gang of people scuffed around down on floor level, twiddling knobs and rapping dials with a detached, mucking-around-with-each-other air. Farther off, there were maybe fifteen or twenty people, each standing on an identically raised platform, and all surrounded by a similar small gang of Zone Securities people and machines. Above all of them hung an Odysseus Hat on long lengths of coiled chain, hovering like some low-budget spacecraft, ready to pounce.

The room was a wide-floored, hollow-noised, oil-smeared, dirty gray shack, littered with broken or discarded machines and stiff with hard, arcing shouts and echoes.

"Please do not cross the yellow line," suggested the woman on the PA again smoothly, "or you may be harpooned."

I glanced around and made out a thick yellow line scoured onto the floor at the far end of this enormous space, but there didn't seem to be anything obvious beyond it, and I couldn't see why crossing it was considered such a big deal. I felt a firm hand grab my arm and, jerking my head down, saw I was on a platform exactly like all the others. The thickset Zone Securities man who was gripping my arm like an iron vise had an air of resigned boredom about him.

"Feet in the clips. Nice and still," someone else cried against the backdrop of machine noise, and I felt two metal pincers snap around my ankles before I even had time to think. The man holding my arm clipped it out horizontally with rough firmness, then plugged my Jab-Tab into a machine that sent a vibration scouring down my arm. Meanwhile, someone had seized my other hand and pulled it out, and I felt a clamp close forcefully around my Skin Media phone. That machine let out an unhealthy, high-pitched squeal and ejected a surprising amount of steam that clouded the whole area.

"You're in the cycle for ten minutes. Can you please sign here?" shouted the first man, whose face was smeared with oil. He pressed a pen into my clamped and vibrating hand, so it was all I could do not to drop it.

"Sign for what?" I shouted.

"To say you've agreed to be decommissioned and you waive all rights to your life and everything associated with it. It's just a formality, to be honest."

"What?" I shouted above a particularly whiny machine that had just started up someplace.

"It's just a formality. It doesn't mean anything."

"I'm not signing it. I want to speak to a lawyer," I yelled rather optimistically, I thought, but the word "lawyer" triggered a change in his facial expression.

"OK. OK." He sighed and swung in a huge bulbous microphone on a counterweighted boom. When it was near me, he said, "All yours," and left.

"Lawyers' fees are controlled by the National Council of Lawyers Fee Board, which dictate that the lawyer is allowed to talk to you for sixty seconds free of charge," a voice howled at me, and I sensed things were moving way too fast. "If you are facing criminal charges, then a further fifteen seconds may be obtainable free of charge. If you wish to insure yourself against saying anything that might incriminate you by employing a man who will speak louder than you at the same time, please indicate to the officer dealing with your case. If you wish to—" but the automated speech was cut off abruptly.

"Tracy 45N. Can I help you?" came another voice from somewhere.

"Are you a lawyer?" I shouted quickly.

"That's correct. You understand my fees?"

"Yes, yes, look, I'm not signing a form saying that I arrhhhhh-hhhhg," I exclaimed as the machine clamped over my Skin Media phone delivered a sharp, stabbing pain into my elbow.

"I see. This may be a nicety of contract law, which I'm not altogether familiar with. Would you like me to put it before council?" came her clipped, but not at all reassuring, voice.

"No. Listen to me, I'm not signing some form saying that I have agreed to this when I clearly haven't."

"Ah, I see, I understand. Well, it is a prerogative of Zone Securities to ask all their clients to sign that particular form, subject to a recent amendment to the Fisheries Act."

"I really don't care. I'm not signing it."

"You have ten seconds remaining," came the smooth, gravelly voice from somewhere.

"Can you sort this out?" I shouted.

"Yes, no problem. My advice is to sign the form under the proviso I—" But she was cut off by the automated voice.

"Your time is up. Your account will be docked a nominal fee to cover health care and shipping."

"Shipping?" I exclaimed, but there was no one to hear. The area around me was empty.

I stared out to the ends of the hangar. Standing on this metal platform with my arms clamped out to the sides by these oil-smeared, bolt-shaking machines that felt like they were gnawing away at my past, I realized that everyone else being decommissioned was in the same position.

Together, we looked like some bizarre group crucifixion. Maybe that's what the person who had designed all this intended. Somehow, I wouldn't have been surprised.

"Down the Avenues and Alleyways" floated in—another easy-listening track washing around the hangar.

The machines suddenly roared louder, screaming with wild, jabbing pleasure, and the searing pain coursed through my arms, tingling at first, then burning into a hot-metaled, liquid soup that poured through my veins. It felt as though the fabric of my life was being scalded away from the inside out. And then, abruptly, the agony faded like water draining away from a large, calm reservoir, and the machine noise whined down to an empty silence, leaving me utterly exhausted.

"All done," said a woman with a clipboard, smiling as I came around. "You had a couple of data viruses but nothing too bad. All your documents are signed and in order and they'll be attached to your Odysseus Hat. Congratulations. You're a Half-Gone."

"I didn't sign anything," I said, finding my voice—which seemed foreign and didn't feel wholly connected to my mouth.

"Is OK," said the man with a heavy Spanish lilt and oil on his cheek. "Is OK. We can have lunch. Is OK."

"All accounted for," said the woman in a matronly tone that I guessed was supposed to draw a line under everything.

"I refused to sign." I tried to shout but it came out as a whisper.

"It's only a formality, honestly. Nothing to worry your socks over." This time she made a gesture. In the distance I caught sight of a lone black figure, running frantically before swerving to avoid being felled by a spear. I opened my mouth in surprise, but at that moment the Odysseus Hat was slipped down over me.

"Please do not cross the yellow line," sang the muffled woman's voice over the PA again, "or you may be harpooned."

14

"You're in with the Half-Gones," chuckled a voice from outside the Odysseus Hat as I was knocked off-balance yet again as the thing was yanked forward.

"They're the mad ones. The psychos," he added, as we trundled off. "It's not the best place, to be honest, not really hotel standard, but Health and Safety turn a blind eye because we fix it for them to have their company baseball game in the A's stadium. But I didn't say that. Anyway, the Half-Gones do make me laugh. One time, one of them collected all his ear wax for several years and used it to try and suffocate one of the—"

"Don't think I want to hear about the Half-Gones," I said quickly, through the metal.

"Come on, you have to laugh about it!" blathered on the man, unperturbed. "Don't you? It's the only way to stay sane in this place. Another time, one of them Half-Gones caught a rat and managed to use its intestines as a stethoscope. He found he could listen to—"

"Thank you!" I shouted from inside the Odysseus Hat, enunciating every word clearly. "Can we talk about something else?"

"OK, if that's what you want," said the voice with a touch of deflated hurt. "Just thought you might want to know what you're in for. Look in their eyes if you want to see which are the most bonkers. That's a good tip. As soon as they take the Hat off, look right into their eyes. Most of them are normal like you probably are, but some of them think nothing of taking a shoe and gnawing at it until it's as sharp as a knife, then—"

"Really. Enough," I shouted. "Honestly. Please."

"OK, OK. As you wish." He sounded dejected and there was a grumpy, hanging silence as we weaved our way onward, pitted only with a few exchanges he had on his voice com. I didn't catch any words, just his general sense of surprise.

Finally, the Hat snapped upright and my momentum rapped my forehead against the metal sides for the umpteenth time that day as he left me.

I waited.

The darkness seemed to suffocate time itself, slowing it to a tortuous plod, then stretching out each second like chewing gum, so I felt dislocated from everything and hung, suspended, in a void of meaninglessness. I became aware of something in my left hand, something I had been clinging to for so long I had forgotten it. I tried to work out what it was and where I had picked it up. It was a crunched-up piece of cardboard and I turned it over, wondering whether it was important, but at that second a thumping clang on the roof of the Hat startled me and I dropped it.

The Hat began to slide up and off and I tried to prepare myself for whatever was to come. What was it the man had said again? Look into their eyes to tell which were the maddest? The Hat rose interminably slowly, letting the screaming white light edge up my legs like a rising flood. I squinted at this new brightness, trying to be ready for whatever the Half-Gones had in store. I could see a pair of feet in smart ladies' shoes marooned in the iridescence. The Hat rose more slowly than ever and was almost off the top of my head when I ducked out of it, blinking into the eyes of a person standing not two feet away. Was this a Half-Gone? I squinted frantically. It seemed like I was in some kind of white light land, where everything shone and gleamed.

"Jonny X—well, look at you. Look at you, my poor love!"

"Sarah?" I said.

"Of course it's me. With nothing but a blanket on! Oh, and what have you done to your wrists? That is absolutely disgusting."

"Yeah. Not pleasant is it?" I said, still barely able to see anything properly.

"You poor, drowned dog. Sit down before you fall down and have a drink."

"Where is this place?" I shambled, now beginning to make out gleaming white surfaces and silver tables from the brightness as I clasped the back of a chair.

"It's the canteen. Where did you think it was, the Staten Island Ferry? I've brought some of your old clothes, which you never picked up even though you promised—sit down, poor love, come on, and please have my coffee. You look like you really need it."

"Yeah," I said, collapsing into the chair. "What am I doing in the canteen? Why are you here exactly?" A torrent of questions lined up in my head, waiting to be asked.

"Zone Securities contacted me as next of kin. Saying you'd been speeding and did I want to pay bail. Which I did. Don't look so surprised. We are still married, you know."

"Yes, officially." It came out whispered.

"What have you been doing, Jonny? And where is your house, for God's sake? That house was wonderful. I loved that house. I painted the bathroom myself." I took the cup of coffee and drank. Next to it was some kind of cake thing and I bit into it, staring off into nothing, trying to take in this new development.

"I'm very glad you're here, Sarah. They were about to dump me somewhere bad," I said slowly. "I owe you one."

"Really?" laughed Sarah with a forced sense of jollity. "For the last ten years I'd say you owe me more like four thousand, eight hundred and ninety-four—and that's just for not returning my calls."

I smiled—and for the first time in a long while, I saw a glimpse of the old Sarah. The funny Sarah, the confident Sarah who was good to be with, who was stimulating and excitable, who could take things and run with them; whom I had deeply, honestly loved and whom I had missed like hell when we were apart. But the feeling was wrapped in the thick, cotton-wool sadness of all that had happened since.

I felt a fuzz of warmth run through me: a warmth of realization that I had friends, people who cared about me, and I was not alone now and I never would be. On the far edge of the canteen, a huge yellow-and-black monster of a machine with wheels the size of Detroit edged its way in like a blind armadillo. On the side of it was emblazoned in large letters: "Wombat Retrieval." My gaze swept up the machine. It had a couple of massive metal pincers, pointing at the ceiling, and I could see the swoop of transparent tubes crisscrossing the roof. As I watched, an Odysseus Hat screamed through one of them with a flick of its silver metal sides and a barely audible hum.

"Jonny. Jonny, are you listening to me?" Sarah's voice broke into my thoughts.

"Yeah," I said. "Yeah. I'm listening."

"You really need to see someone. A specialist. You're all confused, you poor thing, so it's not surprising something like this has happened to you. I talked it over with Becky, who's done a night school diploma course on psychology—although to be exact it's the psychology of plants—but it all comes down to the same thing apparently. She has made me see that you are the one with the problem in our relationship. You need me to look after you, but you can't see it because you have a leaf infection."

"A what?"

"A leaf infection. You have a leaf infection, which stops you absorbing sunlight, and in human terms it means you're not open to the real world and to people's feelings, you poor love."

"Sarah, stop this," I said gently. "Let's not get tangled up now in things we can't resolve. Anyway," I added, "how's Possible Horse?"

"Possible Horse?" she said, shaking her head. "I reckon you always loved that cat more than me. Why don't you come back now and see him? He misses you. Why don't you just come back for a while?" There was a silence as I thought of a hundred things to say and none of them quite right.

"Yes! It's time to add the power of the nuclear bomb to your golf swing," sang out a hologram, a very small man suddenly appearing between us on the table. "Hi! I'm Tony Shappenhaur IV. You know me better as 'The Thinking Buckaroo,' and I'm here to tell you about the amazing power of this driver." I swatted with irritation at the thing, to absolutely no effect.

"They have a virus of these in some zones at the moment," said Sarah. "It's OK. I was given a zapper for it." And she ferreted through her bag, produced a slender unit, and zapped the hologram away, leaving a tiny burning smell.

"Sarah," I said, suddenly feeling that the answer to much of what had happened to me was inexplicably close. "Has anything strange happened to the world? What I mean is, have you noticed anything small that's changed? It might be important."

"Really? Well, I don't know, the MacObrees have a new Crossfield, the 4000 V. Dum Dum. Is that the sort of thing? And my sister got an ear problem after she went scuba diving. I don't know. What are you talking about? Nothing's changed much."

"No, it *has* changed," I said, with more urgency than I was expecting. "Something's not right. Someone has moved something they weren't supposed to," I continued, trying to rein in my voice so I sounded considered rather than just plain mad. "Someone has eaten the forbidden apple or something, and it's messed everything up, and I'm worried it's me that's done it."

"What are you talking about, Jonny? Have you seen yourself? You look like a dog that's been thrown in a mole mine."

"A coal mine, Sarah."

"A what?"

"A coal mine."

"Jonny, what does it matter what's in the mine? Really, have you lost all sense of proportion? It's just as Becky said it would be."

"Sarah..."

"The only weird thing here is you, Jonny. Look at you! Never mind, let's not get you upset, poor love. Come on, get those clothes on and let's go home and get you cleaned up." And I remembered, as I looked at her, that Sarah had forgotten how to indulge in anything that wasn't rock-solid normality; she thought doing that was called growing up.

I walked out into the fresh air on the forecourt of the Zone Securities Headquarters and stood there as Sarah trotted on ahead, unaware I wasn't with her. It was just past midday and for the first time in what seemed like an aeon, I was actually free to do what I wanted.

I didn't have a house. I didn't have a phone. I didn't have a Jab-Tab. But I was free.

I let the sun wash over my face and breathed in deeply, looking at the world with a sense of wonder and detachment. We were in Easy Listening and, as you'd expect, many of the people wandering about the streets were wearing cardigans and slippers. I even saw someone with a pipe. Down the road, a Well-Mall for broken hips looked pristine and clean, and a paint store selling Change-A-Tone paint was touting for business. Change-A-Tone was the paint that sensed your mood from the hormones you gave off and changed color to be the most in tune with you at that moment. So one day your house walls might be blue, and the next day you'd come in and they'd be deep red. That was all very well, but I didn't want my fucking walls telling me how I was feeling, and I think a lot of people felt the same. It was one of those things that some people swore by, but most people swore at.

I sighed. If I was going to start smoking again, I thought, this would be the ideal time. Right now, a cigarette would make life considerably more pleasant. But I didn't have any, and I knew Sarah wouldn't either. I looked about and wondered if it was worth trying to bum one off someone.

"Jonny. Jonny!" called Sarah from the bottom of the steps, "Are you coming?"

"Yeah," I said.

"Because I don't want to stay in Easy Listening a moment more than I have to. This place makes me feel like I'm two hundred years old." I trotted down the steps after her, still itching for a cigarette.

"You don't have a smoke, do you?" I asked, with pointless optimism.

She turned and raised a quizzical eyebrow.

"No," I said. "Just a long shot." We were closer to the road now and the bikes streamed past—a lot of Crossfield 1000s but mixed in I noticed a Swoop Chicken (which was pretty rare), then a Flat Iron Gun. It rasped away—and owning a bike like that meant you had to avoid the sound sniffers in zones like Classical and Swing. A couple of GaFFA 8s thwocked down to the Zone Securities Chopper Bowl, and I let out an audible sigh of relief that it wasn't me in one of them now. We walked in silence over to Sarah's bike. "I got a new machine, see?" she said. "I hated the color of the other one. Why did I ever think I could live with yellow?"

"Very cool," I nodded, seeing the perfect, easy flare of a new Crossfield 1050. "Sarah," I added, after a pause, "I'm not coming back with you to your place. It doesn't feel right. We just haven't had enough time, somehow."

"Jonny, don't be ridiculous. Look at you! Where else can you go? You don't have a house. Do you have a girlfriend?"

"I need to see Teb," I pressed on. "And I really need to see Mat."

"You don't have a proper girlfriend, then? Jonny, you need to get settled, and those two are just drifters like you. They can't ever help you. Come back, come on. Spend five minutes with Possible Horse and just have a . . . a cup of coffee, or one of those Long Island things, and we'll try and straighten us out."

"Sarah, no. Take me to Mat's. Please."

"No. No, I won't. Not this time." She looked at me with a stony, broken face. "This is as far as I go. Becky said you need a firm hand and plenty of bright sun."

"Stop going on about plants!" I shouted, rather too loudly. "Sorry," I added, after a pause. "Look, there's not time to go all through this again and I really must see Mat. Honestly, thank you for getting me out of there and I really mean it when I say, look after yourself. You have a generous heart. Good-bye, Sarah."

I turned and walked away, knowing I was leaving her on the

edge of an emotional cliff, which wasn't at all fair after all that she had just done—but this definitely wasn't the time for psychology about me, about her, and especially not about plants. I was about twenty yards down the road when I heard her high voice, breaking with emotion.

"All right, Jonny," she cried. "All right. You win. You always win. Why is it that you always win?" I stopped and turned slowly, looking into her confused face—tense with fear, anxiety, and desperation—and I thought it wasn't at all like her to soften like that.

"I wasn't trying to win anything," I said, wanting her so much to understand.

"OK," she said, more quietly as I approached. "But I can't keep bailing you out. All that stuff with Eli's brother, Jack—you never let it go. You need to let things go, Jonny. Things change. You have to move on. You have to just be."

I smiled inwardly, hearing words I had said to her years before being pushed back at me. "I know. Things have changed, Sarah; things have changed so much."

She touched me lightly on the cheek, half-avoiding my eyes, and smiled. Then she let her hand drop and slid onto the bike, her crash suit snapping about her. I stood for a moment, allowing the touch to glow on my skin, and wondered if she was crying. But she wasn't able to let herself cry much. More likely she was holding back a flood of emotion in a tight, never-to-be-resolved knot inside.

This was not the time for any kind of in-depth talk, but I wished it was, wished I could drag her to a place where she could see how things were. Wished, simply, that she understood. I sighed and climbed heavily on the back of the bike and felt my crash suit thrum and brrr as it adjusted to my body.

She had a heart of gold and it was such a shame we got so

messed up as a couple, and I thought that could be the epitaph for the whole human race. "Underneath it all they were really quite nice. They just got screwed up. Mostly by stuff that wasn't entirely their fault."

The crash suit was comfortable and that was one of the great luxuries about a new bike; the crash suits don't snap so tightly about you that it feels like you're being bear hugged by an overweight, sweating wrestler who has taken it upon himself to give you a demonstration of the Heimlich Maneuver. How often had I arrived at places red-faced and clawing for breath like a dog at the end of the National Stick-Chasing Championships because of a malfunctioning crash suit? I had lost count. The traffic in Easy Listening was light and Sarah connected her Jab-Tab to the bike, fired it up, and throttled away.

There was no way I was drifting into being a couple again. No way I was even risking going to her apartment. We'd been through all that and moved on, and it wouldn't be good for either of us if we fell back into the old way of doing things. We'd just find the tramlines our lives had run on before and roll through the same arguments, the same frustrations, the same dead-end everything. Although she had a good heart, this woman and I had nothing in common anymore but our past. What had bound us in those final years had been nothing but inertia and fear— fear of loneliness, fear of not knowing whether we could make it on our own, fear of life.

The bike shimmied between lanes as Sarah headed toward Motown in the glaring sun and I tried to relax and let those thoughts go.

Mat lived in Rave, which was three or four zones away, and getting there wasn't going to take an age at this time of day, as long as Motown wasn't having one of their "dancing in the street" days. Then you couldn't move at more than two miles an hour because of the crowds and the constant supply of people climbing on the back of your bike and expertly cartwheeling off it. They always made me wonder why my childhood hadn't involved doing more of that rather than throwing stones into the breakers.

But my mind was still all snagged up on Sarah. There was something hollow about the time when we were married, as if the memories had gone rotten and were about to disintegrate. We weaved our way past a plasi-screen of Elnor Elnorian, one of the government cronies.

"Hi," his voice warbled through the head speakers on my crash suit. "I'm Elnor Elnorian. Enjoy your time on bail. Bail is a beautiful gift that comes wrapped with forgiveness, along with this pink form—"

I snapped the off button down on my head audio. I had as much time for Elnor Elnorian as I did for a skunk that wanted to teach me how to play tennis. He was the last person I wanted to have lecturing me, and I could feel my heart pounding with childish annoyance. His ludicrous corruption speech had been heralded as one of the great honest speeches in American history, which had brought out into the open one of the taboo subjects of our age. I remember it almost word for word:

"If we are going to be corrupt," he had said on Thanksgiving two years before, with a dental plan smile, "and I say, it's inevitable for any government in any modern-day society, I tell you what, I want it to be the best corruption in the world. I want corruption that is superbly efficient. Corruption that is simple to understand. Corruption that makes sense to the homeless, those in hospital, those single mums struggling at home. And most of all, I want corruption that benefits every single member of our nation in the long-term fight for liberty, freedom, justice, and freight haulage."

It had won him a standing ovation. A standing ovation! Sure the audience had probably been paid, and the journalists who wrote about it were likely paid too, but some people actually believed it. They quoted it in bars. But then, some people will believe anything if you serve it up on a plate. Elnor Elnorian was the man pressing ahead with the new science bill that fed zillions into a new space program.

What had made me think of that, for God's sake?

What I definitely needed now, I decided, was a drink—or more specifically, a huge number of Long Island Iced Teas, one after the other, until my brain no longer had the capacity or interest to think about anything.

We flew under the gate out of Easy Listening and into Motown. Sarah leaned the bike into a long cambered corner that just cried out to be taken at speed, but I knew she'd hold back and be sensible about it because that was Sarah. The architecture around us reverted to wooden one-story weather-boarded buildings and stores with flamboyantly hand-painted signs that just made you smile because they were so ridiculously cute.

The City Caretakers had cordoned off the inside lane so that people could dance in the street if they chose during off-peak traffic, and a few were, here and there. Among them I saw a smattering of beehive haircuts and people wearing pointy glasses, but a lot of the others just looked pretty ordinary. Not everyone went to great lengths to live in the style of their zone and thank God they didn't.

I challenge anyone not to like Motown. It's happy without baggage, celebrating life without the heavy self-deluding overtones of so much of Religion. When this is all over, I thought, it would be cool to come here for an ice cream sometime and listen to "Baby Love" play all afternoon in a café someplace.

We swerved between some ludicrously old-fashioned bikes and I felt a pang of warmth that I was going to see Mat. A crazy wave of optimism seared through me, as if my life wasn't messed up at all and I was just heading over for a regular surfing trip.

Sarah opened the throttle and we screamed out of Motown and into Punk, and I felt a small wobble through the bike. Most likely she was a bit nervous about crossing the zone and wanted to take it at speed because Punk was bursting with designer anarchy of varying sorts, and although the roads were generally OK because Zone Securities went ape-shit if they weren't, every now and again something unexpected erupted and it usually involved smashing things. That seemed to be the main pastime of everyone living here—and judging by the wrecked surroundings, they were all pretty expert at it too. Getting insurance to live in Punk must have been almost impossible, and the excess on breakages must have been the equivalent of the income of a small country.

I switched off the air con on my suit, opened the visor, and breathed in the fresh air as I watched the dilapidated, paint-sprayed walls flit by. Somewhere in the distance smoke rose from a fire and loud music suddenly erupted from a supermarket as a man in a suit pushed open the door, looking uncomfortably out of place. A plasi-screen by the road filled up with a blond girl, but I didn't hear what she was saying because I'd switched off the crash suit speaker. Then a lion ate her, and I gathered from the large lettering that appeared that it was an ad for Swedish Spinach.

An outrageously designed mall scooted by, all pink angles and huge flags, and up ahead I could see the gate out of Punk and into Rave loom on the horizon like a wild beast. It was a stainless-steel monolith that blurred past as we hammered through, finding ourselves in the swish expensive malls of Rave, with their neat, white-walled houses.

Rave had some cracking stores and a plethora of superb Japanese restaurants that served some of the best sushi known to man—which is something Mat and his girlfriend, Nina, went on about as though they had found the Holy Grail. And not only that, as if they had found the Grail in the same place as a packet of particularly good chocolate cookies.

I mean, I like sushi. I really do, but it's not something I feel any need to worship.

Sarah eased up behind a gaggle of slower bikes and I wondered how long it had been since she had been to Mat's. I guessed it must have been years, and yet she threaded the bike easily through the corners, as though the route was fresh in her mind. We passed a store called "Ohhhhhhhhhhhhhbang!" that gave the impression from the window display that all it sold were colorful pointy bits of wood, and maybe it did. The people in Rave bought all kinds of odd things, mainly by mistake when they were out of their heads on drugs.

Inside the shop, on the other side of the glass and mixed in with the reflection, was a man who was the spitting image of my boss, Habakkuk, and the whole guilt pang about work hit me like a large hammer. I had clients waiting for dreams; waiting for serial dreams that only I could write, and they would be jumping down Habakkuk's throat, bypassing that small, sticky smile he had creased permanently into his face. Not only that, Habakkuk would kill me when he found I had lost my entire dream library. But he would have to join the line, I thought ruefully.

We rounded the last corner and Sarah throttled to a halt outside a whitewashed block of apartments cascading greenery. My crash suit undid itself with a gentle brrr and I hopped off, suddenly aware of how strange it was to be wearing the clothes Sarah had brought me again. I hadn't worn my leather jacket in years.

She stood looking at me and I felt the emotion hidden behind her eyes. "Look at you! But I'm not going to make a scene, so don't panic. But you do need to sort yourself out, Jonny. You'll never find the perfect partner; she doesn't exist. And we had a lot going for us you know."

I nodded, feeling it just wasn't true. A host of bad memories I hadn't noticed were in my head reared up—of evenings being told I should be doing this or doing that; of conversations about grasping futures that were full of cut-price deals and the latest bikes; of the two of us sharing sad, drunken nights in bars with couples who hated me, or resented me, or didn't trust me, but mainly didn't care or even know who I was. I'd tried to do it for a while. I'd tried to enjoy the world of dinner parties and conversations about vis-programs and zones development, but to me it was a dry, godforsaken desert that howled with a particularly desperate sort of meaninglessness. One that never led anywhere but to another round of shallow gossip, which they spread about liberally over their day-to-day lives to cover the trickling, unacknowledged fear that coursed through them.

"Yeah," I said simply, not wanting to get tangled up in things we couldn't resolve. I kissed her on the cheek, half smiled, then headed on up the steps, purposefully not looking back. The roar of the bike echoed through the stairwell as she throttled away, and I felt relieved she had left, that we had not unpacked too much of the past. Because it's never as easy to repack again, and it always takes up more space than it did before; just like those orange emergency survival bags we used in the mountains. They came packed the size of a tea bag, but once opened you might as well be carrying a bundled-up wedding tent in your rucksack for the amount of space they took.

Sarah was kidding herself about us and about her and about the past, and probably about the future. She was still doing it; maybe she always would. Maybe she'd be one of those people who get stuck in their lives and forget how to move on, spend-ing years in one place while everyone else walks on by. I should know; I had done it too.

I skipped two steps at a time and felt my thighs burn as I rapped up the treads. When all this was over, I was really going to have to get properly fit somehow. But I vowed I wasn't going to buy the Row-master Fitness Experience, which promised to make you an athlete on twenty-five seconds a day but should, by law, have stated clearly on the box that you would only use it twice and after that it was going to take up an inordinate amount of space in the cupboard under the stairs.

I wondered briefly where I would find a fitness program that had a proviso for huge numbers of Long Island Iced Teas, but I was sure there had to be one out there somewhere. And if there wasn't, then I felt I could make a sizeable fortune inventing it. I carried on up more slowly now, my boots tapping on the cool marble stairs, sending an echo out into the empty shade. Mat lived on the top floor, which, as he said, was "dark" (that meant "good" in Rave talk)—particularly as he had a roof garden cre-ated by the previous owner and a terrace that gave a view across the rooftops to the ocean.

In summers gone by, we'd staggered out there bleary-eyed at five o'clock in the morning to see what the waves were doing. If the surf was up, we'd head off for a "dawny," ripping up some rides for an hour or so before breakfast, then scrambling into work by nine. Mat used to design beards, but when he got bored of that, he joined the music company B Gets F.B.T. and ran the Confusing Paper Department. Basically, if anyone in any of the other sections got something that was in any way confusing or complicated, they sent it to Mat, who was an expert in knowing whether to just ignore it and throw it away.

He reckoned he threw away ninety-five percent of the stuff he got, which saved a lot of people doing a lot of other work, so having an expert in charge of whether to chuck things could save a company like that a lot of money. He was quite dedicated to the whole thing, and I always wondered where that serious-ness came from. I guess it was some sense of responsibility in-stilled into his upbringing that had stuck. It was also reflected in his minimalist flat, and especially his highly organized collection of omelette spatulas, which he claimed all had some different culinary use.

So, apart from the inconvenience of actually having to be there when the surf was up—and as far as you can like a job—Mat liked working for B Gets F.B.T. He didn't have any political aspi-rations, but I guess if he'd chosen, he could have worked his way up. Perhaps via the No Shit Department, which didn't take any shit from anyone and was consulted when people thought they were being taken for a ride, or even the Complete Fabrications Board, who made up well-thought-out lies for the company when they were in a tight corner. In fact, it was the stuff produced by the Complete Fabrications Departments of a zillion other com-panies that Mat spent most of his time weeding out. I tapped up the last few stairs, which brought me facing Mat's door square on, and I reached for the buzzer.

"Don't touch that!" screamed the buzzer.

"What?"

"He's not here."

"You're kidding me," I said.

"No, he went out about twenty minutes ago, didn't say where. Got any ID?"

"No," I said, realizing I didn't have any. "He knows me though, anyway."

"Yeah—you know what? They all say that. No ID? Everyone has ID. Even the rats around here have ID. I like you, I really do, but I'll have to call Zone Securities if you hang about much longer."

"What?"

"You heard me. You're out of here."

"He knows me. It's really quite important."

"OK—freeze—hands in the air. I got a live one everyone! Stand back!"

"Shut up," I said.

"No kidding, buddy, I'm not giving you another warning. You're going down."

"You're just a buzzer. Shut up!"

"Oy—apartment C buzzer, you see this one? He's the sort I've been telling you about! I told you, didn't I?"

"Really, dear?" said the buzzer from across the hall. "He looks harmless enough to me. And Mat is in, dear. He's been in all day."

"What? He's in?"

"Well, he may be in...possibly..."

"Right. Unless you ring before I count up to three, I'm going to take out my gun and empty a complete—"

"Ding-Dong!" chimed the buzzer through the flat. "Ding-Dong! Ding-Dong!"

Clearly, the buzzer didn't catch my bluff. I heard the muffled thump of footsteps through from the other side and the door finally eased open, revealing Mat. I guessed straightaway that he had a hangover. There was the faintest flicker of surprise on his face, then he embraced me.

"Jonny X, I'm so glad you're here! I've been having very weird dreams, indeed."

"Me too," I said. "Only mine all seem to be real."

PART TWO

That Which Does Not Kill Us

15

I leaned on the low wall of the roof deck under the shade of a small, drooping palm tree and gazed out toward the sea, guessing the surf was still about three feet and clean.

"It's building. Supposed to jack up to about five feet this afternoon," Mat said, coming over and handing me a Long Island Iced Tea. "But the wind is onshore and getting up too, and will blow it out slightly, but it's not as if we can't get some shelter somewhere. You should try out my new acquisition."

"What's that?" I said, still turning over events in the back of my mind, like a forgotten concrete mixer.

"My new longboard; it's really sweet. You'd like it. You look stressed. You look like you need a chilled-out surf session, then about fifty-six Long Islands."

"Yeah, you're right," I said, feeling the smoothness of the iced-cool glass. "Some very strange things have been happening, Mat. There are some people chasing after me and they may want to kill me."

"Who?" said Mat, looking over with alarm. "Oh, you don't mean Emma's friends? Surely not. They don't like you that much I guess, but I don't think they'd kill you, would they? Even Charlotte's not that mean."

"No, not Emma's friends. I mean real, large, strange people with guns, who have been firing real stuff at me."

"Wow," said Mat. "Why? What have you been doing?"

"That's the thing. I've no real idea. All I get are just these platefuls of random madness being pushed in my face, and I don't know why." I paused and looked over at the ocean. "Emma's friends really don't like me that much, do they?"

"Well, they're a funny lot. You know that."

"Great. That's just great. That's all I need to hear at the moment."

"Jonny?"

"It's really not been my best day, Mat. Everyone suddenly seems to have it in for me. Even your buzzer was giving me a hard time."

"Come on, Jonny, you're feeling too sorry for yourself. My buzzer is the result of some kids messing about. They've hacked into it and fed it lots of police films, I think. It gives everyone a hard time. It accused my mom of being a class-A drug dealer the other day, which at first had her very worried, then very amused. I was going to get Teb to fix it. Look, who's trying to kill you?"

"No idea really. These four strange Riders... We need to see

Teb; he might be able to help. I feel like those kids who did your doorbell have hacked into my life and connected it back all wrong. That's not possible, is it?"

"What are you talking about, Jonny? Are you all right? I don't just mean: 'Are you all right.' I mean: *Are you all right?*' " I sensed his growing comprehension that this was a bigger situation than he first thought.

"I'm OK. Just. But I need some answers." I drank the entire Long Island Iced Tea. "Do you have a cigarette?" I added, eyeing him hopefully, although Mat hardly ever smoked now.

"Jonny," said Mat, holding his hands up. "Jonny. Jonny. Jonny. I know things are bad, but no."

"Come on!" I said, suddenly with an aching for nicotine that seemed to inhabit every cell in my body. "I didn't know my life was going to be put through the weird blender."

"No excuses, Jonny," said Mat, and handed me another Long Island Iced Tea. I took it and smiled back ruefully. Mat had a single-minded intensity that was a pain in the ass sometimes. I had made him promise never to give me another cigarette one drunken night a few weeks before and now I wished he didn't always stick by his word quite so stubbornly.

"You're a pain in the ass, Mat," I reflected, pausing to knock back another gulp of the soothing drink, "but I guess that's why we're still friends."

"Let's hear this whole thing. Who's trying to kill you? And who's brandishing the weird blender?"

So I began to tell the entire story, from the fight with Emma to losing my house, to the Riders and Caroline rescuing me, and the shindig with Zone Securities. Mat took it all in and kept the supply of Long Island Iced Teas coming. I tried to give him as much detail as I could, dragging my mind back to describe the Riders and everything else as clearly as possible in case,

somehow, something small turned out to be key. I had also
hoped that by telling the whole thing straight out, I might get
some flash of inspiration, or insight.

But it didn't happen.

All I got was the feeling of a weight sitting in my stomach—
a darkness that I couldn't reach, couldn't explain, and that
scared the shit out of me. When I'd finished, I felt immensely
tired, and as I sat back in the shade of the palm tree on Mat's
roof terrace, I began to fall asleep with the sound of the ocean
peeling away in the distance. Part of me said life seemed all
right again. I had been through so much and yet now here I was,
in this oasis of calm.

"Mat," I said with my eyes closed, pulling myself back from
the edges of sleep.

"Yeah."

"You know when Jack died?"

"Yeah."

"Has anything come back to you at all?"

"No. Don't go there, Jonny," he said quietly. "Get some rest."

"It feels like it's all tied in to this thing in a way I can't explain.
It feels like I've got to face up to what happened back then," I
said, almost inaudibly, but his reply came back as just a haze of
sounds, because I had drifted into a sleep that was warm and
peaceful, one where I dreamed with delicious clarity. The dreams
fired through me with unnatural intensity, so that they seemed
to occupy my whole mind.

Habakkuk was calling me. I was lying in a crevasse and could see his face through a hole in the roof of the ice,
looking down on me. He was smiling and I wasn't sure why.
Was he pleased to see me? Or was there something more to it
than that? The ice was hard and unforgiving against my back,

and I tried to push myself up with my arms. I could see he was shouting something and gesturing, but no words seemed to be coming out of his mouth. I tried to move again, but something seemed to be holding me back—some weight, some fear. I had to get out. I had to get out of here. Then he waved like he knew something and drew back from the hole but his laughter echoed around the crevasse, barreling down different fissures so it kept returning in waves.

In that moment I was sure of one thing: Habakkuk knew more than I did.

16

I heard the pages fluttering in the warm breeze and knew straightaway that the noise came from a large, open book.

The simple sound was gorgeously intoxicating so I just let it fill my head; let the gentle delicate rustling of wafer-thin pages, tumbling over each other, course through me with a tingle. And I realized the breeze must have stiffened, just as Mat said it would.

The dream about Habakkuk lay fresh in my mind and I turned it over, wondering what it meant—wondering what my subconscious wanted me to see and why on earth Habakkuk should be tied in to any of this, or whether it was just some built-in anxiety about work.

I lay there, letting the pleasant sensation of just being alive have a free run and feeling more rested than I had in what seemed like years. Then something occurred to me. Why was I hearing the sound of pages rustling? I cautiously opened my eyes, sensing something was seriously altered.

I was right.

There were maybe fifty volumes littered about the roof, piled in great heavy towers, and there was even one open volume on my lap.

"Caroline?" I croaked, and saw Mat was asleep on a chair on the other side of the roof. "Caroline?" I cried, getting up and almost tripping up over the things.

"What?" said Mat, stirring. "Whoaaa!" he added seeing the books. "What is this? Books?"

"Yeah. The limpet encyclopedia saleswoman must have left them."

"Dark! This whole thing is genuinely out of control."

"Caroline!" I called, not really surprised when I didn't get an answer. I scanned over the edge of the wall down to the street below but couldn't see even a smidgen of a sign of her. "Well, I guess you could say this is a gentle hint. Why didn't we wake up?"

"That's one reason," Mat said, nodding toward the empty bottles of alcohol.

"Yeah, I guess. Do you think I should buy these things now, anyway? I mean she did get me away from the Riders, didn't she? Maybe I owe it to her."

"No way," Mat said. "They have no right to your Medi-Data, and you don't know anything about her anyway. You don't know what it's about."

"I know, but look at all this." I gestured, then saw a note on top of a particularly large pile. I sighed. " 'Congratulations. Your twenty-four-hour deadline has passed and while we have not got a definite "yes" from you, we assume you are buying our

highly valued encyclopedia collection that will become a treasured family possession enjoyed by you and your wife (separated). As a token of our goodwill, we are able to offer you a free
hologram virus zapper, and a full-sized framed poster of a Canadian moose. Best wishes Colonel Isaac A34.' "

"This is totally dark," said Mat. "Why would anyone want all
these books, when it's all on vis-media anyway? It makes no
sense at all."

"I know, don't look at me," I breathed, catching sight for the
first time of the huge frame containing the Canadian moose
poster. "And why would they think I want that?"

"Beats me. And do you know something else that's slightly
weird? I had such a whopping hangover today that I called in
sick, and I didn't even have a drink last night. What's that about?"

"Everything's gone weird."

"Quite cool in a way."

"Do you think there's something in one of these books that
I'm supposed to find?"

"What? Nah. Chill out, Jonny. If anyone wanted you to know
something, they wouldn't put it in here. It would take years to go
through all of these. There's reams of stuff. Look at it. 'A D-one-
one-three-four is an itch virus that is airborne and attracted to
the shoulder blades of the human being. When scratched and
dislodged, it floats around until it becomes attracted to the
shoulder blades of another human being,' " he read randomly
from a page in one of the volumes near him. "An itch isn't a
virus, is it? They've got to be kidding, haven't they?"

"Caroline E61 doesn't kid about stuff. And yet there's something inexplicable about her. Maybe underneath it all there is
a—Do you know what I think?" I said, with a wave of unexpected
decisiveness that I hadn't seen coming. "I think this whole limpet
saleswoman thing is just a con to cover something up. I'm being
conned and they've gone to a huge length to do it, but I really

don't know why, or how they are tied in with the Riders or my house. If Teb could just trace the leak from my Medi-Data back to their place, we can find out where they operate from and pay them a visit."

"I like it. Especially the 'we.' "

"Yeah, sorry, I didn't mean . . . I just thought you might—"

" 'Course I'm coming! Kidding, OK, Jonny? So what about your house punks then? Leave them to chill for a bit?"

"Yeah, thanks, Mat, yeah. My house will have to wait. I don't have their number anymore. I scrunched up that calling card and dropped it in the Zone Securities canteen by mistake, and my Skin Media is dead."

"OK. And what about those crazy Riders?"

"Well, Caroline found me here, so they can too, I s'pose. All I can think of is to keep moving and hope they take a very long while to catch up. That's my plan, unless you can think of anything better?"

Mat opened his mouth.

"Apart from surfing," I put in quickly.

"Oh," he said after a deflated pause. "In that case, no, I can't."

17

We hailed a taxi in the late afternoon—a three-seater Crossfield Jumbo 140—and scooted through the meandering traffic that was performing its usual delicate weave.

I was on the "rack"—the third seat of the bike that faced backwards—which took a bit of getting used to. But once I went with it, I began to feel relaxed, and found myself looking through the machines darting behind us and wondering if Caroline was out there. Why had she bothered with dropping off all those encyclopedias? Were they really expecting me to pay? There had to be some law against that, but perhaps her company figured people couldn't always be bothered to follow the correct procedures and would just cave in.

Much more worryingly was that the Riders might be out there with their oversized guns and weird porridge. We shifted through Country and Western and into Heavy Thwack, where everything in the zone was a deep electric blue—something that would have done my head in if I'd had to have lived there for any length of time, and I was relieved when we slid over the border into Head Hopping. It wasn't an area of music I liked much, and the people who were into it could really bore you to tears at a party; but it was a relief to be out of Heavy Thwack.

Teb lived in White Noise—a zone that left you shaking your head when you came out because you had spent much of the time in there being perplexed. Given my current state, I wondered if it would explode my head completely.

As we nipped under the East Gate, a chain of elephants was taking up much of the street in some sort of advertising procession for Elnor Elnorian, but the road gradually widened until it was a smooth area that seemed to disappear off into the distance on either side. There were huge expanses of nothing in White Noise, and a lot of the roads were vast tarmac areas with no defined edges, which caused a large number of accidents. The Zone Traffic Police were always furious about it, but someone in White Noise must have had some power somewhere, because it never, ever got changed.

We passed a store that was infamous—it stretched for over a mile, but was very narrow. You stood on a conveyor belt and went past everything, taking what you needed until at the end you paid. Someone had managed to speed up the conveyor belt one day to over forty miles an hour and there had been a lot of broken limbs at the checkout.

Large bulbous towers poked up at the edge of the square and a Ferris wheel that had stopped working years before swung idly on its haunches with a huge broken screen proclaiming

VALDIMAR G78 HAS EATEN MORE— The rest of the screen was missing. I had no idea what it had ever said.

We skipped in and out between a couple of bikes and headed to the far end, where a road ran off in a dead straight line, flanked with faceless stainless-steel structures that went for malls in White Noise. These were broken up by the usual mix of stores, offices, and the shell of the old weather station that had been relocated years before, when the weather control franchise had been bought out by one of the football teams, looking for an edge. For the most part they didn't take much of a role in exercising their franchise, because they found it too expensive. So much of the time the weather was left to do what it felt like, except for the occasional small-scale weather control post paid for by local people, or snuck up illegally by advertisers.

The original theory had been that if they had a big game, the football team would rig it so they got the wind behind them in both halves. They had once even managed to make it snow successfully on every opposition offensive drive, but the NFL got fed up with them and passed a rule saying there was a limit to what they could and could not do with the weather. There was a lot about it in the newspapers at the time, but I don't remember the exact outcome.

There wasn't much traffic following us and I scanned the rooftops of the buildings as the sun peeked over the ridges. The old weather building looked utterly deserted, but I had a nasty feeling about things again—a nasty feeling that there was someone out there I couldn't see. I tried to put it to the back of my mind but the mood hung over me like a bad suit for the rest of the journey and I only snapped out of it with a jolt when the bike stopped near Teb's.

"I rang Teb and told him we were coming, but not much more," said Mat as his crash suit undid.

"Good; very good," I said, wondering why the hell it hadn't

occurred to me. I hopped off the bike, scanning the rooftops for any signs of the Riders while Mat connected up his Jab-Tab to the bike to pay for the ride, but there was nothing there to see.

"You guys have a power day, do you hear?" said the taxi Rider, remounting his bike. I knew he meant it good-naturedly, but instinctively I felt my hackles rise, until they were somewhere near the height of a small skyscraper. I didn't want a power day; I just wanted a normal day without strange things happening. I wanted to sit this man down and give him a forty-five-minute lecture on why I did not want to be wished a fucking power day, but I just gritted my teeth and said, "Yeah, thanks."

The bike blustered off in a scurry of smoke and we found ourselves alone in a backwater of White Noise, where a constant low hum murmured from somewhere that I couldn't place, filling in the space where silence would have been.

Teb's apartment was part of an old warehouse just across the way, so we began to cross over the silent, cool street that epitomized sleepy stillness. We were about halfway when out of the corner of my eye, I saw the sky split open and disgorge a black shape, while a wild explosion of noise reverberated virtually inside my head, like someone had placed an excited road drill in my ear. I instinctively dived behind a Litter Beagle that was wandering up the street as two GaFFA 6s screamed by at low altitude, but I realized instantly it was nothing at all to worry about. Mat was standing looking at me from the center of the empty road.

"Chill out, Jonny, OK?" he called, slightly uncertainly, as the choppers faded.

"Yeah," I replied, straightening. "Yeah, sorry," I added, suddenly aware that things were seriously getting to me.

"Here, Beagle!" said Mat throwing a scrunched-up ball of paper down onto the sidewalk in its direction. The cumbersome-looking Dumpster-sized contraption snorted its way slowly over to the paper and sucked it up through one of its snouts, letting out a gentle "hmm" in appreciation. Most Litter Beagles were pretty friendly, but you just had to be on your guard because one or two rogues sometimes got loose, and they could take your leg off. We hopped up the steps to the entrance to Teb's block as another bike raged past on the road behind us, snorting a change of gear as it went, and I forced myself not to look around.

Mat was right. I had to chill out.

The entrance hall was high, with one vast window that stretched up on the left side, and the whole thing was supported by a flurry of chic-looking pipes and high-tensile wires. Nobody had dusted up there for years, or in fact probably ever, and the tiny lights that pinpricked out of the ceiling looked dimmer than they should have been. No doubt the architects had assured the client at the time that the dust could all be magnetized to the dust trap I could see in the far corner, but Magno-Traps had turned out to give some people headaches, and so most of them were switched off.

Various spiral staircases wound down into this vast space at irregular intervals, and we found Teb's and made our way up. A low deep hum droned through the building, masking the noise the echo of our feet made tapping up the stairs.

When we were about twenty feet off the ground, it leveled out into a gangway that led toward a wall pitted with nine or ten doors, all irregularly spaced at different heights. Teb's door popped open as we approached and warm light flooded out.

Mat shut the door behind us with a heavy clunk.

"Teb?" I called, but there was just a dull hum from somewhere, and otherwise the apartment seemed overly still, as though something busy had just happened and its sudden absence had left a gap. "Teb? What's happening!" I called again, not altogether liking this emptiness, and I could sense that Mat was not reassuringly cool about it, either.

We walked cautiously toward the living room, which was a clean, high-tech, steel-and-wires structure, with a glass roof and a floor littered with enough bits of electronic gadgetry and half-cannibalized machines to power a small country. "Teb? Don't mess about. This is weird. Teb?" A sudden noise from close behind made us both jackknife around.

"Jonny. You want to know something odd I don't get?"

"Teb? Christ!" I exclaimed, as he appeared down the loft ladder, absorbed with a typing gizmo.

"The purring. That's the only bit that still confuses me."

"What do you mean?"

"Purring. Why would they do that?"

"I don't know. Who? Is everything OK here?"

"Yeah, sure," said Teb. "But why would they do it? Just for fun, do you think?"

"Do what?"

"Purr. This is what I've got so far, but it doesn't include purring."

"Teb, will you stop going on about purring?"

"This isn't an ideal time for hearing about your crazy ideas," added Mat. And I thought, No, the best time is when I am too drunk to care.

"Come on! It's taken me three months and about six hundred doughnuts to get to this. Give it a look!" Teb persisted, handing me an open gizmo book scrawled with all kinds of equations. "It's all there. Do you see it?"

"Teb, if I had even the faintest idea what you were talking about, we could have something approaching a normal conversation, but I really don't." I shrugged, and handed it back to him with a brief glance.

"The forces acting on a cat," he said. "In simple black-and-white. It's beautiful! See, those equations are how the forces acting on a cat manifest themselves in ambient conditions.

V equals the wind. G is gravity. R is the random factor that is in proportion to the time curve of a meow. Are you with me?"

"No. What?"

"The time curve of a meow. Now do you get it?"

"Teb," I said, "only you and possibly a few small egglike creatures the other side of the universe who talk in clicks and whistles and eat carpet tiles will ever get this."

"No, it's easy. You see, I began to wonder why cats wander about aimlessly. They look like there's no pattern at all to their actions, but I thought that can't be right, there must be something behind it all. And I found there was! It's linked to the wavelength of a meow. I think you'll find that's not complicated, or sad at all."

"Sounds pretty dark," said Mat.

"Right. But tell me it's not sad. I got suddenly worried about Natasha. Maybe she thinks I'm sad, doing all this."

Teb and Natasha had been going steady since high school. She was stunning, levelheaded, and generous. She wasn't going to change her opinion of him now.

"Teb, Natasha loves you, so chill out, OK?"

"OK. If you think so. Good."

"Look, can I drag you away from cats? Great though that is, I'm really hoping you can help me. There's been a leak on my Medi-Data and I'm kind of hoping you can find the source."

"Love to, but I can't. No way, José," chirped Teb. "The Pit is more corrupted than the average politician. It was shorting last time, and starting it might kill it off forever. Who wants a doughnut? I'm supposed to be cutting back."

"No thanks," said Mat.

"Teb, honestly, I'm pretty desperate. My life is fucked up in a complicated way and I think you are the only person who can help me right now. Is the Pit really not usable at all?"

"Oh." He paused, sensing the depth of my desperation. "Well I could, I suppose. But I don't know. Don't get your hopes up. If it shorts, that's it—and I may not even get past the first wave of viruses with this belly. I tell you, if the Pit goes up, we'll have a bigger fireworks display than the Lady Pom-Pom on night one. And the management committee won't like that."

Lady Pom-Pom night was a pointless tradition invented by a new mayor a few years before, where a zillion girls lined the streets waving pom-poms, while teams of men, who felt they had something to prove, competed in a race to tow burning refrigerators from one end of the city to the other. Don't ask me anything more about it, because the answer is I simply don't know, I especially don't care, and I rigorously make sure I'm never there.

"Takes fifteen minutes to get the system warmed up, so I'll stick it on. Let's get some coffee and doughnuts and you can tell me what I'm looking for. Make a change from cats, I s'pose, but I think it's really pushed back the frontiers of science a bit, don't you?"

"Chill out," I said. "The cats thing is doing my head in."

The Pit was somewhere in the middle of his vast apartment. It wasn't exactly illegal to have made such a thing, probably because Teb was one of the few people who could actually build one; but if Zone Securities had found it, I get the feeling they would have taken it apart.

Probably with a sledgehammer.

There was an area about the size of a double bed sunk into the floor, and stacked around it were a variety of machines that blinked with lights and made occasional pinging noises. Teb crunched down a large power main handle, and blue strands of static electricity arced rather menacingly across the sunken area. More tiny lights than I remembered winked on, skipping their way back and forth across various machines and consoles.

"How did you think of all these things, Teb?" Mat asked, as

Teb whacked a particularly stubborn piece of the contraption until he had coaxed it into life.

" 'There are more things in heaven and earth, Mat, than are dreamt of in your philosophy.' "

"Don't go all Shakespeare on me now, Teb. Where's the coffee?"

"Usual place," he said, waving a hand at Mat, and we both hunkered down on a curved sofa in the little snug area at the side of the machine. Mat made the coffee and I was grateful because he understood the importance of getting it just right. With Teb, it was a complete lottery.

"So what's it all about? Something to do with that Emma is it?" I noticed an edginess in his voice, as the words came out slightly too quickly, and I sensed he was worried about going into the Pit.

"Emma? Why do you say Emma?"

"I don't know. She seems a bit funny, somehow."

"Really? Well, we did have a humongous fight, but I can't see that's connected to this," I said, taking my coffee from Mat and sipping it thoughtfully. He had made it exactly right. "This is what's happened, OK? I've already told Mat, so apologies for saying it all again." And I explained to him briefly what had been going on in the last thirty-six hours but spared him a lot of the details because I didn't want to overload his head too much—especially when he was about to go into the Pit.

"Interesting," he said at the end of my story. " 'Though this be madness, there be method in it.' "

"What?"

"Polonius says it in *Hamlet.*"

"Right. Leaving Shakespeare out of this just for a moment," said Mat, "what can you do in the Pit?"

"Oh. OK. Right. Well, your Skin Media is easy to rectify," he said, "as long as they haven't terminated the source extensions;

that would be annoying and a bit of a pain. The Jab-Tab could be tricky if the credit block has been fixed at a high level, but not really 'tricky' tricky. Those guys are still using codes from the Stone Age."

"And the leak from the Medi-Data source?"

"Depends if it shows up as a thread or not. Sometimes these things are invisible because they've got virtual mustard on them, which kills the signal."

"Right. What," I said, "does that mean to someone like, for example, who doesn't understand how a lightbulb works?"

"Means it might be tricky." He sniffed. "I haven't been in the Pit for six months and things may have changed."

"Six months!" I echoed, with rather too much surprise, thinking no wonder he was out of practice. "Teb, if you don't think this is safe, you mustn't go." The Pit arced, sending blue static forking from one side to the other, and the room lighting dimmed automatically, isolating the Pit like an arena.

"It's OK, I can do it. Piece of cake—or in my case, a jelly doughnut," he said, not altogether happily. "You see that power switch? Throw it all the way up if it looks like I've lost control."

"What, now?" said Mat with a smile.

"Very funny," murmured Teb. "Right." He was clearly nervous, and beads of sweat had started to form on his forehead.

"Need a rollicking bit," he said looking me in the eye.

"Bit of what?"

"*Henry V.*"

"Henry the what?"

"The fifth. Shakespeare? The English guy? Right. Oh, I know. It's obvious. 'I see you stand like greyhounds in the slips!' " he growled, staring around the room, " 'straining upon the start. The game's afoot! Follow your spirit; and upon this charge, Cry, "God for Harry! England and Saint George!" ' " he yelled wildly, before jumping like a sack of cement into the Pit and standing like a martial arts expert, who's learned his skill entirely from out of focus EtherMat pictures of grainy old films.

He's a remarkable person, I thought, exchanging a glance with Mat.

Either Mat or I would have been far more suited to going in the Pit because we were way more athletic, but we wouldn't have had a clue what to do once we were in there. Teb on the other hand knew exactly what to do, but moved like a water-filled balloon.

The Pit floor was about three feet below us, and Teb slowly turned around in a circle, keeping an eye out for anything coming from behind. The first viruses flew at him pretty slowly, like neon butterflies, and he had plenty of time to bat them away with his hands. Then a few more, in waves of three or four, and he jerkily hopped to one side so they floated past before vaporizing as they hit the Pit's walls. He pulled on a strand of light that protruded out across the Pit, and a weird tangle of laser lines drew toward him. He sifted his way through them with his fingers, pulling at some and moving others away, then drawing out more laser threads from the other sides. These lines had some kind of writing on them, but it was too small to see from where we stood. More viruses flew at Teb, some from behind, and he took a couple of fairly heavy blows to the shoulders but regained his balance quickly, whacking them away clumsily as he continued to sift and pull his way along the maze of laser lines.

"There's a lot more stuff in the system than last time I was here," he cried. "It's a lot harder to find any way through."

Without warning, a whole swarm of small green viruses flew at him out of a broken thread. Teb dropped the laser line he was following and spun around frantically to bat them off. One by one, with a squeak, they fell to the floor.

"Hey, I may have been lucky. Look at this! I'm a slither away from the Medi-Data complex already," he shouted, retrieving the strand of light he had been pulling. "It may be that someone's been planting Tiger Bombs, and I don't have to tell you what that means."

Teb for once was quite wrong. I had no idea what that meant, and it always amused me that he assumed more knowledge in those about him than they actually had, no matter how many times you explained it to him.

The Pit was a place he had invented and built from scratch, and it could give him access to pretty well anywhere that had any kind of gadgetry connected to the EtherMat, or vis-media. It wasn't conventional and he usually came out a bit bruised from the virus attacks, but batting them away physically was a far quicker way of disposing of them than trying to do it with written code at a console, apparently.

At least, that's what he told me.

It was this leap of imagination that had given him the idea for the Pit in the first place. As he put it, "You could spend a day trying to convince a terrorist, with reasoned argument, not to shoot, or you could just come up behind him and whack him over the head with a shovel. Which is quicker? See, it's the same with these viruses. Much quicker just to whack them than try to talk to them in code."

You could sort of see what he meant when he put it like that, but Teb did have a very odd mind and I don't think too many other people had approached the problem the way he had. So the Pit was pretty unique.

The viruses were coming thick and fast now in their multi-colored, almost luminous, iridescence. Some of them were as big as small birds but they moved fairly slowly; and although Teb slipped a few times and tripped over his own feet, he dealt with it all.

"I'm at the Medi-Data complex," he cried. " 'Once more into the breach, dear friends, once more; Or close the wall up with

our English dead!' " But at that moment, plumes of smoke began to erupt frenetically from a console on the far side. "Ahh—
it's shorting! Whack that one! Someone whack it, quick!" he
shouted. The light in the Pit began to pulse alarmingly, and it
seemed the laser lines would fade away completely. "Quickly,
it's going!" he cried again.

Mat was on the case, fighting his way over to the machine
through the clouds of thick black smoke. And when he got
there, he hit it with such force the whole contraption shuddered.

Everything in the Pit wound down to a very faint glow.

"Shit," said Mat under his breath. Then, slowly, the lights
around the Pit grew in intensity, the smoke stopped caning out
of the machine, and everything returned to normal.

"You're a very lucky man," cried Teb, pulling his way carefully
along the strand of light. "That thing has enough volts going
through it to widen the Pacific. Medi-Data complex! See?" he
cried, holding up a small, red line of laser light that spurred off
the main thread. "I follow this and find out who's been listening
in, like that."

I had known Teb since we were kids, hanging out in third
grade and getting into some fantastic scrapes together—or rather
Teb getting into some fantastic scrapes and me hanging about
on the periphery, loving it, but not quite having enough guts or
too much sense to get involved. And that's kind of how it had always been. We made a team, of sorts. He took all the risks and I
loved going along for the ride, being the accomplice; albeit a
rubbish one, who spent most of his time laughing uncontrollably from about twenty feet away.

I suppose the most unlikely thing about Teb was that he had
been going steady with the same girl since high school. Natasha
was a lovely, well-organized, conventional sort of girl, and not
anything like Teb at all. With so much chaos in his life, maybe

having a girlfriend he could always rely upon was the heart of his courage.

"I'm going to cut it; everything we need to know should be in here," he said, holding up the same red laser thread but at a point where it bulged into a small pod. He laid it down on the floor and took a knife from his belt.

"This is definitely weird," said Mat, but I don't think Teb heard because he was carefully cutting open the small pod of light like it was a real, solid orange. And suddenly I became aware of his tiny actions as he slit through the last of the Light Skin.

"OK, Teb?" I said quietly, as he knelt there motionless for longer than seemed necessary.

"OK," he echoed, then carefully stood, lifted the bottom half of the pod, paused, and whispered, " 'Now might I do it, Mat.' " And then, abruptly, he flicked the pod over so the contents fell out. Tiny shards of light tumbled and burned in the air like slivers of magnesium as they floated to the floor, where they continued to smolder. I stared at these tiny, blinding lights and realized they were words, coalescing like molten steel on the floor of the Pit.

" 'The play's the thing wherein we'll catch the conscience of the King!' " he said, leaping up out of the Pit. "I think we've got them." And at that moment, the console on the far side began smoking again, and this time it was making a rather ungainly hammering sound as well. Mat was standing there and ready to whack it again, but stopped abruptly as Teb screamed, made a surprisingly agile dive over to the power switch, and heaved it up. "I think we've pushed our luck enough." The Pit lights snapped off, and the lights in the room faded up, dragging us all back to reality.

"This machine could take out the whole block if it went up. And the management committee would definitely send a memo around about that. Probably still wouldn't let up about the parking, though," he added, more wistfully.

"Teb, remind me never to get you to fix my doorbell," said Mat after a pause.

"Doorbell. Yeah," said Teb almost inaudibly, but his eyes were still miles away, as though he were still thinking about the management committee's parking policy.

"Teb?"

"Let's have some coffee to celebrate that we're not all dead," offered Mat.

"Teb?" I said again, as he stood staring.

"Yeah? What?" he said, coming back to life, like a windup toy that has been given a nudge. "Caught one on my shoulder; those viruses are getting bigger, aren't they? Come and see! This is the leak. Here!" And he hopped back onto the floor of the Pit and beckoned me down. I followed him warily, eyeing the machines stacked around the Pit wall. They seemed to look on like beady-eyed crocodiles hiding in a swamp. "Here it is." He was crouched on the floor. "Down here. You see it?" I looked closely where he was pointing and saw that the words that had fallen moments earlier from the pod had somehow coalesced into hard, solid metal letters, fused to the Pit floor like cooled steel. The largest of them spelled out a name: "Argonaut Logistics," and an address was there too, "Branciforte Drive." It wasn't going to be hard to trace them from that. I glanced at the other words, but they didn't seem to make much sense. "Remember the eighteenth of October," one line said. "The acacia tree up on the hill," another read. Teb shook his head. "That stuff shouldn't be there. Must be some security thing gone haywire."

"The eighteenth of October? Didn't something famous happen on that day?" I said, "A battle or something? Do you remember?"

"Don't look at me, I didn't take history; it always seemed to be tubing during those lessons," said Mat. "Want some more?" he added, waving a mug about.

I'd much rather get going, I thought, pulling myself out of the Pit. "D'you mind if we head over to this Argonaut Logistics place?"

"OK. But sure you don't want to chill out, have some more coffee, and get your head together?"

"I can't chill, Mat. There are four psychopathic, porridge-making Riders out there somewhere."

"Yeah, yeah, take your point."

"And anyway, I'm way too pissed off with all of this to chill out at the moment."

18

We left Teb at the flat, hailed a three-seater Crossfield, and burned up toward Branciforte on the far side of town over near Wah-Wah and Klick Track.

Once, the whole area of blanched hills around there had been covered in thick sweet-smelling pine forest, but only a few swathes of trees remained now, clinging uncertainly to the slopes—squashed between the houses, office blocks, and malls like an echo from a misplaced past. It felt like a reflection of my life. A few bits of it were still recognizable, but otherwise it had changed into something quite different.

The Crossfield rack seemed uncomfortable. Perhaps the seat was just harder than usual, and I wriggled inside my crash suit as I kept an amateurish eye out for anyone tailing us. It gave me a flimsy shred of confidence. I left the visor open, letting the cool wind soothe my rising craving for a cigarette. Being on a bike gave me time to think, time to listen to myself, but mainly, it seemed, time to lust after a gigantic infusion of nicotine like at no other moment.

I breathed in deeply and wondered what Mat was making of it all; I didn't want to drag him into anything really serious. If there was music to be faced when the time came, I had to face it alone.

I wondered what we were going to do at this place. Just walk in and say: "Excuse me, but I don't believe you are selling ency-clopedias"? and hope they'd throw their hands in the air and say: "You got us!" I considered this briefly, then booted the thought away. Maybe the place didn't exist. Maybe it would just be one guy with a phone. Maybe I'd get shot the moment I stepped off the bike. Until I knew what was there, it didn't make much sense to plan.

The bike braked sharply, and I was squeezed to the back of my crash suit. Then we kicked around a tight bend and the Rider leaned aggressively from one side to the other, so the road rose up to meet me, then fell away.

When I looked up again, I realized we had crossed the border into Christmas Single and I sighed.

This was a very silly zone.

If anybody got me started, I could rant on about it for a whole evening and still not be through. At least the artificial snow was not too deep today and the snowplows didn't look like they'd be out, but then the Rider decelerated to a crawl. I guessed we were almost certainly stuck behind a sleigh. Usually, I gave ex-plicit instructions to all taxi Riders not to take me anywhere near this zone, no matter what the extra cost.

It was partly that the people in Christmas Single had way too much missionary zeal for my liking, always sending out Father

Christmases to other zones in an attempt to get more people to come and live there. Every few months you would hear a knock on the door and open it to find a big smiling man in a red suit saying, "Ho! Ho! Ho!" and offering you a real estate brochure and a free tinsel pen. The novelty wears off after about the fifth time and you just want to punch him. And although I've managed to control myself, some people haven't, believe me. Perhaps that's why they always have backup now, in the shape of a couple of angels.

The ever-present lights and trees and reindeer always make my heart shudder too, because it feels like under every twinkling light is a problem that someone living in this zone has buried away. This was the favorite zone for people who had problems so big they had decided never to face them. I could have done without being reminded of all this now.

At least Teb was pretty certain he could fix my Skin Media and Jab-Tab by going into the Pit and doing it from there, but he was adamant about mending the console first, so we left him prizing open one of the machines with a serving spoon, even though there must have been at least 150 screwdrivers somewhere in that apartment. If Teb said he thought he could probably do something, that was as good as a cast-in-stone certainty.

He always underplayed his talents.

The Rider accelerated jerkily and we swerved out past a sleigh pulled by a gang of huskies and—mysteriously—a couple of wiener dogs as well. They seemed to have found the art of sliding on their stomachs through the snow, because their tiny legs couldn't keep up. The thing itself was laden with gaily wrapped up parcels and driven by a couple of winged white angels, who were two stoic men in their forties wearing big black boots. I knew Mat would be silently laughing his head off—not just because of the bizarre spectacle, but also because he knew how annoyed it would be making me. Christmas lights twinkled unrelentingly on the strings of stores, and a troupe of Father Christmases strolled past—one of them carrying a shotgun, broken open, and crooked over his elbow. It reminded me I didn't have a gun and I wondered if Mat had brought his.

I had never actually fired one in anger and I couldn't swear there were even bullets in the one I'd had. It was just one of those things that everyone carried because they could. And while most other countries had realized that allowing people guns encouraged violence, America had remained defiant, getting itself into a tangle over our Constitution. I had heard politicians say it wasn't so much the American Constitution anymore, as the American Constipation; the country had been stuck with it for longer than was healthy, and now most things were really beyond the control of anyone, except perhaps the Zone Traffic Securities.

I should have been feeling excited, pumped up like a soldier about to leap into battle, but I just felt tired. I felt worn through, and my reflexes didn't seem to want to care. This was not ideal. I never had been much good at going without sleep and I just hoped the adrenaline would start pumping if I needed it. But I suddenly pictured the adrenaline inside my body as tiny little things bent over in exhaustion. Not exactly positive visualization.

We hammered under the gate out of Christmas Single, almost losing the back wheel in an outlandish slide through the last of the snow, flicking past a final waving neon reindeer telling us to hurry back, and into the relative peace and sense of Wah-Wah. Wah-Wah was a step across the Caribbean to single-story shanty houses and corrugated metal stores, and a road pockmarked with holes as big as soccer balls.

I liked it.

It was laid-back and reminded me in many ways of a poor but happy relation of Chillout. We bounced along the road, the Rider killing our speed until we reached Klick Track, and things became facelessly normal. It occurred to me that this might be why they had put Argonaut Logistics here.

It would be like hiding a casino in the Vatican; it's not a place you would think to look.

As we picked our way through the traffic, someone touched wheels and a couple of bikes slid over, then spun sideways toward us like lazy tops, spiraling down the freeway, growling along the tarmac and grinding off paint as they flew. I closed my eyes when they were almost on top of us, knowing it was inevitable we would go down too; but miraculously one must have gone to each side because when I looked around, a second later, they were gliding to a halt down the road. Crashes weren't unusual and I don't suppose those Riders were hurt inside their crash suits, just a bit bashed and bruised.

We slipped between the fallen machines, which lay lifelessly on the tarmac, and cruised on through Klick Track, until we finally slowed at a junction and I caught sight of a store called "Big Bob's Giant Giveaway Basket Warehouse," which looked about the size of a small cupboard crammed, not surprisingly, with baskets. Outside hung a wickerwork thing that had been woven carefully into the shape of some two-foot-high letters and it clearly spelled out the word "badger." Three people in overalls were painting it red, using brushes on the end of long poles. I stared, wondering what that was all about, and tried to imagine what was in those people's lives, what they dreamed of and cared about and whether they had someone to go home to. Then a burst of acceleration from the Rider sent the shop vanishing into the distance and seemed to leave the thought in the air by their sign.

We couldn't be far from Branciforte and this Argonaut Logistics place now, and a bead of anticipation ran down my neck, but my eyes still ached. And most of all, a heavy knot of confusion lay like a weight in my stomach. It felt as if I'd eaten an extra-large pizza from Raches, the little shack up on Valley.

Why hadn't I let EasyDreams know why I hadn't turned up? Habakkuk would be going crazy.

Well let him.

It wasn't like he would fire me; it was just that if I ever got back to work there, he would give me grief about it for much longer than necessary. He reveled in that kind of thing. It was all ammunition, which he used to fuel the building of his little empire so he could feel like he was in control of all of us. He was a tiresome pain in the ass like that; one of the little people, with little, weasely horizons, but who put so much energy into getting to where he wanted, he inevitably succeeded.

He was efficient though, and he'd placate my clients so that things would carry on. That's why we all put up with him, I guess; he could be bothered, a lot more than the rest of us, about all the dull stuff.

Abruptly, we curved off the road and pulled up. My head cracked the back of the crash suit sharply, reminding me of the bruises I had courtesy of the Odysseus Hat.

I glanced around.

Beside us was a rusting hulk of a steel-framed building. Its panels hung off in the breeze and a sizeable mountain ash was growing out of the first-floor window ledge. Around it, everything felt hopelessly run-down. An old café called Sapid Snacks was boarded up, with a huge sign proclaiming it to be OPEN, FOR HOT SNACKS AND RIOTOUS CAKES, and a Litter Beagle lay slumped over, not showing any signs of life and giving the impression it had not broken down but merely lost hope.

This was an unusual area of Klick Track, at odds with the faceless, calm normality of the zone, and it was a wonder they had allowed things to reach this kind of state. The slopes rose behind the buildings, partly covered in the pine forest that had once colonized this whole place.

My crash suit jammed halfway as I slid it open, and I fought with it while Mat connected up his Jab-Tab to pay.

"Yeah, does that sometimes," said the woman Rider languidly in my direction, without offering me any assistance, or any clue as to how to free the thing. In the end, I clasped my fingers around the edge of the open gap, gave it a massive wrench, and it grated open.

"Argonaut Logistics," she said, with a nod toward the shattered structure, not showing any sign of surprise at its condition. "You have a power day, d'you hear?" she called and was gone with a flare of fumes into the traffic. I turned away and stood there, looking at this building rise up into the midblue sky of the warm evening, too tired to be annoyed with her about the power day thing.

"Looks like business has not been good for them," said Mat, gazing up at the rusting fabric skeleton.

"Yeah," I said, automatically searching for a packet of cigarettes that I knew full well I didn't have. We shambled into what was left of the ground floor, which was completely open to the elements now, and all we could see were the naked rusting girders, propping up the bulk of the building above us. There was no sign of any stairs, or any other means to gain entrance to the upper floors, which from the outside appeared derelict but more intact.

"Ripped the stairs out to stop anyone having raves up there, I expect," said Mat. "It would make a pretty dark venue." A chopper thwocked close by overhead, its blades echoing off the hills and through the shell around us, so the whole place seemed to vibrate like a giant purring cat.

"Guess it would," I said, stopping myself from my ridiculous cigarette search. "I really thought we'd get answers here. Not just this dead end." And we both stood looking vaguely around in the cold silence.

"Come on, head out to East Cliff and catch some waves with me, Jonny. Let's try and get some distance on this thing. You can try out my new longy. It's sweet."

"Wait," I said, as something stirred inside my head. "What happened to that chopper?"

"It flew off, like they do. They're good at that. Come on."

"No, it was overhead just now and it stopped. Don't look at me like that," I added as I saw Mat's expression.

"There's an echo in here like an opera singer's stomach. And I'm telling you, I can smell that surf. The wind has dropped, so it's going to be clean." He headed out into the evening sunlight again and I followed.

"What about if it landed on the roof?" I said, feeling like I was going on about it—but, hey, crazier things had happened to me in the last hours by a factor of about six billion. Mat looked at me and he seemed to be thinking it through, weighing up just how crazy it was—weighing up whether he could bear to leave the surf.

"Tell me something, Jonny. Are you sure Sarah isn't tied into all this? Because there's something bugging me about her and it just sits there in my head."

"Sarah. No. She's mad at me, but she's not crazy."

"Yeah, but there's some kind of weird brittleness about who she is—a sense she's a fake, like she's in the wrong compartment, and when I try and picture you two together, I get a strange image in my head that won't settle down properly."

"Mat, I'm open to any ideas, but I don't think Sarah is the one. She's just . . . Sarah. But what about the roof thing?"

"Yeah, OK, OK. We might as well check it out now that we're here. If we make the second floor, there'll probably be some stairs up from there. Then we'll see if she's an empty shell or not."

I wondered whether that last comment was prompted more by the thought of Sarah than the building, but I didn't say anything. The only small chance of finding any answers was to go up. Mat trampled over the uneven, rubbish-strewn ground, grasped one of the girders with both hands and, lying right back off it, began walking his feet up. He made it look easy, raising his hands one after the other, then his feet, slowly and gracefully gaining height, until I had to crane my neck to watch. He looked down, and said, "Got a really vivid flashback to Clouds Rest. Scary."

I was still looking up at him as he made the window, but the mention of Clouds Rest had triggered a memory that crushed all my other thoughts and dragged me away. Maybe my head craved a break from all the present stuff, because I seemed to be swimming in the intensity of the memory far too easily.

The fresh mountains of Yosemite. The anticipation snapping around us like a thousand firecrackers on a blinding, crisp, clean, blue-skied winter's day. We made an attempt on the north face of Clouds Rest, ignoring the fact it should have been way too technical for us—just going for it without fear, and testing our limits—which was stupid really. But we were young and we didn't understand how Bad Things can have consequences for so long afterward.

The snow lay snugly on the pine trees, weighing down their branches, so when the sun melted the ice in little patches, they suddenly sprung up with excitement. The ice on the climb was satisfyingly hard, and you could tell just from the deep, solid clunk it made when you swung with a climbing ax that nothing was going to flake off. The air was thinner near the top and Mat, who led a lot of the way, got slower; but finally, in the late afternoon, he dragged Jack and me up the last pitch and we all stood gasping on the ridge of the arête.

It was no more than the width of a sidewalk, falling sharply away on both sides to the valley floor, four thousand crazy feet below. We spent twenty minutes there celebrating the view and reveling in our achievement, while all around us the peaks poked their way up through the wisps of cloud and melted into a soft, hazy horizon. The evening sank slowly into such a deep blue it felt like you could jump into it without caring, and an intense stillness bathed the sky so your ears seemed like they could hear anything for ten thousand miles.

Then finally, when a chill ate into the air, we stomped down the footpath toward Half Dome, following the ridge, and camped in the forest by the stream, listening for bears and drinking the cheap brandy I had hauled up while Mat talked of high mountains and Prague and toasted a packet of marshmallows. It had been a trip that fed the soul, and it was good to remember a time before Jack had died. And suddenly, I had a deep, unsettling feeling about that tragic day that lurked just beneath the surface of my memory. Something I had blocked out that needed to be unpacked and faced.

"Jonny? What's happening?" Mat's voice filtered down from above.

"Sorry. Just thinking about Clouds Rest," I said, and saw that Mat was leaning from one of the blown-out windows.

"Yeah," he said, softly.

I looked up and took a breath that must have sounded like a sigh because he called down, "It's just a layback," in encouragement.

I felt the abrasive surface of the rusty steel and I made my way up. It wasn't too difficult, but my arms didn't have a lot of strength and I was relieved to grab Mat's huge hand and let him pull me over the window ledge. I fell haphazardly on the hard floor.

"I would swap my soul for a cigarette right now." I coughed, lying in a heap, breathing much harder from the effort than I would have liked. "Just one drag, in fact. What is the point of giving up smoking again?"

"It'll make you happier, you'll meet the perfect woman and become President of Azerbaijan. Now, come on."

I pushed myself to my feet and walked over, trying to loosen the desire for a cigarette from my head, pleased that it felt like I was doing something positive about the craziness that had swept my life sideways.

The stairs were concrete, covered in a stained green carpet. We made our way up steadily as the late-evening sun slanted gamely in, flopping over the remnants of office stuff that littered most levels—the felled filing cabinets still disgorging their contents; the wires traipsing across the floors; the desks scattered at incomprehensible angles. A lot of the windows were blown, so shattered glass lay in small piles, and the stained fawn curtains flapped in the breeze like dirty prayer flags. One or two of the levels were completely empty, with just the odd piece of paper, discarded and marooned on the exhausted carpet.

We climbed maybe twenty flights, doglegging on every floor, only to be faced by another set of stairs looking much like the last. And with every one of these flights, a nagging doubt grew in the back of my head. Why would anyone run a company selling encyclopedias from the top of a disused building? Cheap rent? To stop people like me from coming after them? It seemed possible, but wildly extreme. Mat was almost certainly right; the chopper had flown off and there was nothing up here. Still, this address was all we had, and since we were here, it felt like we should see it through. We turned the corner on another floor, but a small flash of white light sent my pulse ranting excitedly.

"Mat," I whispered. "See that light in the far corner, behind my right shoulder?"

Mat turned. "A screen is up! Dark!"

"Yeah. It is." My curiosity was deadened by a sense of alarm, that someone was just toying with me for their own amusement, knowing we would be here.

The floor was empty, with just a few desks and a couple of consoles gathering dirt, so we carefully picked our way over sheaves of strewn wires to the screen, which flickered uncertainly as though on the verge of oblivion. I wiped the grime from the console with the tips of my fingers and saw that the big green letters read: "Hello." I felt stupid, right down to my shoes, because I was so out of my depth here with no fucking clue as to what was going on. I simply scuffed away more of the dirt and the thing woke up like a startled squirrel.

"Be bop a loo la! She's my baby!" it sang deafeningly, and I nearly hit the ceiling. "Be bop a loo la, I don't mean maybe!" it went on, and began displaying a picture of what looked like a cartoon duck. "Be bop a—" The machine abruptly flickered, made a crunching sound, and died with a soft sigh. My heart was going for the world record of beats to the minute by this time, and I smiled grimly.

"That was extraordinarily unhelpful," I said.

"Weird."

"Yeah," I replied. "And yet, it doesn't even get in the top ten weird events of the day. It probably comes in at about number thirty-four." I played with the machine a bit, but it was totally dead, and so we gave in and headed on up the building.

We had made maybe forty flights when we turned a corner exactly like all those before, except this time there was just an empty level. There were no more stairs.

We had reached the top.

"Nothing. Nothing."

"Yup," said Mat. The space was pretty much deserted although nearly all the windows were smashed and the glass lay in jagged piles where it had fallen. There was a hatstand lying near one wall and a small plasi-poster hung askew proclaiming: PERSONNEL ARE FORBIDDEN TO SNEER.

"What the fuck is going on with my life?" I said. "Why does nothing have any kind of answers?"

"Beats me," said Mat. "If it had been Teb, I'd have understood more, but why would anyone come after you? Unless it's those guys we trounced at pool."

"Yeah, but even if I did fluke the black, this seems a bit harsh."

We stood in this grimy, stained old office listening to the wind murmur through the empty frames and the distant noise of the bikes herding down the freeway.

"This would actually make a dark place for rave," said Mat. "I think I'll let the crew know. It almost feels like...like we've... but that makes no sense."

19

Not surprisingly, I have never had a fully grown rhino jump on me from an acacia tree. But if I had, I expect it would have felt rather like the sensation I suddenly experienced. I squirmed feverishly on the office floor, felled by this weight, wondering where it had come from. I was confused to find it was Mat. But before I could say anything, a chopper appeared inches from the window, the noise of its blades whipping off the walls with a giant bluster of oil-smoke and gasoline fumes. I froze and watched the cockpit rise slowly out of sight, and as we lay utterly still, poleaxed on the floor, it settled somewhere above us. Its engine wound down from a squeal to a gentle purr, and finally to empty silence.

"Not the top after all, eh?" Mat said with a smile as he dusted himself off. I knew what he was getting at. There could easily be at least one floor above us. Mat edged over to one of the windows and peered around tentatively. Then looking up and holding on to the frame, pulled himself halfway out.

"Mat! Mat!" I called, in an overloud whisper. "Mat." I patted him on the back and he drew himself back inside.

"What?"

I was going to say, "Too risky. There'll be another way," but I didn't. Instead I paused, knowing this was one of those pivotal moments when different futures run off ahead, almost visibly, like two raindrops snaking down a window.

"I'll take a quick look. OK?"

He nodded.

This was my mess, and even though the thought of going out there didn't fill me with joy, I knew it had to be me. I sat on the window frame with my back facing the outside and tilted my head up; there seemed to be two floors above us, judging by the number of windows. Just up and to the left was a satellite dish. The fixing looked good and above that was an air-con unit. Not that technical; just very, very scary, bearing in mind we were at least forty floors up. I really do not like free climbing, but there are moments when I surprise even myself with the risks I will take when my mind is up for it.

I perched on the window ledge, reached above my head for a small cable fixing, and hooked my fingers over it. I gingerly stood up on the window ledge, very slowly turning my head sideways and keeping flat against the building. A gust of wind whipped my face with amusement. I looked down. Heights don't scare me, but this one was interesting, to say the least, and I became very aware of the fact that the hold I had with my right hand was all that was keeping me alive, so I put a lot of concentration into not letting it go. I swept my left arm up along the building until it felt the satellite dish fixing and grabbed it with relief. It was a good solid hold, and I leaned back slightly to rest my arms. That's when it gave way, and my heart walloped my chest cavity with panic. I scrabbled for the edge of the air-conditioning unit with a massive lunge, and caught it as the satellite dish pulled away and dangled down, limp on its wiring.

"Service is overdue by twelve years, two months, and six days," said the air-con unit, abruptly. "The cover fixings will loosen automatically. Please clean filters marked with a red tab."

I swung crazily off the thing, hanging with my hands and kicking my legs frantically. "The dry-bulb outside air temperature is fifty-three degrees. The wet-bulb outside air temperature is fifty-seven degrees...no, make that fifty-five," it continued.

"Please be quiet," I managed to say, as my legs scrabbled against the wall.

"A course of twelve lessons on air-conditioning service maintenance—and general enjoyment of our units—is available at the Institute of Air-Conditioning in Maine. Price available on request." I heaved myself up on the top of the unit. It must have been ancient, because it wasn't a human replicator, just a voice, blathering on automatically. "A shorter course, entitled 'Air-conditioning is cool,' is available for children under sixteen, though an adult must be within one statute mile. Prices available on request."

I got my breath back sitting there, marooned on a small box bolted to the side of the building. The view was awesome and I felt a burst of relief coalesce into excitement. The plate where the duct entered the building was rusty as hell, so I gave it one tug and it came away in my hands. Inside was a small service room, jammed with more ducts and wires, and at the far end was a closed door that led into the building. I was about to head inside and investigate when I heard Mat's voice from below:

"Jonny! Catch," he called, as a loop of something spiraled into the sky. I made a grab for it. It was several strands of cable flex twisted together. Not the sort of stuff most offices bother with now, but this place clearly hadn't been functioning for years.

I shook my head with a smile at Mat's ingenuity and squeezed through the hole into the service room, landing on my haunches on the floor below. I made the end of the flex secure on a massive piece of machinery, leaned out of the hole in the wall, and looked down. Mat was craning his neck to see what was going on, now wearing a ridiculous white knitted hat he must have had in his pocket.

"OK, Jonny?" he called in a loud whisper. I nodded. Then, in one catlike movement, he sprang up out of the window and pulled himself up on top of the air-con unit. He smiled, then tilted his head with surprise.

"Service is overdue by twelve years, two months, and six days," sang the air-con unit, as it jolted into life again. "The cover fixings will loosen automatically. Please clean filters marked with a red tab."

There was a sharp hissing sound from inside the unit and Mat glanced down at it quizzically, then hurriedly launched himself toward me. Another hissing noise and a hard crack as the cover sliced off into the sky, cutting away from us and down toward the ground, like a manic, leaping dog.

"We used to have a washing machine a bit like that," Mat said, pulling himself off me. "The secret was never to ask it to spin anything, or it really lost it."

A further gut-wrenching scream of metal came from the unit and, as we both stared, the whole thing pulled away from the wall. It hung idly for a brief moment by the tenderest of fixings, then plummeted like a felled tree, pulling out the connecting hose that snaked into the room so that it dived between my legs and out of the hole like a frightened cat. It all seemed to make an incredible amount of noise. A second later, there was a dull whump from below.

"Right; that's not good," I said quietly, after a pause.

"I knew we should have gone surfing," Mat murmured, eyeing the door. We both expected a host of security to pile in any second, but nothing happened. I made my way to the door and listened. There was nothing to hear, so I grasped the handle and opened it a touch.

It was so gloomy I pushed a little more. I guessed this was a corridor and we both slipped out quietly. It was deserted. We peered both ways, then edged left in the murky half-light. A short corridor to our right ended with another door. Opposite, to the left, was a door marked ENCYCLOPEDIA RECORDS. My heart lifted. At least we seemed to be in Argonaut Logistics.

We turned right and paused outside this next door; there were distant voices from somewhere, sounding like they were talking rapidly on voice coms, but too quietly to make out distinctly. I carefully pushed the handle only to have it torn violently from my grasp as it was whipped open from the other side by a squat, dark figure. We both stood stupidly, like rabbits caught in a searchlight.

"Marks out of ten for getting my ass kicked?" the man snapped, as he pushed past. "Fifty-six zillion! More probably. This place is worse than the Tree of Woe on a bad day, I'll tell you that for nothing. Never lose an F-51 if you want a life. You're better off emigrating to Utah and living in a colony of marsupials." And then he was gone through the door marked ENCYCLOPEDIA RECORDS.

Mat and I exchanged glances, then slipped into the much bigger room. On the far side was a whole bank of people sitting at screens and monitors, with their backs to us and talking animatedly into voice coms. On the wall was a map of Santa Cruz, with various lights picking out locations. I noticed with surprise that there was a light right on Mat's house. Around the wall were a host of small plasi-screens. "The customer may well be a rude, stupid, lame-brained fathead of a jackass, but respect him," said one. "Always keep a customer alive—it's bad service not to," said another. "Love your workmates, but don't sleep with them, unless you're particularly drunk and can't help it," added a third.

The rest of the floor was empty, except for a spiral staircase to our right. I walked carefully over to it, trying not to attract attention from anyone in the room. The treads flexed slightly as we wound our way up, and I knew now I wanted to find Caroline E. I wanted to find out what this place was about, I wanted to find out more about her, and I wanted to find out what the fuck was going on.

The floor above was bathed in a deep, red glow, as though the main lights had gone down and this was some emergency backup, but I guess it might have been deliberate. If they wanted to keep the place low-key, then having these floors lit up like a Christmas tree, beaming their presence over half of Santa Cruz, wouldn't have been ideal. But then why be in the Street Scanner? Why be in a listing of companies where anyone can find you? I reached the top tread and paused as Mat drew alongside me. This floor was packed with small, underlit glass rooms that faced off from both sides of the corridor. In the ones nearest us were a bed and a small desk, with a screen gently purring away. There was no sign of anyone. We moved gingerly to our left, passing more of these rooms, and I caught the names on the doors. HARRIET M9; then JULIET T32(GF). We moved forward, expecting any moment to hear someone, and I froze. The room on our right was marked with a neat sign. CAROLINE E61.

The blinds were down. I nodded to Mat, indicating the room. I was about to try the door when we heard footsteps on the spiral stairs and a familiar muttering voice floating up.

"Always my ass. Always mine. I come here and eat a hassle salad every fucking day. I live on a diet of hassle fucking salad. Like I'm the only person ever to lose an F-51. Like I'm the only person in the history of the company to ever get the Director General on the phone and think it's the courier."

The balding top of his head came into view but I didn't want to push our luck with this guy, so I flicked open the door to Caroline's room. We scooted inside and I snapped it shut behind us as he grumbled his way past.

I swallowed. Maybe we weren't alone in here.

I turned, very slowly.

20

There are three types of dreams. Those that are made, like the ones I used to make. Those that are normal, and by that I mean the hodgepodges of moments and thoughts of the day past, where your subconscious is trying to organize your head, organize your fears, and organize your future.

And then there are the ones about dead people.

These are different. They have a realism that transcends normal dreams, and they have a quality about them that is comforting and comfortable. They are situations that are fresh, born not from things that can be traced to fleeting images or words from the day before, but a new world that takes you by surprise. They stand alone and they come from another place. Explaining all this means nothing unless you have had them, and if you've had them, then it doesn't need explaining, because clearly you know what I mean.

It all sounds trite and it stinks of needing a crutch to see you through a difficult time when someone has died, but it's not like that. At least, I don't think it is. Dead people crop up in normal dreams too, but the difference is like comparing electricity to pedal power. It's cavernous.

And there is another type of dream I should mention here too, but it's hard to call it a dream because it's off the scale of normal experience. It happens during sleep, when you are near someone who is on the very edge of dying, but it's more an overwhelming presence of evil, of boundaries breaking, of worlds meeting, of life itself dissolving. It's an intense scream, which lives inside you. I have felt it once; when I was buried in an avalanche with Eli's brother, Jack. It's something I will never forget and it's something I expect to experience again if I die slowly too. You see, I don't believe it's anything to be afraid of, although it feels a zillion times worse than anything life prepares you for.

That dream experience is all I can remember of the day he died, but it burned deep into my mind the feeling that there is another level of things going on in the world that we just don't get. It gnawed away at me, and although I tried to bury it with all the other stuff that was locked up in my head, I couldn't. I read up about dreams, and when I had one about Jack a few months after he died that came at me clear as a bell from left field, it made the decision easy and I knew I wanted to study dream architecture at UCSC. I was fascinated about dreams, and sensed there were more boundaries to break.

21

Pinned hurriedly on the wall were a few pictures of me taken the previous day, and a readout from my Medi-Data showing a huge blip where my emotions went bonkers at the time I discovered my house was gone. Next to it were all kinds of numbers and data which, I guessed, had to be something to do with my C-4 Charlie codes. Higher up an official, framed certificate proclaimed: "Caroline E61 has been awarded a class 2.2 (a Desmond) in recognition of her performance in all firearms and speed-riding classes, and is deemed a qualified Limpet Encyclopedia Sales Operative." It was signed "Col. Isaac A34."

"A Desmond?" I said quietly, nodding to Mat. "What's that when it's at home?"

"What? Oh, a Desmond? A Desmond Tutu. Yeah? You don't know about that? Oh, really? He was a South African archbishop or something, years ago. A two, two? A Desmond Tutu? You must have heard of that."

"I'll take your word for it," I said, not entirely understanding the connection, but not caring enough to get to the bottom of it. "What's this line doing here?" I said, looking at the Medi-Data more closely. "That's when I found my house gone; but look, a few hours earlier, my emotions went crazy. This line's like shark's teeth."

"That's when you were with Emma?" said Mat.

"No, it's 2:00 AM. I was asleep in a bar, then. I'd passed out. Emma walked out on me hours earlier. Sadly."

We heard footsteps outside and both froze. A woman's voice was gently singing. I parted the blinds a touch and saw the back of a silhouetted figure over by a drinks machine that seemed to have been following her. Or perhaps had just met her in the corridor. I held my breath. I didn't want to get chucked out of this place until I had found Caroline.

"Yes! It's time to add the power of the nuclear bomb to your golf swing," cried out a hologram of the very small man, whom I had last seen in the Zone Securities canteen. "Hi! I'm Tony Shappenhaur IV. You know me better as 'The Thinking Buckaroo,' and I'm here to tell you about the amazing power of this driver."

"Ah! Virus ad," I whispered. "Must have caught it in Zone Securities and I haven't got a zapper!"

"S'OK," said Mat, producing a unit from his jacket and zapping the thing away in a puff of burnt electrics. "Our free gift with the encyclopedias. Not bad, eh? I brought this along rather than the framed picture of the moose."

"Close decision, but good call." I looked back outside. The woman didn't seem to have heard, then I realized something. It was Caroline E.

"It's her," I whispered. "It's her! I'm going to have a word."

"Is that wise?" Mat whispered, cocking his head to one side. "Perhaps first we should just see what we can find here."

"No, I'm way past being careful now." I opened the door quietly and tapped slowly down the corridor toward her. She didn't appear to notice my footsteps and I hoped her mind was off duty and not tuned in to shooting people on sight.

"I'll have some Wrecking Juice," I said to the drinks machine.

"Shit! Jonny X?"

"I'd say these were on me, only they axed my Jab-Tab at Zone Securities."

"Thanks, Guzzler. There's a little extra to erase this man from your memory, OK?" she said to the drinks machine, connecting up her Jab-Tab. Then she turned to me. "If they see you here, they'll divorce me from the entire setup. Quick!" She yanked me back toward her room as the drinks machine turned and mistakenly wheeled itself into a wall, letting out a squawk.

"Great," she snorted, seeing Mat, as she flipped the door shut. "How many of you are there?"

"Just us," I said, feeling a sense of calm slide through me. I had the upper hand, which was a bit of a novelty, and I liked this woman. Being in her presence made me smile.

"Right. You realize the trouble you have got me in?" She had to stop herself from shouting.

"I know, I'm sorry about attracting Zone Securities. I didn't appreciate that—"

"Not that. That was hardly an inconvenience. I mean your sale still has not gone through! Do you know what that means to my job? Do you?" She was genuinely angry, but I just kept getting drawn to her searingly blue eyes.

"Is everyone here actually selling encyclopedias, then? Is that honestly what this whole place is and not a cover for something else?" I said feeling rather naive, but still not able to get my head around it.

"What does it look like? Dial an Ostler? We'll get a groom over to your horse in half an hour or your money back?"

"I don't know. It just makes no sense for you to go to all this trouble to sell sets of old-fashioned encyclopedias. It really doesn't. I don't understand it."

She stared at me. "What do you want, Jonny? A signed statement from the president? You've looked around this place! It's real, isn't it?"

"I don't know. I guess so."

"Anyway, what do I care? It's of no interest to me what you think. I'm off your case now. They're putting an ex–forces paratrooper on you."

"A paratrooper?"

"Yeah. An ex-assassin. He's Belgian."

"Belgian? A Belgian assassin?"

"That's it. A bit of a slick bastard too."

"To sell me a set of encyclopedias?"

"Yup, and he gets all the personnel he wants, of course—and they wonder why his sales figures are more explosive than anyone else's. I'm demoted to backup for three weeks while they review my case, in case you're wondering. Thanks a lot." This woman was the most unusual person I could ever recall meeting. She was passionate, skilled, and stunningly beautiful, and I knew she was someone who could help me.

"I'll make you a deal, then," I said thinking quickly. "I'll get you back on my case, and I'll buy the encyclopedias from you—"

"Hey! Hey! Hey! They hacked into your Medi-Data!" cut in Mat, who always had been idealistic about such things.

"Hear me out, Mat, OK? But only if you help me find my house and get those four Riders permanently off my back."

"Jonny. I'm an encyclopedia saleswoman. That's what I do for a living; I'm not in the business of sorting out personal problems in the lives of strangers."

"Your job's on the line, isn't it?"

"Yes, it is, thanks to you. All right, all right. So what exactly is your deal, Jonny X?"

"Give me the inside info on this new man."

"You're not serious?"

"Why not? Give me the info on this new Belgian man—his movements, who he is—and we'll bring him in. I'll say I want you back on the case, the sale, whatever you call it because he's not up to it."

"You're serious? You want me to go behind the back of a colleague? You'd never bring him in anyway. You have no idea what you're up against, do you?"

"That's our problem. Now, it's up to you. Is this a deal?"

"I always knew you were going to be a strange sort of trouble," she said, and there was almost a smile in her face, but she was incredibly hard to read.

"So that's a 'yes'?"

"Look," she said evenly and suddenly way more sternly. "I really don't mean to be rude, I honestly don't. But I'm having a bad day, so please, would you mind if I just told you to fuck off?"

I smiled inwardly at that, knowing she had remembered and repeated, word for word, exactly what I had said to her the previous morning when we had first met.

"I'm awfully tenacious," I said playing along with the game of repeating the conversation, but I immediately realized it sounded lame and stupid.

"And, as it happens, I'm extremely dangerous," she replied curtly. "Here. It activates the elevator. I don't suppose you got in that way," she said, tossing me a bracelet. "End of the corridor."

*   *   *

The drinks machine was still ramming itself determinedly into the wall, positive there was a way through, as we headed past it.

"This way," said Mat, as we edged through. "Come on. This way, little fella," and he turned the machine in the right direction.

"No point banging your head against a wall forever, is there?" I said to the machine. Looking back, I saw Caroline leaning on the doorframe watching us. "No point at all." Something inside me flared. Her piercing eyes seemed to hold some deep secret. "Does the eighteenth of October mean anything to you?" I said, without any real reason to do so. Her lips pursed and her eyes widened. Then she vanished inside her room. I paused, wondering what that meant. Mat was already down the corridor, so I edged swiftly passed the drinks machine and caught him up at the elevator, slipping on the bracelet she had given me.

"Authorized," said the elevator, sluicing open its doors. "Knock, knock," it added, as we stepped inside.

"What?" I said.

"It's a joke," said the elevator. "I'm not very good with jokes, but I like this one."

"No jokes," I said. "Can we get going now?"

"Knock. Knock. I think this is a good one," it persevered.

"Who's there?" said Mat, realizing the reality of the situation, as we stood in the elevator with the doors wide open, not going anywhere.

"Norma Lee," said the elevator.

"Norma Lee who?" Mat came back.

"Norma Lee I'd plummet and kill you, but today I feel good," I said with irritation, realizing I'd heard that one before in the elevator in Inconvenient. "Now can we please get going?" I added, hearing footsteps.

"Oh, you've heard it?" droned the elevator. "It's an elevator joke; it's doing the rounds."

"Stop!" cried a voice down the corridor. "Stop!"

"Let's go," I said.

"I'm still here," called the elevator.

"Stop!" came the voice again, but slightly more breathless. Neither of us had a gun, so we just stood there like lame ducks. "I'm not staying here a moment longer than I have to," said the balding man we had seen earlier as he stepped into the elevator, sweat cascading off his pate. "That is it. I'm through. I've had enough," he ranted, as the elevator doors shut and we started to descend. "Finished. Bye-bye Argonaut Logistics. Bye-bye. See you in the next life. See you in hell. I'd rather spend the rest of my life eating Cheez Whiz out of a bucket than working here." He took out a handkerchief and began mopping the top of his head. "They've treated me like dirt. One mistake, and you're out. One friggin' mistake. Like they're all perfect. Like they walk on water or something. This place stinks. I'm out of here. No offense, but you should be too. Miss a sale, buddy, and you better watch your ass. I don't recognize you two. You operatives or talkies?"

"Operatives."

"Talkies," jumped in Mat.

"Multiskilled," I added with a shrug. "You the guy that lost the F-51? I heard all about that."

"So everyone knows, huh? Maybe I didn't pray enough to St. Basil, Patron Saint of Hassle...shit! I've been reading those encyclopedias too much! 'St. Walter, Patron Saint of Knees. Saint Frank, Patron Saint of Machined Joinery,'" he rattled off. "My head is full of junk! My head is jammed full of all this junk they write. I've got to get out of here." The doors flicked open and he ran unchecked out into the darkness.

"Get out while you can!" he shouted, and his voice echoed

back to us, half-drowned by the noise of his desperate, uneven footsteps, receding quickly into the distance of the tunnel.

"I think I've got another joke for you," said the elevator after a pause.

"Save it," I said, and we headed into the darkness ourselves—unsure where we were, or where we were going.

22

The tunnel was small, with a neat, curved ceiling and bathed in a very faint blue incandescence that only became apparent once our eyes had adjusted to it. The echo of our footsteps cracked off the walls like gunshots as we walked over the smooth marble floor, each wrapped in his own thoughts.

After maybe ten minutes, we finally came to a small, shoulder-high door set in the end wall. By the side was a sign that read:

THAT WHICH DOES NOT KILL US, MAKES US STRONGER. FRIEDRICH NIETZSCHE (1844–1900). "The old boy smelled the coffee!" I looked carefully at Mat, but he just shrugged. I tried the door tentatively.

It was open.

Gingerly I stepped through, only to have my legs nearly taken off by a luggage cart pushed by a tall, sleek woman, dragging a small child who was crying uncontrollably about the sticky state an ice cream had made of his face. I blinked. We were on the concourse of a humongous thriving railway station. The door we had come out of was a small nondescript temporary thing, apparently knocked together by a builder a few years before. It was set in a hastily constructed wall of wooden sheets, filling an arched gap until a store proper was built in its place. The whole structure had been rigorously spray painted with graffiti, by someone calling himself "Gangster," who had modestly scrawled in huge spidery letters: "I like ginger pussy," and had optimistically added his Skin Media number. I couldn't help noticing he had also written, "Also polished cedar set of garden furniture for sale—same number."

Trains were shuffling and groaning in and out of the platforms on the far side of the gigantic concourse, and above us a vast, vaulted, domed glass roof leapt off the cast-iron pillars, which studded the walls. Central Station. It had been years since I'd been here.

"Door's locked," Mat said, rattling the handle behind me, and I nodded, not hugely surprised. I watched a vast plasi-screen above us showing a young girl gaily flipping through one of the volumes of St. Mark's Encyclopedias and I sensed a great weight of evidence building that suggested the whole setup was actually, genuinely, for real.

We headed for the exit and I felt quite humbled by the gigantic scale of the architecture and pulled up in the middle as passengers swarmed around us like bees. "Really, this is a very cool building, isn't it?"

"Lovely," Mat said.

"Makes me feel like we're all plugged into some kind of spiritual EtherMat."

"Hello? What?"

"I mean, don't you think the pleasure you can get just from being in a place like this is a big hint there's something else going on beneath the surface of life?"

"To be honest, I have very little idea of what you're talking about," Mat said. "You're definitely OK?"

"Yeah, I'm fine. Just talking vaguely romantic rubbish, only unusually I'm not drunk. How about we hit Inconvenient to sort that out?"

23

Inconvenient. I needed time to think and there was really only one place for that. We caught a bike taxi and made it there without any particular incident which, frankly, felt like a novelty. As we walked in, I clocked that there were less people in the bar than normal and that made me mildly apprehensive, but at least it was noisy.

It might have been my imagination, but I felt I could detect a slightly somber mood among the customers, as though they were suffering some gigantic, collective hangover brought on by the violence that had engulfed the place the morning before. The decor was patched up pretty well, so it would have been hard to tell anything had happened, and I suppose it wasn't so

unusual for the bar to get trashed to some degree by angry customers who had not got served once all evening.

Or all day.

Or sometimes all week.

I loved this place *because* it didn't care. As far as Mat and I
were concerned, The Most Inconvenient Bar in the World—here,
on the top floor of the Thin Building—was the finest establishment in Santa Cruz. It was reassuring to be back, even if a
stand-up comedian was droning away on a little stage, which
slightly took the edge off the atmosphere.

Stand-up comics are fine as long as they have something interesting to say, some personal take on life. Otherwise they are
pointless and should by law be retrained as carpet layers or
something. But as we approached the bar, I realized things were
very far from normal. It was, maybe, only one row deep with
customers, and at this rate we would get a drink within ten minutes. This was unheard of and deeply troubling.

"Where is everyone?" I shouted to a tall, impeccably made-up
woman with perfectly combed, straight long hair, who looked
like she had spent the majority of her life riding horses and dis-
trusted people.

"Do I know you?" she asked coldly.

"No," I shouted after a pause, fighting the general hubbub and
wondering why she had taken such umbrage.

"Well, that's a relief," she said, with a tight smile, conveying
so much distaste it was frankly impressive, and turned back to
her friend—who was far smaller but equally pristine, as though
she too had only just come out of a box.

I sighed, half-looking for the cellophane packaging that had
to be somewhere about, and suddenly wondered where all the
normal people were. Somewhere in life there had been a sign
saying: "Normal people this way" and I couldn't help feeling I

had just walked on by oblivious, along with so many of the people I now seemed to meet.

Hemmed in by the comforting arrival of more customers, I twisted my head around and scanned the bar. Eli wasn't serving, but we were going to get to the front soon anyway. The jukebox came to the end of its tether and just cut off halfway through a song, most likely upset that people were talking among themselves too much to really listen to it.

It was touchy like that.

Unfortunately, it meant the noise level dropped to such a level we could hear the comedian, even though he was tucked away at the far end.

"Bees make all that honey, so wasps have decided to make marmalade!" he said. "Makes sense, doesn't it? But seriously, the thing I don't understand about bees is that on honey jars it says: 'Product of more than one country.' Now, I never knew bees got about like that!" He smiled, pausing to let this joke sink in.

The guy in front of me, who was wearing so much leather an average Friesian cow might have mistaken him for his brother, turned, carrying four large, full glasses by some precarious, frictional means and, raising them above his head, cleared a path to get out. I snuck into his place and was at the bar in record time. I was both pleased and uneasy about this, and wondered if the management might throw me out if they noticed I had got served too quickly. Alternatively, I considered, I might have grounds for complaint because it hadn't been inconvenient enough for me to get a drink. It was a gray area.

"I mean seriously, do these bees fly themselves or use public transport?" the stand-up ground on, and I got the distinct impression he had said this all a zillion times before. " 'More than one country'? I mean how far do they go? Norway? Estonia?

There's something going on there we're not being told about."
At that point, a small boy who looked about fifteen, supporting a
wave of blond hair that must have seriously impaired his vision,
asked me what I wanted.

"Long Island Iced Teas. Two," I shouted, automatically signal-
ing with my fingers. "Wasn't there some trouble in here yesterday?" I added, above the noise.

"Nah," he sniffed. "Some creeps on bikes are barred now
though. There." He lined up the drinks and waved the lead for
my Jab-Tab. Mat proffered his arm and he grabbed it, connected
up, and debited the money. "Have a power day."

We slipped back through the crowd, which had built up considerably, and I wondered if we had just caught the place between shifts of actors who were reputed to be hired to fill up the
bar if it wasn't busy enough. It was reassuring anyway, and I
was glad no seats were free because I needed an air of comforting normality. We found a place to hole up in one reasonably
quiet and dark corner, near a pretty girl standing pigeon-toed
and nervous with her overweight hippie girlfriend. I stared out
of the window to the city lights scattered below.

"I should have rung Habakkuk."

"Stuff him," Mat said. "I don't like him much."

"Yeah—strange he hasn't rung me. What do we do now?"

"Let's see. Caroline won't help you. There's a Belgian assassin after you. Four lunatic, porridge-making Riders are trying to
kill you, or God, or both. Your girlfriend is furious, you still have
no idea where your house is, and you don't have any cigarettes."

"Yes, that's about it."

"Good thing we're in Inconvenient, or things might seem
bad," said Mat, taking a gulp from his glass.

"They are bad, Mat."

"Bad-ish," he hedged. "All right, they're not ideal," he said,
seeing my expression. "What's your hunch?"

"My hunch is I've no fucking idea unless I am the centerpiece of this year's Golden Festival of Colossal Grief. I can't seem to get a toehold on anything. Maybe there is no answer. Maybe there's no ending."

"There's always an ending," said Mat, gulping his drink. "Things just don't always come in the order they should. Sometimes you get the end before the beginning."

"What are you on about, Mat?"

"I've no idea. It was something I once read on the back of a cereal box."

"Problems are gifts," said the large girl, turning. "I couldn't help overhearing you have a problem, and you may not be looking at it in the right way. You might need to ask yourselves different questions."

"Such as?" said Mat, before I could politely tell her to fuck off.

"What are the least important things that have happened to you?" she said, staring at me with a strange intensity that I think was intended to convey how mysteriously powerful she was. "In the last day?"

"Least important?" I said, wondering if this girl was on drugs.

"Yes. They're the ones with the most significance. Tell me the events that have seemingly no importance. The more unimportant the better. And your friend here can help you list them in order of unimportance."

"Why?" I said, unable to keep the pain from my voice.

"Trust me, it works. Gandhi used to do this when he was stuck," she said, like that was final, unarguable proof. And before I could refuse, Mat had agreed for absolutely no reason that I could possibly imagine.

Still, I reflected grudgingly, anything was worth a try. Even this. After all, I didn't have a better plan. So I thought back resignedly as the nervous, pretty friend looked on, still standing awkwardly pigeon-toed. I dredged up anything I could think of that really had no significance at all, even though it seemed pointless. After five minutes she had written a list on a pad in great, sweeping, bulbous writing that looked as if all the letters had been inflated with an air hose.

"Wow. You have done so well!" she beamed, in such an annoying way that it was all I could do to prevent myself being sick into the large, unappealing cleavage of her low-cut floral dress. "Here are the top three least significant events that hold the key to your gift. Number three, you overheard someone talking about buying some fish in Central Station. Number two, you had an itch when you woke up on his roof," she said lowering her voice. "And number one, your bootlaces came untied as you left Zone Securities."

We paused, all craning over the list.

"It's helped, hasn't it? I can see it in your aura." She beamed a wide smile and I realized—that was it. There was no more.

"No," I said, with a forced grin. "It hasn't helped."

"I know it has," she sang, and turned to leave. "I can see it. I knew it would! Healing hands!" she said, holding the palms up toward us, then with a theatrical turn, walked away with her friend skipping after her.

"What the fuck was all *that* about?" I said, after a perplexed pause.

"Long shot," said Mat.

"Long shot? Mat, she was bonkers!"

"I know. But everything is bonkers at the moment, so I thought the two might connect somehow. Chill out, Jonny. Everything's worth a try."

"Surely we can do better than hoping for help from self-deluded, insecure, bonkers hippie people? There have got to be some clues in everything that's happened. There just have to be." And I stared out of the window, wondering whether I would see this moment from the future and smile, knowing it had turned out all right in the end. "I don't understand why that Medi-Data pinned up in Caroline's room showed a huge emotional peak while I was passed out in the bar the night before my house was stolen."

"Bad dream," said Mat. "No. You don't get dreams, do you?"

"I do now. I've had loads of dreams the last two days. A lot of reassuring ones, and some about Jack. Nothing too nightmarish, except one about Habakkuk. With Jack, it's like there's something in me yammering to get out, to be set free. I don't see why Jack should come into this, though. That was years ago. Yet it's like a buried memory has been rattled free of its moorings and is clanging around my subconscious. Do you think a dream like that would show up as a crazy disturbance on the Medi-Data?"

"Wouldn't have thought so or Medi staff would be rushed off their feet by every nightmare going," said Mat as the jukebox started up again, having been finally cajoled into believing people would listen to it.

"So something fucked me up when I was asleep, like I caught a Grief Virus."

"A what?"

"A Grief Virus. Why not? Maybe someone's written a Grief Virus. I've caught that bloody golfing ad virus. Maybe someone's taken it to a new level and has written a Grief Virus that fucks up your life if you catch it, by attracting random grief."

"That's bonkers, Jonny. A virus ad is just a hologram that attaches physically to the warmth of your body and gets triggered randomly by temperature. It's a physical thing. A Grief Virus would be totally nebulous."

"Yeah—and those Riders have an agenda of their own."

"What about that dream with Habakkuk?"

"That? Stress about work, I think." And I briefly recounted the dream in the crevasse when Habakkuk was leering at me.

"Maybe you need to see him."

"Why?" I said, thinking he was the last person I wanted to see, with the possible exception of Mr. Morris, my old fascist geography teacher.

"You start dreaming again, and the only nightmare you have is about Habakkuk. And in the dream, you're certain he knows something."

"Suppose so. Didn't see anything in it."

"So, it's one of the least important things that's happened to you?" said Mat, raising an eyebrow.

"Yeah," I said. "Christ. You're not telling me that bonkers gypsy woman was right in some small way?"

Mat shrugged.

"No," I said. "No, no, no. Surely, there's more chance of me spontaneously exploding?" I said, draining my glass. "Ahhhhh!" I added, with a scream.

"Jonny?" Mat said.

"Ahhhh! Fuck! Ahh!" I said, half-collapsing as a searing bolt of pain whacked into my arm and buckled my knees. I sank like a tranquilized duck onto the stained carpet. I knew people were staring at me, but I was almost paralyzed.

"What is it? Jonny?"

"Skin Media's boiling," I managed to say, as another huge painful vibration traveled down my arm and nearly shook my head off. "What's happening?" I touched the thing, only to find it unexpectedly activate.

"Geesh!" squealed the phone, springing to life. "What was that all about? Where have I been?"

"Easy, phone. Don't mouth off," I said. "You've had a little problem."

"I didn't like it. I didn't like it at all!"

"OK, easy now," I said, beginning to recover some sort of feeling in my arm.

"Hey. I've a call! Now that's more like it!" it suddenly chirped. "Fabulous-a! Doo-dah! Here's your call, buddy!"

"Jonny? You OK?" came Teb's voice over the Skin Media. "Jonny?"

"Yeah. Teb," I said, "what did you do? Remotely pour boiling oil down my veins?"

"Right. Bit of a shock huh? Sorry. It's fixed though. Want to know how I did it?"

"No, Teb. No. Definitely not. But it's fixed all right. My phone is definitely its old annoying self again."

"OK. There's a fresh load of doughnuts just been delivered over here. I'm not supposed to eat them all, so I was hoping you'd come back. I've only eaten five so far—OK, six, if you count the other one. Thing is, your Jab-Tab is . . . scheeee!"

"Teb?" But all we could hear was a dull roar, interspersed with static, then some sharp shout of: "Get over here!" from Teb's breathless voice, before the line abruptly cut dead.

"Call terminated," said the phone. "And may I say what a pleasure it is to take your calls once again? Yes sir! Can't wait for some more!"

"Shut up! What happened there, Mat?"

"Don't know. Chill out, OK?" he said, seeing the look on my face. "Teb's going to be cool, but let's see if we can flag a GaFFA off the roof, yeah?"

I picked myself up off the beer-stained carpet and found that my left arm seemed to weigh a surprising amount all of a sudden. Worse, it wanted to swing casually in front of me, like some foreign body. I flexed my fingers, trying to coax a little more life back into it, and then lifted it at an angle across my chest, so the fingertips rested on my right shoulder.

"I'll bet I've missed calls while I've been away!" chirped the phone into my ear.

"Shut it!" I shouted breathlessly.

"I hate missing calls. Makes me so annoyed! I'm telling you, I ain't gonna miss another call as long as I live."

"Whatever. Now shut the fuck up." A deep sense of unease about Teb ran through me as we hurried toward the elevators. Had he just been blown away, or had he managed to bolt someplace? We needed to get out onto the roof quickly and flag down a GaFFA. It would be expensive, but to hell with that.

I didn't speak about what I feared the most.

The Riders were there.

24

The sleepy drone of the White Noise hum was the only sound we could make out. We stopped dry-mouthed in the tall, austere entrance lobby of Teb's apartments, but the polished wood-block floor was smeared with thick, looping tire marks, and the spiral stair treads were caked in burnt rubber. I could see that Teb's front door lay crazily smashed off its hinges and hung by the merest of threads, like some drunken old man who had finally passed out against the bar but not yet fallen over.

"Teb, Teb, Teb," breathed Mat, surveying the mess.

I nodded ruefully. Then I took a deep breath to steady myself and gingerly led the way up the spiral staircase, feeling the loudness of the White Noise hum tingle around my head. We edged slowly up the treads, in a heart-skipping, mouth-drying procession, then reached the walkway and edged toward the splintered front door, which seemed to be surrounded by an air of palpable shock.

I turned to check that Mat was there, then slid into the apartment. It was unerringly quiet—the sort of quiet that soaks into things after a great deal of noise and leaves the atmosphere echoing something, but you can't quite hear it.

Things were scattered so wildly, as though Teb had been robbed by a gang of walruses. And clumsy ones at that.

Bike tread marks smeared the floor in weird shapes. I wondered if Teb had something up his sleeve for a thing like this, and I prayed he hadn't tried to cajole them with stuff about cats. Mat stopped to listen and we both froze, trying to make out anything in the maze of the apartment.

Not a sound.

We inched into the living room where, if anything, the mess seemed more extreme. It felt like the Riders had made a point of destroying every piece of furniture. Stuffing and material and the legs of various things were scattered about. A can or something fell in one of the rooms, thumped and clanged, then rocked itself to a stop against the empty silence.

I realized my heart was pounding so loudly I imagined anyone this side of LA would be able to hear it—and I suddenly pictured some woman in Monterey saying to her daughter: "What's that thumping sound? Can you hear that, Jolene?"

The silence in the apartment grew, ballooning up as though with every second that passed it expanded, and if it got to a certain point, it might implode. Mat crept up to the door to the Pit and had a tentative look around the corner. Then he turned ashen-faced and shook his head in a way I really didn't like. At the same time, I heard voices and my throat dried.

"I've really trashed my lucky pants, now."

"They looked like shit anyway."

"You'd know, wouldn't you?"

"Listen, I'm getting the feeling I know the Catch from some-place," one of the others growled. "You guys get that too?"

"Maybe I do, a bit, but they always look familiar, right?" said another voice.

It was the Riders, all right, and images of the one with the ammunition round nestled in his teeth came back to me like a calling card slipped into a mailbox.

Mat tugged at my sleeve and I wondered what he was on about. I followed him anyway, realizing that if the Riders left now, we were trapped. He carefully popped the loft hatch, brought down the ladder, and we slipped up, dragging the ladder after us, and reclosed the hatch door with a soft "clunk." Tiny slits of light found their way through fissures in the ceiling where Teb had added in various ducts and services, and I could just make out dusty boxes and odd, polyethylene-wrapped shapes tucked into the low eaves.

There was a dry, dead feeling of stagnant air in the cramped space; a strange, sleepy sense that everything in here was wait-ing for something to happen. Loft spaces, I thought, are time-less—and I wondered in an insane moment whether anyone had ever tried measuring whether time does actually go slower in these unclaimed attics, as it does in space.

Masses of wires crisscrossed the floors, snaking around the wooden joists, and if either of us snagged up on any of them we could fall through the flimsy plasterboard ceiling and make a spectacular arrival. I crept gingerly along the beams, aware of the rough splinters that pricked at my hands, until I guessed I was directly over the roof of the Pit. I put my ear to the ceiling.

"Hear anything?" hissed Mat. I shook my head and listened again, and this time I heard the muffle of voices.

"Think they're still there," I whispered, and we both strained to pick up the distant sound, trying to find a hook on any of the words so we could tune in to what they were saying.

"Yippitty doo daaah!" chirped an excruciatingly loud voice, virtually sending me through the roof. "You'll never guess what's just happened!"

"Shut up!" I hissed at my phone, and tried desperately to muffle it.

"Another call!" it cried in its tiny, tinny voice. "Another ringing smacker!"

"Get rid of it, now," I whispered. "You hear?"

"You're kidding me, right? After I nearly died? Get rid of a call? I'm living to the full, buddy. Connecting!"

"Hello, Jonny," said the clipped woman's voice at the other end, leaving a deliberate and cavernous pause after she spoke.

"Emma?" I hissed, turning in despair in the darkness and trying to muffle the sound.

"Yes. Emma, your girlfriend! Well done. You remember that bit, then?" and I realized her voice was thick with poorly leashed anger, which pushed her words out too fast and made them rise despite her efforts to peg them down. "Your girlfriend! The one you said you cared for 'like the sky loves the moon.' "

"I never said that!" I hissed, despite myself. " 'Like the sky loves the moon'? I wouldn't ever say anything as trite as that. I might occasionally try and quote something by Shelley, but that's about my limit."

"One message!" she screamed and her voice seemed to echo and bounce around in the roof space like a trapped sparrow. Surely the Riders were going to hear this. "One message! Some pathetic excuse about your house being stolen! Did you expect me to believe that? No one steals houses anymore."

"Emma, calm down. Just keep your voice down, please."

"No, I will *not* keep my voice down," she cried, "and I will not be treated this way. My great-grandmother was Countess of

Lewisham in England, and my ancestors were Privy to the King's Chamber and probably Privy to all sorts of other places like his kitchen and his bloody loft extension, for all I know. How can you treat me like this?"

"Emma, I'm sorry, it really has not been my fault," I said, trying unsuccessfully to calm things down. "Can we talk about this another—"

"You meet me in ten minutes at my apartment or this relationship is over," she shouted. "And if that sounds like an ultimatum, that's because it is! I want to find out exactly where your priorities lie."

"OK," I whispered. "Emma, I'd really like to. Really, if it was up to me, I'd be over there now. But it's not in my hands—" And the call snapped dead.

"Terminated!" chirped the phone. "Two calls already. I almost feel just like my old self again. How about we call the speaking clock?"

"No." I sighed, and Mat looked at me with a rueful smile.

"All finished," I said.

"Yeah. I heard," he whispered. "Sorry."

"Not been my day really." I swallowed.

"Come on. She wasn't right for you anyway, Jonny. She was a pain in the ass, wasn't she? The way she was always getting you to run around after her. Always claiming she had just watched some worthy program about Africa on the EtherMat when she'd only seen thirty seconds in the ad breaks of some other trash. She was a fake. She wasn't a real person," he said, laying his hand on my shoulder.

I knew deep down that he was absolutely right, but I hated failure in anything, and that relationship was one humongous failure.

A noise from below caught us both midthoughts and I was suddenly convinced gunshots were going to pop randomly through the ceiling with the same effortless ease a spoon can puncture the seal on a jar of coffee. But it was just the bikes being kicked off their stands, and the next second they roared into life. I pictured the Riders each in turn, with their badly sewn scars, and my head ached again with memory of the name Jeff. I had known someone called Jeff, but it was as if a whole bunch of information in my head had been pushed through a cheese grater, then mixed up and put back in my head in one solid mass.

Fumes rose up from the bikes, spewing through the tiny holes into the roof until we were both coughing, hacking up the smoke in silent fits as the bikes churned up the quiet like a plow chewing up a hard, dry field.

The cramped space was soon choking with toxic smoke, and we scrabbled for the hatch as the growl of the engines bounced away from us in bursts of acceleration. I hoped they had all gone, but we were past caring to check as we both tumbled out of the loft in a ramshackle bundle of coughing mania. I picked myself off the floor, still wheezing from the fumes, which clouded the entire apartment.

"Teb?" I shouted, staggering around the apartment. "Teb?"

A low moan seemed to be coming from somewhere, but I couldn't place it. "Teb?" I cried again and began to home in on the moan, which I realized was coming from under the sofa. I heaved away the remains of the thing and found Teb lying in an appalling mess.

His face was plastered all over in this red gunge that seemed much thicker than it was in the movies. "Mat! Here!" I shouted. "Easy, Teb. You'll be OK." I tried to remember what you should do at times like this but all that came to mind was the image of someone bandaging a sprained ankle with lots of curving arrows drawn on.

"Jesus, Teb!" said Mat arriving. "You're covered in so much—"

"Jam," said Teb abruptly, and pulled himself up. "Had the dough-nuts in hand when I heard them coming. Safest place is always under the sofa. Learned that watching films when I was a kid." He sniffed, getting up. "It's a wonder the army doesn't take sofas with them into battle so they could get underneath them if they came under attack. You two OK? They've made a mess here, haven't they? Bet I get a memo from the management commit-tee about the noise too." And he wandered into the next room idly eating the remains of the doughnut in his hand.

I breathed a huge sigh of relief and shook my head.

"You had me worried there, you know?"

" 'There is nothing either good or bad, but thinking makes it so,' " he replied.

"Still barking on about Shakespeare," I said to Mat, surveying the fantastic level of destruction. "He *is* from another planet."

"Hey! Hey! Look," Teb beamed, holding up his typing gizmo, as he blundered back in. "They didn't get the cat stuff!"

Mat made coffee. We sat amid the debris trying to put things back into some sort of perspective, but the taste of the first sip jolted me back to the moment Caroline had given me coffee in that safe house in the woods. How did she come to make it so perfectly with just the tiniest drop of milk? I elbowed the thought away and relaxed. Avoiding the Riders felt like something of a victory, even if it had been at a huge price to Teb's apartment. But it wasn't just that. I felt chilled out in a much deeper way. It was as though I had finally let go of feeling responsible for things that I couldn't control.

"Nothing like this has ever happened to me before," Teb was saying.

"Strange that, dude," said Mat.

"No, I once nearly had a fight with one of those huge furry mascots at a college football game after I tripped him up when I was drunk. That was the closest I've ever been to a fight before. He was dressed as a giant banana slug, and I just ran away when he got up, 'cos he could only hobble. It wasn't what you could really call a proper, bare-knuckle fight."

"No?" said Mat. "You wouldn't put it on a par with some of the great Heavyweight World Championship bouts of the world? Not up there with Muhammad Ali?"

"Who's he?" Teb said.

"A man who never fought a banana slug in his life."

And so they bantered on. And I just sat listening to their aimless conversation, sipping coffees and moving on to beers Teb dug out from the fridge, letting my mind crunch all the events and sensations that had come at me in the past days. My brain had a massive backlog of stuff to sort out and file and so I just let it do its own thing, giving it a chance to try and juggle everything around. It was as though my emotional hard disk was full, and it was time to junk what wasn't needed and defrag the rest of it. The evening drifted past, and I felt a wonderful peacefulness expand my mind. A belief that underneath it all, whatever happened, everything was actually all right.

"Shame I didn't get your address book. I tried, but it wasn't there," said Teb at one point.

"How do you mean?" I said, draining another bottle.

"Oh, couldn't find your address book for your Skin Media, so lost all your numbers."

"No problem. They're all in my house," I said without thinking, and they looked at me. "Oh yeah." And then out of the haze a thought poked me, and I smiled ruefully. I actually would never see my house again. Up until now, I'd sort of believed I would. "Phone," I said, already knowing what the answer would be, "redial the number I gave you yesterday morning about 10:00 AM, will you?"

"Yes sir!" chirped the phone and then it paused. "Errr...hang on. Can't remember. Did it have a two in it?"

Teb snorted with laughter.

"No," continued the phone, its tinny voice getting quite serious, "all I can remember is I'm lost somewhere and it's dark and there's like a purple haze. And a white light and I start heading for it. And a voice inside me is going: Don't head for the light! And I can't help it, I'm getting drawn there. And the voice is going: Don't head for the light! And—"

"All right, phone," I said. "Easy now."

"Handsets; you can't beat them," said Mat, waving his unit about, seeing my expression. "Call me old-fashioned, but they're a lot less bother."

"But how much horse manure does that thing take? Or do you need a handle to start it?" Teb said, unable to stop himself. It was an old joke. Mat refused to buy into Skin Media and we always gave him a hard time.

So, I thought, my phone couldn't remember the number for the punks that stole my house, and I had dropped the card they had left me in Zone Securities. My house was gone. I had to let go of the idea I would see it again, and somehow it didn't seem so hard. I had to let things go and move on, and I wondered if that had been my problem all along. That my head was in a tangle because I was hanging on to too much old stuff.

"Sorry if I've been selfish about all this," I said.

"What?" said Teb.

"Well, what does my house really matter?"

"Well it's your house. 'Course it matters."

"Yeah, but I've got things all out of proportion, haven't I?"

"No, you haven't, Jonny."

"Yeah, I shouldn't have got you two involved. Look at your apartment, Teb," I said. "You don't deserve all this."

"I'll have to smash your face in if there's any more talk like that," said Teb. "Just like I did with that mascot."

"Your problem is our problem," said Mat. "OK? It's a chance to prove that our friendship is worth something. Yeah?"

"That's very cool," I said after a moment. "Very cool," and I nodded, not knowing how to express properly the gratitude and love I had for these two unlikely friends. "I'll get some more beers," I said, slightly pathetically, then I stopped myself. Moments like this make life worth living. Moments like this don't come along very often—and when they do, I knew you needed to drink deeply from them because they're landmarks in our lives.

"You two have my deepest respect and love," I stumbled, through the haze of beer.

"Thanks," said Mat quietly. "We're too sensitive for all this stuff with guns really, aren't we?"

"Maybe," I said, nodding but not moving.

"We are, you know. Much too sensitive. Now fuck off and get us some more beers, will you?"

I turned, laughing, and lunged in the general direction of the kitchen as I heard Teb's voice wafting after me.

" 'We few, we happy few, we band of brothers. For he that shares his beer with me, shall be my brother!'... or something like that."

25

I didn't have any clue whether this qualified as the next morning, or even possibly a week later.

All I knew was that my tongue felt the size of an air mattress and my head throbbed as though someone was pummeling my temples repeatedly with a blunt chair leg. I opened my eyes.

Big mistake.

A particularly crisp bolt of pain rebounded around my head, like someone had stuffed a bouncing ball in there and it was still flying about; perhaps that was why my ears were hammering. I'd had a lot of hangovers in my life but this had to be in the top ten. Then again, that's how I always felt the morning after about all of them.

I was torn between trying to get back to sleep so my body

could repair itself without me noticing and getting up and taking charge. I closed my eyes and thought about anything other than spinning. I saw the image of a big, leering face, very close to mine with a round of ammunition where one of its teeth should have been. Then, in some confusion, I tried to work out whether my eyes were open or closed and decided they were closed. I tried to drift off, but felt something tickling my forehead, and when I scratched it I found that it was very hard and very metal. I roused myself as well as I could and saw the same image of the face again.

A great rocket-propelled grenade of adrenaline smashed into the base of my stomach.

There was a gun at my head.

And there was a Rider leering at me.

Fuck.

I didn't see Mat and Teb. I expected they were just sleeping elsewhere in the apartment, oblivious, as the Rider dragged me out and downstairs to where the others were waiting.

"Ah-ha! Ah-ha! Haaaa!" he called, sailing across the entrance hall.

"Oh God," said the bearded one. "He was right. Now we'll never hear the end of it."

"I have the Package. I told you! Didn't I?" said the one dragging me. "Didn't I?"

"You have cost us a lot of time," said one of the others to me.

"Didn't really mean to escape," I mumbled vaguely. "Someone tried to sell me some encyclopedias," I added, fighting the fact that the inside of my head had decided to do an impression of a bass drum with such fervor it made some imaginary metal garage door, located somewhere else in my head, continually vibrate.

"I knew he'd be there," continued the jumpy Rider. "I had a weird sense of it."

"Yeah, last time you had a sense of something we knocked off a pet shop because you thought there were diamonds stashed in the kangaroo pen," spat another Rider.

"I was misinformed. I explained it."

"I tell you, if another kangaroo ever punches me, I'm going to blow his fucking head off," spat the first one again.

"Get going. Come on," nodded the bearded one, and he gestured I should get onto the bike. I eased myself on gingerly; the crash suit slipped around me, and we all cruised off. No doubt we would be breaking more speed limits and as I was the only one with a C-4 Charlie, it would once more look to the sensors as if I were driving.

I really hoped the clever thing Caroline had done with my C-4 was still in force; otherwise, I could just see Zone Securities taking great pleasure in throwing the book at me.

Followed by the shelves.

Then probably the whole wall.

The crash suit had a blacked-out visor so I couldn't see where we were going. Not that it bothered me a great deal, because my head was seriously throbbing now from my hangover. Part of me insisted I was still actually lying down in Teb's flat and that this was a drunken dream, but a superior part of me knew that was a lie and it was all very real. I had no idea where we were and didn't especially care, but I did once hear a loud stern "Shhhhhh!" as we hammered along, and that had to mean we were in Classical and breaking the noise restrictions. That always triggered the huge "Please be quiet" signs they had everywhere.

We cruised on for a long time after that, so it didn't make a slither of difference. I couldn't mentally try to follow the route and, besides, I couldn't shake my headache. It felt like being closely followed by the entire percussion section of the San Diego Philharmonic.

After they had taken speed.

And then smack.

And then found out they had won the lottery.

I tried to think about other things but any fresh thoughts kept getting drowned out. Pain has a way of invading every nook of your soul so there's nowhere else in your head to go. It's like someone coming into your house and throwing all your things out of the window. In the end, no matter how hard you try to block it out, it gets to you.

So I just took every moment that went by as another one I had got through, and I knew if I strung enough of these moments together, eventually things would change. It doesn't sound a big deal, I know, but believe me—in the shape I was in, it was.

After an eternity of cambered bends and long open-throttle freeways, we slowed, meandering through tiny corners and finally climbing some bumps, which felt like a flight of small steps. At a snail's pace, we lurched over a much larger hump, circled slowly, and stopped. I guessed we were here, wherever that was.

A huge bell struck somewhere overhead, beating out long, slow seconds, and the echo rang around like an energetic terrier. The vibrations resonated deep within my throbbing temples, expanding my skull, it seemed, to three times its actual size. The bell tolled a final stroke, and the note slipped about me before retreating to some distant corner to curl up.

I felt hands on the crash suit and guessed the Riders were now about to ask me to assassinate God.

26

I wanted to lie down and turn my life off for an hour or so until my head stopped giving me such a hard time, but the Riders were already bundling me out of the crash suit and across the hard, uneven stone floor. The air was cool and I wondered where the hell we were. Around me seemed to be huge, squat stone columns, ragged with age, that sat belligerently in this silent, dingy half-light.

I looked up and, despite the pounding behind my eyes, took in the vaulted ceiling rearing above us, supported on a babble of ever-more-slender stone columns. The roof was falling into ruin, and great jagged edges of stone were silhouetted against the sky like biting mouths.

I tripped over a pile of masonry on the floor. It molted dust and I stumbled on through pale, slanting fissures of light that fell through the stained glass. I was in one of the replicas of Lincoln Cathedral, England. It had to be. There were about twenty of them in Plain Song, in various states of disrepair—put up by some property speculator a hundred years earlier who'd bought the franchise rights to the design. He'd created a whole heap of them before the bottom fell out of religion and he went bust.

Religion had hung in there, though, and I knew parts of Plain Song were in revival now.

Buddhism had been the first of the new religions to sweep America in the last century, but it came as a feeble orange color wash—a pale shade of its true self. And other religions had followed in its wake, spreading out like weakening ripples on a pond.

A new religion, launched with much publicity and pizzazz, didn't make much of a lasting mark in the end. It was called The Temple of Profound Pauses and they said God existed only in pauses. And so they spent their time "shaping pauses," whatever that meant. There were five hundred thousand followers in Milwaukee for a time, but it lost its appeal when the central minister was found to be using the money to fuel a heady cocktail of prostitutes, snowboarding holidays, and a rare collection of Victorian military cap-badges. Sometimes, he pursued all three at the same time, the papers had claimed.

Generally, though, religion remained a backwater because it seemed that somehow, all at once, people cottoned on to a feeling that it was religion that had caused so much of the pain and war in the world by putting such an emphasis on secularizing different peoples.

Or maybe it had been the well-publicized note from one leader to another that simply read: "Think the 'eye for an eye, tooth for a tooth' policy isn't working. Say we both ditch it?"

Now the emphasis was on seeking peace rather than clinging to spurious explanations for our existence—and once the focus moved toward peace, religion seemed to lose a lot of its hold over the masses. Religions never had been interested in peace that much, anyway.

The Riders pushed me past more collapsed brick clutter until we reached a tiny set of rickety spiral stairs, near the organ. The whole contraption looked rusted as hell. Many of the fixings had wormed their way out of the wood, so that a few of the huge pipes leaned forward precariously, like they were standing on a precipice and peeking over the edge. I guessed the thing hadn't been played in years.

We trooped on upward past shining steel girders that lay hidden from down below and were clearly not part of the original eleventh-century design, and I guessed they'd cut corners in these cathedrals to make them cheaper to build. My mouth cried impatiently for water as we finally reached a level above the organ and an unexpectedly large carpeted gallery that had a view of the whole cathedral on either side. It was surprisingly well organized, with settees, a couple of computers, and some familiar-looking equipment that jolted away the pain from my head with a jab.

That was a dream-making machine. The La Poderosa model—exactly the one I used at work, and they weren't that easy to get hold of now. Mostly because they were made in Miami, which was one of the entirely Spanish-speaking cities. The Mayor of Miami had, in fact, recently passed a local law there declaring no one was allowed to speak any English at all. Not that that would have been a problem, but they had developed a unique Spanish dialect that confused casual visitors. The Spanish government had tried to sue the inhabitants for intellectual property misappropriation or something—and had, in fact, received some form of compensation. But the upshot of it all was that it was now extremely hard for anyone to make any form of meaningful communication with anyone in Miami now.

We opened one of our orders for dream-making machines a few months back and found a selection of prime alfalfa and a variety of multisized joist noggins, along with a note that no one could decipher. Maybe they were just fooling with us; it seems the most likely explanation. But either way, Habakkuk went through the roof and immediately got someone on the inside up there. She secretly speaks English as well as their weird Spanish, but it's all a bit risky because she'll get a three-year statutory prison term if she's caught.

"Right," said the lead Rider to me, and I sensed he was about to launch off into some complicated explanation of everything. While this is exactly what I had been craving for some time, when the moment finally came I had other things on my mind.

"One moment, OK?" I said, holding up my hand. "You get me a pitcher of water the size of a Scottish loch, or I swear I'll throw up over this console." I was aware it wasn't the best bargaining threat that had ever been made. Normally, people suggest they'll blow up buildings or shoot people; but it was all I had. The Rider paused, shook his head in a tired way I couldn't help sympathizing with, and gestured to one of the others to get it for me.

"OK, Jonny-fucking-X. Business."

"Assassinating God," said War, distracting himself by balancing his shotgun on two fingers. "Blowing up His Holiness into oblivion," he added.

"We're not mad. I can see you think we're mad," the one with the beard went on.

"Apart from him. He is fucking mad," said the chirpy one, nodding. "He likes the Bee Gees. Always playing the fucking Bee Gees. Drives me insane."

"The first album is unsurpassed in modern music," said Famine.

"Shut up," said the leader. "This is business."

"Yeah, but it's Death. All right?" said the chirpy one.

"For fuck's sake. Then shut up, Death!" cried the leader.

"Yeah that's me." Death smiled. "He's the Pestilence thing now. Death," he said, straightening his shoulders. "Mr. Death, when I'm in a more formal situation."

"Do you want me to fucking shoot you? Right. Can we do the business, then? Right, Jonny X, you are going to write a dream on that thing, in which the dreamer believes God doesn't exist. OK?"

"How does that assassinate God?"

"Obvious, isn't it? Now, get on with it."

"There," said Famine, presenting me with what appeared to be a huge glass flower vase full of water. I didn't argue with him about the cleanliness of it. I was way too thirsty, so I just took it and drained the thing, feeling the water hit my stomach in a block, which made me unusually aware of its shape and position in my body. It gave me an instant kick and I offered it back.

"More...if that's doable," I added, and he took the vase back. I sat down at the desk and sorted out the computer, finding a sheet of stuff on the desk with a list of things I was supposed to put into the dream, and it was quite well thought out. Sometimes, when people ask for various stuff to put in dreams, you have to explain why it won't work. It usually comes down to cost. For example, there are oddities like—the color purple is expensive to use in dream architecture, and it's difficult to get horses looking right—but this brief had been done by someone who really seemed to know what they were doing.

I settled down to work.

None of the shortcuts were programmed into the console,

and none of the virtual tools were personalized, which was a pain. I realized it was going to take a good few hours to get anywhere. The Rider brought back the vase full of water. I took it from him and stood it on the corner of the desk, sipping it gratefully now and again, feeling the life ebb back into me as the ball of pain in my head began to smooth away.

I get quite absorbed in designing dreams, and even now I found myself immersed in a bubble of concentration, working out the initial framework, the dream parameters, the color hues, and animating the basic blocks. As dreams go, it was quite an interesting one to design, and only once did I wonder why they had chosen me. There were loads of dream architects in the business, and most of them were more efficient and more dependable than I was. I was way too prone to disappear off in some curious, unexplained alley of dream theory and waste a surprising amount of time and clients' money. I put their choice down to their ineptitude, and lack of research.

Quite how they thought this dream was going to assassinate God, though, was beyond me. Sure, people might believe a dream they have now and again. Maybe if they had a dream that God doesn't exist night after night, maybe eventually they would come to believe it. But how you would get people to swallow the dreams, I couldn't really tell.

Did they intend to give this to some prominent person like the president, perhaps?

Then I threw away the thought and just beetled on, and after working for maybe four or five hours, I had got the dream into a basic shape. There was still a great deal of detail to put in, and all of the sound to mix—and I figured they'd want music, which makes a good impact but requires skill so it's not too intrusive. But I was exhausted and needed a break. "I need five minutes to stretch my legs and have a cigarette," I said, trying to make my voice sound smooth and controlled.

"OK. No more than five." The lead Rider nodded. I pushed my chair back from the table and stood slowly, suddenly aware of the heaviness in my stomach.

"Want to hit some golf, X?" War eyed me, jabbing a golf club in my direction, and I stared at him.

Call me old-fashioned, but golf wasn't the thing I most craved at that moment. In fact, golf wasn't something I craved, ever. Golf is a game of constant boredom, punctuated first by moments of alarming surprise at the state of the clothing worn by everyone, and second with guffaws of derision at the idea of women using the clubhouse bar.

Most golfers probably still had a secret belief William Wilberforce had helped outlaw slavery rather too hastily, and that the American Revolution wasn't actually over as historians claimed, but merely pausing for halftime. Even leaving all that aside, a tired, crumbling cathedral wasn't the setting I normally associated with the game.

"No," I said. "Definitely no golf." He shrugged, unperturbed, set a ball up, and smashed it with the club from the gallery into the grainy darkness of the nave below.

There was a pause and a tiny smash of glass a second later. He turned and smiled.

"Nice swing," I said, imagining that was the sort of thing golfy people say.

He shrugged, set up another ball, and hit that out into the nothingness too. A second later, there was a clang. I leaned over the balcony, massaging my forehead gently, wondering if I would ever get to sleep in a warm bed again.

Somewhere, something had happened—like a shear in normality, or a tear in my life that had left the ends floundering. I looked around at these guys and realized they had a total belief in this cause that was actually quite impressive, and in many ways enviable. And, when I thought about it, it seemed that way with so many people I knew; they felt comfortable committing to something. Mat to his surfing, Teb to Natasha and his mad schemes. I felt too confused to do that, preferring the warm comfort of a beer in Inconvenient and a haphazard see-what-happens sort of approach to life. Maybe it was even deeper than that, I thought. Maybe I wasn't even committed to who I was.

It was a cold, unpleasant thought, and I wished I hadn't disturbed it. Maybe I was holding the real truth back for some reason—perhaps alarmed that who I was wouldn't fit in, and in the end I had completely lost track of who I was myself. I had got tangled in a web of false habits and torpid reruns of the past, just like that girl Tanya who had been Sarah's roommate, and maybe that's why she had made such an impression on me.

I didn't like the way these thoughts resonated about my head. Who the fuck was I exactly? "Do you have a cigarette?" I asked War, trying to distract myself from all this, and found he was in midswing. He stopped with the club at its highest point of the backswing.

"How am I ever going to get my pro tour card if no one gives me any fucking peace?" he said. "I need one thousand percent concentration!" I held up my hands in apology and he settled again and drew back for the swing.

The bell above us struck like a cannon with impeccable timing and the whole gallery vibrated. He spun in anger, raising his club as the other Riders doubled up with laughter, but the repeated clanging of the giant bell drowned out all noise, so all I saw were their animated faces. The bell chimed its way through the hours, then stopped, leaving the echo of the last ring to scurry this way and that like a frightened mouse looking for a way out.

I walked over and pulled the chair back, settled down at the comfort of the desk, and carried on with the design of the dream. The clock in this cathedral was fucked, I thought. It hadn't struck anything for hours, and now it had just struck fourteen. I began sorting out the audio tracks on the dream, only vaguely annoyed by the constant thwacking noise as the Rider resumed smashing golf balls into the chasm below. I prefer to work in silence rather than the atmosphere of the eighteenth tee when the green has been stacked full of crockery. Still, I added the music, tidied up the detail in the images, and made sure the whole thing didn't have any glitches.

I was bursting by now, and they let me use the toilet. When I got back, I reviewed the whole thing, and the entire dream sequence felt like it had come together. It's possible to spend days designing dreams, and there comes a point when you just have to stop or you start unraveling what you've already done. You could say it's like climbing a mountain and that, sooner or later, you get to the top. And, if you don't spot that moment, you'll start going down and be back at the bottom again without noticing. So, all in all, I decided I was done.

"That's it," I said, pushing back my chair. "A dream that tells the dreamer God doesn't exist. All here."

"Good," said the lead Rider, nodding.

"Fucking good," said the chirpy one, who lay on his back and didn't move. "Fucking, shit, good," he added, then, after a pause, he went on, "Fucking, shit, bloody, fucking, good. No, I'd already used 'fucking' once in that one, didn't I?"

"Just shut up for once, Death, for goodness' sake!"

"Death! That sounds sweet. My name is Death. How do you do, I'm Death...no, just Death...no, no first name. No, you don't recognize me from that high school. I am Death."

"What are you on about? Shut up! I mean Christ! OK? Jonny X, time for the Dream Virus bit."

"What's that?"

"The Dream Virus. This is the list of DNA we need to be susceptible," he said, handing over a sheet.

I was genuinely perplexed, and wondered whether they had read some article in a newspaper about the future of dream architecture and thought it was real.

"You've got me," I said, and he stared at me.

"Yes, we have got you. So get on with it."

"With what?"

"With this," said War. "We're really not so stupid," and he plonked down a folder of paper notes as thick as a pile of sandwiches. I stared at the thing. On the top was scrawled: "The Dream Virus Project," and it was unmistakably in my writing. And yet, I had no memory of it at all. I was so enwrapped by this turn of events, I assumed the excruciatingly loud organ music that suddenly started playing was solely in my head. The feeling was reinforced when I began to recognize the tune as a very bad version of the theme from *Michael, the Very, Very Magic Horse*—a children's program from when I was a kid.

After a moment I looked up to where the Riders were standing, wondering how I would explain to them I might have lost part of my memory, when I saw they could hear the music too and were slightly alarmed by it. I realized the obvious.

Somebody was playing the organ.

27

The Riders were staring down the stairs in child-like confusion, for once knocked mentally off-balance. I guessed Death was probably oblivious to the fact he was actually mouthing the words along to "Michael, the Very, Very Magic Horse." But someone swung the butt of a shotgun into his chest and motioned him to follow them down to check it out, and that snapped him out of it pretty quickly.

My head was still sloshing the news of the Dream Virus Project backwards and forwards like a stricken ship suddenly awash with seawater. I ran my fingers over the file, trying to trigger anything hidden, but nothing came. I carefully picked it up. The organ player was probably some student who had blundered into the cathedral, but it gave me some breathing space to try to think of my next move.

That is, if I got a next move.

The music continued, but the force of the air through the tubes was too much for some of the old, cobwebbed pipes, and I heard them rattle and clang as they fell to the floor like fainting grandmothers. I gazed at the first page of scribbled notes and tried to make some sense of it all. It looked alarmingly like my writing—but then again, I suppose, it could easily have been forged. Though why anyone would forge my writing was beyond me. Was there some conspiracy to set me up with this?

But why?

My head kept coming back to the question: why? I was a nobody. Why any of this? Could the Dream Virus Project be for real? It seemed unlikely. There were always rumors of outrageous breakthroughs in all kinds of fields, but that's generally all they were. Rumors. I flicked through the notes and diagrams and chemical formulae and understood only bits of it, but enough to see that if this was a hoax, it was a very detailed one—and there did seem to be some kind of interesting logic to the idea. I turned over another page and my eye caught a note scribbled in one corner. It said simply: "Moss Landing. Killer waves, five- to six-foot."

I felt like my head was being stirred with a cold spoon.

This was the echo of something, but whatever had made the original noise was long gone. I was always making absent-minded surfing notes like that when on the phone to Mat, and seeing it written out sent a divot of memories somersaulting around my head. I leaned back and drew in a huge lungful of cool, heavy air as another organ pipe clanged off its mountings and bounced to the floor. Whoever was playing was still tugging away maniacally at the stops, or whatever it is you do with organs—oblivious, or perhaps just not caring, that the whole thing was collapsing about them.

Clearly the Riders hadn't got to them yet, but I knew it would only be a matter of time, and I hoped they just set whoever it was on their way without anything more than a massive shock. "Michael the Very, Very Magic Horse" went the lyrics, and there were gaps in the tune now, where parts of the organ were missing. "He can jump down from the clouds, of course!" Although the person playing seemed to get stuck on this line, playing it over and over. "He can jump down from the clouds, of course!" I saw in my mind's eye the picture of the rainbow-colored horse jumping down through a hole in the clouds as it always used to do, and instinctively I looked up.

My heart rebounded off the walls of my chest and nearly went out through the top of my head.

A dozen thoughts sprang at me and clamored for attention all at once. A tiny figure was dangling on a wire that threaded in through one of the huge holes in the roof, maybe a hundred feet up. It looked a lot like Caroline. Or maybe I was being optimistic—but in the situation I was in, any reason for optimism had to be grabbed with both hands, teeth, and anything else that came to hand, like adjustable torque wrenches. In the back of my mind I knew it could be the Belgian too, and that a whole new chapter of grief could be about to unfurl, but frankly that seemed preferable to staying here.

The two Riders left up on the gallery were still pretty distracted by the organ music, and certainly hadn't seen the suspended figure. I slowly got up and walked to the edge of the gallery, which I guessed was about the point directly underneath the wire. They didn't seem to take much notice of me.

Still the music thundered on.

I stood as coolly as I could, hoping if they did see me, they would think I was just stretching my legs, and I hoped to God they didn't look up. I didn't dare look up myself now, but instead tried to guess how long it would take for the figure above to reach me. I realized it would be at least another thirty seconds and I knew then that a lot of things would happen at once—and judging by past experience, I would not have much to do with any of them. I looked around and noticed the Dream Virus file lying open on the desk, and as I've said before my curiosity can really get me into a lot of trouble. Curiosity killed the cat, as they say, but I have a strain that can also kill half the farm animals in New England. So despite the voice of reason screaming at me not to, I sauntered back to the desk like a bad B-movie extra. Walking seemed unexpectedly foreign, and I wondered how I'd ever done it so easily all these years. I reached for the file and picked it up at precisely the same moment the organ music abruptly cut off. And in the sudden, deathly silence, I felt the eyes of the two remaining Riders fall on me like a sack of elk meat. I froze, knowing somehow that this did not look good. I lifted the file, turned slowly toward them, and smiled inanely.

"I know what you mean about this," I said, seeing the depth of humorless disinterest in their eyes. The sullenness. I sensed images of violence trapped in their memories that doused them both in a comfortless torpor. They were in another place, where the consequences were different, where different rules applied. Where life meant something very different.

They said nothing.

"It's not as though I'm going anywhere," I added.

They seemed to accept this. So they were perhaps even more surprised than me when I was scooped off my feet in the very next second by the black figure who tore across their line of vision, suspended on the steel wire.

Gunfire broke out in fumbling showers. We swung above the floor, then paused at the end of the arc, before swooping the other way in an effortless loop toward the nave. I hung on to the black figure desperately, feeling the preciousness of life envelop me. I didn't want to die. Not now. Not after all this. Masonry fell in thumping clumps from the roof and dust blew after it in swarms. The noise of gunfire echoed and cracked, filling the cathedral in a chorus of earsplitting chaos. Masonry rained down in ever-larger sections, smothering any sign of the original floor like spewed-up lava. I was pincered in the legs of the figure and I tilted my head back slightly wondering who it was, but my rescuer was clad entirely in black, with a balaclava on. It could as easily be the Belgian as Caroline, I thought.

Another trainload of masonry screamed past us on its way down, and as the dust cleared above for a brief second, I saw exactly the reason it was falling with such fervor. The wire we were suspended on was cutting through the roof, dislodging the great stones like a razor saw, and I guessed we had to be suspended under a chopper. We lurched sideways down the nave, about twenty feet off the ground, bringing down more sizeable bits of the roof. At least the dust made it impossible for the Riders to see much; but they fired anyway, splintering the columns around us with random intensity.

We seemed to be dropping down, and I twisted my head to see the floor rise up. A dust-clad figure was running below, trying to keep to our pace as falling masonry exploded around him.

I didn't like this at all. My only option would be to kick at him, and somehow I didn't feel that was going to be enough. He made a wild dive for the tail of the wire, caught it, and was dragged along the floor through a substantial pile of chairs, then a faded display about flowers. He hung on doggedly and was scooped up off the ground as we swiftly gained height, so there were now three of us on the wire.

I clung on.

Our sideways momentum increased and I turned my head to

see where the hell we were going. In front of us was the towering, arched west window of the cathedral, glowing with stained-
glass figures. The main figure had his hands wide apart in a
welcoming embrace and we were swinging straight for him.

"All ye who come unto me shall be free," I couldn't help reading below the figure. The wire above us scythed through the last
of the roof and its momentum tore us through the body of the giant figure in the window in an explosion of colored glass, plaster, and masonry.

We swung free into the warm midday sun, trailing a dust
cloud like a swarm of bees who'd just had a flour fight. Plain
Song spread out around us in a pincushion of spires—some lying collapsed in long, shattered lines like dinosaur fossils. I felt
my fingers begin to go numb in the cold with alarming speed as
we gained height, and massive gusts of buffeting wind swayed
us in looping circles below the chopper. I clung to the Dream
Virus Project file and hoped all the papers weren't fluttering
away in the breeze behind us. Then I turned my head from the
direction we were going, so it was sheltered from the roaring
air, and saw the dust-covered figure below me, still hanging on
to a handle twisted into the wire.

I stared, and as we rolled wildly in a great arc past another
double-sized replica of Lincoln Cathedral, I finally understood.

28

The wire hawser drew us steadily up toward the chopper and we swung level with the empty rear cargo bay. The door was missing and the panels of the GaFFA 6 were conspicuously beat-up. I was yanked aboard by the black figure and rolled over on the pop-riveted metal floor in cold exhaustion.

This was no cure for a hangover, I thought.

But I couldn't relax yet. Heaving myself up, I reached out of the door, found Mat's hand, and lugged him into the GaFFA 6.

"Nice work," I cried above the engine howl, "but 'Michael, the Very, Very Magic Horse'?"

"You recognized it then?" he gasped, with a face shorn of all

emotion as he flopped beside me. Caroline slipped off her balaclava, looking composed and alert.

"This doesn't mean I'm accepting your offer," she shouted,
"so don't get any ideas, but events took a bad turn at Logistics
HQ when they realized your Jab-Tab had been terminated."

"A bad turn?" I cried, wondering what she could possibly
mean. As if things weren't bad enough.

"I felt in part responsible," she cried, "and I pride myself on
being a professional." She clambered forward into the cockpit,
flipped the straps over her shoulders, and locked herself into the
copilot's seat. "This is Marius," she called back above the gravelly
whine of engine noise, pointing at the pilot. "He saved your ass."

I nodded, wondering what she meant by "events took a bad
turn," but I didn't let it bug me. I was free from the Riders, which
was very cool, and I couldn't help liking her.

She was independent and knew her own mind—and for someone who had lost track of his own, that seemed pretty attractive.
But there was also a whole other side to her—a great dark area I
knew nothing about—and I wondered what lurked there. What
events from her past pushed her forward with such visible intensity? Maybe she was running away from stuff just like I felt I
was, or maybe she was running toward something she knew
was real. That's the thing; it's not always easy to tell one from
the other.

I could see that Mat's hangover was still haunting him, and
his ashen face gave him a strangely waxy appearance. I should
have known it was Mat playing the organ. We had often sung
"Michael, the Very, Very Magic Horse" at the tail end of drunken
parties, when a guitar had surfaced and everyone else had got
through their repertoire of dull, heartfelt love songs. Clearly he
had been trying to give me a hint with that second line of the
song.

I really can be quite dumb sometimes.

I stared out of the chopper door, watching the malls and roads slip by in neat blocks, and felt that the tide had turned. My old life was probably gone forever, but somehow that didn't matter anymore. I wasn't sure I wanted it back, anyway. What mattered were the people around me now. What mattered was regaining who I was, because the pleasure of being alive is not pining for different lives, or different things, but just being. Just being.

There was a pungent smell of engine fumes in the cargo bay that broke in strong waves around us, only to be immediately washed out of the missing door by the whipping breeze. I edged closer to the opening to try and breathe the cleaner air and looked at Mat, but he was poleaxed on the metal floor. The Dream Virus Project file was still clutched in my numb white hand, and I was relieved it had a large number of sheets still in it—though some were on the verge of escaping, and I tucked them back in. Probably I had lost a few, but this was still something to go on, and it bulged in my mind like a Christmas stocking waiting to be unwrapped.

I didn't bother to take in where we were, or where we were heading. I would find out soon enough. Instead, I just watched the odd cloud flop by, and the birds roller-coaster about on the breeze. It felt good just to let life slide by for a while, and I had always liked travel where you could watch the world go past and put your mind into neutral. Much sooner than I would have chosen, we hovered above some building and began the familiar, gentle sink onto a pad. I nudged Mat, who was still lying on the metal floor, knowing that getting up and gaining any sort of momentum again was going to be a wrench for him.

"This is where you get out," Caroline said over her shoulder, as the skids scraped down and the chopper sank onto its haunches. "The Riders won't find you here. I've arranged for a Medi-Data leak on their file, anyway."

"Why?" I shouted, wondering what that was about, but she just pressed on.

"As for the Belgian on your case now, he's all your problem. This will unmask his C-4 Charlie and trigger plasi-screens if he is in the area," she said, tossing me another wrist bracelet. "He's called Luke K34. It's more than my ethics allow. He may be arrogant, but he's my colleague and I've signed the limpet encyclopedia salesperson oath like everyone else."

"An oath?" I repeated.

"Yes, and this is really testing my conscience."

"Thanks, then. What did you mean earlier about 'events had taken a bad break' or something?" I pressed, sensing I might not get another chance to see her and that these snatched answers might turn out to be precious.

"When people don't have the means to pay for their encyclopedias, the company can get very angry and hand clients over to the debt collectors, to *Le Volci*—'The Voices.' When you hear The Voices, it can be very scary. It can ruin your life forever. They decided to turn you over to *Le Volci* if you don't pay," she said with a shrug of the shoulders, staring at me with those deep blue eyes. "And since you were in my care when Zone Securities snatched you, I felt in part responsible. Now, leave. Go on."

"But I don't want any encyclopedias! Did they not factor that in at all?" I protested as Marius wound up the rotors to a howl.

"Don't kid yourself, Jonny. Everyone succumbs in the end. Even the president has a set," she shouted, as Mat and I collapsed out of the cargo bay and onto the concrete as the chopper eased up off its skids. "Drinks are arranged," she cried as her voice receded. "See the man with the earrings." And then any other words were swallowed up by the engine growl. The

GaFFA 6 hummed happily up for about ten feet then yawed away, sliding off into the clear, empty sky.

Two ludicrously dust-clad figures stood marooned on the top of a building someplace in downtown Santa Cruz, looking like they'd just robbed a flour factory.

Badly.

29

The roof was familiar, and I realized we were on top of the Thin Building, just one floor up from The Most Inconvenient Bar in the World.

"I think I'll just lie here for a bit," said Mat, gazing up from where he had landed when he'd flopped out of the chopper. "It feels like all the cells in my body are vibrating." Then after a pause he added, "She's very cool, isn't she? Very cool."

"Caroline?"

"Don't you think?"

"Yes I do, but she sells encyclopedias. What is all that about? I really just don't get it. People who sell encyclopedias don't have guns normally, do they?" I yawned, walking to the edge of the building, looking down to see the familiar graveyard of reclaimed bits and pieces from old houses strewn out across the wasteland.

"She likes you. She likes you a lot, even though she tries to hide it."

"Mat, don't go there. How can I go out with a woman who takes an oath about encyclopedia selling?" I turned when he didn't reply, and saw his hangover had taken a solid grip on him again, so I gazed back over the city.

After a few minutes, we got ourselves together enough to stagger into an elevator, which was preoccupied with trying out different sorts of ping, which could accompany the doors opening.

"I like this one," it said. "It's more me. What do you think? Ping!" it went with a high-pitched ringing sound.

"It's great," I said. "How about we—"

"But then there's this one, which is a bit more traditional. Ping!" it went again, with a barely perceptible difference. "Better?"

"Inconvenient," I said.

"Please," added Mat diplomatically. "And I prefer the first ping." Thankfully, this seemed to satisfy the elevator, and it closed the doors and headed down in silence. "Here we go. Ready?" said the elevator.

"Yes," I said.

"PING!" it went, as the doors slid open. "Oh, that was good. Wasn't that good?"

"Unbelievable," I said. "Utterly stupendous," and we walked out into the delicious buzz of Inconvenient.

It was heaving, and that was good.

I could immediately see the time-honored mix of annoyingly pretty women; men with shirts drizzled with color in such a way that made them look like idiots; people with hair sculpted into a variety of shapes, some of them quite possibly with practical uses such as opening bottles; and Mat and myself, still covered in a quite remarkable amount of dust, despite having spent some time hanging underneath a moving helicopter—which, you would have thought, would have dry-cleaned anything. But then again, maybe that explains why dry cleaning never works. Blowing something about isn't going to get it clean, no matter what they tell you. Otherwise, parachutists would arrive back down gleaming, wouldn't they?

"Hey!" said a voice, slapping a heavy hand on my shoulder from behind. I turned and saw the thickset bouncer with OTTER tattooed on his forehead and wearing two large earrings. It had been him and his mate who had got me served quickly by Eli a few days before. "You're the two donkeys I've been waiting for. Come on," he sniffed, clearing away a gap through the crowd with slightly unnecessary force. "Ever done a liver transplant?" he said, turning back to me after a few steps.

"No," I said.

"Went on a course, didn't I?"

"Did you?"

"Did my first one this morning. See, I've got a badge!" he said, pointing at a small badge he was wearing, of what I took to be a liver that was dripping with blood. "It's not that difficult. Long as you follow the facts sheet." He grinned. "Right, this is your space," he added more seriously, frightening away a teenager who was wearing a T-shirt that I couldn't help seeing had written on it: HE WHO LAUGHS LAST DIDN'T GET THE JOKE RIGHT AWAY.

"Drinks coming," he said. "Give you that number of the liver transplant class. Here!" he said, handing Mat a card.

"Thanks."

"A course makes a nice present to someone," he added, and left.

"He gets a cut," said Mat. "It's all a big selling thing. I've had the spiel in here before. It takes five years before they let you anywhere near a liver." I was relieved to hear this, because the idea of that man operating on my liver was deeply unsettling.

"Four Hangover Whackers," said a waiter in a white coat, to my shock.

It was impossible to get any sort of drink from the waiters in Inconvenient; they were exclusively there for effect. They were primed just to nod and say things like, "I'll be with you in a minute," or just gesticulate and smile in a meaningful way, then never reappear at all. Generally, the drinks they carried weren't actually for anyone. Sometimes they even took orders and people new to Inconvenient were often under the illusion that this would lead to a drink being served at some stage.

How naive they were.

It was a steep learning curve, getting used to the ways of Inconvenient, but this waiter had actually served us four drinks and I can tell you, that caused quite a stir in the people around us. They moved back slightly as though we possessed some kind of ethereal force field that they wanted to be well clear of.

I tried to ignore them as Mat and I dragged ourselves up onto the stools we had somehow managed to acquire and leaned on the shelf that held our drinks. Hangover Whackers were a concoction that were reputed to cure hangovers faster than any other known substance. What was in them was supposed to be some kind of gigantic secret, because it dealt with the alcohol in a holistic way or something. An even bigger secret seemed to me to be the fact that they did fuck all that a glass of water couldn't do, but it was liquid of some sort and that was all that mattered. Mat took the first one and drained it right off, then paused. "I've been dreaming of that," he said croakily.

I smiled as he caressed his second Whacker, and I could see speaking was still way down on his list of easily attainable activities. "Chill out, Mat. I've got some stuff to check out here," I said, opening the folder.

The whole Dream Virus Project idea was intriguing, if bonkers, but maybe there was some tangential clue in here that would unlock this whole thing.

"I'm glad the psychopathic Riders made sure you took some paperwork home with you," Mat commented weakly, then laid his head down on the shelf, having seemingly used up all reserves of energy, and by all appearances went to sleep.

I sipped my drink and began to pore over the contents of the folder. Some of the sheets seemed to be out of order and some of them didn't have anything to do with the project at all as far as I could see, and some were torn hurriedly from books, so the whole collection was a weird jumble of facts and ideas. There were mathematical fractals, some complicated dream psychology, and quite a bit of stuff about DNA. The DNA pages triggered something one of the Riders had said to me. "This is the list of DNA we need to be susceptible." They seemed to have believed the Dream Virus could somehow be specifically targeted at an individual's DNA. That was a very weird idea.

It would mean you could release a virus and only the people you had singled out would catch it; the ones you had specified by attaching their DNA somehow to the virus.

But a Dream Virus? That was another step along the line. A virus that gave people serial dreams night after night that you simply uncorked someplace and let find its targets by spreading out like a disease? It was an idea from so far out in left field that I had to get my head adjusted to the whole concept. It was like being told the earth is actually flat after all, and a mixup with some of the adding and subtracting in the seventeenth century led generations to think it was round.

You have to take several steps back and try and readjust your whole mental landscape, while not allowing yourself to shout,

"Stop talking complete and utter bollocks!" at the top of your voice.

"A Dream Virus that only infects a person whose DNA has been written into the program and gives them the same dream night after night," I said to myself, trying to keep an open mind. Suppose such a thing was true. Suppose that's what these pages actually did show. Where did that get me? I still had no idea what this had to do with me. Or why the file seemed to be in my handwriting. Or really how it would assassinate God. Or come to that, why anyone would want to assassinate God. There were still way too many questions. It was like getting an exam on a different subject from the one you were expecting.

I sat back and took a gulp of my Hangover Whacker. It had a slightly sweet lemony taste, and gently fizzed in my mouth in a pleasingly medicinal kind of way. Actually, it wasn't bad. Not the sort of thing I would have normally ordered, but surprisingly ideal for when you've had a hangover and been lugged alarmingly about underneath a helicopter. It did give the impression it was actively sorting out my insides, which was rather wonderful, and I was beginning to revise my scepticism about the whole subject of Hangover Whackers. I looked at the file again.

Having got hold of it was a step forward, and ideally I needed all my research stuff to help me dissect it in detail. But that was in my house. I tried to think of a way to get in touch with the punks who had stolen it, but other than go back to Zone Securities on my hands and knees looking for the lost business card, my mind drew a blank. I took another gulp and let the Hangover Whacker slide down and saw that on the back of the teenager's T-shirt it said: WHEN YOU CAN'T FIND THE DOOR TO YOUR FUTURE, REMEMBER, EVERY ROOM HAS A DOOR SOMEPLACE. I wondered whether he'd considered the possibility someone could have built the room around him while he was asleep. My thoughts skidded on the idea, but the significance of it eluded me—and the more I thought about it, the less sense it made, until I had to let it go.

"Mat, here's the deal. We need to break in to Zone Securities and find a card that is as big as a chocolate cookie," I said, returning to the problem of my house and knowing full well that Mat was unconscious. I took another gulp and began to feel that my head needed to slow down and take time-out properly.

"Yes! It's time to add the power of the nuclear bomb to your golf swing," sang out the hologram of the annoying small man, suddenly appearing just in front of me again. "Hi! I'm Tony Shappenhaur IV. You know me better as 'The Thinking Buckaroo,' and I'm here to tell you about the amazing power of this driver."

This was all I needed—the ad I had caught in Zone Securities. I stared wearily at the hologram, unable to face the prospect of waiting for it to run through its whole spiel, and I was about to ask the teenage kid whether he had a zapper when the waiter reappeared from nowhere.

"Can I get that for you, sir?" he said in a smooth, accentless voice, producing a neat white zapper and snuffing out the virus ad instantly. I tried to thank him, but I was way too surprised. Not only had the waiter served us drinks, but now he was being helpful. I suddenly sensed people around us were getting uneasy about this.

"Never seen a waiter be helpful in here before," said a man in a baggy suit, looking utterly perplexed. "The whole world is going weird." I nodded and tried to ignore the whispers around us.

"There was a helpful waiter," and "I'm telling you he was really helpful," were a couple I picked up from the melee, which seemed to be buzzing in our vicinity all of a sudden. Clearly, Caroline E had friends in high places to make all this happen. I sensed she probably had friends in low places too, come to that, and quite possibly she had friends in places that were as close to sea level as makes no difference if I'm going to be pedantic. But the point is, when waiters start being helpful in Inconvenient, it makes you know you are part of something very big that you really don't understand.

"I have an idea," said Mat, still lying with his eyes shut.

"What's that?" I said, caught slightly off guard by the fact he wasn't unconscious.

"I have an idea, but my head is too tired to tell you now," he added without moving.

"Right. Good. Well, you know, don't forget it," I said, wondering if he knew he was talking.

"Where to now?" I muttered. "Where to now?" I picked up the file and began to reread bits of it more carefully. While parts of it made some sort of sense, a lot of it was beyond me. And yet I had this feeling in my mind somewhere that it was stuff I would have understood years before, at college, when my dream theory classes were still fresh in my mind. The more I read, the more I seemed to be able to get my head around the idea of a Dream Virus. Maybe it wasn't such a crazy concept, after all. "Come on, Mat," I said, poking him. "Time to leave."

"Oh. What flavor of people have come to kill you this time?" he groaned, without moving.

"Nobody yet, but we're leaving." I helped him off the barstool and onto his feet, and he reluctantly began to readjust himself to the complicated scenario of walking. A couple of waiters hovered close by ready to remove our stools into storage the moment we were gone, so no one else could use them. We staggered into the same elevator we had used earlier, which was possibly a mistake.

"I've been thinking, maybe it should be more dramatic and not just a ping," said the elevator.

"Ground floor," I said, hoping to stem its enthusiasm for inane conversation.

"Please," added Mat weakly. The doors swooshed shut and

we began to descend in silence. But just when I thought we'd demoralized it, it started babbling on again. "It's like the big moment, isn't it? The crescendo of the whole journey. You arrive! The doors open! And all you get is a 'ping.' It's not enough, is it?"

"It's quite enough for me."

"But what about something bigger?"

"No. Really," I said.

"Just see what you think."

"Oh, God," I sighed, as we reached the ground floor with a smooth bump.

"Uhhhh," went the elevator, sounding like a woman about to reach orgasm. "Uhhhhhh!" It carried on more forcefully, and the elevator doors began shaking. "Uuuuuuuuuughghgh" it cried. Then "Yessss!" as the doors flew open accompanied by the dramatic final chord of *Also Sprach Zarathustra*.

Mat and I exchanged glances.

"I preferred the 'ping,' " said Mat, and we both stepped out into the long, cool entrance lobby of the Thin Building.

It was empty, as it nearly always seemed to be, and our footsteps echoed up into the vast ceiling, reminding me of the sound of ice cracking in a crevasse. We'd crossed about halfway toward the giant, heavy metal doors when we came to a bench on our left strewn with bunches of flowers.

I stopped, curious, and saw there was a small card. I carefully picked it up. It read, "Rest in peace. Or do whatever it is dead people like to do most." I hesitated for a moment, and the image of the old man who had been lýing here asleep a few days earlier came to me and I wondered if this was all for him. I recalled his face with unexpected clarity, then seeing Mat ahead of me, trotted after him, catching up as he struggled with one of the vast doors. I wanted to say something about it, but didn't know what it was exactly I wanted to say, so I said nothing.

We heaved open the door and stepped out into the fresh

afternoon sun, but the image of the man stayed, cloaking me in a feeling of unexplainable peace. We weaved our way through the reclamation yard, past a variety of classical stone entrance porches that hadn't seen a door in years, and through an intricate wrought-iron rose pagoda that was folding up onto its knees with rust.

"We've somewhere to go," I said to Mat.

"Giving Habakkuk a visit at last, are we? Excellent. I might actually be sick over him right now rather than just really wanting to be," said Mat, who had taken a surprising dislike to him considering he had only met him twice.

"Not quite yet," I said, "but we will soon."

PART THREE

All shall Be Well

30

Waddell Creek was deserted. Mat cut the engine and the gentle noise of the sea lapped inquisitively up to us in the thumping silence.

I had seen too many confusing and, frankly, bizarre people recently, and needed some time-out in a place where there was explicitly no chance of an elevator giving me any sort of grief. I could smell the salt in the spray and felt like a kid skipping class. I shouldn't be here. I should be someplace being shot at.

I hauled myself stiffly off the bike and felt the sand crumble under my boots like stale sugar. The surf wasn't that big, perhaps about four to five feet, but the waves were clean, breaking effortlessly in long lines, like someone gently unzipping the water. I watched the glassy, unbroken peaks roll lazily over into bluff explosions of white foam, and it felt like seeing a circus trick over and over, never understanding how it was done. I heard a cough and glanced back. Mat's hangover seemed to be more under control now. He was unclipping the boards from the carrier hooked onto the Crossfield, and chucked me a wet suit with a smile.

Hitting the surf had always been his answer to problems, and it wasn't such a bad call; it was finding something real to believe in again. Call me a dork, but the world seems a different place when you've just been surfing with a friend. It all feels more chilled by a factor of about ten zillion.

A rip was sucking out a little to the left of us, and to the right I could see the beach run away north toward Half Moon Bay in a frazzle of dunes that poked up like unshaven stubble. I peeled off my clothes and tried not to think about anything and just tune in to the stuff around me, like the gentle breeze sliding across my chest and the noise of the sea; but the image of Caroline staring at me with those blue eyes kept surfacing in my mind.

I wondered whether that stuff about my Jab-Tab and The Voices was really true. Maybe she just said that so she had a reason to get me out of trouble, because she didn't like to see people floundering in stuff they couldn't deal with.

Maybe.

Nothing about her made much sense, and I still had very little idea who she was exactly, but I regretted not asking her about that date again—October 18. Why had she reacted so strangely when I threw that at her inside Argonaut Logistics? What had happened on that day? It seemed to touch a nerve inside me as well, but the memory, if there was one, lay hidden—and it felt like sitting in an exam trying to reach back for information you hadn't really been paying that much attention to in the first place.

I took a breath and told myself I had to let all this stuff go for
a while. The waves were calling and I needed to stop wheeling
these events around in my head or I would go crazy. So I threw
on a rash vest and took hold of my beat-up old wet suit. I stuffed
one foot, then the other, into the legs, tugged them through,
then folded it up over my shoulders, wriggled into the arms, and
pulled up the back zip with a haul on the long strap.

Mat passed me his new longboard with a smile and grabbed
his old faithful, which was thick with combed wax and scuffed
with dinks, which all had a lengthy story of a wave or a rock behind them that he could go on about until you stopped him.

Which, frankly, you normally had to do.

We attempted a run, which ended up as a sort of half trot to
the water's edge, and it felt like someone had ratcheted up the
tension in my leg muscles so tightly, all I could manage was this
achingly heavy cardboard-stiff plod.

Finally, we stuttered into a walk, then stood for a moment,
double-checking the shape of the waves as we watched some of
the sets come through, and wrapped on our ankle leashes. How
often had we done this together? I wondered. Hundreds of
times. Thousands even. It was a cool moment. There was always a freshness at this time, a prickle of anticipation and a
feeling that all the things you thought were problems were
nothing but brittle illusions that the paddle out would wash
away, together with any lingering feelings you should be somewhere else.

Surfing was a miraculous rebirth, a baptism of saltwater, and
the power of it never ceased to surprise me. As we stood drinking in the moment, it occurred to me the only other thing that
came close was climbing. I didn't climb mountains because they
were there, as people were fond of quoting. I climbed because if
you went up into that otherworldly environment, then returned
unharmed, you felt reborn.

In winter, the effect was magnified by the cranky, irascible weather that scooted about the peaks, snapping like an angry sheepdog. It's as though weather gets confident in the mountains and loses its shyness. In cities, we forget weather can be like that because it seems almost anonymous, slinking about the streets with only the homeless for company. In the hills, though, the weather will take you on and try and kill you. I remember chewing all this over with Jack on a warm, windless evening on the beach, by a cracking fire of driftwood. Eli's brother, Jack.

I let his memory and some of our times surfing together course through me; his crazy smile, his deep-set eyes and laid-back, have-a-go attitude. His wild kickbacks. Maybe it was slipping into a past I should have let go a while back. Maybe it was sentimental, but to hell with that. The kid had died and we had loved him, and he had left a hole that still shouted. A gap that we filled clumsily, like we were still surprised that it was ours to fill.

And he left me something else too. An uneasy, flailing feeling about the day he had died.

We waded into the chill of the water, pushed the boards onto the foam, and paddled away. I let my uneasiness slide. This was heaven; the gentle lap-lap of the water on the noses of the boards, the chop of small peaks as they jostled inanely about us, the sun reflecting off the water in blinding, random shards. We met the first wave in a crazy snap of froth that ran a chill down the backs of our wet suits as we duck-dived and emerged on the other side like clumsy seals, only to be smacked by another charge of seething white water.

And another. The waves seemed a good four or maybe five feet. We kept paddling on through the slicks of foam, and after a while rode over a pregnant hump of swell, which meant we were out beyond where the waves were breaking. I let the board drift, then pushed myself up, my legs dangling in the sea and the nose of the longboard rising out of the water like some phallic symbol. There was a peacefulness out here. It was a place where time didn't happen so much, where you could sit and let the waves go, or turn and catch the next one in. We lazily scanned the horizon, keeping an eye out for the next sets; but in truth, we were in no hurry and allowed the lines of swell to ride under the boards as if, as someone had once told me when I was a child, the long tail of a dragon was snaking through, lifting and dropping us, as the humps slipped beneath us. I turned and watched the waves boulder up as they passed us, then strained their necks like leashed dogs before they crashed, stretching for the shore with white fingers of foam.

"I can definitely see you getting the Nobel Prize for Unhelpful Grief this year," said Mat, as the wind kicked up a halter of spray, making a tiny rainbow that instantly fell and died.

"Well, that's always been my main aim in life, obviously. Along with winning a Harvard Exhibition to study the history of the table-tennis paddle. My head feels like a phone book where someone has altered all the numbers, but just ever so slightly— so although they look familiar, I don't quite know the difference. D'you have any sort of feelings like that? You said you woke with a hangover a few days ago and didn't drink the night before…"

"Yeah. Doesn't exactly compare with some Riders wanting you to assassinate God, though."

"But I think it's all connected somehow. All of it. Remember that date Teb found when he was tracing Argonaut Logistics?"

"No."

"Well, it was the eighteenth of October. I threw at Caroline, and she looked really huffy about it."

"Well, she's a limpet encyclopedia saleswoman who was assigned to you; that's enough to make the Pope huffy. I say we surf now."

"Yeah, we'll surf, Mat. It's just that it feels like I have all these loose wires flapping around in my head and they keep connecting to each other and giving me shocks that set my fillings on edge, and I can't seem to tie them down. The Riders had this really weird idea. Really weird."

"I say leave it now, Jonny, yeah? Let's just surf. Let it go for a bit, and we'll come at it fresh."

"Yeah, but, Mat, there's this tiny, tiny bizarre chance that they have something of mine. The file they gave me looks a lot like my handwriting. Really it does. I would swear it was my handwriting but I don't remember anything of it. Explain that." Mat stared at me with tired, resigned alarm and I shrugged hopelessly. Then I found myself talking and the whole thing spilled out in one great fur-ball of words. Sentences shambled over one another like lambs to an udder as I tried to convey too many ideas at the same time. This thing had been fizzing about my head and wanted out.

"So, it's something to do with a dream that's released like a virus, but can only be caught by the one person it was written for?" said Mat, raising one eyebrow in that way I had never learned to do.

"Yeah, that's about it. That seems to be what they're on about. Why, I just really don't know."

"Dark," said Mat. "Very fucking dark, in fact."

"Sorry, Mat. I just needed to get that out. Come on, let's surf, dude." Although my hands were a touch blue from the chill, I could see from Mat's pale complexion that his hangover was catching up with him again. That often happens if you stay in one place too long. A hangover gets a bit tired trying to keep up once you are doing stuff; but if you stay in one place too long, it can find you again, climb back in and say "Ah-ha! I'm back!"

"This one's all yours." I nodded as a line of swell breezed in happily toward us. Mat spun his board around and paddled hard. The peak surged up, and he skipped to his feet, smoothly ripping toward the shore so I could just see the top of his body behind the shoulder of the wave like a bird belly-skimming the water.

I turned slowly and shivered. The vast ocean seemed inhuman all of a sudden. Alien. A galloping mass of cold power on an unimaginable scale. Then I became aware of a strange liquid feeling in my brain, as though warm, molten nectar was gently dripping from a small cavity inside my head, and the sensation was both intoxicating and alarming.

As the next peak arched forward, I wheeled around and paddled, waiting for my board to pitch down as the swell grabbed me, then I kicked to my feet. Not so much like a coiled spring, it has to be said, but more like a spring in need of some oil and perhaps a week at a reenergizing retreat.

But at least I was on my feet and surfing. The world burned through into another layer of perspective in one swift movement. I was above the sea suddenly, as though I was skipping over it, being gently juggled by nature rather than being crushed by it. I cut a wide, sweeping bottom turn into the wave, then rode up the face before twisting back with an easy snap of my hips. Mat had been right; his new board felt really sweet. I was wonderfully at peace now, divorced from the mindless man-made flotsam and jetsam that had been flying at me with destructive casualness the past few days.

It had been a fantastic decision to come here.

After a while the peak chased me down and broke, leaving a commotion of wild froth yapping about as the power drained from the wave. I could see Mat already paddling back out, so I spun the tail and flopped into the sea. He was heading for the rip and I paddled after him as the remains of the next wave came cruising down at me. I tried to duck-dive, but somehow the nose of the board wouldn't sink and the white water smacked into me like a pack of annoyingly playful dogs. I always thought being wiped out, even by broken waves like this, was like having a massage from a large, frustrated masseuse. After being pounded for a while, you felt a lot more relaxed but also slightly bruised all over.

As the froth scurried away, something else seemed to dislodge inside my head, and it suddenly felt like my brain was vibrating ever so slightly. I paddled hard toward Mat, not knowing what to make of it, and just concentrated on getting out the back. I sat up on my board when I reached him, breathing hard, and let the tightness in my chest loosen.

"My head feels weird," I said.

"Really?" said Mat. "What sort of weird?"

"Weird, weird. Like it's vibrating slightly and there's warm liquid running through it." Mat stared toward the shore. "I only said it felt weird," I added when he still didn't reply.

"I had something like that yesterday," he said.

"Really? Warm honeylike liquid, dripping around?"

"Yep."

"What the fuck is going on, Mat?"

"I don't know, Jonny. I really don't know. But I don't want to think about it now. Come on. Let's catch some waves, and we'll talk about it all later when we're chilled."

I nodded, guessing he was right, and spun the board and paddled. As I turned to see where the peak was, it reared up suddenly, much bigger than the earlier ones, and it struck me that the tide was on the push and the waves would probably grow all afternoon. As it lunged for me, white water broke from the lip and the board tipped acutely forward. I knew I had to be very quick and snapped to my feet the next instant, exactly as I had done a thousand times before.

Except I didn't. I'd timed it all wrong.

There's a brief moment before a big wipeout where you can't believe it's really going to be that bad; you can't believe the wave won't back off, and say: "Yeah well, could have had you there if I'd wanted to." But "God doesn't play dice," as Einstein had once said. He doesn't play charades either if it comes to that, or Scrabble. At least, there's no mention of it in the Bible, anyway. There's no parable of the man who chose all vowels and a "z," as far as I remember. Either way I was fucked, sprawling headfirst, midair, like a teenager who has just shambled off the high board in the Santa Cruz swimming pool, misguidedly hoping to piece together the skills needed for a perfect dive on the way down. I hit the water with the dexterity of a bedroom wall, and the wave collapsed, crushing me like a discarded cigarette packet.

Under the surface, I was torn about in a wild world that foamed with dumb light; the sky swam above out of reach, and undefined images, boiled up by the water, cut and pasted around my head. The board felt like it had gone rabid, and seemed about to break my ankle as it jerked at the leash. Deep inside, I became aware that my brain was going weird again, and it seemed like warm golden liquid was trickling from cavities where it had been holed up. My head broke free from the water and I grasped at the air, taking in lungfuls of the stuff, then I grabbed my board and slid onto it as the next wave steamed in and I just had time to duck-dive.

I paddled back out wondering how I could have been so stupid to miss a takeoff, and felt the saltwater stinging at my eyes so I couldn't see a thing half the time. When I got far enough out, I sat up on my board but saw that Mat was almost at the shore riding a wave in and I realized I must have passed him on the way.

What was going on with my mind? Images and memories were sliding about like icebergs in the summer sun, cut adrift from the glacier and floating free. I suddenly felt as though part of my mind was melting to reveal other parts underneath, and I had no idea which was my true self. Like when they x-ray a painting and find another one hidden below. Which is the real painting?

And that was how it seemed for a second. As though I had another life that existed beneath the life I was living, but I didn't know which was real, or which one I should fight to keep. The sensation lasted for only a moment, then was gone—and the details of the other world I had seen echoed away. All I was left with was a sense of something. A feeling. And I wondered what the hell it meant.

"Did you see that?" called Mat, paddling up. "Did you see? I nailed a one-eighty! That was the bee's knees, the wasp's ankles, and the butterfly's goddamned elbows! A one-eighty!"

"Sorry, didn't see anything. My head is really weird, Mat. I've suddenly got this sense that October 18 was a marriage thing. Where did that come from? Do you know anyone who got married on October 18?"

"Shit, Jonny! Didn't you hear? A one-eighty! I did a one-eighty. Stop meddling with all that stuff in your head and start actually being here. It's five-foot and clean! Come on, dude! Let's go! Let's surf!"

And so I did try to let it go, and as we surfed on for the next hour, my head seemed fine again. The weird experience cooled until I could hardly imagine what I had been on about, and I remembered almost nothing of it, like the vivid images of a nighttime dream burned away by the harsh morning light. I didn't feel in any sort of shock from everything that had happened, as I suppose I might have done, but instead seemed to sink back into the past.

For a while it felt like we were kids, skipping eighth grade again. It felt like time hadn't passed and we were the young, impetuous idiots we had been back then. It even felt like we might meet Jack out the back.

For a while.

Mat nailed another couple of one-eighties, and I think he surfed with a freedom that you only experience occasionally in your life. Maybe it was the relief of still being alive, after the chaos of the morning.

"I'll tell you my idea now, if you like," he called, as we sat out the back waiting to catch a final wave in.

"What idea?" I said.

"My idea. I told you in Inconvenient I had an idea. Well, I do."

"You had to be unconscious in Inconvenient," I said.

"Only partially," said Mat with a smile. "And that's when I'm at my sharpest."

"Christ, I'm learning new stuff about you even now. What's this idea, then?"

31

Ad virus control," said Mat, but seemingly too quietly for the guy because he didn't move an iota. And, frankly, he gave the impression that had there been a whole bag of iotas right in his way, he wouldn't have bothered to move those either.

"Ad virus control," I repeated, but it came out slightly louder than I had meant to, as though my throat was swollen.

I took in a deep, slow breath and assessed the full extent of this tired, stomach-bulging security monkey slouched in the chair behind the counter. He had hair that might have been cut by a family of overeager bears who had learned only the basics of scissors control and a complexion that suggested he ate most meals with a side salad of grease.

"Ad virus control," I said again, after a pause, trying to rein in my voice so it had the right mix of authority and don't-give-a-fuck nonchalance of a workman.

But the guy still just stared off at the screens.

I exchanged a glance with Mat. His overalls were decidedly dodgy. He looked like he'd used cheap soap powder or something, and his washing machine had got so touchy about it, it had shrunk all his clothes by rinsing them in water hot enough to cause nuclear fusion. Seeing him standing there like that made me shudder inwardly. We were treading a thin line, and even if the line had been fatter, I wasn't that sure how good at treading on lines we really were anyway.

"What is it this time?" huffed the man, still transfixed by the banks of security screens. "A new strain of the ad that goes on about hot ice cubes?" I knew the one he meant.

"Plink! Plink! Fzzz! Fuck!" had been their slogan—which, I have to say, I liked. Particularly as it had been accompanied by a picture of a woman dropping a glass of bourbon because the addition of the ice cubes had suddenly made it excruciatingly hot to grasp.

"No, it's golf. 'I'm Tony Shappenhaur IV!' " I went on, trying to give the impression of disinterest. " 'You know me better as "The Thinking Buckaroo." ' You come across it?" We both looked at the guy, but he seemed to have got sucked into whatever was on the screens again.

"OK. Well," I pressed on, "your canteen is the Mother Area for the thing on our ad virus maps. See?" I held up some sheets Teb had concocted. "And we need security clearance so we can zap it before it becomes an epidemic."

"Ha! What are the chances of that, do you think?" he laughed, and his thick eyebrows danced across his forehead. "Fly that plane, Chico!" He paused. "We had a dog like that once." He nodded at the screen, suddenly getting enthusiastic. "Used to leap the fence and come and meet you when you turned into the street, just because he somehow sensed you were there. I mean, how did he do that? I could never work it out. He could sense other things too, like whether people were going to be friendly, or whether they were only faking it."

In one unexpectedly athletic movement, the man swung onto his feet and leered at me. Maybe it was the stench of hamburger on his breath, or the sheer bushiness of his eyebrows, but I sensed a trapdoor drop open to a rather alarming side to his character. "He could smell out the fakers a mile off," he said, revealing an urgent need for dentistry, then he made half a sniffing gesture without breaking eye contact. "Just by doing that. Do you believe that's possible?"

"I don't know," I said. "Perhaps it depends on the dog. So, don't mean to press you, but how are we off for security clearance?"

"Yeah, that's it! Some dogs have it and some don't," he said, having some kind of feeding frenzy on the subject. "Tom there is a bit of a dog himself in some ways. The good ways. He doesn't piss over people's front lawns if that's what you're thinking." He nodded to a small unshaven man snoring impassively in a chair. Tom definitely needed a shave, a clean uniform and, ideally, I guessed, some kind of basic body odor training. He had a large complicated gun laid across his lap, and I don't suppose anyone had thought it worth the risk of trying to tell him.

"I'm telling you, he looks like he's asleep, but he can smell a thief from fifty yards, and a drug dealer from twenty."

Although I told my brain to stop being so fucking witty, I couldn't help wondering if they had worked out Tom's yardage on every sort of criminal going.

"Hands in here for Blood Clearance, then," he said, tapping a machine on the counter that looked like an old-fashioned lever-arm orange press. The things had become obsolete twenty years

before in most places, and this one looked like it was held together mostly with Wrap-A-Tap-Tape—"the tape that cannot
stick to itself."

"Can I tell you something?" he said, as we both shoved our
arms into the machine.

"Sure." His hand fingered the lever arm as a voice in my head
pleaded with him to get the fuck on with it.

"I want to get a dog again," said the man, "but my wife likes
cats. So I say, well let's get a cat *and* a dog and she says, 'How
about a cow? My friend Berlinda has just got one, and she
swears by them.' So now we have these two cows. Pedigree
Friesians, they are. Very nice. But to be honest, they're no fun.
You can't take them for walks really, and they never sit when
you ask them to. I think dogs are just better. I think we should
get a dog. What do you think?"

"Sure," I said. "I'm all for dogs."

"Seeing Chico here has got me all excited about dogs again,"
he said, and finally crunched the handle down. A sharp stab of
pain arrowed through my wrist, as if a hedgehog had mistakenly
thrown one of its spines into my arm while re-creating some
great moment in Olympic javelin history.

"Ahh!"

"Yeah, sometimes does that; never found out why," said the
man, wiping his nose with his hand. "Canteen's first on the left.
That's an hour you've got in your arms. Don't be any longer;
they say the pain is worse than childbirth if you're late. Catch
some of Chico on the screens when you can. He's great. He
makes me laugh, but he has a serious side too."

"We'll try," I said, my head unable to clear away the pain fast
enough to fully grasp what he was on about.

"Zap those ads till the cows come home," he chuckled, "or as
I say to my wife, until they get within mooing distance." He settled back to watch the screens.

We grabbed the toolkit Teb had given us and lugged it clumsily toward the canteen. The overalls suddenly seemed to fit more badly than ever.

"Did you really, honestly think it would be quite that easy? I mean, get a life!" cried the security monkey from behind us.

I jerked to a halt. Had Tom's nose sniffed us out? Was he now standing miraculously alert behind the desk, wearing a loose, toothless smile like those pleased-with-themselves cowboys used to have in Westerns, and pointing that contraption of a gun at my head?

I turned slowly.

"Chico's coming, man. Go get him, Chico! Go on, boy."

Tom was still asleep and the security monkey had no interest in us at all. He was simply engrossed with the bank of screens. From here, I could now see there were about twenty monitors all showing the same picture of a rather excitable collie dog in grainy black and white. My mind squealed into gear, and I remembered one of the Zone Securities guys telling me that a hacker had dug into their security system and was playing *Chico the Dog* on all the security camera circuits twenty-four hours a day.

We turned, exchanged a glance, then sauntered down the corridor.

Tony Christie was crooning quietly over a PA somewhere as a faint reminder we were in Easy Listening, and I strained to hear the lyrics, but his voice got buried by a commotion up ahead as some poor idiot in an Odysseus Hat blindly staggered around the corner. Behind lumbered an overweight Zone Securities woman.

"Jesus, what is it with these people!" she managed to shout, breathing hard. The person under the Hat was gaining ground and shuffled frantically down the corridor, taking irregular, glancing blows off the walls and gouging out scrapes of plaster. Mat scooted into a doorway and I flattened myself on one wall, but the person in the Hat blindly veered toward me. I shifted to the other side, but the Hat clanged off the far wall and still staggered straight for me like it had a homing beacon or something.

I could hear the desperate person inside breathing furiously, like some unfit monster from a swamp. I jumped quickly to the other wall and watched the feet of the person in the Hat shuffling maniacally, his knees painfully banging the inside of the metal.

At the last moment, the Hat swerved for me again. This time there was not a cat in hell's chance to get out of the way, and I stiffened for the impact.

The clang was earsplitting.

The Hat shuddered an inch from my nose, wavered for a moment, then keeled over backwards like a felled redwood. I stood for a second as my mind took a frantic inventory of my body and discovered that I hadn't felt anything.

Then I noticed Mal nodding to something on the roof. The top of the Odysseus Hat had smacked a beam that protruded slightly lower than the rest of the ceiling, halting the poor sucker in his tracks just in front of me.

"What a waster!" said the woman loudly as she plodded up. Mostly, I suspected, for our benefit. "Some people have no manners! I preferred the old days when you could tar and feather them."

"Right," I said, wondering whether she was referring to the seventeenth century or just a time when she had actually done it herself.

"It's the paperwork I'll get for this," she huffed on, "but I just write 'C.B.B.' on everything they give me." She snorted, winding a leash over the Hat before grabbing a fire hose, slipping the nozzle expertly into the open end of the tube, and dousing down the person inside with water till they came around. " 'C.B.B.' Cannot be bothered," she said, enunciating each word proudly, before dragging the guy in the Hat to his feet and leading him away, dripping, to God knows what fate. "Never had anyone complain about it," she called back. "Not a soul!"

"We have an hour in here," I said to Mat. "An hour. And that is more than enough time to last me for the rest of my life."

We found the canteen easily enough and hunkered down on one of the shiny white tables, which I now realized were designed in the shape of pairs of handcuffs. It was virtually deserted and strewn with paper cups and discarded discharge forms. If they did have a Litter Beagle, it wasn't working. Perhaps they had assigned it to some other inconsequential task, like Chief Commissioner.

I watched Mat carefully unpack Teb's humongous toolkit, and he pulled out a couple of machines that were supposed to detect and zap the spores that gave rise to ad viruses. Why Teb had such things, I don't exactly know. But then, asking questions that contained the words "why" and "Teb" in the same sentence rarely got you anywhere, and I had learned not to do it.

"Come on, look busy," Mat said, handing me an Ad Sniffer.

"Do you have any idea at all what to do with these things?"

"Absolutely none. Now, let's get going."

I slipped the goggles on and stared at the thing with a mixture of confusion and vague temerity. I'd seen pairs of Virus Ad Cleanup staff in our office wandering around, usually showing faces of utter boredom that they tried to pass off as concentration, wheedling out ad spores that had somehow taken root in EasyDreams. It really didn't look that taxing.

The machine extended to about six feet and came with a harness that appeared to be something more appropriate to a parachute. There was a snout on the end, looking like a dog's muzzle, which made an unnecessary chewing sound when destroying a spore. I hauled the shoulder straps on and slung the thing out, then flicked the switch. It hummed like an overloud bee that'd spent too much time at the poppy flowers and was high on opium.

I kept my eyes peeled for any tiny scrunched-up bits of card among the flotilla of paper on the floor, and headed off. A skinny cop sat alone at a table, staring motionless at an ice cream that was topped with a gaily sizzling sparkler. Across the ice cream it declared "Surprise! Your Retirement Today!" in curly chocolate writing. The sparkler burned down to a stump but the guy didn't move. I didn't get too close.

A few tables away, a group of smart men in suits were earnestly examining a football-sized model of a chicken, and pointing at it animatedly. For what reason, I had no idea.

There were a few other cops about, and one seemed to be trying to chat up the Hispanic girl who was serving the coffee. And he was having some success, judging by her laughter. Or maybe she was just being polite. Either way, I think the cop was more interested in the size of her chest.

I wandered on through the canteen, picking up the odd bit of paper here and there, but finding nothing but scrunched-up cards for prostitutes or drug dealers—the latter with badly drawn sketches of lines of smack or coke next to a sketched nose.

To my right, a counter ran down one side of the canteen. Pictures of food turned slowly around on the plasi-screens, except for one that baldly announced LASAGNE IS NOW ILLEGAL. I had read someplace that a judge had decreed lasagne was a risk to public safety because someone had slipped over some and won a large damages claim. It had been withdrawn from menus as a result—although in some places they got around the ban by, apparently, calling the dish "Wheat Flaps Extra," which was permitted because of some bizarre, pedantic loophole in the law.

I edged more to the left of the canteen.

A squeal of outraged metal sang out from the midst of a group of people in the far corner, who were taking the reflective ribbed panels off the walls. They were some sort of maintenance team who had cordoned off the area with enough yellow tape to truss up a buffalo.

I continued to scan the floor, kicking over any bits of card that looked hopeful, but they were mostly empty sugar packets and discarded envelopes of teeth-cleaning "fuzz"—the powder you put in your mouth that eats all the plaque. Dentists hated the stuff because it cut into their profits, and there was even an armed wing of the Dentists Union that occasionally made raids on the "fuzz" factories to put them out of commission, claiming the stuff caused disease, but there was no evidence for it. It was just another case of someone trying to cover up their own greed or fear with the pretense of caring for others.

Without warning, the Ad Sniffer began shaking violently, like an excited dog on a leash. It sniffed out an ad spore and chewed it up in a flurry of vibration and unpleasant noise. Great, I thought. Now I'm a success at this job.

I pressed on, but the harsh, inhumane artificial light and soporific atmosphere lay heavily on my brain, and I drifted into a dreamy torpor. Events from the past days shambled through my mind in snippets, and it felt like my body was operating on backup power.

The next thing I knew, I was wrapped up in the yellow tape spooled around the cordoned-off area. Ahead were a herd of arc lights, burrowing into the darkness of a hole that spewed wires and ducts like a decomposing whale. All about the place, oversized machines with razor-sharp claws and excessively pointy pincers—each stamped WOMBAT RETRIEVAL—were poised to do God knows what.

"Hey! Can't you read?" called a woman who I guessed had

long brown hair, but it was coiled up in a series of tight complicated plaits so that it swam around her head like cats' tails.

"Sorry?"

"Jesus, we've got a Wombat in here. Can't you read?" she
bawled, marching over to me as I untangled myself. "Or should I
call a cop?" she added, stressing the cataclysmic irony of this
last idea. "See?" She tapped the tape. I glanced down at the lettering, and saw it had the phrase JUST FUCK OFF repeatedly printed
in neat black letters down it.

"Just swabbing for ad viruses to keep us all safe," I said, giving
her an answer to a question she hadn't asked—a trick workmen
love to use.

Over her shoulder, I saw a tiny sweating blond girl emerge
from the hole and cry, "Pincers! Wombat located! She's off the
rails and kicking! We may need to douse her like we did with
that Sally woman." And that got everyone scurrying to start up
one of the machines, and the woman with the brown cats' tails
was gone. She'd no doubt take her tightly reined-in indignation
out on some other sucker soon enough.

I scanned the room for Mat and caught sight of the men with
smart suits who had earlier been animatedly discussing the
model chicken. One of them was crying, and the others were
gathered around comforting him. Another was repeatedly offering the crying man the chicken. For what reason I had no idea.

An Odysseus Hat slashed through the transparent tube in the
roof with a battling swoosh and dislodged a butterfly of paint
from a beam. It floated down jerkily.

I pressed on with the virus scanning. There was no shortage
of scrunched-up cards scattered about the floor, and I gingerly
unraveled another. It was from a person who guaranteed to
guard your cat when it was wandering about outside. "Make
your cat the top cat," it said. "I'll follow your cat and tip the

balance in fights with other cats. I'll make sure your loved one is safe from the wheels of a bike." People really did pay for services like that, mainly because there were morons out there who had so little sense you would've had no trouble persuading them their mothers were badgers.

I picked up another ball of card and, crouching down, unraveled the wrinkled edges. "Don't you hate it when this happens?" it said. I smiled. I had found the fucker!

A hard, cold object tapped the back of my neck, and my excitement immediately drained away through my feet, sucking pints of my blood with it. Or so it seemed.

I heard a voice.

It was speaking English, but the words had a lot more vowels in them than I had been brought up to believe were necessary. It took me a moment to realize it was a deep Southern accent.

"Drop what's in your hand and turn around sloo-ly, mister," the voice said.

There was no fucking way I was dropping this card again. My brain raced for an idea, and I suddenly wished I had paid more attention to the magic set I had been given when I was seven. Then maybe I could palm this card, but I didn't even know what the phrase "palm this card" meant. I mean, palm it where? Detroit? The image of a trick that involved pulling some twisted bits of metal apart came to mind with unhelpful clarity. Seconds ebbed past and I stood up slowly, then shuffled around to see the unshaven cowboy, Tom, from the front desk pointing his tree trunk of a gun at me. "Said drop waaaas in your hand, mister!"

I opened my palm and the card fluttered to the floor like the entire consignment of confetti at a very tightly budgeted wedding.

"Jesus, man, can't have youse getting in with those drug dealers. Come on, I've a job for you," he said, dropping his gun and breaking into a broad smile.

This abrupt change of gear threw me. Tom clapped an arm around my shoulder with the strength of a brown bear who'd been at the steroids and bundled me toward the door like we were best friends.

I caught the eye of the guy sitting with the retirement ice cream and swiftly broke his stare. It was the man in the suit who had interrogated me in here earlier. There was a flicker of something in his eyes and I wasn't sure exactly what it was, but I wasn't hanging about to find out.

"Basically, they have the biggest moment of the year, of the decade—of the whole millennium—going on in Decom."

"Wha?" I said, with a guttural nonword.

"Sure! It's a huge celebration. Huge! Decommissioning our ten thousandth person. Can you believe that? Isn't that special? But there's some awful ad virus spreading in there. I'll introduce you to the Chief of Whoever-it-is. Come on!" And with that, he manhandled me out of the canteen and down a corridor jumbled with Odysseus Hats. The nearest was casually slapped with a smattering of colored labels, reminding me of an old-fashioned clothes trunk that had done its share of rail travel. Tom made no allowance for the fact I had a bulky Ad Sniffer slung about me, and it rang and clanked on almost every Hat as he blithely hustled me along. The effect was like a stuttering peal from a set of cracked old church bells.

Rooms off the corridor flashed by, and I only caught snippets of the conversations that flew out of them.

"Oy, Frenchy!" a young lad with greased-up hair cried. "I watched that film *Agincourt* last night, and your lot lost!" More Odysseus Hats. Then a whole bunch being wheeled on hand trucks so that they virtually blocked the corridor.

We squeezed our way through. The Ad Sniffer scraped down the metal sides of one Hat with a squeal that sent my ears into meltdown.

"Thank my huge great cock!" shouted a sweating mous-tached man, suddenly appearing from nowhere in front of my face, then running alongside me with massive effort. "Thank my cock! You're the Ad Sniffer guy, right?" he puffed. "I'm from computers. Computer's the game. Frank's the name. We've two Base Ones and a Klimy. I think it's the Klimy doing the damage in there, although the Base Ones may be eating the Damsen. Hoo! We had one a few months ago. They took out a whole egg!"

Despite everything, I felt duty-bound to draw a line in the sand here. I knew this sort of person, and this sort of computer jargon, and I hated it. Call it a deep-seated prejudice. Call it just plain stupid, but I pulled up doggedly, bringing our little party to a halt. Then I turned to this guy and said slowly, stressing each word, "I have absolutely no fucking idea what you're talking about."

There was a pause, and I watched as his face tried to pull an expression that was appropriate, but he just couldn't think of one and his broad smile remained there, with only a slight flick-ering in his eyes giving away any sign of uncertainty. In his mind, we were friends, compadres. In my eyes, he was the sort of dickhead I had never had any time for. I'm sorry, but there it is. I found, with this sort of person it's better to cut to the chase. Or ideally, cut to the bit after the chase.

"You better leave Mister here alone," said Tom, cutting the pause short. "He's a job to do, double quick." And he lugged me away as the moustached man's voice floated down the corridor after us.

"Good stuff!" he cried. "Just thank my cock you're here al-ready."

Somehow, I felt Tom and I had bonded over the incident, which was a little weird. We turned a corner to another corridor, where windows looked down onto one of the wide streets in

Easy Listening. As I glanced out, I saw a man sitting on a bench smoking a pipe, and a plasi-screen above him with some ad about cardigans that began targeting someone with the name Luke K34. An alarm bell didn't so much ring in my head as explode, then a variety of other alarm bells came to see what the excitement was about.

That was the name of the Belgian assassin Caroline had said would come after me to sell me those ludicrous encyclopedias. How had he found me? My brain coughed like an engine struggling on a cold winter's morning. I had to get that card and just get out of here. Time was definitely ticking.

"Here's we are, mister," drawled Tom, cutting into my thoughts as we came to a couple of pointlessly monumental double doors that gave the impression we were entering a particularly crucial Roman temple.

Stamped across them in dramatic bulging metal letters, ten feet above our head, it said:

DECOMMISSIONING.

32

The doors sliced apart, allowing a sliver of light to escape, then the gap widened into a blinding door-to-door salesman grin. I squinted involuntarily, and tilting my head down saw a deep wound gouged in the wood of the doors where the Odysseus Hats must have chafed and torn each time they had been wheeled through.

There was a sudden, unexpected smell of grease and cauliflower, then a faint whisper of music that sounded like a swing band wafted about. I looked at Tom and he nodded faintly, with the serene smile of a cat who not only got the cream, but also quite a bit of the salmon mousse and possibly a couple of large brandies.

He ushered me through into Decom with a proud chew of his

gum, and I realized he clearly felt a part of all this. I moved warily into the glaring curtain of arc light that made it impossible to see anything for ten yards, then stepped beyond into a pool of soft shadow and let my aching eyes readjust.

We were nestled on a wide balcony flanked by two stone ramps that meandered down on either side. I followed Tom's gaze and saw far below the familiar little decommissioning areas, each with its own gaggle of machines huddled around, except that everything was turned on its head.

There was a carnival going on down there now.

The place was decorated with delicate midsummer party lights and streamers that wound like Shakespearean ivy over everything. People in cocktail dresses were swanning about, and others in less-well-fitting outfits were not so much swanning as waddling like startled ducks. There was an ageing swing band playing with the enthusiasm of a group of teenagers who were more drunk than they ought to be, and a stage area hooped around one of the decommissioning areas, with a banner whirled about it proclaiming: "Our ten thousandth decommissioning! Thank you, boys and girls!"

And there, marooned and ignored amid the bustle and chatter, was a tired, middle-aged lady with her arms outstretched in the decommissioning machine, and her feet in the clips, simply waiting alone and in confusion.

Around her in the melee, waiters swooped with canapés and drinks. People mingled gaily, and a little party of officials were huddled on the stage just behind her, laughing at jokes that probably weren't all that funny as they fidgeted with the nervous self-importance of those about to make a speech.

"On the stage," said Tom at last, more to himself than me, and grabbed my arm with a waft of body odor that nearly sent me unconscious. "He's got his tail in a twozzy," he informed me at one point on the way down, and I got the feeling this was part of

a much larger sentence, but the rest of it was drowned out by
the expectant hubbub of the purring crowd. We scooted down
onto the floor below, and hit the melee almost at a run, so I was
certain we would collide disastrously with one or two cocktail
dresses and maybe a few waiters. But a passageway opened up
before us—the same way the crowds part impossibly late for a
racing cyclist on an alarmingly steep mountain, and I put it
down to Tom's somewhat terrifying presence coupled with his
smell. It would certainly have had any self-respecting skunk
reaching for the deodorant.

Chiffon dresses in shiny blues and pinks slipped past, and the
ring of glasses and squeals of excited laughter fell around us like
blown rose petals. The next moment, I was hauled up on the
stage and directed to shake hands with someone who was partially bald. And then someone else. I cried at my brain to catch
up with events and still not be dawdling on the images it had
seen on the way through the crowd. The men I was meeting had
wide business-meeting smiles, firm handshakes, and jackets
that reached around them like wrestlers' bear hugs, betraying,
all in all, that they'd had a few too many desserts over the years.

The second guy took me aside on the stage.

"Jesus, man. It's a godsend you were in the building," he
growled, and I recognized him with a shock as the politician
Elnor Elnorian—the man who had made the feted corruption
speech a few Thanksgivings before. His silver hair looked thinner,
and his eyes darker from the plasi-screens. "Not that I mean God
had anything to do with it at all. Thank God I'm an atheist, eh?"
he corrected himself, staring at me, gauging my character as
people in politics do—weighing up my likely beliefs and desires
and mentally looking for weaknesses. "My ass saved, though."

"Your ass in my hands? That's a privilege, sir," I said, not
breaking eye contact, and fortunately the comment didn't get
past his thick smile, which was just as well when I realized what

I had just said. "What's the lady here for?" I added, nodding at the back of the woman in the decommissioning stand to change the subject.

"Probably tried to take over the whole world!" he said, widening his smile to impossible proportions—and, I guessed, trying to inject some humor to cover his ignorance. "Mr. X...I've a feeling we've met somewhere? X. Did I award you a Sparkling Citizen Kitchen Colander?" I could see his brain ferreting about in his memory and I didn't like this. We had never met, but I didn't want anyone to start making inquiries as to who the fuck I was. And I'd certainly never won one of his Golden Colanders, which were handed out to people when he needed to look caring.

"No, I think I would remember that, sir," I said. "What's your problem here?"

"Yes, good. Right. I've caught an ad virus on the way here, the damn thing keeps going off every few minutes, and these zappers they throw at me can't cope with it at all. You appreciate I've a speech to make, and it's central to my campaign."

"Another of your famous speeches, eh?"

"Oh, yes. It's time to reassure the record companies how confident I am in their ability to take us forward into a new era of space exploration. I'm moving the emphasis away from God, you see. He's only made real by belief after all, isn't he? So I'm going to stop that belief at the source. Shazam! You see?"

"I'll happily leave that kind of thinking to politicians."

"Oh, come on! Don't be so coy, Mr. X. Look, it has an equation: G equals B squared over F," he said, pointing to a huge sign hanging behind him. "You know what that means? Simple! God equals belief squared over fear. You see that? It's as simple as that."

"That's a pretty weird idea; a lot of people might think you're some kind of power-crazy dickhead, sir."

"No, no, it's all proven by professors and cleverer men than us. It's been through the mill, as they say, and come out solid as a rock. G equals B squared over F. It's the way the future is going for all of us, so you'd better come along, because the train is leaving, Mr. X."

"I've always liked walking. A lot."

"Well, I can see you're stubborn as hell, but it's a great future, Jonny. A future of truth," he said, slapping me on the back. "Now, let's cure this damned ad virus, shall we, my boy?"

"Of course, sir," I said, nodding and staring at him, trying to force my desire to keep my cover overpower my intense desire to deck him.

But it was impossible to cure his ad virus.

The scanner I had merely ate the spores from which people caught the ad viruses, but once in the body it was like a disease. You had to wait for it to run its course while the blood built up immunity. This was first-grade stuff and he should have known it, but I guess he didn't have much time for actual thinking, being a politician and all.

"Hold still," I said, realizing the truth wasn't going to get me anywhere. I flicked on the scanner and the thing hummed and fussed. Elnor held a powerful eye contact with me, and I felt vaguely uncomfortable until the moment was broken by the scanner detecting a spore on his clothes. It began vibrating excitedly before eating it in its ludicrous way.

"Ah! Well done!" said another official, barreling up at that precise moment with a rather flimsy woman hanging off his arm. She was wearing more makeup than the average clown.

"We need more people like you," said Elnor with unexpected jollity, and I realized he was playing to these people. "Here's my card. Ring me if you ever need anything. And I mean anything!" He handed it over with a firm hand and flitted back to the little group of officials at the back of the stage, wiping the memory of me away in three short steps.

I glanced at the card. "Elnor Elnorian. Whatever I said, don't get any ideas about contacting me, ever, OK? I'm a busy man," it read in italics. I shook my head. At least he was open about being two-faced.

"Whole place is full of spores, mister. Chief wants you to sweep it right off, or we might get sued or something," said Tom suddenly, at my elbow. I nodded, inadvertently making eye contact with the lady in the decommissioning stand. From the balcony above, I had thought she had looked scared and lonely, but from up close I noticed something far more remarkable. There was a strength in her eyes, and a stillness, as though she had already accepted what was going to happen and was not afraid anymore. It was so unexpected and powerful that I paused, but as I opened my mouth to speak, Tom bundled me off the stage and the Ad Sniffer immediately got interested in a spore on one of the waiters. He tried to swat me away with furious indignation as the thing nuzzled under his jacket and began humming with pleasure, but the Sniffer was pretty persistent. It had that one, then leapt immediately on the tail of a woman's dress. I could hardly control the excitement of the thing.

And so it went.

It turned out there were spores everywhere on the floor of Decom, and I realized someone must have released some sort of ad virus bomb in here because I couldn't go ten feet without finding one. I began to see that discovering one on Elnor Elnorian had not been such a coincidence, after all. The Sniffer started becoming riotous—either not used to dealing with quite so many spores, or it was a rogue one Teb had not quite fixed properly. It began making other satisfying noises and finally, after eating an apparently huge ad virus off a woman in a blue dress, flagrantly burped in her face.

I'd had enough by then, and I'd finally managed to lose Tom, so I struggled for the OFF button and whacked it before the machine noticed. It took me a second to realize the lights had dimmed and the swing band had halted.

I scanned the place. I was in a hurry, but something made me hang back as Elnor Elnorian stepped to the stage. Despite everything, he had a certain magnetic presence, and I wanted to hear what the bastard had to say.

An expectant hush rippled through the crowd, who were buoyed up by the alcohol and ready to applaud anything. The thought occurred to me that many of them might well have been paid to be here.

"Ladies and gentlemen, boys and girls, brothers and sisters and..." he paused, with a well-rehearsed twitch of the mouth, "...and that elk they've supposed to have trained up in Nebraska to read..." Huge laughter. "Seriously. We all belong to one thing—to this universe. A universe that talks to us with its math and its geometry and its order and its mysteries. A universe that is telling us it is the power behind our lives. We have no evidence for some mystical God—nothing but a lot of stories— but we do have the universe. We can see it every day of our lives, and that's why I believe the space fund and space exploration are things that are fundamental rights of every man, woman, and child on this earth. To support renewed space exploration and to cut the budgets of all religious institutions is the clear way forward, for all of you."

I didn't like the sound of this. I didn't like the way it connected to thoughts of assassinating God. Maybe it was a coincidence but it was an uncomfortable one.

"Technology can only be good. Technology can only serve to smooth our way through this world. I give you these words," he crooned with faked sincerity. "I give you these four simple words, to hold and caress as each and every one of you moves forward with your own lives. Four words—"

"Plink! Plink! Fzzzz! Fuck!" cut in a voice from his ad virus deciding to play itself with impeccable timing. "Plink! Plink! Fzzzz! Fuck!" it sang again, as it was picked up and amplified over the whole place.

Everyone watched as Elnor's face wrestled painfully with the moment.

"Hot Ice Cubes!" chirped on the hologram. "Buy some tubes... today!"

The crowd of officials started clumsily battling with a number of zappers, but the ad virus wasn't responding—probably because it was a different strain.

"I'm sorry. Technical problems." And Elnor smiled aggressively at the audience.

"Hot Ice Cubes are the technology of next week in your pocket," ranted on a holographic voice from the ad virus. "Use them to warm up drinks or soup. Keep them for emergencies when you..."

"Right," cried Elnor, trampling supremely loudly over the words from the hologram as he tried to rescue the event. "I would like to declare the ten thousandth person here...decommissioned!" And he ceremoniously tugged down a huge lever by the woman in the clamps, then acknowledged a response that didn't happen.

Finally, uncertain applause broke out from the party of officials on the stage, which began to firm up as people in the hall became more confident about joining in. And then a slight buzzing of chatter built up.

I saw the jolt of pain slip into the poor woman's arms as the machines kicked in, but she blinked for only a second, then seemed to let it go. I watched, transfixed by her strength as she stood there marooned amid this sea of chatting people with her arms outstretched. There was no anger in her eyes, but something calmer. My head started to feel weird again, and the sensation

I'd had before of warm melting syrup dripping out of spaces in my skull where it had been cooped up began to overwhelm me. I looked up and felt as though the woman was staring straight at me.

It seemed as though her eyes were burrowing into my head with some message, but I didn't know what that message was. The people around me began to fade, and I was left in a strange defocused tunnel with just me and this woman at the other end. My brain gave the sensation it was melting like hot cheese, and thoughts began to slide perilously around, like cargo that has broken free on the deck of a ship. It was beyond my control, and yet it was happening inside me. I tried desperately to focus on reality, but all I saw was the woman in the clamps still staring at me, and now she seemed annoyed that I didn't get what she was trying to convey. My eyes creeped shut, forced down by some outrageous weight.

I swayed unsteadily.

An aching pain jabbed at the base of my skull, and then erupted into an unearthly fork of agony coursing through my head. I screamed silently as my life seemed to slip into some other place, and I battled with bits breaking down, cells breaking down, my own self breaking down into its constituent parts. The clutter of things said and things left unsaid swirled inside me and somehow dislodged something pivotal—unleashing a white light that burst through me like it was fracturing open some dark forgotten area of the universe. And in that moment, a chunk of memory tumbled back in one great lump.

It was a while before I could dissect what was in it; a long second before I could make sense of the images and words and feelings that were there.

And then I realized what had happened.

I had remembered about Eli's brother. I had remembered all the events from the day Jack had died.

33

"Jonny! Jonny!" I heard a voice somewhere. "Jonny!" And then a tugging at my arm. "I've got it! I got the card. Jonny! Come on! Let's get out of this fucking place. Jonny?"

I stood motionless, still struggling to reattach myself to the reality around me. The woman was gone from the decommissioning machine now, but a few of the crowd still hung about draining the last dregs of free hospitality from the event, and I had no idea how long I had stood there.

"Jonny? You OK?" Mat's voice wavered.

"I have to see Eli," I said, "I've just remembered what happened that day on the mountain with Jack."

Mat's face softened and he put his arm around me, knowing I had somehow unleashed a plateload of inner demons.

"Oh, Jonny. What a time to be dealing with that too," he whispered.

"Yeah," I said. "I must tell it all to Eli. She has to know."

"OK, that's cool. Come on." Then he added, "We've only a few minutes of security clearance left in our arms, so let's get out of here."

We scurried over to the stone ramp and scampered up toward the gargantuan entrance doors. I tried desperately to put what I had remembered out of the way until a time I could go over it all properly, but my mind was seeping sadness and guilt into my soul. It ran through my body like an upturned bottle of olive oil in a handbag, finding every corner.

Mat sensed my head was all over the place and eased me down the corridors, weaving us through the ever-growing traffic of Odysseus Hats and generally making a path. I wondered about Eli; it was almost a certainty she'd be at Inconvenient. She worked most evenings there, too generous to take the time off she was owed.

"Thank my huge cock!" cried a voice from a room as we passed, and I fell back into the present moment with an aching sigh of annoyance. "Thank my cock!" cried the same man I had seen earlier, hopping out after us as we shimmied onward through the crowds toward the entrance. "Computer's the game! Frank's the name! You nailed it, right? And it was a Klimy, wasn't it?"

He babbled on, not waiting for my response. "I knew you'd nail it. I could tell from your eyes. This man is going to nail that Klimy! I thought. Nice job, soldier."

That was too much. I halted abruptly with a cocktail of frustration, annoyance, and bottled sadness scouring through me.

"I'm going! I'm going!" said the man, holding his hands up

before I could say a word. "Just thank my cock!" he cried back from down the corridor. "Thank my huge great cock!"

Mat had carried on ahead, unaware I had stopped, and now he bobbed in and out of my sight, skipping among the crowds of Zone Securities personnel and Odysseus Hats, probably assuming I was right behind him and I was an idiot not to be. The corridor seemed busier than ever. I struggled to pass three Father Christmases who must have been here from Christmas Single for some reason. They were "ho-ho-ho-ing" to such a degree that sending them on a lifetime tour of especially dull areas of Finland would have not been too harsh a punishment, as far as I was concerned.

I barged forward, trying to get Mat back into sight, but a Hat coming the other way wobbled off its hand truck and fell sideways across the corridor, blocking the passageway entirely. The sadness that coursed through me quelled most of my frustration. There were about three minutes before the hour in my arm ran out, and that was still enough to get me out of here.

I watched the Zone Securities woman take a huge, worn wooden mallet out of a case on the wall and smash at the Hat repeatedly until it scraped free, taking gouges of plaster with it. The cries of the man inside the thing rang on after each blow, and I guessed he wouldn't be able to hear jack shit for hours. Perhaps he'd still be vibrating too much to notice, anyway. The Securities woman replaced the mallet in the case and I sprang over the Hat while it still lay poleaxed on the floor. Everyone else was hanging back, waiting for the poor man to get up, but I had ditched politeness sometime earlier.

Mat was nowhere in sight now, and I guessed he'd hold up for me outside, realizing that I was caught up in this porridge of madness. The corridor became less crowded, and I pushed on as quickly as I dared without drawing too much attention to myself. I wondered about the guy on the front desk; he was the last line of security in this place, and it would be ideal if he was still engrossed in Chico the Dog. A sensation of something light touched my neck, then a hand yanked me ferociously sideways through a set of doors, like the snap of a mousetrap.

"Let's have a look at you," said a man in a suit, holding my neck with the overpowerful grasp of a madman. "Yeah, you're the guy that I saw yesterday, and now look at you in this fancy costume. You're no ad virus worker. You were some dream architect. Well, how do you do? You're my ticket back into a job here."

The day before this man had sent me to the Half-Gones, and earlier he'd been the one hunched over the retirement ice cream. His suit was more crumpled, and he looked like someone had battered his ego around the block with a heavy spade, but it was the same man all right. There was a terrified nervousness in his eyes that reminded me of a lost puppy that had spent the night wandering the streets on its own, its whole life-support system suddenly gone.

"Surprise retirement! Well, have I got a surprise for them," he hissed, his eyes bulging.

"Surprise?" I said, trying to generate some kind of relationship with him in the hope it might lead somewhere.

"Yeah," said the man. "Surprise!" And at that moment, an Odysseus Hat slammed down from the ceiling above and covered him with a wild clang. I stood stunned for a long second, wondering what had happened. No one in the canteen seemed to notice anything. The cop on the far side was trying to put his arm around the Hispanic girl. She was resisting with a worried smile, while the Wombat Retrieval team were all gathered around the hole in the wall with some machine or other making a grinding noise like a steam train sliding slowly off a rusty tin roof. Sparks spluttered out from the hole like sprays of luminous phosphorescence. I guessed all that racket had smothered any noise from the Hat. Otherwise, the place was pretty much deserted.

I put my ear to the Hat but I couldn't hear groaning of any kind. The guy was out cold.

There was no sign of Mat, and I had an uneasy feeling about this. The only other people who could want me free from Zone Securities were the Belgian encyclopedia salesman or the Riders.

I decided not to hang around to find out which of them it was. I only had about thirty seconds' security clearance left in my arm anyway, and I unashamedly bolted for the door.

Outside, Mat was waiting at the top of the steps. "OK?" he said, as I crashed out, breathing hard.

"Yeah. You didn't drop one of those metal Hats on some guy just now, did you?"

"Not me," he said, shaking his head.

"Well, someone did, thankfully. Come on. Let's get over to Inconvenient. Eli will be there, and I want to tell her now. I can't hold on to this anymore," I said, heading toward the steps.

The warm afternoon sun wrapped over the scattering of buildings and plasi-screens that squatted sadly in this chewed-up part of town as we skipped down the steps toward the bike. Someone was probably following us, but right now I wasn't looking back. I was thinking about Eli.

And I was thinking about Eli's brother, Jack.

34

Mat's bike was parked in a narrow street, tucked in next to a boarded-up bar that hunched over a small side alley. We carefully checked around, but the whole area was deserted, so we squeezed out of the ad virus uniforms before tossing them to a Litter Beagle that was nosing about in a doorway.

It grasped at them gratefully, battling with sudden excitement to suck the sheer weight of material down one of its nozzles. We folded up the ad scanners and shoved the whole bulging toolkit hurriedly onto the bike carrier. Then I slid onto the back. The crash suit hummed as it bustled around me, fitting itself snugly. Mat's did the same.

The memory I had back seemed to lie cold and detached in

my head, making the other images in my mind look faded. It was as though it had a different weight to it that made it stand apart. I guessed I had suppressed it for so long now that suddenly being out in the open allowed it to pulsate in this weird way. Mat fired the bike, and we roared away in a shock of smoke, heading off through Easy Listening toward the outskirts of Jazz, Compilation, then on to The Most Inconvenient Bar in the World.

I didn't pay too much attention to the journey, and most of the images I saw tended to pass through my head without getting digested. Maybe I should have been on the alert for the Riders, but I had reached saturation point and there was no longer as much room for fear in my head as there had been.

Jazz was its usual self-indulgent mix. I was accosted by a memory of ordering a pizza just around the corner from the street we were on, only for it to arrive topped solely with olives and nothing else—not even cheese—because, I was told, "that's what the chef is really into at the moment." That was one of the reasons I avoided Jazz—not because I had any deep dislike of the people there, but merely because I liked normal pizzas and Long Island Iced Teas that didn't come made with sherry and cloves "as a new experimental form."

We banked a corner and cruised into Compilation, which was a silly zone and tended to attract people who tried to avoid making decisions about anything. There was a bland mix of all the zones here, which they always earnestly argued gave the place the very best of everything. But in reality, it was nothing but a stodgy characterless mess, which—sadly—summed up many of the people who lived here too.

It was the sort of place dull people gravitated toward. The sort who had got to be forty before they were thirty—men who were going bald before their time and running around in over-neat clothes as though they had been dressed by their mums

that morning, who also combed their hair and packed their ter-
rifyingly ordered bags.

Mat throttled down and turned into an alley that contained an
unexpectedly chic bar called Flame Rouge. It bristled with shiny
metal and wires that zigzagged around it like some sort of
homage to the wings of a Wright brothers' plane. Flame Rouge
filled all its bars with "edible smoke," whatever that was, but the
result was you couldn't see a foot in front of your hand. It was
popular with students who liked things that make no sense—
perhaps because it reminded them of their essays.

Mat throttled to a stop and we both snapped off our crash
suits and hopped from the bike. We were as close as we could
comfortably get to the FBZ around Inconvenient. A frantic noise
of someone slamming pans about, together with raised Chinese
voices, wafted in from one of the tenement flats somewhere
above and suggested the preparation of one meal was not going
as smoothly as it might have.

For some reason, it triggered a craving in me for a beefsteak
tomato and mozzarella salad, strewn with olive oil and fresh
basil and served with another plate containing a neatly sliced
ripe peach. The image was tantalizing. Down on the street, a
few young boys milled about with some girls, laughing and trying to impress them with their macho style and showy, gym-
honed muscles. Behind them, blue smoke funneled orgasmically
out from an open window at the side of Flame Rouge. As I
watched, it drifted carelessly about, staining the sky in dark random patches.

We started down toward the tight, dark path that was snuck
in between two crumbling brick warehouses and beyond was
the footbridge, which crossed where the river had been. The alley was cold and I shivered, feeling we could get trapped here
and there would be no escape, so it was a relief to reach the
small rusting bridge that flaked red paint. The river was still

missing and I guessed the cleaning firm who'd removed it had probably sold it on the black market somewhere, then slipped away to set up another shady company somewhere else.

We walked into the old reclamation yard and wound our way through three vast French-style staircases, swaggering up to floors that didn't exist anymore, their treads worn down by groups of kids who came to play here now. When I was younger, I could have sat on the top step myself, legs dangling into the air, smoking a cigarette with friends and watching the sun draw long shadows across the glory of the Thin Building on the horizon.

We headed on in silence, past some graffiti proclaiming "Rock and roll is our epiphany" in spidery letters, scrawled on a discarded, peeling old door, and I realized Mat was probably wrapped up in thoughts of that day we were all on the mountain together too. The three of us had been inseparable then, but I knew he'd understand why Eli had to be there when I told the story. I owed her that, and so much more.

We weaved our way past strewn piles of rotting sash windows, a whole clump of collapsed greenhouses that shed glass like tears, and a pair of outsized ornamental stone ostriches, which stared unblinkingly as the acid in each passing rainstorm gently stroked away their feathers.

The brass doors of the Thin Building shimmered warmly in the late-afternoon sun, burning like a wall of golden flame. But as we got closer, the mirage died away and the brass turned an ethereal white. We snaked past some pitted enamel baths and I noticed, with a start, a piece of motorbike lying inside one. It must have ended up there the day the Riders rode me out of the window in Inconvenient. We reached the doors and I gripped the small, twisted box section of brass that swooped out as a handle, and it swung forward with a stiff swoosh.

The long, thin hallway with its vast, cathedral-like ceiling hummed with a deep resonating silence—the sort of silence you would somehow expect to only find in the emptiness of outer space or when a dull lecturer has asked a particularly pointless question. Then three sets of elevator doors broke open almost together and people spilled out in unexpected numbers, fanning out across the hall from the far end, and I felt like I detected a collective slouch of annoyance from them as we threaded our way through. We scooted into one of the elevators before it could leave.

"Inconvenient," I said.

"Yup," said the elevator simply, and the doors slotted shut with a thwump. I was half-waiting for some sort of hassle from the elevator, but it seemed remarkably subdued and kept a stoic silence until we were almost there.

"What's it like in Europe?" it said eventually, as though it had been pondering this.

"What do you mean?" I said.

"What's it like in Europe? I was thinking of going. Or perhaps even to Panama."

"You're an elevator! You can't go anywhere except up or down," I said with more vehemence than was probably a good thing.

"Well, I . . . haven't tried," said the elevator.

"It's dark in Europe," said Mat—sensing, perhaps, that I was just going to pointlessly antagonize the thing. "And in Panama they have some great waves."

"Cool," said the elevator. "What about Baja?"

"Baja. The wide beaches crawl down to an ocean that is peeling with right-handers. We've had some good times down in Baja and Isla Todos Santos. We went there one time with Eli's brother and Jeff, and surfed with the dolphins."

"Who's Jeff?" I said, almost involuntarily, as though motivated by a part of my brain that I didn't know existed. "Who's Jeff?" I repeated, more insistently, staring at Mat. He looked at me in confusion.

"He's...he's...Jeff. Um...fucked if I know. What am I talking about?"

The doors slid open. "See you guys around," said the elevator. "Either here or in Baja."

"Yeah," I said and we stepped out into The Most Inconvenient Bar in the World.

It was completely and utterly deserted.

35

The lights were dim and there was no one about, although after a moment, I made out a couple of voices talking earnestly somewhere. The jukebox was jubilantly playing steam train sound effects for reasons known only to itself, and there were tables and chairs stacked carelessly in riotous piles. I was frankly impressed that Inconvenient even had that many chairs, and glanced at Mat hoping he had some theory that would explain all this, but he just shrugged.

"Closed! Closed! Closed!" said the huge bouncer with OTTER tattooed on his forehead, striding over. "Elevators have orders not to bring anyone else up here. What the fuck was it thinking about?" he shouted as the thing shut its doors quickly. He began to usher us back impatiently. "Come on! Out of 'ere!"

"Where's Eli?" I said, ignoring him, but he didn't appear to hear.

"Caroline E61 sent us," Mat added, and it was the mention of her name that broke the bouncer's stride.

"Oh. You two," he said stepping back and suddenly placing our faces. "OK, well..." He paused reassessing. "I can do you one drink, but that's it. And you'll have to wait for forty-five minutes."

Mat scanned the place. "Dark. But there's no one else here, is there?"

"Standards to keep, don't we?" cried the bouncer, with an impatient gesture, as though this was one thing he would gladly kill a man over. "This is Inconvenient. Just 'cos there's no one here doesn't mean you don't have to wait in line! You stand at the bar for forty-five minutes and you might just get served. I don't care what asses you've been licking. Take it or fuck off."

"That's cool," I replied. "It's cool. Is Eli here?" The bouncer dropped his shoulders and nodded, then motioned us with his eyebrows to go through to the bar as though he had used up his quota of words for the day. Bouncers are, of course, the masters of understatement and can talk to each other in a secret language called "laconic." This consists entirely of raising their eyebrows, shrugging their shoulders, and occasionally sniffing. You watch them next time you have a chance. You might think they're just standing there outside a club staring into space, but actually they're having a deep conversation about quantum physics or something.

We wandered into the bar area and found it had been turned virtually inside out, so we picked our way over the assorted debris, righted a couple of stools, and hunkered down on them. The bouncer had gone off somewhere—possibly to give the elevator a hard time for bringing us up here—and the jukebox now began to play the noise of old-fashioned racing cars, followed up with some jungle noises.

"Weird," I said, gesturing at the room. "Definitely weird."

"Yup," said Mat. "But hell, let's be cool about it."

"Yeah, I guess. Can I use your phone, please, Mat? I could ring Eli, then call those punks who stole my house." As I've said before, Mat stuck with a handset and had never signed up for Skin Media. He'd held out for so long, handsets had almost become interesting again.

"Might be low on horse manure," he said, throwing my standard joke back at me with a satisfied smile.

"Yes," I said. "But as long as it's wound up that shouldn't matter."

I tried Eli, but she wasn't answering and I was partly relieved. I didn't know how much I wanted to say over the phone, anyway. Mat dug out the crumpled card and handed it to me before I had to ask.

"Fuckers," I added, thinking back.

"Fuckers," echoed Mat and I smiled, tapping in the number. It sounded like the same hood as last time picked up.

"Eddy-yo!"

"You still got my house?"

"Hey! Moose! It's you!" he cried. "I knew you'd call! It's the Moose again," he shouted to someone farther off.

"You still got my house?" I repeated.

" 'Course! We love your house, Moose. I was getting worried about you, after all that shooting last time. Did you try the singing thing I told you about to calm down?"

"Listen," I said, trying to keep to the point, "we had a deal. The books and things I want from my house for the information you need about how to work the lights in the bathroom and where the stairs are for the roof garden."

"Sure, Moose. I'm cool about that. Our client hasn't asked about delivery yet, anyway. Come on, try some singing for me. Just for me."

"Forget the singing," I said, "I'll be over tonight. Now, where the fuck are you?"

36

I handed the phone back to Mat, feeling a vague sense of shock that I finally might get some answers. Outside I caught a glimpse of a bike in the FBZ and had a terrible sense of déjà vu, but when I looked again it was gone and I put it down to my brain being overloaded. Eli appeared at the end of the room and my throat swelled.

Seeing her made the sadness from the day on the mountain fall over everything again like a thick velvet blanket.

"Hey, you guys!" she said with a kick of surprise, and ran up to give first Mat, then me, a hug. "This is cool. A final drink together in the old haunt. That seems appropriate, doesn't it?"

"What do you mean?" I said.

"You've not heard? We got a call from the management ten minutes ago, saying the bar was getting too convenient, so they decided to move straightaway. Customers weren't happy," she said, indicating the mess.

"Where to?" I said, considering where actually could be more inconvenient than this place.

"Nebraska," she said. "At least, that's the rumor the guys have heard. They've decided not to give out the address so it's more inconvenient to find. Even for staff. You have to hand it to them, I suppose."

"Shame," I said, thinking I would miss the place.

"Are you OK, Jonny? You look really tired. Is it Emma?"

"No, that's all finished now, but I'm cool about it. It's something else, Eli. It's Jack."

"Jack?" Her whole tiny body seemed to stiffen with surprise.

"I've just got my memory back about the day."

"Oh, Jonny. You didn't have to come here."

"I did, Eli. I had to tell you. I have to. Please."

"Jonny," she said softly, and I sensed she had always known this moment would come, but she had not expected it now. I could see her eyes glisten with sadness as her love for her brother Jack shone through.

"I have to tell you. I want you to know how it was. I have to get it all out. Please."

She sat down on Mat's chair, eyes wide with held tears.

"You know Jack and I got separated from Mat on the snowed-up ridge, as the weather swamped us?" I said, and she nodded. "Mat had gone ahead to check the route, and we waited for half an hour, then knew we had to get moving or we'd freeze." She had heard all of that before, but I wanted to make sure she remembered.

She looked at me. And I suddenly realized how difficult this was for her—suddenly saw the depth of her loss—and I wondered if it was too selfish to tell her like this. But she had to know and I sensed, deep down, that this was the right thing to do.

I took a breath, immersing myself in the memory, and told Eli and Mat everything.

37

I had been roped up with Jack, but by the time we got sorted, Mat's tracks were pretty well bleached away by the wind and whipping snow. We were scared about Mat, but the only plan that made sense was to make our way along the ridge and hope for some reason he had gone on ahead and we'd catch him. It didn't even cross our minds he might have got disoriented and was walking down one of the other arêtes, but as it turned out it was just as well that he did.

I was leading Jack out, prodding with my ice ax to make sure we weren't strolling out onto some gigantic cornice, when the wind just exploded in a freak gust. I turned to see the whole side of the mountain bend like plastic, then shudder before it gave under us in a neat slab of avalanche, like a curtain pole tearing out its fixings and the cloth falling in one single, smooth sheet.

I remember watching Jack go, almost transfixed by the sight, then in the next sliver of a moment I went too, legs sucked down the mountain in a screaming swarm of white. It was as if I had been standing on an old-fashioned haystack that had broken up beneath me into a rain of tumbling bales. I was tossed about, all the time terrified I'd land on my ice ax. I kept thinking about how you are supposed to try and swim to the top of an avalanche, so when it settles you aren't frozen in, but I might as well have been dropped through a never-ending stack of greenhouse roofs for all the control I had. The seconds stretched like chewing gum, each one on a knife-edge of confusion and survival, then abruptly the gray light of the world shut off, everything snapped pitch-black, and I just fell, for ages and ages, as though I had dropped into another sort of world.

I stopped in the darkness with a jolt that pulled every limb out of its socket. It took me a moment to get my breath and find my senses, then I found I ached—chronically. I moved my arms and legs; nothing was broken. I tried to focus, but found I was hanging. I reached out with my arms and just spun, like a sycamore seed in the darkness. I felt for the pencil light around my neck and tilted it up. There was a bulging shadow about fifteen feet above me and I stared, because it seemed somehow familiar. Then I recognized the shape of a boot, and the whole thing clicked into place; it was Jack up there. I shouted for maybe five minutes, but I got no reply, and my throat swelled with worry.

I trained the thin pencil beam of light up into the darkness, but it just vanished into nothingness. We were both hanging in some gigantic crevasse, and all I could think was that the middle of the rope must have snagged somewhere above us, perhaps over a snow bridge, leaving us both dangling on either side like two limp bits of fishing bait. I checked my harness, hoping to find some gear, but it had been ripped off. All I had was one crampon on my left boot.

I tried to climb the rope, but the vibration just caused it to drop a couple of inches with an alarming shudder. Whatever was snagging the rope above, it wasn't that solid, and it wasn't going to hold forever.

I flicked the flashlight around. The right-hand side of the crevasse was perhaps fifteen feet away, but to my left the light just dropped away into thick darkness. Primeval creaks were groaning from the depths of the chasm, and I knew this was not a place meant for humans. I felt a horrible fear ache through my chest. I put the flashlight in my mouth and, trying not to shake, carefully took the crampon off my left boot and slipped the straps over my right hand so the crampon spikes faced outwards. Then I leaned back and began to make the rope swing, gaining momentum, but when I was almost within reach of the ice wall, the rope gave, jerking downward alarmingly. I closed my eyes.

After a moment, it steadied.

I summoned the courage to try again, flashlight in my mouth. Another swing and I almost reached the wall, then another and I was able to scrape the crampon along the ice. The next time, I came at it hard and thudded the crampon on my hand straight in so it held. I hung off it precariously, scrabbling with the numb fingers of my other hand to find a fissure in the wall to hold. Then I kicked about for a ledge and slowly put the weight of my right foot on a tiny lip. When I was balanced, I gingerly twisted the crampon free, reached up above my head, and swung it into the ice again.

My breath was stuttering in tight staccato bursts with the intensity of each action, and I was trying not to think about the terrifying situation we were in, just focusing on each little movement.

I pulled myself up with my right hand, and the tightness in the rope eased off slightly. Jack dropped down a little bit in the darkness, taking up the slack in the rope. I searched about for more holds and slowly made my way up the ice wall like that.

With every step I went up, Jack dropped a little on the rope.

Eventually, I had made about ten feet and reckoned I was level with him. I hung the flashlight back around my neck, took a deep breath, and let go of the ice wall, swinging out into the deep nothingness of the chasm.

I collided heavily with Jack above the abyss, and bear hugged him wildly. After a few seconds, I was suddenly aware I was shouting his name, and tried to calm myself down. I touched his head and felt warmth, then I heard him cough thickly.

"Jonny?" he said faintly. "Are we nearly home?"

"Not quite, Jack," I said with tears of relief. "Another little climb."

"I'm cold," he said weakly.

"Yes," I answered, and hugged him. "Just hang in there." I held him in that moment with a wave of love that seemed to defy that whole place. Maybe it was triggered by the fear of dying, and I was saying good-bye to him and to the world, I don't know.

But after a few minutes, I wiped the tears away and got more of a grip. I searched Jack's harness and found he still had a full set of ice screws and climbing gear on him. I thought if we could both get to the wall, we could climb our way out.

It felt like a flicker of hope.

"Jack," I shouted. "Wake up. Come on. Get a grip. Jack!" And I could see his eyes were fighting some inner voice that was cajoling him into a warm, dangerous sleep. He had taken some kind of injury but there was nothing I could do about that here.

"Eyes open, Jack. Come on. Don't mess about!" I cried, and he eventually forced his eyes open in a glassy stare.

"Ready," he said, with no real idea where he was.

"Good. We've some climbing to do. Understand?"

I joined our harnesses together with a quick-draw, then I swung us clumsily together toward the ice wall, feeling the rope cutting frighteningly through the support above. When I was in range, I lunged at the wall with his climbing ax so it gripped, and we both froze at the end of the arc. I fumbled with an ice screw and, holding it awkwardly with my free hand, somehow managed to twist it into the wall. Then I took a quick-draw and clipped one end onto the carabiner on Jack's harness and the other on the ice screw, so he was attached to the wall. I did the same for myself, then worked as quickly as I could with my numb hands to get another ice screw into the face and clipped us both onto that one too.

That felt good.

There was a flutter from above, and the body of the rope dropped heavily past us, snaking into the chasm below, the ends yanking at our harnesses like playful dogs. That felt bad. Very bad. I shuddered at the thought of not being attached to the wall and crashing down into that blackness below. I wound in another couple of ice screws and found my hands were shaking. Then I leaned back and saw Jack was asleep again.

"Jack!" I shouted. "Jack! Come on! Help me!" He opened his eyes and smiled drowsily.

"OK," he said.

"You mustn't sleep, Jack!" I shouted.

"No, no sleeping," he said, with a weak smile.

I put my one crampon back on my left boot, stuck the flashlight in my mouth, took all the gear from Jack's harness, and clipped it onto the one loop that was still intact on my own. Then I started to climb up the crevasse wall in the darkness. I swung the ice ax, jabbed in the toe spikes of the crampon, then heaved myself up.

Resting there, I twisted in an ice screw and clipped myself on. And so I continued up, always clipping myself onto gear I had put into the face, feeling it was too risky to free climb. My hands turned blue with the cold, my mouth went dry and raw with the struggle to hold the flashlight; but I edged my way up, bit by bit, until I could no longer see Jack below in the darkness.

Once or twice I called to him, but he didn't respond.

The rope was still attached to my harness and to Jack's, so I knew if it went taut I would have climbed a hundred feet, then I would somehow have to pull him up. Above, I suddenly noticed a faint glow of light on the ice, and my throat swelled. I wondered if I was seeing things, but the glow seemed to pool on the wall.

I climbed feverishly, now focused on this light.

I still couldn't make out what it was, and even when I had almost reached it, I was confused. Then I put my hand on a solid lip and realized it was a small cave—a fissure about six feet wide with a smooth floor of soft snow leading off to a glimmer of daylight maybe a hundred feet away up a slope. If I could just get Jack up here, we'd be OK, and I felt a whack of adrenaline.

There was a way out of this thing.

I heaved myself onto the smooth floor of the fissure, then feverishly got to work twisting a couple of ice screws into the roof to hold two carabiners. Then, I untied the rope from my waist and threaded it through the gear, stuffed it into the belay device on my harness, and retied the end. I yelled to Jack to unclip the quick-draws from the ice wall so I could haul him up. I yelled and yelled, but each time I hauled on the rope, I couldn't budge him, and I knew he must be asleep and still clipped firmly to the wall below.

I wanted to cry, but I got a grip and tried to focus, pulling the rope out of my belay device and tying some huge shanks so the end couldn't slip through the carabiners in the roof. I tugged it to make sure it was secure, clipped the ice ax to my harness, stood on the edge of the fissure, and eased myself off, back down to him. Hand over hand, I scraped my way back down into the crevasse, as my fingers screamed with cold.

"Jack!" I cried, clipping myself on as I reached him. "Jack! Fucking wake up! Wake up."

"Shot in Quebec," he whispered. "Here it comes again."

"Jack!" I cried. "Wake up!" And I rubbed his face and hands.

"Don't leave me," he said with sudden clarity, looking into my eyes. "Please don't leave me."

"No one's going to leave you, Jack!" I said, unclipping the quick-draws, so all his weight was taken by the rope that was belayed at the fissure above. He swung away from the ice wall, and I realized the crevasse must be at a slight angle. "No one's leaving you. Now just stay awake! Please!" I began to climb back up the ice wall again. At least this time, all the gear was fixed in place, but I found it hard to locate in the fading glow of my flashlight and I scrabbled about with my numb hands until I felt each of the small metal fixings so I could clip on. My hands had all the dexterity of bear paws by now. I knew they were frostbitten, but I reached the cavelike fissure after about twenty minutes, slid myself onto the ice floor, then took the loose end of the rope and forced it to bend so I could stuff it through my belay device. I struggled to untie the shanks I'd put in the rope as a stopper knot because they had Jack's weight on them now, but when they eventually pulled free, the rope strained on my harness. I heaved on it and felt Jack move up a few inches. It was going to work.

I hauled again, and tried to lose the pain I could feel in my hands in the rhythm of the never-ending flow of some beat. As I did so, I called to Jack to keep alert, to keep feeling human, and I was wild with hope that some part of him would hear my voice and lock on to it. "Stay awake, Jack! Stay awake!" I remember shouting, then I was suddenly flooded with a sharp, distinct memory.

"Remember when we went out with those two girls and ended up skinny-dipping in the river? Remember the warm evening that was thick with crickets and a moon so full it was like a bulging sack of presents? That girl I was with had the bluest eyes I have ever seen, and I was so deeply in love with her, I could have skated over that water. Then we lay, rolled in blankets under a massive sheet of stars, and drank margaritas and rum straight from the bottle. You remember all that, Jack? You remember I cried, because the moment was so full of being alive? You remember?"

I was hardly able to believe it myself.

I heard a scrape of ice, and realized Jack hung just below the fissure. I took the whole strain of the rope with my right hand, reached over the ledge with my left, felt the icy smooth material of his jacket, and took a big, firm grip. Then I hauled with everything I had, and he landed onto the floor of the fissure like a deadweight.

"Jack, wake up," I whispered breathlessly. "Fucking wake up!" I tried to shout, lying spilled on the ground next to him, but I found I was utterly empty, as though my adrenaline had run out and the bottles needed changing.

The ice felt warm and comfortable against my face, so I closed my eyes just for a few seconds. There was a desperate voice telling me not to, but it was just too quiet, just too far away, just too small.

38

I slept immediately, dropping into a weird restless doze, where shadows moved. I didn't dream exactly, but just met some formless, towering thing that reared up screaming in my mind, and I knew I had blundered into another place where I wasn't meant to be.

There was the sense of boundaries breaking, of whole other worlds grinding against our own, of life being sucked away, of love and evil sweeping unchecked, flowing across the surface like blown sand. I fought this formless screaming thing that had got inside of me, knowing I must not bend or run, and for minutes we locked in a battle of will, until my sheer stubbornness seemed to tire its patience and it melted away.

I awoke pretty quickly after that, and I knew Jack was dying for sure. I knew that this thing I had felt had come for him but had left us both, and I had one chance to get him out of there.

And that chance was now.

I took hold of his harness, and heard a deep, hollow shudder bellow through the ice, which seemed to almost split right across my own chest. The noise died, then it sounded like someone trying to squeeze a full-sized wooden sailing ship into a small suitcase. I glanced up and saw that the ceiling was running with thousands of silent cracks, and the next second the whole fissure began vibrating, sending ice and powder down like clouds of white soot.

Chasms appeared on my left and crunched shut, and awful noises sloshed in and out as vast empty caves yawned open around us and slid off downward.

I grabbed Jack's collar and lugged him toward the small pool of daylight that shone through the haze of powdered snow at the end of the fissure. I just focused on the light and kept going, scrambling over the rocks of ice, balancing on ledges that were sliding away, trying to fend off bits of roof that were collapsing on me like cinder blocks being dropped carelessly from a scaffold.

I kept going, and each time I fell, I looked up and saw that the daylight had moved, but it was still there. I pushed and pushed into the chaos of sliding ice and noise, gripping Jack's collar with my frostbitten hand. I was close enough to smell the cold wind whipping in from outside, near enough to believe that the old world existed after all; near enough to dream of drinking coffee out on the pier at Capitola again. I glanced back to Jack and my stomach ran with fear.

My hand was empty.

It was so frostbitten and numb I had no idea I had let go of Jack. I stood transfixed as a weight of ice felled me unconscious.

I don't know how long I lay there, but when I came to, it was evening. I didn't remember anything. Didn't know where Jack was. Didn't know what had happened to Mat. I managed to dig my way out and found the weather had eased, and somehow staggered down alone and found someone in the ranger's hut.

39

I looked at the two of them and realized a deep silence had pooled around us. Even the jukebox had gone quiet.

"That's the story. I let go of Jack in the fissure when that was the one thing I promised him I wouldn't do. Said I wouldn't leave him." I realized my hands had gone numb during the telling of the story, so they ran with purple veins and white blotches.

Eli didn't say anything. She just reached over and hugged me.

"There's nothing to forgive," she said finally, looking at me with her deep brown, tear-smeared eyes. "You see that, don't you? In the end, all you can do is all you can do."

I held her and felt a thickness in my throat.

"And Jack would have been proud you tried so hard," she

said, leaning back and holding my shoulders gently with her palms. "Of course he would."

Eli was one of the special people, the way she took all that sadness and just swallowed it and never felt any resentment, or anger, or frustration about anything, as though she had an inside that shone with white light and everything that went in was purified. "Long Island Iced Teas," she whispered suddenly, looking into my eyes and, springing up, wiped her nose. "These are definitely on the house."

Mat reached over and hugged me with a grip a brown bear would have been pleased with. "Don't beat yourself up," he said. "There's nothing to forgive, but the hardest thing is to forgive yourself. You see that, don't you?" Eli lined up three Long Island Iced Teas.

"To Jack," she said slipping her neat, long fingers around one of the glasses.

"To Jack," Mat and I said. And as I held the Long Island Iced Tea there before me, in that one elongated moment, I sensed the whole of Jack's life, from beginning to end, like a finished, complete thing. I saw it in a way it had never quite looked before, and I didn't think it would appear so clearly again. The intensity of his presence rolled around us, like an undulating map, and it was as though his birth and death and everything in between existed all together.

I took the first, cool sip of the drink and the strangeness of the moment began to break up gently and move off, and I was content to watch it go. I had carried something of Jack with me all these years, and now, I realized, he didn't want me to carry him anymore. We had different ways to go.

"Jack was always scared of the mountains," said Eli, "but he loved them too, and I know he wouldn't have missed those trips for anything." She threw her hair back. "He'd like the fact you two are still drinking Long Island Iced Teas and catching waves at ridiculous hours of the day."

Yeah, I thought. Actually, he would.

The jukebox woke up and started playing the sound effects of applause from a concert hall, punctuated with raucous cries of "Bravo!" And somehow that seemed as appropriate a statement to Jack as I could think of. Bravo Jack! Bravo! I thought. And we all sat there as amusement mixed with our sadness, sipping Long Island Iced Teas without saying a word as the cheers and whistles echoed around the empty room.

"Anyone want a seriously messed-up jukebox?" said Eli finally, with a slow shake of the head, as the applause began to die. I smiled, looking around the place, knowing this would be the last time I would come here and wanting to fix the moment in my mind, so I could come here again when it was all gone and think of this drink in celebration of Jack's life.

Several of the elevators pinged and the doors eased open. The bouncer would be livid other people were still getting in here, I thought, then the roar of bikes slashed across everything and I was off my seat and running before I could even think what I was doing.

Somehow, though, Eli was ahead of me, reading the basics of the situation through my eyes and tugging at my collar. "This way," she shouted. "This way," and she hauled me physically around the back of the bar to a hidden elevator.

"Staff elevator," she cried, as Mat flew in next to me and the doors slipped shut with a solid swish.

"Oh," said the elevator. "Normally I have a lunch break at this time."

"Get us the fuck out of here, now!" I cried.

"Please," added Mat.

"Knock, knock," said the elevator.

"Normally, I'd plummet and kill you but today I feel good," I said. "Now let's fucking *go*!"

40

The elevator began to descend in slightly stunned silence, and the roar of bikes thankfully melted away.

"Riders?" Mat said.

"Had to be," I said, snorting like a small dog after a session chasing a particularly elusive stick, but also sensing, even in the flurry of this moment, that a great weight had gone with the telling of the story about Jack. "Had to be. Thought they were off our tail, but apparently not. Still keen to assassinate God, obviously." Then something in my head made a connection. "Did I tell you I met Elnor Elnorian in Zone Securities?" Mat looked at me. "He wasn't that hot on God, either."

"You met Elnor Elnorian? Really? And you think he's tied in to all this?" Mat said.

"I don't know." Something struck me like a crisp packet full of water dropped on my head from a great height. "Although the Riders called their boss Double E. Coincidence, do you think? Elnor Elnorian? Double E?"

"Criminal, the bar closing," said the elevator cutting in. "Criminal! It gave me a new lease on life when it came here. Not sure what I'll do now if no one takes the place on."

"Another elevator wanting to go to Baja?" said Mat as I felt my patience burning up at the interruption.

"No. What would I want to go there for?" said the elevator. "No, I was thinking about becoming a fridge. Listen, I can make the noise: Mrrrrrrrnnnnn," it hummed. "What do you think? Authentic? I've been practicing."

"You're an elevator," I said flatly, despite myself. "How are you going to keep things cold?"

"Well, I'll leave my doors open quite a bit," it suggested, after a pause.

"Nice thinking," said Mat. "You've got a good future being so...proactive like that." Then he added, "Jonny, the Double E thing. It could be a possibility; Elnorian's been going on about trying to get funding for his space project and cutting spending on religions."

"Yes," I said. "I smell half of one small answer."

The elevator decelerated to a stuttering halt and, after a tiny pause, suddenly jolted down another three inches just before the doors hustled open. Why do elevators do that? I mean, why not just go down to the right level to begin with? I looked into the small dingy room it had brought us to, which was lit solely by a wall covered in neon signs.

One of those I saw said: "This way!" in squiggly purple, with the outline of a hand next to it; another read: "Jazz Bar!" in fluorescent blue; and another, in wiry yellow neon, bizarrely said: "Osprey Housing Should Be Available to Everyone!" I had no idea what floor this was, or why it should be lit with neon signs that seemed to be collected from forgotten places.

"Staff exit is up the spiral stairs," said the elevator. "I don't open in the main hall, with the riffraff."

I nodded and stepped out but I had a bad feeling about this.

"Think of me if you ever want some milk kept cold," the elevator continued. "Listen. I have it perfectly." And it started making a humming sound again: "Mrrrrrrrrnnnnnn!"

I tried not to get too irritated. I knew I had bigger fish to fry and probably a variety of other seafood to poach if it came to that, but in that moment if I could have got my hands on the person responsible for programming that elevator, I would have given them a very passionate and massively dull talking-to.

I snapped out of it and headed for the well-worn spiral staircase that jutted into the room, knowing this wasn't the time to start arguing with an elevator about where exactly we were, and particularly not one that was doing a very bad impression of a fridge. My feet scraped bluntly off the worn iron treads and I could hear Mat right behind as we snaked our way up. I felt my back twinge slightly with the strain of twisting up these over-corkscrewed stairs.

At last, we came to a chic stainless-steel door that seemed to be hung at a rather unsettling and wonky angle. A small business card was stuck neatly to the middle of it saying, "Jonny and Mat, please don't be late for the party!"

I ripped it off and simply stuffed it in my pocket for a later time, when my head would be able to consider such a thing.

I gripped the handle, ready to heave the door open, but it swung easily, and suddenly we were staring out across the familiar reclamation yard.

It was quiet.

I stepped hesitantly through, and saw that the door was actually a run-of-the-mill one from an old tenement someplace, but now with a steel lining. It had been hung at a weird angle to disguise it, so that it blended in with the piles of discarded doors that were heaped around in that part of the junkyard.

"Dark," said Mat, closing it behind him, and glanced instinctively up at the Thin Building. "There goes Inconvenient," he said toward the flicker of lights on the top two floors, and I knew what he meant. I would miss the place too.

Things change. Things always keep on fucking changing. If only they would just stay the same for a bit I could get a grip on them all, I thought.

It was terrible for Eli, losing her job, then me appearing like that, but that was just the way it turned out. There's never a good time for some things. I wondered for the millionth time how it was we had never managed to hook up together. I guess I shouldn't have fallen into becoming good friends with her if I had wanted to date. That easy, comfortable warmth of intimate friendship kills passion like nothing else. Except possibly peanut butter sandwiches.

Mat shambled into a run and I saw his point; it would be good to get back to the bike before the Riders sensed we were gone, but frankly I hate running. The reason is simple; after a hundred yards my lungs were clamoring for oxygen and a series of cigarettes in their habitual way. I would settle for one cigarette, I thought, trying to taste the first drag in my mind, which always made the craving worse and not better. When all this was over, I was going to make a point of starting smoking again. I was going to hold a party to celebrate the first new cigarette packet the same way people hold parties to celebrate a new house.

The running began to take its toll and I felt my stomach tighten unnecessarily; then a pain wormed its way across my chest, and my thigh muscles decided to tell me they were as tight as fence wire. I ignored their shouts and just tried to revel in the basics of breathing, which wasn't easy. We bashed on through areas of old, ornate, crumbling fireplaces that cried for the houses they had lost. Then we dodged around piles of gigantic wooden beams ingrained with knots like crocodile eyes that might have crisscrossed the Pacific at one time as part of ships that were long gone. And all the time, we headed in the direction of the discarded staircases that perched like claws on the horizon.

I heard what sounded like distant trumpets echoing off a warehouse on the other side of the river. They faded, and I shook them from my mind until a loud screech of brass set my ears ringing. About twenty yards away, the nose of a wedding conga spat out from one of the bridges, fawning over the dusty ground with a howl of bright, garish colors that beat up the senses the way the first neat whiskey of the night bites the back of the throat. The shouts and laughter of drunken celebration flew off the small crowd like acrobats flipping about a trampoline, and these people seemed to virtually pulsate with the beat of their own drums, making the atmosphere of what had gone before seem as shy and sedate as a dead walrus.

It was a traditional wedding conga, all right. The bride and groom were being carried on wedding chairs through their neighborhood, as a public demonstration of their love, commitment, and—on this occasion—appalling clothes sense.

They would all finish at a reception someplace, burning for more alcohol and laughing good-naturedly at the nervous, mumbled speeches. The conga was a tradition begun by the now defunct Ministry of Reassurance, whose job it had been to make everyone feel that everything was OK. It was said at one time they hired four hundred good-looking women to walk around bars and tell men how great they were and how good the world was. But once the record companies needled their

way into power, a lot of government ministries were mysteriously closed and the Ministry of Reassurance had been one of
them. Wedding congas had survived despite this, though, having been taken to heart by the populace.

This procession spun toward us, not seemingly led by anyone
in particular but giving the appearance of a lot of bees that
had decided to swarm off for reasons known only to the bees
themselves—and probably a couple of men with beards deep
in the bowels of the University of Idaho who studied bees because they had some innate fear of human relationships, which
might well have had a sad tale behind it.

The conga twisted our way, presenting an impenetrable wall
of red-faced people.

We hesitated, looking for a route around it among the crumbling, dank, water-filled ornamental fountains, but there wasn't
an obvious one. And before we had made any definite decision,
the crowd engulfed us in a foaming froth of excitement, snapping us into a tangle of wine bottles and cheering. Of heavy
breath and kisses; of sharp hats and little-worn suits. I was flung
backwards through the waving arms and trumpets, the hatted
fruit and sprays of limp flowers, and for a dark second I glimpsed
plumes of dust rising like explosions near the Thin Building and
knew immediately they were the bike trails of the Riders, who
were already ferociously on our case.

I unsnagged myself from the gigantic earrings of a middle-
aged lady who had already started telling me about her hernia
and was wheeled around into the steely-eyed, unrelenting stare
of a man who simply said: "You're not part of this, are you? And
I know what you're thinking. You're thinking: Where can I get a
set of encyclopedias?" And then amid this crush of people he offered up a volume.

It had to be the Belgian Caroline had warned me about, and

I stared at him, suddenly suspended in the eye of a storm of people.

"Listen," I found myself shouting, "tell whoever is in charge that I do not wish to buy any encyclopedias. I'm *never* buying a set. OK?"

"OK," said the man with a barely audible accent, but I could see by his smile he was mocking me. "You don't want to buy any encyclopedias? OK."

I wrenched myself from the edge of the crowd, like a suction cup pulled from a glass door, and chased after my feet as they ran ahead, only regaining my balance with huge unwieldy steps as though I had been shoved off a moving walkway. As I straightened, I saw Mat do almost exactly the same thing. The Belgian hadn't flinched and was watching me with a calm, unnerving stare as the conga swirled around him.

I screamed at Mat to run, and we both pounded for the flaking red bridge, clattering over it, down the narrow alley, and back toward the Flame Rouge, where we had left the bike. I just had time to see that the windows of the Flame Rouge were all thrown open. Colored smoke was pouring out uncontrollably, while a group of bored staff stood waiting outside, marooned in the road, the chef still wearing his white hat and clutching a ladle, as we skidded up to the bike.

It was covered in balloons and streamers. I couldn't begin to understand exactly what that was all about. Some student prank perhaps? Or some advertising campaign? We snatched at them, but there wasn't time, so I just hopped on the front, then fired up the engine as our crash suits eased shut, and screamed away—trailing streamers and party decorations.

It wasn't the ideal start when you're trying not to look obtrusive.

I love bikes. I love their character, but I'm not that big on them as things to worship. I'm not one of those people who gets excited about the smell of a new carburetor, or the curve of a particularly swoopy fuel tank, or the extra shininess of some new exhaust. But I had a lot of decisions milling around in my mind waiting to be resolved, and I couldn't decide which one had priority. Maybe if I drove, my subconscious would lead me in the right direction.

It was a long shot, but it was a trick I had used before.

Normally I ended up in a bar someplace I had forgotten about, or a spot down in Big Sur I'd camped as a kid—although once I woke up in a motel in El Salvador, which was a bit of a surprise. But that's what happens if you drink mojitos when you're not used to them, I guess.

I dropped the bike onto the freeway and gunned it, swinging up my visor to feel the crisp, cold wind across my face and hoping the sheer brutal force of it would clear right through my head. Balloons thudded, like some boxer was giving them a working over, then, one by one, they were torn off and ripped out of sight down our slipstream. Why had someone put balloons on the bike? And what was written on that card I had picked up off the door? "Jonny and Mat, don't be late for the party." Were the two things connected?

My head reeled.

I was far enough into this thing to deserve some answers by now surely, I thought, rather than more confusion. I flicked the bike through the traffic, as we wound down the main street of Compilation, and I just wanted to get out of this zone because it always gave me a bad feeling—the same way I got a bad feeling from a room where the lighting was harsh and inhumane, or when I saw a dying vase of ignored flowers, or when I heard the fidgeting whine of a badly tuned-in radio. Some things are not meant to be.

Just as some things are meant to be. Like Mozart. Or the

cheesecake they served at the Wham-Wham Bar. Or the dawn paddle out at Todos Santos.

I opened up the throttle, implicitly trusting that Teb really had masked our C-4 Charlies, and the road fell away, smearing into a blur as we whipped in and out of the toiling traffic. I was driven by an insatiable urge just to get the fuck out of here. A helicopter yawed around above us, skidding and sliding through the air like a drunkard on an ice rink.

The Well-Malls and Sniffer Alarm stores and Chair-Crazy warehouses, the bars and whorehouses and Kitchen Guerrilla shops bounded past as I let the bike go. Just let the big dog eat. The helicopter rolled past again in a wild flurry of blades, rocking like a ship on the sea as it banked, then finally settled high above the freeway, a hundred yards ahead. It could be anyone, I told myself. It could be anyone. But it was following the road now, and moving at our speed.

The rear door yawned open like a loose jaw, and I caught a glint of something shining in the bowels of the thing. Then, as the freeway curved gently around, the chopper banked and the sunlight flooded into the rear bay, and I saw the front wheels of the four bikes; the four figures and the familiar absence of four crash suits.

It was the Riders. Fuck it.

41

The bikes fell from the rear of the chopper like evening swallows searching for insects, as one after the other, engines fuming with white-blue smoke, they dropped in a heart-stopping, slow-motion arc that would surely smash them to pieces when they hit the tarmac.

Instead, when they struck the ground, the bikes all skipped back up into the air like tennis balls poured from a tin, bouncing out of time in great, jerky, bucking movements. Eventually they settled heavily onto the road and surged toward me through the scattering traffic, the wrong way down the freeway. My throat swelled, and the saliva in my mouth vanished as I wrenched the bike instantly off the freeway, thumping down a soft grassy bank and skidding uncomfortably onto a small gravel road in the backwater of Compilation, crashing through the gears until we ripped down the quiet lane. Here the shops were sleepy as hell, and the single-story wooden houses were shored up with neat metal crutches.

I whacked the heads-up display button on the bike, and a faint translucent green screen appeared obediently. I toggled gingerly through the menu, keeping an eye on the road, until I found the setting that activated the rear sensor, and the ghostly image slid up in front of me, blurred by the vibration of the bike.

I let my eyes adjust to what I was seeing, and eventually understood that the small shivery green dots were the Riders, hammering their way after us. My attention was wrenched back to the road in a crack of movement as I whipped the bike sideways to avoid someone ahead I had hardly seen.

I felt the shock inside settle back down through my veins like the sediment in a murky pond after the dive of a kingfisher.

Our sheer speed meant corners were appearing in wild bursts, charging up to meet us, and I leaned into them at such an angle that the world seemed to slide away. Up ahead, a wall of white lights marked the separation of the zones, but I had lost all sense of orientation and didn't know where we were now.

The bike shook as I sent it through the jinking corners, then ripped into the next zone, scything through thick snow, which instantly clawed and choked the back wheel so it slewed wildly and began wagging from side to side like the tail of an excited dog.

It would have to be Christmas Single.

I fought with the sluggish, overheavy steering that felt like it had been drugged, and I screamed at myself not to hit the brakes too hard or I'd lose the thing for sure.

And all the while fresh flares of slush sprayed up in a brown-white fog.

The bike skewed again, knocked almost sideways by a drift of hard-packed snow, and we virtually careered into one of the huge smiling angels that were plastered up along that particular road, each with the name of some generous sponsor being blown from a trumpet. A sleigh appeared out of the snowy fog, pulled by four reindeer, and tramped past us while the smiling, unshaven Santa inanely grinned in our direction with an expression like he had just slept with his neighbor's wife or something.

We screamed past advertising slogans saying: "Come and live the fairy tale!" And I just had time to think: "Come and live with a lot of sad deranged people who should know better," would have been more accurate.

I gripped the handlebars as loosely as I could, absorbing the bumps and jolts and trying to convince myself I had some slippery sort of control over the bike now. We stumbled on much too slowly for my nerves, bumbling over the ruts and crunching over the mounds of artificial snow they spent so much pointless time and effort creating. I felt anger pour through my veins again, but one glance at the display screen found the Riders still on our tail, but closer now.

Much closer.

I threw the bike down a small side alley, not caring that it might not go anywhere. I had to do something, or we were just a couple of lame reindeer. The place was lit with white fairy lights that gave a gentle pale glow to the snow. We roared farther down this twisting alley, and the garish overenthusiasm of whoever did the decoration soon swamped everything. Fountains of lights erupted, adorning every conceivable cranny on every building, like a creeping, shining plague.

I took a sharp right, then a left, hoping the narrow streets would make it impossible for the Riders to keep up. My throat bulged with anxiety, and my heart pumped so hard I was sure I would soon run out of blood. At some stage, they would start shooting and I mustn't be startled by it. Almost immediately, I felt a dull, solid whump across my face. I wiped snow away from my eyes and wondered if my adrenaline was masking some pain that would seep slowly through, gradually chilling my body. I felt another dull whump on my arm and, looking up, saw it was just playful kids laughing and chucking snowballs from the top of a flat roof many stories above. No doubt brimming with glee at their accuracy.

I cajoled the bike on, letting it snap over the bumps and wondering how the Riders had suddenly found me at Inconvenient. Maybe it was just a lucky guess, just like it had been at Teb's place. I flicked left down a wider, tree-lined street where the snow was almost pristine, with only a couple of other tracks scratched over it, and knew I had to get away. It was suddenly obvious I had to get over to my house, whatever happened. I opened up the throttle, realizing it was all or nothing now— realizing there was no point getting caught lamely somehow trying to play safe.

The bike skewed and skidded. I took the next corner with my feet sliding across the ground to keep from bouncing through the shop windows, but the Riders were still gaining.

I dodged two more sleighs, slewing over the sidewalk to get out of their way. One was pulled by men dressed as angels, and the other by excitable huskies, who barked and tugged as we screamed past, rolling the sleigh sideways out of control and scattering presents wrapped in glossy, bright paper all across the slushy road in a chorus of tiny sleigh bells.

I kicked up through the gears, leaving the chaos of the sleigh behind, and skated down the wide street, flanked with rough two-story log cabins, that sprawled their wide, rustic porches down onto the sidewalk. Ironic, I thought, as they blurred past, how they had hijacked the style of the gold rush and presented it as something magical and romantic, when speculator towns had been cold, harsh, and ferociously brutal. Humans had a habit of being careless with history like that, treating it as something bendy and pliable that could be reshaped into whatever was most amusing.

Gentle flakes of snow began falling, taking the edge still further off any kind of sense of reality, while the thumping bumps of the icy ruts threw us up against the walls of our crash suits like we were inside a lettuce shaker. Up ahead, I could see the road broaden into a wide square, so I eased the throttle, wondering whether to double back down one of the side streets, but it was clear from the screen that one of the Riders was too close behind me.

There was a gaudy fountain in the center gushing snow from the mouth of a huge, triumphant angel, and on the near side was a massive neoclassical building with wide steps and a gigantic white illuminated star outside the front door. I kicked the bike sideways around the fountain, trying to decide which might be the quickest way out of the zone, when I saw him.

My chest tightened like it was trussed up with piano wire and my stomach sank as though it was an old rag dropped in a bucket of water. Screaming smoothly out from the streets opposite came the shining, fuming, laid-back Rider.

I slewed away from him.

A second Rider swung out from another street, blocking my path, and I realized bleakly they had somehow got ahead and were bearing down on the square from different sides.

I hurled the bike around, spraying up a curtain of brown slush that fell lazily across the road. Then I gunned the bike back the way we had come, but as I accelerated I saw a third Rider wallowing wildly down the middle of the road toward us, like a wild horse that has been spooked by a fox.

I spun the bike again and scrabbled, catlike, up the first few steps of the large stone building, thinking that from up there, at least, I would hold the high ground. The front wheel of the last Rider's bike nosed to a halt at the top, and as I looked, I saw him unsheathe a gigantic gun.

I twisted away instantly, veering back down toward the fountain, when I heard the blown-out, rasping howl of a shot, and felt the bike buck like a bear that had trodden on a hornet.

The ground lurched and swiveled, merging with confusing slices of sky. We scrambled through the dead air, then I felt the hard, back-shuddering, screeching crack as we hit the base of the fountain. The crash suits scraped across the hard, unforgiving stone, and we came to a raw, dull, aching halt that left a trail of eerie silence behind us. As everything settled, all I could hear was the slow slap-slapping of the thick slushy snow falling from the fountain above us.

Everything stayed like that for the next few seconds, as though time had moved on without us—as though the warm comfort of lying prostrate and snug in the crash suits on the felled bike might last for hours.

Then I saw the familiar boot of one of the Riders and realized he was looming over me. I released the crash suit and rolled over in the crunching snow, and found they were all there, silhouetted black against the large bright star that sat at the top of the steps I had tried to climb.

"You are a pain in the ass," said one of them, prodding me with his gun. "If you've broken anything, we'll kill you."

"Ho! Ho! Ho!" I heard a Santa shouting from somewhere, "Ho! Ho! Ho!" And from where I was lying, I saw a young, fresh-faced man excitedly run over toward us. Whatever was going through his head, I could not possibly imagine. One of the Riders leveled a gun at him as he reached us.

"Ho fucking...oh!" he said, tailing off, and turned and fled.

"This place is weird, I'm telling you," said one of the other Riders. "The whole population dresses as Santa Claus."

"Get the Package," the lead one said.

I opened my mouth, thinking I might as well get it over with there and then.

I couldn't do what they wanted.

I didn't even have the file anymore, because I had left it with Teb to see if he could make sense of it. Maybe there would be another chance to escape, maybe there would be more last-minute reprieves, but they would simply come after me again and I was tired of it all. I wanted to face the music now; I couldn't make a Dream Virus and I couldn't carry out their weird plan to assassinate God.

"Come on, Package! Come to Mummy," said the one calling himself Death, leaning down, and I just caught sight of the round of ammunition in his teeth when a voice cut through the artificially chilled air.

"He's mine."

There was something assured and steady about the tone that made the Riders hesitate, when normally I sensed they would have turned and fired. Over their shoulder at the top of the steps, silhouetted by the giant white star, was the relaxed figure of a man—and I knew exactly who it was.

"Who the fuck are you?" said Death, waving his gun wildly about.

"I am an encyclopedia salesman," said the man with the merest hint of a Belgian accent, still with his arms loosely folded.

"A what?"

"An encyclopedia salesman. And the Package, as you call him, is mine. You can go now."

"We can go?" said the same Rider as though he had just been told his best friend had cooked and eaten his pet hamster. "We can go?" he repeated, more insanely, and I felt the safety valves breaking in his mind. His broken tone seemed to be laying the groundwork for some hugely violent act that was to follow.

"Yes," said the Belgian, holding up a finger as one of the other Riders went for his gun. "Naughty. I have backup." He smiled, and a thick swarm of faceless armed marksmen suddenly appeared on the roofs of all the surrounding buildings with such density even the Riders were taken aback. "They will kill you very quickly," said the Belgian with a forced smile. "So, as I said, you can go."

The Riders stared, amazed at this development, but the guns were there and they were real. They'd begun to walk self-consciously toward their bikes when one of them stopped.

"You're an encyclopedia salesman, you say?"

"That's it."

"That's what I thought you said. We could do a deal if—"

The Belgian cut him off. "No deal," he said, smiling. "Good-bye."

The Riders strolled casually to their machines, drawing out the moment, perhaps feeling there was a good chance this bizarre man and his backup might disappear as quickly as they had arrived. This lasted until they fired up their bikes, when it all seemed to get too much for them, and they screamed off unnecessarily quickly into the distance, roaring out their frustration.

The Belgian stood, poised and relaxed, as they burned off. I stiffly heaved myself up off the snow, my clothes damp at the knees and elbows. I glanced around at the rooftops and took in the alarming number of guns that still seemed to be pointing directly at us.

"I don't think running is a serious option," Mat said.

"No, they might notice even if we just walk quickly," I said, with a halfhearted attempt at a joke. The Belgian began tapping down the stone steps toward us in the ice-cold silence.

"They are all having Christmas dinner in the town hall!" he

322   Tim Scott

cried, opening his arms—explaining, I guessed, why there was
no one about. "Turkey," he went on, getting closer, "with all the
trimmings."

I looked at him. He was a much smaller man than I had imagined, with a rather too-neat, pristine appearance, as though he
had a hairdresser lurking just out of sight, ready to attend to him
at any moment. His walk was crisp, but not manic, like a squirrel who'd eaten all the nuts he could ever want and had chilled
out a bit. I suddenly got the idea he was the sort of person who
was fastidious about not storing anything in his attic because he
couldn't stand the mess, but quite where that came from, when
there were at least sixty guns pointing at me, I really don't know.
Caroline had made it clear he was an assassin, and this was not
a good time to take any liberties even inside my own head.

"So," he said, reaching us, then holding up a single thin sheet
of paper, "I suggest you sign." I smiled at him, and reached for
the paper and pen without much hesitation. There really was no
point arguing; he held all the aces. He probably held all the kings
for that matter, and quite a few of the other cards as well. And
really, if I'm going to be pedantic, he pretty much held the card
table and probably all the air. I wasn't going to get away with
saying "Thanks but no thanks" to his encyclopedias this time;
the stakes had gone up by infinity.

"Thank you," he said, "you won't be disappointed. Half a million drawings, one million color photographs, with detailed explanations of every conceivable subject in the world today. They
are a valuable addition to the quality of your life. You will never
be short of answers now."

"Thank you," I said, wondering if he knew how ironic that
statement sounded.

"We know you have a minor problem with your Jab-Tab, but
we are working on it and will deduct the money from you at the
source."

"Tell Caroline E I'll see her again," I said ignoring the stuff about the Jab-Tab and handing back the signed sheet, not knowing exactly why I had said it, but feeling it was worth saying anyway. He looked at me quizzically, like a teacher listening to a child who has just used the word "owl" instead of the word "pencil" by mistake in a question.

"Who?" he said cocking his head.

"Caroline E61. One of your representatives. She was on my case."

"Ah," he said nodding to himself. "Ahhh," he added more finally, after a pause, then turned and walked away without giving any indication as to whether he would tell her anything. As he clipped up the stairs again, I realized all the figures in black had melted from the rooftops. The Belgian reached the top step, heading for the solid stone building, pushed open one of the large doors, and slipped inside.

There was an empty pause after the door thunked shut, and Mat let out a breath. I guess he had been holding it in for some time.

"Fuck-ing he-ll," he said, as we stood there, marooned in the silence of the empty wide square with the noise of the fountain suddenly lapping louder again. In the distance, a large group of people was singing "Jingle Bells" and the words filtered through to us intermittently between the splashes of the falling slush.

> Jingle Bells,
> Jingle Bells,
> Jingle all the way
> Oh, what fun it is to run
> Away from men with guns! Oh!

I looked at Mat to see if he shared my surprise, but he was righting the bike. I put what I thought I'd heard down to my head feeling as confused as if it had spent an entire week on a tour of the dullest paper bag factory there was in Kansas.

With an otter as a tour guide.

"Shame about your bike," I said, knowing how attached Mat was to it.

"Yeah, it's pretty much had it," he replied. "Back wheel's all over the place."

"Guess we'll have to leave it for now and start walking unless you have a better idea." I sighed. At that moment, we heard the faint ring of approaching sleigh bells and I caught Mat's eye.

"Oh no," I said. "Oh no, no way. Don't even think we might do that." But Mat didn't break eye contact with me, and a smug, immovable smile spread across his face.

42

I had never been to the Buena Vista Industrial Village before. As we crossed through the first few miles, I saw it wasn't so much a village as a sprawling, smoke-belching litter of pipes, urban machinery, and chimneys that stained the ground with leaked oil and gagged the sky with gases and vapors that their white-teethed spokesmen always cheerily explained weren't doing anyone any harm. But the miles of dead, inhumane wasteland around us said otherwise as brutally as if the place had been covered in dying, gasping badgers. Maybe it's inevitable industry kills everything around it, cleansing all sense of nature and humanity, so the science-y things they do can have center stage.

Maybe, but probably not.

The taxi Rider cruised between the factories and rusting holding tanks, dwarfed by the sheer scale of their awkward bulk, and I realized these were the cathedrals of our generation—not the showy, shiny, make-believe, high-tensile things architects were always trying to impose on us. These things sat ignored and shoved out of sight, but still with a gritty, stubborn character all of their own. They stood in part for greed and a certain sort of carelessness with the world, but there was an element of triumphalism about them too—a sense of sticking a marker down to show we were here. I liked the kick that entering this foreign, grinding land gave me. It's like smoking, I thought; it's bad for you, but hell, it's a really deep, satisfying buzz.

I sighed and wished I hadn't stumbled across the thought of smoking again, because now it would plague me, and I tried unsuccessfully to lose the idea in a backwater of my mind.

We had left Christmas Single a half hour before. Mat had reveled in the fact I was consumed by a fire of embarrassment and anger at finding myself in the back of a sleigh covered in presents, and was doubled up with laughter for just about the whole journey, which made things seem somehow normal again. The "Ho-ho-ho-ing" Santa had taken us through the snow to the edge of the zone, and from there we had hailed a taxi bike to the Buena Vista Industrial Village.

If I had been given a dollar every time that Santa said, "Ho! Ho! Ho!" on that short journey, I would, at a guess, have something like forty-two dollars. I visibly winced every time he said it, which of course made Mat laugh more, and the Santa saw that as a sign of encouragement. So the whole thing just snowballed.

And snowballed.

I prodded myself back to the present, and my eyes took in more gangling hulks of factories that were slipping by with welters of chimneys and oddly shaped outbuildings circling around them. I wondered why on earth they had brought my house to this godforsaken industrial wasteland when they could be on an isolated beach in Baja, or tucked away in the outreaches of Yosemite, or down in a forest clearing in Oregon somewhere. I guessed they thought this was the last place anyone would come looking for them, and maybe they were right. We were also not that far from downtown Santa Cruz, and all its services would be easy to tap into here, so I s'pose it wasn't so stupid.

My house was about two hundred yards away and to our left when I finally saw it, looking like a lost, crying child abandoned in a city of giants and surrounded by an air of shock. It was exactly where the punks had said it would be, and I realized I had been reining in my expectation, paying heed to a sense of something inside my head that this was all going to turn out to be some hugely dull and frustrating joke. But there it was, tiny and improbable, elegant and stupidly out of place, like someone who had gone to a party making a real effort with the fancy dress chicken costume, then found out when they walked in that it was black tie. The taxi Rider throttled back as we approached, pulling the bike lazily over a little way short as we had asked and hopped off, unconcerned at the bulging strangeness of this whole situation.

I guess taxi Riders see so many disparate pieces of people's lives that they cease to have any grounding in what is strange and what isn't. Or perhaps they just stop caring and let things skid by like signs on a freeway. Either way, this woman might have been dropping us off at the theater for all the interest she showed in where we were. "My son's birthday is today; know what I'm getting him?" she was saying with a rise in her voice and a shake of her long auburn hair.

"You tell me," I said, eyeing my house, and suddenly full of doubt—feeling this was a gigantic trap we were walking straight into and wondering how stupid we must be to approach so brazenly in the open.

"A chair. A good solid chair. The sort of chair you can take with you through life. My dad once gave me a chair when I was nineteen, and that chair has gone everywhere with me. I can come back to that wonderful chair at the end of the day and sit down and feel I'm home. I'm really, actually home. And, on top of all that, I'm getting great lumbar support at the same time. You know what I'm saying?"

"Yes," I said distractedly, still keeping an eye on my house and pulling myself up when I finally registered what it was she had actually said. "Well, actually no. I don't really have any idea at all." I saw her hesitate and added, "But then, I don't have kids." And I realized I had made an attempt to be vaguely polite when normally I would probably have been incredibly irritated. Maybe my temper had been blunted by the relief of having escaped the Riders.

"Oh, well, you should," she went on, connecting up the Jab-Tab to Mat's arm. "They're great. I love all my kids, except when they sit on my chair; then I see black. Very black. Anyway, have a power day, d'you hear?"

"Yes," I said, "our day has certainly been brimming with power already, thank you."

She nodded, not sensing my irony, mounted the bike, then squealed off, curving away into the gray, smoking landscape, down the wide, savaged road we had come in.

And there we were, utterly alone, dwarfed by these massive industrial carcasses, and I wondered why, when stumbling upon them like this, their scale made me feel far more acutely alive. It was as though they focused some great, unseen laser beam of self-awareness right down on me.

I watched my house for a few seconds, but there was no sign of movement. I turned to Mat. "If we're walking into a trap of some sort, it's already too late, because they'll have seen us an age ago. So we might as well just stroll up as though we're going for Thanksgiving dinner."

Mat smiled ruefully, and it reminded me of the sort of expression he normally reserved for when he had just spent the morning in a dull meeting, while all the time the surf at Steamers had been eight-foot and clean. We began walking, leaving dim footprints in the skim of black dust that had settled on everything, crunching over the brittle, irregular black nodules that were scattered liberally about. They looked like something made at school by a teenager in chemistry that seemed to consist partly of chemicals, but mostly of melted lab equipment.

There was still no movement from my house, but above the hiss and flutter of the factories, the grumpy, dull thuds of distant machinery and chirping whines, I became aware of another noise—a human voice that was singing, straining away, trying to reach the top notes of a song I couldn't begin to recognize. Mat had heard it too, and was looking at me, but I just shrugged and pressed on. Maybe these punks who had stolen my house were just straightforward, happy-go-lucky punks whom I might have shared a wave and a laugh with at some time in my life at East Cliff or Steamers.

Nevertheless, I thought, the fuckers had stolen my house and I shouldn't forget that. But boy, whoever it was singing, was really having trouble hitting those top notes. We reached the door and could hear the beat of the music clearly now. It was an old David Bowie track called "Changes." I thought about trying the door, but I didn't want to surprise whoever was inside, so I just knocked loudly. And then we waited. The singer belted on, and the music was probably loud enough to mask out pretty much any other noise. After a minute, Mat was about to try the handle, but I stopped him. I waited for the track to come to an end, and knocked again in the relative silence.

There was a heavy pause and some audible scrambling. It opened very slowly and carefully, and a Caribbean Rasta with short, tight dreadlocks poked his head extremely gingerly around before exploding into a broad, white-teethed smile.

"Moose!" he cried. "Hey, it's the Moose!" he shouted to someone inside and, as he threw open the front door, I saw the other man, who was overweight, pale-skinned, about thirty, and looking sceptically in our direction.

"Kill him," this other guy said nonchalantly.

"No," boomed the Rasta. "It's the Moose! See?"

"We should kill him," said the man, totally unconcerned that I could clearly hear every word he was saying.

"Sorry, please ignore John," said the Rasta, turning back to us. "He wants to kill everyone."

"We did kill the last one," said John, still ignoring us.

"Will you please just drop it?" cried the Rasta. "Ignore him, Moose. Come in. Make yourself at home! We didn't kill anyone," he added.

"We should have killed him, though, just like we should kill this one," said John. "I want it on the record that I wanted to kill him."

"This is so great that you are here," went on the Rasta, shrugging off the last comment. John now hung back, deliberately keeping his distance. "Did you try the singing thing like I said?"

"The stuff I need from my house for the information you need about it. Right?" I said, wondering what we had walked into here.

"Chill out, Moose! Chill out. Come on, let's have a drink. We've been stuck in here together for days, and it's just great to see someone else."

I nodded. A drink seemed quite a good idea; it was going to take me a while to sort through my dream library, and I needed to calm down and think straight before I started. We walked through into the living room, and everything was pretty much where I had left it, except I had the weird feeling all the objects were vibrating slightly as though in shock at being wrenched here, and I couldn't quite seem to focus on the sharp edges of anything. Looking around, I felt a rising tide of materialism and a desire to hang on to all my stuff, but I reined in those thoughts; staying alive was better.

"Long Island Iced Tea, right, Moose?"

I nodded.

"Same for me, please," Mat said.

"Fine," said the Rasta, smiling. "And, as it's the only thing in your drinks cabinet, why don't we all have one?"

"Tch," said the other guy, John, shaking his head and turning away.

"He'll be OK once *Sarah the Space Chicken* comes on later; he loves that program. I am so glad you are here, Moose!" the Rasta went on more loudly, fixing the drinks.

"How did you know it was me?" I asked, not greatly caring about the answer.

"Your pictures, Moose, all the pictures of you and your wife about the house."

"My wife?" I said, knowing I was pretty certain there was no picture of me and Sarah anywhere.

"Yes, and doesn't she half-look pretty with those blue eyes?"

"Sarah has brown eyes," I said, staring at him.

"Well, then, someone's been messing around with your photos, Moose, because your wife has the bluest eyes I have ever seen."

My mind began to thump. Something was not right here. There was a yawning gap, like a crevasse in reality, and I didn't know whether I dared to go any farther and look over the edge.

"What's the name of the person you stole my house for?" I said quickly.

"I can't say, Moose. You must see that."

"Yes, you can. Give me the name. Just the name." And he was taken slightly aback by the new, steely tone of insistence in my voice.

"Don't tell him. It's classified," called the fat white man smugly, sensing his indecision, then spitting on the floor to prove some point about his status. The Rasta looked at me straight in the eyes, holding out my drink.

"Some guy calling himself Exodus," he said. "What does it matter?"

"Oh! Now we will have to kill him," said the sweating guy, outraged and still keeping his distance, but no one was really listening to him.

"Exodus?" My throat went dry and I could hardly speak. "Exodus is my alias, my work alias."

"Well lucky for you," said the Rasta, sorting out Mat's drink.

"So what happens when Exodus arrives here?" I pressed on, feeling something inexorably building here.

"This Exodus guy is going to give us the password, and we'll take the house to a desired location," said the Rasta.

I swallowed heavily.

Events and images from the past few days suddenly melted and ran like hot lava through my mind. Things were merging and forming, and for a sliver of a second I had no idea what I would end up with. Perhaps nothing much, like those cold, hard black nodules that lay everywhere outside. But I could feel everything that I had taken for granted was suddenly molten, then abruptly, all kinds of ideas cooled quickly into more solid form that would take hours to explore in detail. But already I had a big sense of something that ripped through me.

"Cheers," said the Rasta, and we clinked glasses.

"All shall be well, and all shall be well, and all manner of things shall be well," I said, and the Rasta choked on his Long Island Iced Tea, spitting it everywhere.

"Fucking Hell, Moose! Moose?"

"Is it right?" I said, feeling a burning in my eyes.

"What's going on here?"

"Is it the right password?"

"Yes. It's the right one, man. How did you know?"

"How did I know?" I said, asking myself the same question.

"What the fuck is going on?"

"We should definitely kill him now," said the big sweating guy.
"No question. You kill him first, then I'll make sure afterward,"
but he made no move to do anything.

"Listen to me," I said ignoring him, "I am Exodus; I arranged
for you to steal my house," I said, not really believing it myself
but just letting my mind run with it, because I had nothing to
lose. I saw Mat look at me with the sort of expression of surprise
he normally reserved for when he was told he would not be allowed in the VIP section of the 49ers' lounge because they only
allowed VIPs in there, and not just people who asked nicely.

There was a pause, and the Rasta stared at me. "You understand it was me?" I said. "That password about 'All shall be well'
is the one I use at work."

"OK, OK. Just chill out, Moose. This is very weird."

"Exodus asked you to leave this card, didn't he?" I said,
pulling out the "Don't you hate it when that happens?" card.

"Why would he do that?"

"Pah!" spat the white guy, as though this didn't prove anything.

"You must believe me. I'm Exodus. I am him," and I realized I
was suddenly sounding too desperate and everyone knew it.
The delicate spell I had been weaving was broken.

"Come on, Moose. I'm not buying it. You haven't even got the
tattoo."

"Which tattoo?"

"The tattoo he told us about."

I could feel panic spreading more forcefully through my chest, now. I didn't have a tattoo. What was he talking about? Maybe I had been completely wrong after all; maybe the desperation I felt was because I knew I was grasping at straws, grasping at anything, hoping that somehow I could make everything all right just by convincing these guys some crazy idea I had was true.

"The tiny tattoo on your left butt," he added.

I had come this far, and now I had driven into a roadblock of sand, but some part of me put faith in a feeling that made no sense, that had no ground in reality.

I didn't have a tattoo. I hated tattoos. As far as I was concerned, they were badges of stupidity that had to be worn like a sentence through life, long past the time when they ceased to mean anything to you. Like an outrageous haircut that refused to grow out, like a pair of silver boots that got stuck to your feet. Nevertheless, I unbuckled my belt and dropped my pants. The Rasta looked on, appalled.

"Come on, Moose. Don't do this. We both know you haven't got the tattoo. I'm not buying the bluff, but it's a nice try."

But I slid down my underwear. "What does it say?" I said quietly.

There was a prickling pause.

"The Dream Virus Project," said Mat finally, and I heard the tension breaking his voice up.

"Jesus," said the overweight guy, and the empty, shocked silence that followed said all I needed to know. My head almost broke open with emotion, because I sensed I had crossed a line in the sand and was on the way home, finally.

Even though I didn't understand it at all yet, I knew that events had an unstoppable momentum all their own, that I could ride without looking back.

I was Exodus.

I had told these guys to do this myself, although I had absolutely no memory of it. The Rasta exploded into a smile again. "I knew I liked you, Moose. You're as mad as hell. Fucking hell, Moose! You got us to steal your own house! What was all that about?"

"Not sure exactly," I said, breathing with relief and pulling my clothes back on. "But I know where to find out."

"Good! That's good!"

"Take my house to this place," I said, scribbling down the name of a cove Mat and I had been to on trips to Baja.

"It's the north end of Isla Todos Santos," I said, aware this whole idea had no real logic to it, but things were falling into place and this was one of them. I just had to trust myself when things felt right, and this felt like the thing to be doing.

"Is my bike still in the garage?"

"Guess so."

"Good. We'll meet you at that place as soon as we can. Now, you'd better get moving."

"OK, OK, sure you wouldn't like a cookie? John's been busy with them all day."

"OK," I said, fizzing with adrenaline. "Let's have a cookie."

"This is classic, Moose! Classic!" said the Rasta, passing over a plateful. "You are one weird person, and I like that. I knew I liked you!"

"Dark," said Mat, shaking his head as he ate his chocolate chip cookie. "I'm hoping you have some idea of what is going on now, Jonny, because otherwise I suggest we go to Hawaii forever."

"Yeah. We need to get over to see Habakkuk, but I don't know whose side he's on in this. So be ready, OK?"

"For what?" Mat said.

"Beats me. But I guess you'll know if it happens."

There was a knock at the door and we all froze. The Rasta

made a pressing-down sort of gesture with his outstretched palms that I took to mean "Keep quiet," then tiptoed rather pointlessly over to the door before opening it as gingerly as before. I noticed the overweight guy had sheepishly sidled out of sight behind a pillar. There was a familiar and wildly out-of-place voice.

"Can I see Jonny, please?" said Teb, like an eight-year-old wanting to know if the neighbor would like to come out to play.

"Jonny. Hi!" said Teb, bustling in red-faced and breathless. "I've been through the file. I don't exactly understand it, but my feeling is, Habakkuk does, and he will try and kill you."

"Wow!" said the Rasta, "that's one bad messenger. Here, Moose, you'd better take my gun." And he tossed me a pistol with an overlong golden barrel.

I looked at him.

"So I like gold," he said with a smile.

43

I understood now why Habakkuk had not hounded me over my absence from work. I was guessing he knew about all this—or at least he knew about some of it. Maybe he had been even partly to blame for the insane events, but for what possible reason I had no idea other than it was something to do with that file. I swung the bike into the Nineteen Seventies Zone, which meant we were only three blocks from the EasyDreams office, and my brain felt like it was so fired up every cell had its own separate opinion. I hadn't even looked at the wedding photos the Rasta had been going on about, but never mind. Maybe subconsciously, I hadn't wanted to anyway, in case I was wrong—and I really didn't want to be wrong now.

I tried to nail my feelings down, to stop them from slopping about in the massive soup of adrenaline that was washing through me. The Dream Virus Project had to be the key. That's what linked Habakkuk, my house, and the Riders; it seemed obvious, although the details in my head were sketchy as hell. The Riders had gone on about an airborne Dream Virus that could find one specific person and trigger the same dream night after night; that was crazy, but what seemed to be happening to me was all one step beyond even that. What would I say to Habakkuk exactly? "Hello. What the fuck have you done to my head?"

There again, if he knew nothing about this, he was going to shovel work-related grief down my neck faster than even your average anaconda could swallow. Well, let him, I thought, revving the bike across a junction with Mat and Teb on the back. What did I care? My job and my dream architect clients seemed so far removed from anything that meant anything that I could live with losing all of that.

But there was something else. I was nervous about meeting Habakkuk, and it wasn't just Teb's weird warning. Some undefined thing was gnawing away at me about him, and I couldn't sense what it was. We passed a group of office staff trolling down the sidewalk in silver flares and wide-collared shirts, and I began to feel a cordial of tension slither through me. I was about to open a Pandora's box and Pandora had spent far more time packing this one than the one you read about in the classics. What was I going to find at the office?

Some bizarre connection in my head suddenly made me think about those tweed-clad Victorian archaeologists, sweating in the dark with their flaming torches in the airless stone chambers on the outskirts of Cairo, about to prize open an Egyptian tomb with worn metal tools, unsure whether they would find dusty skeletons or twinkling treasures in the sarcophagus beyond.

I tried to breathe deeply and retain some sort of logic in my head; I didn't want to blunder into his office like a bull in a china shop—or indeed, like any kind of dairy animal visiting any sort of consumer outlet.

We weaved on through the traffic, sliding by a heap of massive textured-concrete slabs that were pitted with slanting windows and looked vaguely like a twentieth-century concrete gun emplacement that had been mistakenly built out of jelly and immediately begun to melt. This 1970s-style building was the head office of the S.C. Cookery Vets Practice. They were essentially vets and tried to save pet animals, but as a last resort—if they had to put them down—they cooked them on the spot into a special commemorative meal for the owner.

I flicked the machine between a couple of other bikes—some Flat Iron Guns and a Crossfield 23M—but my thoughts were still wildly jumpy, going off like firecrackers in my head. What the hell was I going to find? And why did I have a terrible lung-aching, hollow-stomached, dry-throat feeling that Habakkuk was setting me up? The dream about him suddenly spun back to me, and I pictured his face laughing from the top of the crevasse. That had been one unsettling dream, and maybe that was the root of my unease.

We were only a block away from the EasyDreams office. The company felt that the Nineteen Seventies Zone gave it some kind of retrocredibility that dream clients of all ages were comfortable with. They claimed it was good marketing, and maybe they were right; or maybe it was all part of creating a nice little easy-money marketing job for themselves.

Up ahead, I could now see the building, flashing with reflective glass and twirled in steel, rising like some giant, organic thing. It wasn't exactly 1970s in style, but that was frankly a godsend, because it freed the place up from having to look terrible.

I pulled in to the bike lot, throttled right down, and snuck into a parking space. Glancing around, I saw that too many of the familiar bikes that should be there were missing, and I didn't have a good feeling about that.

Where was everyone?

The three crash suits undid with a whirr, and as we all slipped off I realized it was a balmy late afternoon and the sun was still drifting in between the buildings, so that I could feel its reassuring warmth across on my back. I breathed in deeply.

This was it. This was fucking it.

We walked quickly over to the arched front doors without saying a word, my legs moving a little quicker than I intended, as though they just couldn't wait to take me to see what was going on. As we slipped into the foyer, I realized I didn't have any kind of ID and Teb had masked our C-4 Charlies so we could get into Zone Traffic Securities. I prepared myself for a battle with the girl at the desk.

She was engrossed, as nearly always, with painting her nails. Those nails must have had more coats of paint on them than the Bay Bridge, I thought. Her painting output would have rivaled Gauguin and Matisse put together if she had chosen to paint canvases instead of just her nails.

She half-looked up with a disinterested sneer as we approached, but didn't say anything and her eyes wandered away from us as we got closer, as though it was inconceivable we were actually going to want to speak to her.

"Hi, Karen," I began, wondering what the best way was to tackle this. "I've worked in EasyDreams for seven years, okay? But my C-4 Charlie is acting up." She slanted her eyes toward us and carried on dabbing her nails.

"One moment," she said eventually, with enough disinterest to kill a cat at fifty yards, but made no move to do anything. The three of us exchanged glances and stood, marooned in the silence that followed, feeling as helpless as if we had been abandoned unexpectedly in the middle of a remote colony of puffins.

Finally, she plonked the tiny brush back into the bottle of nail polish, slipped off her chair, and disappeared through a door behind her, clacking her heels across the hard floor. She returned moments later with several plastic wristbands. "Three passes. Can you sign for them here?" She slid over a SignatPad, and managed to convey with her manner just how much trouble she felt we had put her to and how the next time she would probably have to call in the army for this kind of misdemeanor.

"Thank you," said Mat with an impressive amount of charm under the circumstances, and we all signed, one after the other in flourishing scrawls, then bounded into a waiting elevator.

"EasyDreams," I said, feeling the strange familiarity of being back here again, as though it was any other day at work. Except, while everything here was the same, now I was like a spectator looking in from the outside instead of being an integral part of it.

"Knock, knock," said the elevator.

"What?" said Teb.

"Knock, knock," said the elevator again.

"Oh! Let's just use the stairs," I said, not having the patience to be screwed about by an elevator again.

I headed out and toward the first flight, without waiting.

Mat was close behind while Teb did his best, but his diet of doughnuts left him straggling, and I decided we might as well let him get there in his own time. So I pressed on ahead.

"Wait!" I heard the elevator cry. "Wait! Please. It's just a joke," it went on, its voice fading as we thwick-twacked through a set of double doors.

It was four flights, and I began bouncing up them, happy to be free from a time-on-its-hands elevator and a receptionist who felt her whole job was a flagrant imposition on her leisure time.

I hadn't used the stairs for years, and clearly not many other people had either; they felt foreign and were dusty as hell, echoing the noise we made like some yawning crevasse. I got a flashback of that feeling I'd had in the ice with Jack. Fire escape staircases are alien territory, I thought, and no place for humans.

We reached the second floor as Mat came up alongside me, leaping two treads at a time, and suddenly the idea that I had arranged for my own house to be stolen came back to me with a wild jolt. How could that have happened? Was I really the Exodus they had been waiting for? What had blocked out such a chunk of memory that I could have no recollection of it? One more floor, and tension rose through my chest again as a lash of nervousness ran across my neck. I sprinted up the last few steps and clattered through the double doors to the fourth-floor landing, heading straight for the main doors of EasyDreams. If Habakkuk knew we were coming, the less time he had to prepare the better. I walked brazenly into the open-plan atrium at a fast walk, expecting to skip across the bustling floor and straight to Habakkuk's office on the far side, but I broke my stride almost immediately.

The place was utterly quiet, and incomprehensibly dark.

Like a forgotten Egyptian tomb.

44

I heard a spectacular clatter as Mat went headlong into a potted plant in the achingly black room, and it occurred to me that if you really want to stop an invading army, you just had to put a lot of potted plants and knee-high coffee tables in their path, then see how far they got with their night assault. They'd be too busy rubbing their shins to do anything.

"Have we got the right floor, Jonny?" Mat hissed as he pulled himself up on my left arm.

"Yes, right floor, but probably the wrong universe or something. It's not Sunday, is it?" I said, realizing I was speaking in a half whisper as well, for reasons that were beyond me. We both stood hovering there stupidly and I tried to think of a possible explanation. Habakkuk was fastidious about people working the correct number of hours, meeting deadlines, and that sort of thing. He could be incredibly dull about it, so to close the office down would be a big deal for him. A very big deal. Maybe the marketing people had upped and moved everyone to Klick Track or Wah-Wah as part of some new sales initiative, but somehow I didn't think so. There was a massive, hollow, shuddering crack behind us, and everything in my head said the moment had come.

But all I could do was turn.

The doors were already flicking shut, and I swallowed.

"Jonny?" wavered Teb's voice, after a pause.

"Jesus, Teb. I wondered what that was," I breathed as he stumbled forward into us.

" 'When shall we three meet again?' "

"Teb?"

" 'In thunder lightning or in rain!' "

"That's definitely enough Shakespeare," I said, catching his drift, but he muttered on with it.

" 'When the hurly-burly's done! When the battle's lost and won.' "

I looked around, feeling the soft rub of my coat across my neck, and inexplicably made out some large red numbers dancing in the dark, like a large clock that was counting down at a ferocious rate, shoveling through hundredths of a second as though it was flicking through the pages of a book. Part of it read: sixty-four, fourteen, thirty-four, and I was trying to understand if that meant anything to me when the world imploded into a searing, scorching firestorm of light, suffocating the darkness, burning straight through my eyes, and searing across my head.

The sheer white-hot blaze of incandescence ahead of me

made it feel as though God Himself had chosen that moment to finally descend to earth, perhaps to ask everyone what exactly they thought they were doing, precisely. And had anyone seen His glasses or something. All three of us cowered there while a voice cut through the white air.

"Kill it!" it cried, and I felt myself go numb with fear. The momentum from my run up the stairs suddenly washed away and my legs were violently heavy with inertia, as though I was stapled to the floor.

Then time stopped, but not literally.

I could somehow still see the red figures of the clock, and they froze, then hung in the air like a person who had opened his mouth but forgotten what it was he wanted to say. As I tried to think of anything in this vacuum of confusion, the fierce light blinked out with an audible, implosive "kaboof," and a myriad of softer, warmer lights flickered on around and above us, gradu ally pulling the building out of the darkness and patching together the familiar atrium in soft blurred areas, which hardened into focus as my eyes readjusted. The four or five balconies that looked down from above were stacked with people I half recognized but couldn't place with any certainty, and I suddenly realized they were clapping.

"Sixty-four hours, fourteen minutes, and fifty-six seconds," the cold, clipped voice cried, somehow finding its way over the cheers. My eyes scurried around to see who it was, and as it did, I wondered whether we should all just run now while there was still a sliver of a chance. But Teb could never make it, and we couldn't just leave him.

Besides, we were not dead yet, and, although I wasn't buying into this strange welcome, maybe there was a chance to find out what had been happening.

"Very commendable. I calculated you would take at least four

days, but you've made it here in less than three." The voice went
on and my eyes settled on a figure directly ahead, hunched on the
second-floor balcony next to a massive old-fashioned searchlight that was now switched off, but still faintly purring with a red
glow.

My heartbeat stumbled as I wrenched the person into focus. It
was Habakkuk. Habakkuk was standing there with a thin, weasel-
like smile, his bald head glistening with perspiration, clapping
with only a veiled gesture of effort, and I wondered why I had
not known it would be him all along.

"It's Habakkuk," said Mat, quietly. "I knew that bastard was at
the heart of this."

"He certainly knew we were coming," I said, above the
lengthening noise of the weird ovation from the crowd.

"Habakkuk. Do you mind awfully if I ask you what the fuck is
going on?" I said, deadening the applause so it stuttered to an
embarrassed halt.

"Oh come on, Mr. X, surely you've worked it out! A genius
like you?" he said into the echoing silence, reveling rather too
openly, I thought, in my confusion. I didn't like the way his
words seemed to curl up at the ends either, almost as though
they had been soaked in some sort of acid. Now I understood
why Mat disliked him so much; maybe I had always made a bit
of an effort to put up with him as a necessary pain in the ass because he was my boss, but as he stood there, leering down, all
that goodwill just dried up.

"Did you do all this stuff to me?" I cried, but his face just broke
into a strange, stifled wheezing laughter that seemed to be
throttling the life from him. His whole expression reminded me
of a gargoyle carved by some mischievous medieval stone-
mason that looked like a cross between a hobgoblin and a
strangely shaped potato. It suddenly occurred to me I had never
actually seen Habakkuk laugh before, and he clearly needed a

lot more practice and possibly some training. It drew my attention away from the fact the rest of the crowd seemed to find my last comment pleasantly amusing too.

"You haven't worked it out at all, have you?" he said eventually, as the murmured laughter faded, and I could see he was still reveling in the pleasure of having me so neatly under his thumb. Then, without any kind of warning, I felt something give deep inside my head, as if it was crumbling under the sheer intensity of this moment. "You disappoint me, Jonny X. Honestly. You were so adamant about it beforehand."

But I hardly heard him, because my brain felt like it was running with the same thick treacle that had been dripping and slopping about when we'd been surfing. There was a warm, dull, distant ache near the crown of my head. A tiny cracking sound ran through my skull as my eyes defocused, and I was overwhelmed by vivid slabs of memories from the past few days coming to the fore, then sliding away from my consciousness, like the ice shelves calved off a glacier. Huge, knifelike crevasses cut through the very sense of who I was. I had a heart-burning, tearing sensation that a foreign part of me was careering through my mind, grasping an older me by the collar, trying to drag it free from this melee before it was totally crushed and lost.

"I did this," I said, before I had even been aware of knowing it, and the words sat neatly on the heavy silence that felt like it had piled up thickly across the floor, as though having some strange, liquid quality. I realized my mind was working in a very weird way to be thinking like this. "I did it all," I went on almost automatically, knowing somehow it was incontrovertibly true, but still not understanding any of it.

"Oh, bravo!" cried Habakkuk, exploding with sarcasm as he began clapping alone, so that the noise of each clap echoed, bald and naked. "Bravo, Mr. X. Give that man a banana!"

"I got them to steal my house, I put the Riders after me, and I got those encyclopedia salespeople to come after me too. It was me, wasn't it?"

"Top of the class! For a moment there you had me worried. Bravo!" he cried, still clapping. "But you always like to think you have something up your sleeve, don't you, Mr. X?"

"Why did I do it, Habakkuk? And where the fuck has my memory gone?" I added, realizing I was sounding too much like a child who had lost a favorite toy.

"Come, come! This is a party. See?" he said, gesturing to the balconies of people—and for the first time I properly took in that there were streamers and balloons hooked over the balustrades and hanging gaily from the ceiling. "We even have fireworks," he added.

My mind kicked sideways. "Jonny and Mat, please don't be late for the party!" I thought, remembering the words and pulling the card out of my pocket. I had picked it off the exit door on the Thin Building. They had just been toying with me, playing me like some dumb animal.

"The prodigal son has returned to the scene of the crime," he cried, mixing his metaphors like a cheap cocktail. "I'll see you later. You have some things to tell me. In the meantime, enjoy yourself!" And he backed away from the balcony, setting alight a low, excited murmur in the bulging crowd. But that didn't feel right; it didn't make sense to get drawn into all this without getting any kind of answers.

"Now, Habakkuk! Why don't we have the answers now, so everyone can hear them?" I shouted, but he brushed aside this comment with a limp waft of his right hand and a too-smug smile and began to leave. I don't even remember thinking about it; I simply drew the gun and there was a confusing sense of déjà vu about the whole moment, as though I had done this a million times before, so that I felt like a detached observer to my own actions. The gun was satisfyingly cool in my hand, and I carefully leveled it at him. It would be crazy to shoot, I said to myself. It would be the end of me, I must not do it, but my personality seemed frighteningly split, and I heard the jolt of the explosion crack around the atrium, echoing bluntly off the hard stone walls like a thin, wild cat skulking about maniacally to find a way to freedom.

Habakkuk wavered, and I was convinced he would fall in an easy swallow dive to the floor, felled like a deadweight; but he rode the moment, then glanced back, alert and brisk, as he watched the glowing parachute of the purple fireworks drop, lazily smoking down into the atrium until his eyes rested on me.

I had the gun in hand, still aimed directly at his head. I couldn't have fired the thing at all, I realized. It had simply been fireworks excitedly ignited by someone in the crowd. Habakkuk stared in my direction now with a hard, cold, pinpoint glare that had no human warmth to it at all.

"No real bullets in the guns anyway, Mr. X," he said with a quiet, flat, dull expression. "They were all fake; all of them. You arranged it. You planned it. Fire as much as you want. You won't hit a thing." The triumphal edge to his voice had completely gone now, and his tone was flat and serious, as though we had moved into an arena he had hoped to avoid.

I swung around and pointed the gun at an oversized ornamental vase that stood on a plinth not five yards away and pulled the trigger. There was a much louder, ear-cracking spit from the gun, and the noise bounded around the atrium, running up and down the walls until it exhausted itself and died.

But the vase didn't so much as wobble.

"You want something from me, Habakkuk. You have to explain here and now, or we're leaving. And you won't find me again. I promise that."

I was clutching at straws so furiously that I might have snatched enough to build a haystack and perhaps some rather fetching corn dollies, but the idea of me leaving seemed to hit a raw nerve and he hesitated. I saw his weaselly eyes dart about, and his head was alive with sharp, angular movements. It occurred to me that, whatever he wanted, it must be pretty important.

"It's your party," he said, turning back and breaking into a thin smile to cover his nervousness. "We'll play whatever game you want. What would you like to hear? Let's see...how about that you caught a virus that affected your head and overwrote your memory?"

"I caught a disease?" I said, momentarily stunned into almost mute confusion.

"Exactly! Your fake past is just a disease that you caught, but once under its grip your mind was controlled by it. You'll recover; your body will build up an immunity to the virus and the disease will die, leaving your memory as it was before. It will take you another twenty-four hours, I should think, before your mind is back to normal."

"What the fuck are you talking about?" I said, knowing that if part of my memory had been overwritten in some way, it would explain everything. It would explain why so many of my memories seemed paper-thin and insubstantial; why I'd been plagued by the uncomfortable feeling that I had lost track of who I was, as though my real self had deserted me and just left a mush of papier-mâché in its place.

"What else would you like to hear, Mr. X? That you invented it? That you wanted to try it out first of all, along with a collection of volunteers?" He was warming to his theme again, reveling in his role like a circus ringmaster. "The Dream Virus Project. A waking dream that you catch like a disease, but which can only infect you if your DNA has been written into the virus. Sound familiar, Mr. X?"

My mind was torn apart, a side of me knowing this was the truth, but finding nothing in my head that could verify it. I furiously riffled through my mind, like a burglar plundering a filing cabinet, tossing papers over his shoulder, but there was nothing tangible to be found. Just file after file of blank white pages, and all the time I had a growing unease about Habakkuk.

"Then that file about the Dream Virus was all true?" I managed.

"Mostly. Yes." Habakkuk was confidently tapping down the stairs toward me, with the crowd silently slipping in behind him, like some weird cult procession. "You see, you wanted to give yourself plenty of clues to the truth; you wanted to find out how successfully the disease would work. Just how much of a trigger would it take to make you remember. As you can see, it worked so well, you remember almost nothing."

"So who were the Riders, then?"

"Come on, Jonny!" said Habakkuk, snapping across the floor to meet me with a shake of the head as the atrium filled with people. "Don't you understand? They were all your friends. All these people here," he said, gesturing around. "You wrote each one of them a separate Dream Virus. They all had their own false memories, so each would play a part in your...experiment. It took you a full year to plan. Trays and trays of glass phials, each with a separate Dream Virus. Don't you remember?"

" 'It is a tale told by an idiot, full of sound and fury, signifying nothing,' " said Teb quietly, and I looked around at him wondering what planet he was coming from now, but Habakkuk wasn't done.

"Jonny X. You must see it, surely?" he said, putting his arm stiffly on my shoulder in a gesture I was meant to take as friendliness.

I stared at him, and I did see it. I saw it all.

The crowd was swarming into the atrium now, bunching around us, glasses filled with champagne, all with smiles of concern and excitement, each trying to catch my eye with an "it's all true" raise of the eyebrows.

I looked around and saw the bouncers from Inconvenient; the Zone Securities policemen; the mad guy from the encyclopedia offices; Sarah, my ex-wife who was probably not my ex-wife at all; the Belgian assassin; even the Father Christmas sleigh driver. And as I turned farther, there, up on the balcony, I saw Caroline, all alone, staring down on the crowd.

"So there never was such a thing as a limpet encyclopedia salesperson?" I said, still staring up at her, and she looked back with an easy, gentle smile. Someone in the crowd chuckled, and said something like:

"You got it, Jonny. That was all your idea." And then I felt myself loosening up. What the hell was I worried about Habakkuk for? I had set this up; it was all my doing. I had masked my own memories with a disease, and soon I would get those memories back. And if I had been worried about Habakkuk, I would have put in some kind of safety net to catch myself. These people were all my friends, and I had written them each a different past so they could be part of my crazy adventure, only they had got their real memories back before I did, for some reason. Perhaps I had deliberately given myself, Mat, and Teb a stronger version of the virus, one I felt was too risky to expose everyone else to.

Caroline was still staring down at me, and I felt my heart smack into the pit of my stomach. I pushed through the crowd, making for the stairs, and she tilted her head quizzically, just as she had done the first time we had met when she had dropped from the helicopter.

Her eyes cut right through me, and I felt a thickness in my throat and a coolness on the back of my neck. I jumped up the stairs, not caring how public this was, and swung around onto the balcony, where she still stood, almost hovering, it seemed, stunningly alive and calm and set well apart from the madness and small-mindedness that seemed to infect people like Habakkuk. I stared into her blue eyes, which swam with the deep color of a vast summer sky in the warm, tender moments before sunset, and I drank in the soft, unbending pleasure of it all.

"Forgive me," I whispered, and touched her lightly on the cheek. She nodded almost imperceptibly, as though I had given her the answer to a question she had been asking herself.

"Welcome back, Jonny X," she said, with the smallest of smiles, which nevertheless transformed her face. "You nearly remembered our anniversary. That's pretty impressive, you know." I didn't even try to think what she meant by that, because I was on fire with emotion, so I just took her soft, warm cheeks between my hands and kissed her.

Fireworks exploded about us, as some romantic smart ass set them off, and the moment sent another sweet spiral of adrenaline ripping through me. The crowd let off cries of surprise and squeals of shock amid the flashes and cracks, as the fireworks coughed smoke and spat sparks, dangerously close to highly expensive office electrical equipment, but no one seemed to care.

And then, as I held her close, I saw a faint change knock the softness from her eyes, as if she had suddenly remembered something. She leaned over and spoke above the noise of the firecrackers. "You never wrote me a virus, did you realize? I was the safety net. You called me your guardian angel and I followed you everywhere, but Habakkuk never knew; he thought my memory was overwritten like everyone else's."

My throat dried and a shiver dropped through me like a shovelful of gravel. Although I had sensed this, I hadn't put it into thought, but it explained so much about her actions. But far more worryingly, it set alight a forest of uneasiness about Habakkuk again. Why had I thought I would need Caroline as a safety net? I scoured the atrium floor and just caught a glimpse of his shining head, reflecting the blue showers of the fireworks as he slipped away to his office.

"You know who all my friends are?" I said above the noise of the firecrackers, trying to get my feet back onto the ground.

"Of course."

"Good. Come on, introduce me. I want to talk to them all." We headed toward the stairs and a particularly insistent, whizzing sort of fireworks cracked off the balcony near us like a cornered squirrel with its tail on fire.

I grabbed up a couple of glasses of champagne from a white-linened table near the balustrade at the bottom, touched Caroline's arm and handed one to her. We made a silent toast, for a moment dropping away from the splutter and madness of the firecrackers. I looked into her eyes and the white-hot sparks of love I felt inside for this girl seemed to burst across the whole sky and scorch the well-manicured lawns outside in line after line of smoldering grass. And then we were engulfed in a barrage of slaps on the back and hugs of congratulations as the crowd swooped down on the pair of us.

I shook hands and laughed and thanked them all as we bundled our way over to Teb and Mat. Caroline poked fun at them, because they couldn't remember who she was at all and consequently were way too polite. I just smiled with a sense of relief, excitement, and pride in this girl, but with a feeling too that I was trying to cover a nervousness that lurked inside of me like a lungful of bees.

As Caroline explained, Mat, Teb, and I were close friends, exactly as our memories had it, and, I hadn't ever doubted it would be any different; the feelings I had for the two were too solid and strong to be something manufactured on a computer. We drank a glass or two and mingled with the ever-growing crowd, sliding among the little groups. I met so many of my friends all over again for the first time in a flurry of handshakes, spilled drinks, congratulations, and red-cheeked, alcohol-driven laughter. I had stepped outside my own life, and now I was getting it all back in one gigantic spoonful.

Sarah was there, flaxen-haired and laughing, explaining how she was my sister, regaling me with tales of growing up and family holidays. Eli was my first girlfriend, she said, divorced now but happy, with two fantastic children. She explained how we had kept in touch all this time, and knew each other back to front. We often wondered in drunken moments what would have happened if we had stayed together and ridden out the fires of teenage frustrations that had split us apart all those years ago.

The Belgian assassin was a surf mate called Luke, whom we had got to know sitting in the line up at Steamers; and one of the Riders really was called Jeff, and I had studied dream architecture with him at UCSC. He said we'd spent many reckless nights together, getting drunk and taking too many raw dreams that frazzled our heads. The last few days were like remembering a foreign holiday when you are back at work, he explained; the excitement and vibrant memories were being smothered by the mind-numbing familiarity of everything you thought, just for a moment, you had left behind forever.

He wanted to know the details of the virus and how it came about, but I couldn't tell him anything with my memory still wiped, then he started on about what was going to happen with the Dream Virus Project next.

It was like being kicked heavily in the stomach by a wild horse.

When you reach the top of a mountain, you have to remember amid the lash of explosive excitement at seeing the view that actually you're only halfway there, and it doesn't count for anything if you don't make it back down. And right now, I suddenly realized, I was only halfway there.

A band kicked off, careering into a wild, guitar-fueled song that was pitted with neat tunes and surprising harmonies, and after a few bars I could see that the noise would make it impossible to hear anything else, so I made an "it's too loud to hear" sort of gesture, shook Jeff's hand, and wound my way out of the crowd to the edges of the atrium, where I could think.

I found a quiet spot in the shadows, perched on a marble edging to a small raised garden area containing some manicured plants and an acacia tree. It was very weird seeing all these people talk about stuff that ran so completely contrary to the memories I held about them. My mind told me to run like fuck from someone like Jeff, but he was as gentle as anything, and the whole experience made reality seem incredibly brittle.

But either way, I realized I still had a nervousness about Habakkuk lying tightly curled somewhere inside me, and I had to sort it out. What was to become of the Dream Virus Project? A person could control pretty much anyone else in the world if they had their DNA; they could change all of their memories—which meant not just altering their hopes and desires a bit, but transforming their whole selves. This thing could whack away a person's character overnight. I had given myself a pretty tame dose; I had still known Teb and Mat and Santa Cruz, come to that. But what if you scrubbed everything and gave someone a memory that overwrote a whole new past? What if you gave them a virus from which the body could never recover? Would they start to live another life, unaware of everything that had gone before? Would they believe a lot of fake memories someone had written on a computer about who they actually were? My mind fought over this, spinning it around, watching the alarming, monstrous possibilities of it all. If the technology of the waking Dream Virus got out, it would mean people in small rooms could play God, and their victims would never even be consciously aware they had been hit.

Had I really bounded into this whole project blind to that? Had it just seemed like a bit of fun? Or had I been too wildly eager to stagger greedily across some virgin piece of scientific ground and stick a flag in it?

And what about Jack?

What about Jack?

The thought swept through me like a cold mountain wind, and I realized that I hadn't talked about it with Eli. Jack wasn't at the party, and the realization spread slowly through me like a cold, upturned bowl of ice cream that he wasn't coming later on either.

However much I wanted him to, however much the aching tightness in me asked God for him to be here, I know it just wasn't going to happen. My memory of the crevasse was too real, too hard-edged and vibrant to be anything fake and there was a deeper feeling too that cast the thing in stone. I didn't need to ask Eli about her brother.

Jack was dead, and it was all just as I had remembered it.

The frenetic activity of the virus in my head must have knocked the memory slightly so I was suddenly aware of it, just as a startled deer darting across a mountain slope can nudge an avalanche rolling into a valley below.

I breathed in deeply, feeling my way back to the present, and saw Caroline's face bobbing among the crowd as she laughed with the bouncer from Inconvenient who had OTTER tattooed across his forehead and still wore the huge earrings. I hoped for his sake that the tattoo was not actually real and was just some crazy random detail I had thought up in a drunken moment when organizing this whole bonkers charabanc of an adventure.

I had come so far, covered so much ground to be here, and yet wasn't I almost back where I had started? What had all this been for? And did I still have control of events or not? I prayed that I wasn't trying to shut the barn door on this whole thing after the horse had bolted, but something was nagging away at me saying that not only had the horse bolted but the farmhands as well.

And I had a sinking feeling they had taken the entire barn along with them.

"Weirdest party I've ever been to," said Mat, dropping himself down next to me, waving a glass in the direction of the crowd. "I don't know anyone, and they all know me really well."

"Yeah. Jack really is dead, Mat. I don't want you clinging to false hopes. Everything I told you before is true, even though our memories are screwed up," I said, guessing doubts about Jack must have been playing across his mind too.

"Ohh." He sighed, swallowing heavily. "I was hoping that he might—are you certain?"

"Yeah, I'm sorry. Why that memory came back like that was odd. I think the virus must have dislodged it somehow, because of all the weird stuff going on in my head."

"So what happens now? Do you know?" he murmured, perhaps, wanting to move on from Jack, not wanting to face up to the prospect of losing him for a second time. Not wanting to admit how much hope he had been nurturing.

"There's unfinished business with Habakkuk," I said. "And then it's all done and we can leave it behind. Forever."

"Good. I need some head space. We should just drop out and go surfing for a while."

"Yeah." I nodded quietly. "I'm still nervous about Habakkuk, although I don't think there's anything he can do. He's just a pen-pushing bureaucrat. Tell Teb and Caroline they shouldn't worry."

"Yeah, sure. If you're certain. There's one thing I still don't really understand though...Did you really not see me pull off those one-eighties today?" he asked with a sad grin.

"To Jack," I said, holding up my drink. "And to your mythical one-eighties, which, actually, I don't believe."

"Jack. And to all our friends here even though we don't have any idea at all who they are," Mat said, and sank the last of his champagne.

I wanted to just stay here and get drunk like Mat, but I knew I couldn't.

The time had come to finish this once and for all.

45

I found Habakkuk hunched behind his desk in his office, skimming through a lot of papers; but I sensed he was not taking a lot of it in, and I wondered exactly why I was here and not gunning down to Isla Todos Santos with the surfboards, ready for the dawn paddle out at Thor's Hammer.

As I've said before, I guess I'm way too curious. I can only think one of my ancestors was a cat, or something.

"Ah, good. Good," he said, jerking his head about, slipping the papers around to no obvious purpose, and I realized it was because he was nervous—there was something he was nervous about saying. There again, maybe he just felt embarrassed about his performance in the atrium now that we were face-to-face. He stopped to wipe the perspiration from his head as his mouth and eyebrows flitted about like yellowthroats in a tree. "So, you've had an amazing few days. The whole thing was a triumph, a splendid triumph, and the investment EasyDreams made in you seems to have paid off."

"In what way?"

"Come on, Mr. X. In every way! We spent a huge amount on this; on offices, helicopters, staff, and we had a deal. You said if you got back safely, you would give me the formula. So here you are!"

"You seem to be unaware that I don't remember anything about any formula. I don't even remember my own sister," I said, hugely relieved I still had control of this. I had built in a safety net, after all.

"But you will very soon, I'm sure," he said, with a thin smile that I didn't particularly like. "It was part of the deal. You would write the last bit of the formula on the board in there. I thought that was why you had come to see me now."

"No, and I have no intention of writing any formulae for anyone till I've had time to get my head together. Do you know how dangerous this thing is? What were we thinking?"

"Of course we knew. Please don't worry. We went through everything. I'm sure you will get your memory back soon."

And that's when I felt a skull-splitting crunch that cut through my head like someone was trying to cure my toothache by dropping an anvil on my head. I winced with the shock, which receded in a wave—but only slightly.

"Don't fight it, Mr. X. It's out of your control anyway. Your mind will decide these things for you, because they were written. Come!" I heard his voice echo somewhere, and I didn't like what he was saying—mainly because I had no idea what he was talking about. I felt reality sway alarmingly under my feet as though it had buckled, like the hull of a ship as it ran into an unseen iceberg. He guided me, staggering, through a door, and it felt like my legs had passed out before the rest of my body.

My vision swooped in and out. On the far wall was an old-fashioned blackboard, scribbled with waves of equations that ran and tipped as I tried to focus.

"Your work. Obvious stuff. But I need the real thing," he said, and I didn't like this. There was something going on here and I wanted to get out, but I couldn't do jack shit.

"I can't help you," I whispered, but my head was burning now and I felt like I was falling into an ever thicker darkness.

"Oh, but you will, Mr. X. You see, I wrote another virus. I wrote it, me! And then I slipped it into one of your batches, so you converted it into a disease with your secret formulae. You thought it was one for someone out there, one that you had written; you had so many to do, you see. And I wrote you a virus that would take a little longer to incubate, but would surface like a bolt as the other one retreated. It was one that would make you happily reveal the secrets of the whole project to me. The first symptom of my disease was that you would think it a good idea to see me in private. So you see, Mr. X, there is nothing you can do. Your mind is not your own and the beauty of it is, you did this to yourself!"

My thoughts seemed to sideslip, so that every time I opened my eyes I was somewhere else, yet still in the same place. Time hopped past in great lumps, taking gouges out of reality as it went.

"It's happening. It's happening! I thought it might be another few hours yet. Good. This is better than I thought. This is most convenient. I shall leave you to it. I have things to do. Here is the chalk," he said, picking up the box that was on the blackboard. "Here. Now, soon, you will be writing it all out, I'm sure."

I saw the shadow of his shape over by the door and tried to say something, but my mouth didn't seem totally connected anymore. "You always kept something up your sleeve, didn't you,

Mr. X? But I knew about your wife. I knew you didn't give her the virus. You see, I was always one step ahead. I had cut the strings from your safety nets before they were even in place."

My head ran with pain, and I knew that the other disease was taking a terrifying hold and I must not give in to it.

I had to be strong.

I looked hazily inside myself, trying to find the pathways to who I really was, trying to make the connections that I knew must be there; but for the moment, I just could not feel them. Even as I staggered wildly, I found that the chalk box was in my hand and my mind was splitting in two—one foreign half, standing off somewhere at the end of a long tunnel, looking in on me somehow. This other half was calm and cool and was willing me to write letters and numbers in strange combinations that meant nothing. I saw my hand pull a piece of chalk from the box and scrape it across the board, but it snapped in two. And while my vision swooped and dived, I caught a glimpse of something strange and glasslike that seemed to be embedded inside the chalk.

With enormous effort, I forced myself to hold the white stick an inch from my eyes as my mind rocked. Then part of me smiled, and my body kicked with silent laughter. I shouted Habakkuk's name as loud as I could, and the noise from my mouth seemed to come from another part of the room. He appeared blurred at the corner of the door and I beckoned him over, staggering wildly like a drunken tramp, and sweating like the kid at the school disco who never understood why he didn't get the last dance.

Habakkuk sidled toward me, saying something that I could not hear as I beckoned him closer, until I was near enough to whisper in his ear. Then I simply took his hand and pressed something into it and closed the fingers. He stared at me, then looked down to see what it was. In his palm was a small, slightly chalky glass phial with a shattered neck, spilling out liquid. On the side, in small, neat handwriting, it simply read, "Safety Net."

I saw the confusion in his face contort into twisted understanding. Then sheer panic.

The next moment, I passed out.

Epilogue

Mat, Caroline, and Teb said I acted like a mad-man for two whole days. I was constantly ask-ing for a pad and paper and writing reams of stuff and asking when Habakkuk would be there and could they mail it to him, or courier it, or send it by pigeon, or was he in the vicinity and was it worth shouting.

No matter how many times they explained that I should just chill out, I didn't seem to take it in—although they said they could see something in my eyes that told them I was still in there and battling.

After two days, the virus wore off and the fever passed. I came to in my bed with no real idea which reality I was in, but with Possible Horse, our cat, purring on my stomach. I lay there

in the white sheets and looked out between the trembling curtains to the darkness outside, and realized I could hear the sea,
gently lapping at the beach with each folding wave, and the ci-
cadas buzzing their legs off about how balmy the evening was.
There were soft voices laughing and chatting somewhere, and
the crackle of a fire shaking puffs of sparks into the thick night
sky.

I swung myself off the bed and shuffled over to the window
and peeked out. I saw Caroline, Mat, and Teb, and the Rasta—
who was a close friend, Jamie—hunkered down, lying on blankets by the flickering fire, cradling drinks. And even from here I
could feel the warm, easy pleasure they felt simply from being in
one another's company.

I walked achingly downstairs, trying to absorb the strangeness of my house being by the sea and piecing images together
of how I got here that still lay in a jumble in a box in the back of
my mind as though it hadn't been unpacked yet.

But it was all there—just very foreign, unreal, and shuffled.

"Hey, look who's here!" said Caroline, as I stepped out of the
back door, feeling the sand under my toes and breathing in the
night air from a sky that spread out above like the mind of God—
twinkling and sinking away with infinite, incomprehensible
depth. Caroline skipped over and reached up. I felt her soft,
warm hand touch my unshaven face, and I could see she could
tell the disease had passed and all my memories were my own.
I ran my fingers through her long hair, watching the sparkle of
the fire in her eyes and smelling the sweet perfume of the pine
branches as they burned, spitting and crackling excitedly, as
though in some sort of hurry.

But there was no hurry.

At last, my mind stilled and I could clearly see everything that
had happened, reaching back into the past in a long line like a
river, twisting and turning miles and miles from its source, until

it reached the sea. I kissed her tenderly, feeling the soft warmth of her slender body beneath my hands, and wondered how I could be so lucky to be here now, with this remarkable woman. And with such good friends.

"You know what the date is?" She smiled.

I shook my head playfully.

"October 18."

I looked at her, and she waited to see if I understood.

"Happy anniversary," I whispered in her ear, and slipped a bottle of champagne I had plucked from the fridge under her nose. Then, putting my arm around her waist, I swung her over to join the others. I could sense they were so chilled out, their bodies seemed loose and heavy with contentment.

"Hey, Teb, Mat, Jamie!"

"Hey! Hey! Hey!"

"You are one mad motherfucker," said Mat. "The first person I have ever met who struggled to give up smoking before he had ever even started."

"Good to have you back, Moose," said Jamie, slapping me on the back.

"Good to be here. Better than good. So great to see you all. That was a crazy adventure! I'm never ever doing anything like that ever again." I smiled. "Ever."

"Ahhhhhh! We'll see," came Mat's voice.

"No, I'm serious. What was I thinking? That was way too serious to be getting tangled up in."

"Yeah, but that's what you're like, Jonny. We all know that."

"Well, I'm officially retiring from all that kind of stuff as of now. Anyway, I have an announcement. It's our wedding anniversary today. Six years to the day since we were all gathered under the acacia tree for that photo."

And they all applauded, like we were a pair of enthusiastic street acrobats.

Later, lying there wrapped in a blanket by the fire, with Caroline nestled into the folds of my body, I told them everything. I told them how Habakkuk had realized that I had squeezed a phial containing a virus into his hand. He didn't know exactly what sort of Dream Virus it contained, but he wasn't stupid. He knew it meant when he caught it he would lose his past, probably forever, and he ran in a fit of panic, hoping he could get away.

"He passed out in the atrium," said Mat. "Came screaming out of the office and tried to squeeze through the band at the back of the stage. The guitarist yanked him forward to take a bow and he just blacked out. Everyone thought he was drunk or fooling around except Caroline—who hit his office like an express train and found you."

I became aware of the curving shape of her body close to me again and sank into the feeling, kissing her lightly and offering her an awkward swig of champagne. Then I began to explain how Habakkuk had made some kind of breakthrough, but he didn't have the knowledge to make the final leap of dream theory, which I was able to do. I told them my doubts about the project all along; I told them how I thought testing out the virus was a way to find out what Habakkuk's motives really were and whether he could be trusted.

And now, finally, Habakkuk was not a threat. He had caught a hugely powerful virus from that phial I gave him as he had feared, and now he had a different past forever.

"He's working in an orphanage in Mexico City. Those are the only memories he has, of wanting all his life to work in that orphanage."

"Is that fair?"

"I don't know. It's a tough one, but I think so. The whole project is so dangerous. He has lost his past life, but it means many others will not lose theirs. I think, in balance, it's justified—and he should be content there, because I wrote that into the virus.

But you can be sure I'm burying the whole thing forever now, and I hope nobody else stumbles on it for a long, long time."

I looked back in my head at the past days, and as Jeff said it would, it felt like gazing back at the memory of a holiday in some wildly different place that had slipped away too quickly, before I had time to get my hands around it. I'd laid clues in the adventure as I'd written the viruses—having people make me perfect cups of coffee; visiting our winter bolt-hole cabin in the mountains; pushing my credulity with the idea of a limpet encyclopedia salesperson or Four Riders wanting to assassinate God.

I never twigged that they were the bad guys and that the good guys were called Mat (Matthew), Mark (St. Mark's Encyclopedia), Luke (the Belgian assassin), and John. I guess it was all pretty obscure, and it wasn't like they were all obviously on the side of good anyway. I even planned to end the story here at Todos Santos: "All Saints."

I sure as hell didn't see the symmetry of the four Riders being balanced by Eli, Caroline, Emma, and Sarah; the four women

The night it started, I went on my own to the bar, got extraordinarily drunk, then broke open the phial I had written for myself. My fictitious girlfriend Emma hadn't even been there. The virus knocked me out cold, and I woke with a hangover and a whole set of new memories. The virus tended to do the same thing to everyone, whether they had been drinking or not. I'm certain that was why Mat woke with a hangover that day too.

We had released the viruses from the other phials a few hours earlier in the day, on the rooftop of EasyDreams. The thing was as contagious as bad hair. It could pick out a person's DNA in a five-mile radius from the faint vibrations it gave off. We named it the DNAura. It was almost like a phone call.

We knew the diseases were all going to get through to their targets. Everyone in the story was going to play their part.

There was a risk someone might have got hurt, but we

rehearsed many of the situations we knew would happen, so our subconsciouses had something to go on. We rehearsed the shoot-out at Inconvenient, with the planted charges to blow the walls apart, and the fall through the big windows with the parachute; we rehearsed the climb up to Argonaut Logistics. It was like being part of a film and doing your own stunts, but thinking all the time it was all for real. Sure, things could have gone wrong and that's why I put Caroline on my tail. She was both part of the story and outside of it, just as Habakkuk had guessed.

Maybe, I had sensed there would only ever be one trial run of the Dream Virus Project, and I wanted to push the limits of the experience. It was a dangerous thing to do but that's me all over—going the whole way, all or nothing, and too much curiosity for my own good. And that made the success of being back all the sweeter; the success of seeing if who I was was just my things and my job, or whether there was something more.

Things turned out well, and I wondered if you just hung in there long enough whether things always turned out well, as long as you kept believing.

In the morning we'll go for a dawny. In the morning, me, Mat, Caroline, and Jamie will paddle out the back at Thor's Hammer, just as it's getting light, and sit on our boards and watch the sun rise over the beaches on Isla Todos Santos.

We can all ask ourselves if we really know who we are, and sometimes it's hard to find an answer amid the clutter of life. I feel I found an answer by taking away who I thought I was, putting everything I cherished on the line, then somehow holding things together and coming through it all.

Perhaps that's why I did it.

I have always believed heroes are not born in the moment of victory but in the lonely hour when everyone has abandoned them; in the hour when there is nothing but dying hope, in the hour when they must stand alone against the rising tide of defeat. In that moment, even they may doubt, but they fight on anyway, because a memory of something lives deeply in their souls. In their selves. They put their trust in a belief they cannot see, or touch, or always explain, and while others plead with them to flee, so filled with fear their real selves cannot be heard, those who have this belief stand firm. This is the lesson life wants us to learn and tell our children.

Listen to your true self and trust it.

The mind is a distraction that should not be allowed to control our lives, or we die in a holocaust of meaninglessness, in a foray of paperwork, in a mountain of councils and neatness and nothingness.

Passion. Art. Nature. Love. These are the things that can lead us to who we are.

We are shaped by our experiences. We test the mettle of love under the heat of confrontation, but none of this means anything if we don't know our true selves. The true self that doesn't know fear, or jealousy, or hatred, but only deep love. So when things are lost and you are left to face the world alone, trust deeply in who you are; trust in its supple strength and strive, with every sinew, simply to be. Hamlet asked, "To be, or not to be?" There's a fucking simple answer, Hamlet:

Be.

Be with a passion.

Be.

About the Author

TIM SCOTT lives in England and writes for television. In 2003, he won a BAFTA. This is his first novel.

If you have enjoyed
Outrageous Fortune,
be sure not to miss

LOVE IN THE TIME OF FRIDGES

the next madcap novel from
the twisted mind of
Tim Scott.

Coming in Summer 2008

Turn the page for a special preview...

LOVE IN THE TIME OF FRIDGES
Coming in 2008

Trust me on this; common sense was regarded with suspicion by the Seattle police. If they ever came across it, they tended to stay well back and call for assistance. And common sense said that I had been in Attila's Diner eating chop suey that tasted like it contained more MSG than actual food.

But the summons was routine.

They had thrown up some roadblocks and snagged me on one as I headed back to the motel the night before. And now they wanted to print out all the images stored in my memory from the last thirty-six hours, because some hoods had pulled off a robbery in the area. The downtown police were trawling for evidence from anyone who came close to being a witness.

I guess they were pretty desperate.

Or maybe it was the kind of wild sweep they did all the time in Seattle. I didn't know the place well, and I'd never wanted to come here anyway. As far as I was concerned, we should be in Florida. At least the cheap hotels there didn't have mattresses that were as malleable as wet toast, or fittings that a paleontologist could have dated.

And anyway, I had a very bad feeling about this summons for reasons of my own. I really did not want some police cadet poking around in my head.

Frankly, I was nervous.

In fact, I was probably scared. But over the years, I had forgotten how to be properly scared, so all I was getting now was a rush of feelings that didn't know where to settle. Or how to form themselves into a simple, easy-to-grasp emotion.

I was in a four-person Pod on my way to Head Hack Central. The Seattle police had a reputation for being a pain in the ass when it came to doing stuff by the book, and I knew if I ignored this summons or faked ill health, they'd be on my case until they got bored.

Which might take years.

It might even take until after I was dead. They might visit my grave just to heckle me.

I had been on the run before, and it was tiring. It was a bad way to go through life. And it had confused things between me and Anna. In moments when my mind drove back into my past, I still regretted that.

So I was going to the summons, however much the idea grated on my nerves or wound up my heart until the beats just sounded like one continuous drone.

After all, it was only routine. And I would be out of there within the hour.

I'd found space in a Pod with an alarming crack running through the roof. In fact, the whole car was going to split in two at some stage, and I was gambling that it wouldn't be in the next few minutes. The odds were just about in my favor.

But not by as much as I would have liked.

The thing had been programmed to cut corners so aggressively that it slewed and screeched like a cat in a fight, and I saw people on the sidewalk cover their ears as we peeled past.

The suspension was fucked, and that meant that my head hit the roof with pretty much every pothole. And these downtown streets had so many potholes, it was as though Maintenance saw them as a feature they should encourage. As though in the future, they might be able to close the highway and open some sort of sanctuary.

The only other person in the Pod was an old lady who sat opposite, clinging firmly to a small umbrella. She had a smile resolutely frozen onto her face and seemed to be taking this journey in stride. The crack in the domed roof grated alarmingly as bits of Perspex showered down between us.

We both ignored it. She did a pretty convincing job.

I braced myself into one corner and scrolled through my phone book. It was stored on a data-fingernail, which threw up a tiny heads-up display of my numbers. Some people had features on all their nails. I just had a phone and a phone book on two fingernails of my left hand. The numbers glowed a faint, blurred blue as they hung in the air above my hand, and after a certain amount of messing about I selected Miranda's and dialed just as we hit a particularly deep pothole. My head cracked the roof like I had been hit with a sledgehammer.

"Fuck!"

Miranda had already picked up. "Is this a sales call?" she replied.

"No. It's me."

"Oh, Huck. What's up?"

"Did you find her?"

"No. They said she'd moved on."

"Great. Look, I'll be back at the motel within an hour, and then I suggest we get out of town. We never should have come. This police Head Hack thing terrifies me."

"What's the big deal with this, Huck? It's routine."

"I know, I know. I'm just scared of someone poking around in my head. It's a thing with me. Arrgghh!" I cried as we hit another pothole and my head smashed the roof.

"Huck? You okay?"

"Yes . . . no . . . This is getting to me."

"Well, just think of it like a new experience. When I was in Paraguay, I met this shaman who was always saying that you should search out new experiences."

Yeah, well, shamans say a lot of things. Most of them utter crap.

"Huck, you've fallen into a really dull rut. You need to get out of your comfort zone."

"But that's just it. I'm happy with being dull. I'm good at being dull. I could get a degree in it."

"Don't think like that! That's not why I hooked up with you."

"It's not just that, Miranda. I have this innate fear of my head getting damaged...Ah!" We hit another dip that threw me against the roof, and a scream of pain forked down my neck.

"Huck?"

"Why don't they make these Pods bigger? And better. Jesus."

"Huck, I can really feel your negative karma. I'm going to have to do some random act of kindness to balance things out. Accept what life throws your way. Who knows where it might lead? Talk to you later."

"Miranda, listen. Did I ever tell you my father died when I was two, from some people who were...Miranda? Who were messing around inside his head...Miranda? Miranda?" I ended lamely, realizing the line was dead.

"I'm sorry about your father," the old lady said, her voice vibrating as the Pod rattled furiously over the bumpy road. Or maybe that was just how she always spoke.

Perhaps age had put a crease in her voice.

"Oh, that's okay," I said, but I was touched she had taken an interest. She was one of those people it was easy to like straight off. It was a quality I had never mastered.

Not even slightly.

"My father died before I was born," she said, "when he tried to swallow a stoat. They say it was for a bet."

"A stoat? Is that so?" I tried to take this in. Was she joking?

"Yes. At the autopsy, the cause of death was just recorded as 'stoat blockage,' " she added. "Amazing, isn't it? Don't you think?"

"Yes," I said. And then I looked at her. "You don't think it said 'throat blockage' on the report, do you, and someone misread it?"

She stared at me and her eyes grew larger, but the moment was broken as the Pod slowed to a halt and I smashed my head one final time on the roof.

"This is the office of Police Head Hack Central," said the Pod voice.

"It's actually one more block," I said. "It's down there. And you really do need to get this suspension fixed."

"This is the office of the Police Head Hack Central," repeated the tinny voice. "Please leave the cab now, or you will be arrested under section forty-three of the Seattle penal code."

"It's one more block. There! It's down there."

"Your lucky number today is seven. Your lucky color is blue with some green. This is the office of Police Head Hack Central. Get out of the cab, or you will be arrested. Your receipt is being printed."

"I don't want a receipt."

"Please take your receipt," insisted the Pod as reams of paper spewed out.

"All right, all right. I'm sorry about your father, however he died," I said to the old lady, heaving open the curved glass door and grappling with the receipt.

"Oh, that's all right. Death is just an opening to another place, isn't it?"

"Is that right?"

"Oh, yes," she said. "And I get the feeling there'll be bluebells there."

I nodded and slammed the Pod door shut, and the whole thing rocked like a life raft on a swell.

Bluebells, I thought. Was it going to be like that? Was death a door to someplace else?

Or just a door to oblivion?

Then I was involuntarily sucked into the crowd. The sidewalks of Seattle writhed with such a wild cross-section of fashion statements, anthropologists might have struggled to classify the people wearing all this stuff as a single race.

I squeezed past a heavily manicured woman with a small dog encased in her hat—and then I noticed she was with a man who had an identical dog in his hat. And then a group of nuns went by, clad neatly in pristine wimples but carrying clear plastic riot shields, so they could keep the crowds away from the mother superior.

You didn't get this kind of stuff in Florida. People just wore normal clothes and hung out. It was as though the population here was trying to distract themselves and everyone else from the terrible weather.

"Hail Mary, Mother of Grace," said one overly large nun, whacking a businessman out of the way with her shield on the word "grace."

It took about fifteen minutes of being pummeled by this annoying shamble of people until I was outside the massive offices where they based Police Head Hack Central. I walked partially up the massive flight of steps and stopped.

The place was built of cheap stone and was meant to look like it came from ancient times, but it probably more closely resembled something from a very bad film set about ancient Rome.

I unscrunched the summons from my pocket, looked at it one more time, then walked up the remaining steps.

Police officers were flooding down in knots of twos and threes. They were conspicuously carrying small red truncheons and red guns. The use of the color red was restricted in this city, and the police must have had the franchise on it.

I walked through the doors and noticed that the huge Hessian doormat was printed with the words HANDS WHERE I CAN SEE THEM, BUDDY!

The front desk was dead ahead and was split into various areas by signs that flashed behind them. There were long lines at some of the windows. I tracked down the "Witness" one, and found the line consisted of just a huge man with a long, pointed beard and a drunkard in a cheap suit who was trying to flatten out a filthy piece of paper he had just removed from his pocket.

Someone had made a sign and stuck it up farther along, over one of the closed windows. It said: TRAMPS WHO JUST WANT TO COME AND SHOUT AT US. I was guessing this was a joke. But all the same, a couple of people were waiting patiently in line behind it.

Just being in this place trawled up a host of bad memories. There was some kind of palpable heaviness in the atmosphere, as though the echo from the frustration, pain, and anger of all the people who had passed through was almost too much weight for the air to bear. And at some stage, the air would give up and the place would become a vacuum.

The man with the beard seemed to have brought an actual filing cabinet with him on a dolly, and he was delving into various drawers again and again for papers. I guess he wanted to have all the bases covered.

A woman appeared slightly to my left, as if she had materialized out of thin air.

She had black hair wound tightly into a bun, and an unblinking expression. She pointed at me and mouthed something. It was unsettling, and my heart began buffeting my rib cage like it had a point to make. This woman had the words "Porlock Inc." printed across her top pocket, and as I stared at her she flickered and faded away.

She had been a hologram.

I stood for a moment, trying to take this in. You didn't see holograms anymore—not since they were banned by the military many years before. No advertiser in their right mind would mess about with them.

And this one had been really sharp. I had a bad feeling about this. There was something about her that had struck something deep inside me, and my thoughts sucked me away from the present. I rerolled her appearance in my mind, trying to recall her face, and what it was about her. I tried to reconstruct her lips and work out the words that should have been there.

"You, sir!" I vaguely heard the voice, but I was still trying to cling on to the image of the hologram so I could unravel its significance. "Next!" The rotund face of an overweight policewoman prodded at the edge of my consciousness. "Can you hear me, sir? Or is your head just too full of crap like the rest of them?"

I focused. The policewoman behind the desk had the sort of bad haircut that looked like it had been done on the move. Possibly at high speed. And a set of braces on her teeth that could have raised a passable amount of cash for its scrap value.

"Sorry...yes." I handed her the piece of paper with the summons seal and witness number.

"For a Head Hack, sir?"

"Yes."

"Weird what you can have stored in your memory and not know about, isn't it?"

"Is it?"

"Oh, yes. At the Christmas party, they had a look in my head for a laugh, and found an image of a man riding a bear and holding a candelabrum. Now, how did that get into my memory? I **would swear I've never seen anything like that. You'd remember** something like that, wouldn't you?"

"Yeah," I said.

"Then again, we have had some pretty wild parties here. Maybe it was one of those."

"Maybe."

"So, here's an album for you to keep the images. The copyright is yours once they've got the security clearance."

"Is that right?"

"And put these on, please," she added, pulling some big red clown shoes down from a shelf behind her and handing them to me.

"Why?" I wanted to say something more cohesive, but the confusion of the moment had stopped the supply of words from my brain.

The woman sighed. "We've got a reputation for being too serious, and our image consultants said it would lighten up our profile if prisoners and witnesses wore these around the building. So put them on."

"You're actually serious?"

"Yeah. Put the fucking shoes on, will you? What's the matter with you?"

"Right."

"You can pick yours up when you leave. Just take this form to Footwear Claims, and then they'll give you a chit you take to Footwear Return."

As I said, common sense was not a big player with these people.

I took the shoes stoically.

The drunken man watched me as I struggled to put them on. "Cheer up," he said. "It might never happen. And if it does," he added conspiratorially, invading my personal space with a massive waft of gin, "there's bound to be a cop nearby with a big stick to hit the fucker."

I looked at him. He smiled a thin smile and, just for a moment, I wondered how his life had led him to this. To be here now, drunkenly lost, washed up in this terrible building. It was as though this place was the unacknowledged end of something, the place where people collected when their lives had gone irretrievably wrong.

I plonked my own shoes on the desk.

"Follow the HEAD HACK signs," said the woman. "And don't forget your album. And I'll bet they find something in your head you never expected!"

I flapped off down the corridor in the long red shoes, carrying the album and wondering what I had let myself in for. There was nothing in my head that I wouldn't expect, but I still felt a weight of anxiety. A cold mass of dread was ballooning up in my mind. So much so that the space for other thoughts was getting crushed.

I tried not to think about my father, dying from someone doing something like this, but all I could see was the photograph I had of him on my desk at work. He was about my age, all slicked-back hair and a wide, generous smile. He looked happy to engage with whatever life had to offer. So why, exactly, had he died? What had been so important to him that he had let someone fool about in his head? I knew practically nothing about it.

The walls of this corridor were virtually alive with anticrime posters. I even saw one that was framed. It was some kind of certificate. "Seattle Police are proud to have won the national award for the 'Best Stakeout,' " it said. They were also runners-up in the category "Best Riot Shields." Next to these was a small trophy of a policeman inscribed with the epigraph: "Most Imaginative Use of a Riot Shield on Duty—Officer Lenny Gretchen—Interstate Police Awards—Second Place."

I kept following the signs for "HEAD HACK CENTRAL," and all I saw were cops wandering about or slouching in offices. It was clear these cops could slouch with the best. They'd already put in rigorous hours of training.

Eventually, I came to a huge sign that read: WITNESS HEAD HACK PROGRAM. PLEASE RING THE BELL.

I reached for it when a girl in a white coat appeared and smiled pleasantly.

"Mr. Runner?" she said.

"Yes?" I replied.

"Your Head Hack is next."

At hologram control in Porlock Inc., they were having problems. Holograms were going AWOL all over the place.

Somehow they had been hacked into. And whoever had done the hacking had created a major meltdown.

Most were just dying in a froth of electronics, but a few were singing a rather catchy, bizarre children's song about a puffin that started: *Every puffin has a dream. Every penguin has a spleen.*

The reputation of the people from Porlock Inc. (Seattle) was being shredded. The future of the whole business was collapsing, spectacularly, before their eyes.

It was calculated that Porlock Inc. saved the country two billion dollars a year by preventing all kinds of people from doing stupid things. Doing Stupid Things, or DTS, as it was known, had been proven to be one of the biggest waste areas of the country's economy. And cracking down on the whole DTS problem had been made a priority.

They still couldn't do much about people doing fairly insignificant stupid things, of course, like calling the zoo and trying to sell them a locust, or taking a golf cart and driving it as fast as it would go into a lake.

But they could do something about the Big Stuff.

They could detect the abnormal brainwaves that were generated when people went into DST mode, and then instantly dispatch a hologram.

Normally.

But not today.

Nigel had called in everyone who worked at Porlock. Everyone. He'd even called up people who didn't work there. He'd basically called up everyone he knew.

"Another missed target!" shouted an operative at a bank of screens. "In Souk twenty-three. That's thirty-three major DST alerts today, including a massive one an hour ago at Head Hack Central."

"Jesus," said Nigel. "This can't go on. What's going to happen? If all these people don't get interrupted, they'll be DST without any kind of control. *What's going to happen?*"

No one could give him an answer.

Not even his gardener.

"What on earth are you doing here?" he said to the man, as he stood hopelessly holding a flowerpot. "This is supposed to be a secret establishment."

"You called me."

"Did I? Yeah...Yeah, I probably did."

Nigel went into his office and closed the door. If they didn't get this situation under control soon, they'd take apart his career and spread the pieces to the four corners of the earth.

He poured himself a drink.

"To Kublai Khan," he said quietly, raising his glass.

And drank it without noticing its taste.

The woman took me through a small operating theater that was unexpectedly clean.

"I'm Francine, your nurse today. Can I get you a cup of coffee?"

"No, thanks," I said.

"Or a glass of wonker?" She smiled, but her eyes were not a part of it.

"Wonker?" I repeated. "What's that?"

"Wonker? It's like water. But not as good."

"Okay. No, thanks." I had no idea what she was talking about, but this wasn't the time to ask. The room had no windows, but one of the walls was glazed and looked into a small viewing room. In front of me was a massive padded chair that looked like it would recline, and there were various clinical bits of machinery in the room. It was like being at the dentist.

Only worse.

"So, sit yourself down and pop on the bib," said this girl, bringing out the same smile again. "And pop the safety goggles on for me as well."

A balding man hit the room at speed. I sensed his mind was not entirely here, and that he was wallowing in his position of responsibility. Maybe it gave him a reason to feel he had a valid role in life.

"I'm Dr. Phillips, and this will only take a few seconds. We're just going to get a few images out of your head. Have you done this before, Mr. Runner?" He sat perched on the desk, clipboard in hand, staring at me.

"No," I said.

"Are you on any medication?"

"No."

"Any problems with headaches?"

"No."

"Any allergic reactions ever to Alf-Alfa?"

"No."

"You're certain? No swelling? No sneezing? Anything like that?"

"No." The questions rattled out so quickly, they trod on my answers. It was as though this man felt that by cutting out all the pauses from his life, he might gain an extra half-hour in the day.

"Good. Look forward and hold your head nice and still for me. That's it. And fire the Head Torsion, please, Francine."

Two flat boards on the end of some kind of hydraulic arms squeezed onto my cheeks, clamping my head in a tight vise. My mouth was forced open until I was doing a bad impression of a fish.

"That's fine. Francine is going to put some gel on your head. It may feel a tiny bit cold. Gel type 3-B, please, Francine."

And I felt the cold slop of gunge all over my hair. The girl swept it around with her rubber gloves until I could feel it dripping down the sides of my head.

"Good. Well done. So, this will take only a second or two. All you will feel is a slight tingle, and then we'll download the images from your short-term memory. Francine has a card of safety instructions in case there is a fire. Prepare the Vault for the images, please, Francine."

They exchanged a few other words behind me, and Francine gave me a card. It was a map with various emergency exits and corridors on it. It would have been impossible to go anywhere while I was trapped by this machine, so it was a pretty pointless exercise.

Then the doctor's voice was much louder. "Head hack in five—four—nice and relaxed for me—two—one. Fire!"

My throat tightened, and the lights dimmed and then flashed, and I felt a faint tingling at the top of my head, but the sensation was only fleeting. A deep unsettling darkness swept from one side of my mind to the other. It seemed to echo and tumble. Then the image of the whole room writhed and elongated. Images from my past pinballed about my head in splintering colors. And it felt like my brain was being drawn out through my nose with a pair of chopsticks.

I opened my eyes and saw a strobing white light, and I was swamped with the sensation that it was burning away the essence of who I was and leaving nothing but blank emptiness behind. I began to snap in and out of consciousness, vaguely aware of more people gathering in front me.

They looked like terrified carol singers who had been told they were about to be put to the torch. This bizarre thought lodged at the front of my mind for a moment, then was swept away. My whole body began shaking.

It felt like I might shake myself out through the ceiling. More people came into the room, and I realized the doctor was shouting orders, the tired, smug expression gone from his face. Instead, it was replaced with sheer, unfettered panic that stretched his skin taut and gave his eyes a hectic glitter.

Then I screamed and blacked out.

I came around a second later in a shriek of voices and cries. I knew I was going to die in the same way that my father had.

The old lady had said there would be bluebells. I wondered if there would be bluebells. Somehow I didn't think there would be bluebells for me. She would get bluebells because she had such a kind manner. I would just get pain.

More images ballooned and were crushed. Numbers. Reams of numbers. In walls. In sheets. Cascading through me. As though the universe was breaking down into mathematics and all of it was flowing through me. As though that was all there was—numbers and numbers.

Oceans of fucking numbers.

And then with a jolt I remembered the hologram woman. Her image cut through everything and just sat there in my head.

And I realized instantly what it was about her.

She hadn't been random.

I knew what she had been saying now.

She had been mouthing my name.

On the hill, three refrigerators huddled together as lightning nibbled at the edges of the darkening sky.

It was impossible to make out what they were saying because they were speaking in their own language, which consisted entirely of humming. They all had a battered, shambolic look to them, like they had seen their fair share of lettuces and mayonnaise. Like they had kept a truckload of milk cold in their time. Like they never wanted to see another remnant of a meal placed carefully in a small bowl, sealed in plastic wrap, positioned on the top shelf, then ceremoniously thrown away a week later.

They had seen that all before.

A thousand times.

More lightning snapped at the trees in the evening gloom, but the rain was still holding off.

A woman in a swirling kaftan made her way toward them. As she approached, all the refrigerators closed their doors so that their lights went out, and they hunkered together, trying to blend in.

As much as large, white objects can blend in against a grassy hill.

Which, actually, is not at all.

She walked over, knelt down, and began talking to them. The refrigerators didn't bolt. Instead they gradually opened their doors—just a bit—as though she was winning their confidence.